FORTITUDE SMASHED

Copyright © 2017 Taylor Brooke
All Rights Reserved
ISBN 13: 978-1-945053-36-8 (trade)
ISBN 13: 978-1-945053-42-9 (ebook)
Published by Interlude Press
http://interludepress.com

BOOK AND COVER DESIGN BY CB Messer
10 9 8 7 6 5 4 3 2 1

interlude press • new york

For the wild ones

"*Sometimes our fate resembles a fruit tree in winter. Who would think that those branches would turn green again and blossom, but we hope it, we know it.*"

—Johann Wolfgang von Goethe

AUTHOR'S NOTE

DUE TO SOME SENSITIVE SUBJECT matter in *Fortitude Smashed*, I've decided to include a list of warnings for readers who may need them. Chapter numbers are given below.

Discussion of Mental Health—portrayals of depression, panic attacks, disassociation, anxiety
Instances of general anxiety, minor panic and depression-induced habits appear throughout the novel.

Dissociative episode
Chapter 33, Chapter 39, Chapter 40

Discussion of off-page sexual assault
Chapter 18, Chapter 35

Discussion of on-page physical assault
Chapter 18, Chapter 34, Chapter 35

1

A ROUTINE TRAFFIC ACCIDENT AT a gas station turned out to be a drug bust. Naturally, the patrol officer phoned Shannon, who looked at his half-eaten plate of curry and gave an unsatisfied sigh. The station was quieter than usual: an undertone of hushed conversations, rushed fingers tapping on keyboards, and file cabinets opening and closing. Simple brown desks littered the square room, and offices lined the back wall next to a holding cell. It wasn't a big station, one of the smallest in Orange County. Shannon didn't let its size deter him, though, and had spent many sleepless nights buried in his studies to get there. He set the takeout box on a stack of manila folders and adjusted the bronze placard next to his laptop.

Detective Shannon Wurther—Laguna Beach, California

How long had it been? A year, almost, since he'd passed the entry exam and was promoted from officer to detective. It'd taken too long, he thought. After three years as an officer, another spent studying, finally he'd done it. He was twenty-five years old, the youngest detective in Southern California and the first to pass the exam in one attempt in more than five years. Shannon ran at things full speed. What he'd done in three years, most officers hadn't done in six, and still, he was sure it'd taken too long.

"Cruz, we've got a call." Shannon peered around the edge of his computer. Karman de la Cruz sat across from him at their conjoined desk, separated by two laptops and a mess of files. Her long unruly curls were bundled into a braid. She wore rich brown lipstick, three shades darker than her skin, and her thick eyebrows were penciled in, perfectly arched. She was also eating curry—green opposed to Shannon's red—and frowned around a forkful of rice.

"Who called it in?" she mumbled, searching out the straw in her iced tea with her tongue. "It was Barrow, wasn't it?"

"Of course it was." Shannon snorted a laugh. He closed the container of his mediocre dinner, stood, and slung a messenger bag over his shoulder. "It's the gas station off Main. Do you have to pick up Fae?"

Karman shook her head as she shoved another forkful of rice into her mouth. "She's staying at a friend's house tonight. They're working on one of those solar system diagrams together. I thought they were a little young for planetary assignments but..." She finished with a shrug. "Drinks after we wrap up?"

"Sounds good to me. Is your car still in the shop?" He dug in his bag for his keys, and then patted his waist to make sure his badge was snug on his belt and his gun was holstered alongside it.

Even after five years of police work, he still wasn't used to the weight of a sleek black gun on his hip. He'd grown up accustomed to hunting rifles, the smell of horses, fresh cream, and peach trees. Sometimes the West Coast still overwhelmed him with its mysteries and majesties laid out for all to see. Sometimes Shannon prayed he'd never have to use his gun.

Karman groaned, keeping pace as they walked out the back door. "Yeah, I guess there's something wrong with the transmission now. I need a new car, man."

"I've been telling you that for two years, Cruz."

"Yeah, yeah. Well, when you have to pay for private school and violin lessons, we'll talk all right? Cars are expensive; six-year-olds are even worse."

The Jeep Cherokee's doors squeaked, and the engine thrummed to life. A twinge of pity squirmed in his gut as he glanced at Karman's hands folded casually in her lap. She worked hard for her daughter and herself. No one waited for Karman at home; there was no help to be had, or breaks to be given. Her index finger rubbed back and forth over the top of her right thumbnail. It was a nervous habit, one she'd had since he met her. The translucent tint beneath her fingernail was an eerie reminder of her Rose Road and how she'd lost it.

On his own hand, wrapped tight around the steering wheel, glowing numbers counted backward, second by second, a flicker beneath his thumbnail. Tonight, mere hours from now, Shannon's Camellia Clock was going to time-out, and he would face his Rose Road. He'd waited his whole life for fate to make up its mind, and sometime tonight he'd find out what it decided. The numbers marched: 3:28, 3:27, 3:26.

Karman cleared her throat. "Green light, Wurther."

He tucked his thumb behind the steering wheel. The inevitable wasn't worth worrying about.

A four-lane road snaked through the middle of the city and merged into the Pacific Coast Highway on the north and south ends. Dark roads spun away to wind through quiet coastal neighborhoods where beaches stretched between apartment buildings, high-end resorts, and reservation-only restaurants. Laguna Canyon cut a path inland, home to the summertime art show *Sawdust Festival,* and *Pageant of the Masters'* outdoor theater, surrounded by the Laguna Coast Wilderness Park's sprawling rural hills. It was an easy place to live, safe and manageable, with a median income of a hundred grand, a downtown full of good food, and enough artistic charisma to woo Monet. But even "safe and manageable" had its crime, and crime was something Shannon was good at. Dealing with people, uprooting their secrets, getting the truth: those were all things he did too well for comfort. They were in his blood.

They pulled into the gas station on the outskirts of the canyon road just before eight o'clock. Karman stepped from the car first and flashed her badge to Deputy Barrow. The deputy clasped a meaty hand over her shoulder and grinned. Shannon stole another glance at his thumb. The white numbers 3:05 sent a chill down his back. His heartbeat thundered. *Don't panic.* He dug in his messenger bag for a pair of black gloves and tugged them on. *It'll be fine. It'll be exactly what it should be.*

"Evening, Barrow, what's going on?" Shannon folded the sleeves of his white dress shirt up on his forearms. Karman examined the notes and handed them to Shannon. As he read the charges, Barrow said them aloud.

"Three counts felony possession of prescription drugs with no prescription. Full bottles, too." Deputy Barrow was a round man with a bald head and a dark goatee. He looked more threatening than he was, with cheeks that always stayed red and eyes that always looked glassy. He was a good police officer, though. Shannon considered him a friend.

"And the vehicle?" Shannon prompted.

Barrow heaved a deep sigh. "Vehicle is registered to the driver's stepmother, and the driver claims the drugs aren't hers."

"Of course," Karman muttered.

Shannon shook his head and smirked. "We're in Orange County." He glanced at Barrow, who shrugged. "The drugs very well might not be hers. Did she mention anything about the prescriptions?"

"Just that her stepmother is a 'crazy bitch addicted to pills,'" he quoted, curling his fingers, "and that she borrowed the car so she could study for finals at the coffee shop on the south side, what's it called, The Klatch?"

Shannon nodded and rubbed his gloved hand over his chin. "She's nineteen?" His eyebrows slanted down, and he waved dismissively to Karman. "That's all you. You're good with these young ones."

It wasn't that Shannon *wasn't* good with cases like this one—he liked to think he was—but there was no denying the motherly nature of Karman de la Cruz. She soothed her way to the truth, whereas Shannon dug for it. When there was a teenager with stepmom's car and three bottles of pills in the glove box, he was sure Karman would be better suited to figuring out the details. While Karman crouched beside the open back door of Barrow's patrol car, her hand on the teenager's knee, smiling gently and nodding, Shannon paced.

He chatted with Barrow about what was going on in his life, how his kids and his wife were doing, and adamantly directed the conversation away from his own internal dilemma. He wanted to ask, *what happens when the Camellia Clock stops?* What happens to his heart, his head— his life?

Waves of uncertainty flooded his stomach, swirling the curry. Barrow said something about his oldest girl making the volleyball team, so Shannon smiled. He talked about his anniversary, and Shannon said, "That's great, man." But inside his head, like a swarm of hornets, the buzzing, ticking, humming Clock beneath his thumbnail drove him mad.

THE STREETLIGHT ILLUMINATING THE SIDEWALK outside of Laguna Beach Canvas & Sculpt flickered, casting eerie shadows around the decorative bushes that lined the walkway.

Vague suspicion told Aiden he should turn around and go home. Tonight wasn't a good night; tonight the streets were telling him it wasn't worth it. Superstition, he thought, what a way to bow out. Anyway, he hadn't walked under any ladders lately. No black cats had crossed his path.

His lips wrapped around the end of a cigarette. Gray smoke leaked from the corners of his mouth. Then again, maybe he was the black cat.

Downtown wasn't crowded at night, not in the middle of the week. The only witnesses he might expect were homeless kids, and he could bribe them with alcohol, or weed, or food. He'd learned his way around street kids and travelers during his extended trips up north, when he'd played in Seattle, dabbled in Los Angeles, made enemies in San

Francisco. It was no surprise he'd overstayed his welcome in the latter. He probably wouldn't see that foggy city again for years.

As he lifted the cigarette to his lips, Aiden caught the glow of white numbers beneath his thumbnail.

1:32

"Well, look at that," he said to himself, as though he hadn't been aware of those numbers for twenty-two years. "Looks like my soul mate is right around the corner."

Aiden believed that when his Camellia Clock timed out he would be alone. No one out there waited for him; no one was set aside to be his Rose Road. He'd believed that since he was sixteen, sitting in the front pews of an unfamiliar church with his brother's arm over his shoulders and the smell of hydrangeas and carnations tickling his nose. The realization that fate wouldn't come for him had been sudden, like a spider bite. One minute Aiden Maar was sure he was on fate's good side, and a second later he was convinced otherwise.

Aiden flicked the cigarette butt into the middle of the street. The worn sole of his boot was propped against the back wall of an ice cream parlor; his shoulders were growing cold against the scratch of old paint. He adjusted his black beanie, mentally checking the list of had-to's and would-be's that made up the before and after of a burglary. He'd left his bike in the parking structure off Fifth—a few blocks away, but easy to get to if he took back alleys and cut through the market.

The painting he was after was small—hardly noticeable in a gallery full of tall canvases. He was in it for all the wrong reasons this time. There was no buyer lined up; he didn't have a listing on the dark web for a one-of-a-kind canvas stained with pressed flower petals and colored pollen. The conceptual piece of artwork he'd seen weeks ago, a miniscule thing called *Fortitude Smashed*, still hung on the wall opposite the staircase, and he wanted it for himself.

The streetlight went out, bathing the front of the gallery in darkness. Aiden took that as his cue, glanced left, right, took long strides across the street, and disappeared around the back of the building.

"ALL RIGHT—YEAH, I'LL MEET YOU guys there." Shannon waved to Deputy Barrow and Karman as they loaded into the patrol car and took the handcuffed, still-crying girl to the station. Their shift was over, which meant the team there would process her, and Barrow, Karman, and Shannon would be free to enjoy the rest of their night. He was looking forward to not having to worry about anything except a cold beer, conversations between friends, and going to sleep before two a.m.

He climbed into his car. The buzz in his mind was long gone, replaced by Karman's rambled overview of the case.

Fast cars, too-rich bachelors, and women with nothing to lose but themselves made up the lackluster circle of criminals who actually committed any crime in Orange County. There was a horrific number of traffic accidents, sometimes gang-related incidents that trickled down from Los Angeles, and an occasional murder. As few and far between as the murders were, Shannon didn't aim for the homicide department. He didn't have the constitution for it, no—that was his father's thing.

Detective Wurther was a seeker. Breaking up drug rings on college campuses, handling informants, busting street racers, that was what Shannon did, and he was good at it.

He took the route through the shops downtown to get to the Whitehouse, Karman's favorite watering hole. Leaning his elbow on the lip of his window with his chin resting on his thumb, he watched ocean mist settle over the streets. It dampened his windshield and confirmed that the seasons really were changing. It also broke up the light that danced off the glass front of the gallery to his right, where he could have sworn he caught a flicker of movement. He clicked his headlights off. The car rolled to a stop. It had to be the owner, but… no; it was too late for anyone to be inside without the lights on. It was probably nothing. Shannon sighed and shook his head. He turned the headlights on and stepped on the gas.

No, he *had* seen it.

He slammed on his brakes and swore as his seat belt cut into his shoulder.

He saw a flash of pale something. Light glinted off a pair of eyes. Someone ducked behind the staircase.

After turning into one of the curbside parking spaces, Shannon trotted around the building. The alley was bathed in shadow. A soft glow from the streetlights on the other side of the block broke up the darkness. The back door was ajar, barely, but noticeably. Whoever was inside had expected to be in and out quickly enough that no one would notice.

Shannon's first instinct was to call for backup. It's what he should've done.

Instead, he slid his hand around the door and pulled it open; his other hand rested on his holstered gun.

The scent of oil paint and clay wafted strong in the stillness. The room was too open, a wide space with nowhere to hide. Shannon took a step, another, and glanced at the desk, where abstract patterns swirled on the screen of a hibernating computer next to a dimmed, decorative lamp.

Movement. Footsteps, heel to toe, slow and quiet, behind him.

Shannon swung around. Someone—the thief—gasped. He grabbed the fabric of a shirt and shoved whoever was wearing it against the wall.

"You're under arrest," he growled. The body, a man, squirmed and cursed. The one time he didn't play it safe and call for backup was the time he might need it. Shannon forced the thief's hands against the wall. "Spread your fingers."

The thief complied. "Of fucking course." Shannon heard him rolling his eyes.

"Breaking and entering is a crime, you understand that? So is taking things that aren't yours."

"I didn't take anything. I didn't get the chance to." Whoever he was, he was unapologetically bored with the situation. Shannon spotted a bold tattoo on his side where his shirt was bunched up from their abrupt collision. The man sighed. "Can I have my hands back now?"

"No, you can't, because—"

Shannon's entire being screeched to a stop. His spine straightened; his knees locked. He couldn't breathe. Beneath his glove, warmth spread from his right thumb into his wrist. The Camellia Clock vibrated, gentle but convincing, a purr that alerted him to the 00:00 that now read in glowing numbers under his thumbnail. Saliva pooled in his mouth. Heat coursed through him. Blood rushed—high speed traffic in his veins. His heartbeat, steady and then not, pounded in his ears.

He stared at the hand spread out on the wall. On the thief's right thumbnail, the same numbers glowed 00:00. Shannon squeezed the man's wrist a little tighter.

A shaky breath quivered from the chest in front of him. Apparently, Shannon wasn't the only one surprised.

He swallowed, and his grip tightened again before he let go and ripped his hands away. Eyeing Shannon carefully, the burglar spun. He had a straight nose and a sharp jaw; he was all angles and edges and pale skin. His skittishness reminded Shannon of a deer—maybe not a deer. The stranger's lips twitched into a straight-toothed grin under hooded dark eyes. Yeah, maybe not a deer. Maybe a wolf.

A breathless chuckle trickled past a clever smile. The thief gave a slow shake of his head, disbelief and curiosity stitching a genuine expression across his face that Shannon hated. "Aiden Maar," he said, too confidently to be taken lightly.

Shannon's jaw was set so tight it ached to open his mouth. "Detective Wurther."

"Pleasure's all mine, Detective." The rasp in his voice made Shannon's stomach jump.

Before Shannon could yell, or grab, or get another word in, the thief—Aiden—was gone, darting past him and out the door. His head swam. Still reeling, he couldn't have caught Aiden if his life depended on it. But he was going to have to, because, according to the Camellia Clock, Aiden Maar was his future.

According to Shannon Wurther, the Camellia Clock was wrong.

2

AIDEN DUCKED IN FRONT OF an oncoming car and made his way across the street that divided downtown from Main Beach. The empty beach was a shelter of pitch darkness. He gulped and panted hard. His heavy boots flung sand this way and that. Waves lifted and curled, slamming against the shore. They drowned the panicked drumming of his heart and gave him something to focus on besides his burning lungs.

Slithering out to sea, climbing high, crashing down—the ocean was a constant loop, a soundtrack that played his favorite song again and again. He hid at the base of the black rock cliffs where Laguna's finest boutique hotel perched, overlooking the city. He climbed the first set of boulders, an expanse of slippery onyx rocks covered in dark green kelp. *Focus.* A patch of seaweed snagged his ankle. He slipped, but caught himself before his face smacked a rock. He crawled the rest of the way and dropped onto his rear once he was safely on the other side.

Far out on the horizon, stars peppered up and up until the moon's glow diffused them. Sea spray misted his face. Rise, fall, repeat, the waves continued to roar. Aiden decided to blame them. If fate had a conscience, it lived in the ocean with the rest of the world's mysteries.

"A cop!" Aiden yelled. Maybe somewhere out there, fate could hear him. "That's what you decided?"

He pulled out a blue pack of cigarettes and lit one. *Steady.* He stared at his hand, the one where a number no longer glowed under his thumbnail, and willed it to stop shaking. *Keep breathing.* It wasn't supposed to happen like that. One breath. Another. It wasn't supposed to happen at all.

"You totally fucked me!" he called out, scowling at the waves when they didn't shout an apology.

Aiden rolled his eyes. The back of his head rested against the cliff. He thought of Detective Wurther: short auburn hair, arranged to look willfully messy. Bright blue eyes, probably nice to look at when they weren't filled with disgust. Maybe it wasn't disgust: Maybe the cop looked like that all the time. *No, he couldn't.* The detective's face was soft, with nascent smile lines edging the corner of his eyes. That was a good sign.

He tried to remember Wurther's features, but all he saw was his expression. The cop's face said *no*, but his eyes said *you*, and that made Aiden want to punch a goddamn wall.

He smoked the cigarette until the filter burned his fingers and then flicked it at the sea. "Choke on it," he hissed, head lolling back as smoke drifted from his parted lips.

He stared at the half of the moon not cloaked by blackness and listened. Maybe fate would whisper. Maybe fate would come from the sea and take Aiden's face in its hands and say *you'll be fine.* He'd been waiting six guilt-ridden, dysthymia-filled, fucked-up years for that.

Fate didn't come for him, though. No, fate had sent a cop.

Aiden lit another cigarette and looked at the sky.

SHANNON STRUGGLED WITH HIS PHONE for ten minutes. He slid his finger across the screen, dialed the police station's number, pressed "end," glanced at the three missed texts from Karman, started to text her back, and backspaced everything he'd written. He had to do the right thing. He had to call it in.

Sweaty palms dampened his gloves. He paced along the back wall of the gallery with his cell phone pressed against his ear. "Cindy, it's Shannon. I'm calling in an attempted burglary at…" He craned his neck and glanced at the sign above the door. "Laguna Beach Canvas & Sculpt. Yeah—yeah, that's the one. No, I tried to detain him, but he ran off. Just…" His bottom lip stung under the weight of his teeth. "Just a kid, I think. He didn't take anything; there's no damage."

The lie tasted salty and thick.

"No—no, yeah, he was tall. About my height. Caucasian, no, I didn't—a tattoo?" Shannon rubbed his temples. "Yeah, briefly. On his side, yeah, yeah. I can't be sure—could be."

Cindy asked, "Was it a bird?"

Yes. Shannon remembered feathers curving from high on his side to low on Aiden's hip. He hadn't seen it all, but he'd seen enough. He closed his eyes and said, "I didn't get a good look."

"It could be him, the San Francisco thief. I'm not sure. I'd have to see a picture. None on file? Convenient. I'll stay until the deputies get here. They'll need my statement… Dangerous?" Shannon chewed on his lip again. Yes, he probably was dangerous, but something about his smile, endearing and genuine, made Shannon say, "No, I don't think so. Just some kid."

Just some kid.

"Cindy, wait! Hey, can you… Can you do a search for me? Aiden Maar. Yeah. Yeah—no, no it isn't a big deal, just someone my landlord wanted a background check on. Leave his file on my desk, all right? I'll stop by and grab it."

Shannon hung up. He waited for the patrol officers, gave his statement, and drove to the station. What was left for him to lie about? He glanced in the rearview mirror and spotted his reflection: ghastly pale, wide-eyed, looking as guilty as he was for lying to protect a mistake made by the Camellia Clock.

"WURTHER!" KARMAN WAVED HER HANDS. "What took you so long?"

The Whitehouse was quiet, typical for a weekday. Karman and Barrow sat by the front window at a high-top table, a half-eaten basket of fries in front of them. A handful of people chatted in the restaurant portion of the establishment, sipping expensive glasses of wine and eating fresh-caught seafood.

Shannon took a deep breath and slung his messenger bag on the back of the chair. "A gallery downtown was being broken into while I was driving here. I stopped to check it out and almost made an arrest."

"They got away?" Karman laughed. Disbelief and surprise scrawled across her face. She arched a brow. "Was there more than one person? Wait—why didn't you call me?"

"Just a stupid kid." He batted his hand at her and slid onto the tall barstool. "I would've called you if I thought I couldn't handle it."

"Apparently, you couldn't," Barrow said, chuckling around the lip of a beer bottle.

"Yeah, no shit. What the hell were you thinking? Did you at least get a good look at the guy?" Karman stood up, walked to the bar, and swatted the glossed wooden bar-top. "Yeah, another, and a Sam Adams for the rookie," she gestured to Shannon with a flick of her wrist.

"Not really." Lie. "It was too dark." Another lie. "He slipped out the back door before I could get a good look at him." The biggest lie. Shannon remembered every nook and cranny of Aiden Maar's face. He remembered his ashy breath, his dark, dark eyes.

She slid a frosty glass in front of him and set a beer bottle next to it. "Don't be pullin' shit like that again, Shannon. You call me next time, all right?"

He nodded and sighed through his nose. She had a right to be angry. He would've been, too, if the situation was reversed. "How's Fae doing with her violin lessons?"

The change of subject was surprisingly smooth. Karman's long lashes fluttered. She sipped her cocktail and shook her head. "You know, I get that learning an instrument is supposed to increase brain activity and everything, but that shit isn't easy. Poor thing has calluses on her fingers, but she wants to keep going, so I'm gonna to keep paying for it."

"I know how that is," Barrow chirped. "My wife and I are trying to plan something for our anniversary, but we've got volleyball, soccer, photography," he counted on his fingers as he went. "It'll be ten years in a couple weeks. Who knew, huh?"

"Is she your Rose Road?" Shannon nursed his beer.

"Oh, yeah. Yeah, we've been together since the day we met. That's how it's supposed to be, right?" He laughed, full-bodied and warm, a sound expected from a man of his stature. "Timer goes off, meet the person you're gonna fall in love with, fall in love, end of story. I couldn't see myself with anyone else."

Creeping cold inched its way up Shannon's back. *That's how it's supposed to be, right?* No, Shannon was sure it wasn't. He was positive that his future wouldn't be defined by what the Camellia Clock decided, especially if that decision was Aiden Maar.

Karman snorted and shrugged. "Sometimes it doesn't work out," she mumbled.

"How so?" Barrow tilted his head; his thick, bushy brows slanted down.

"Maybe I just got bad luck, but my Rose Road turned out to be a crock of shit." She laughed, a winded, sad laugh Shannon had heard before, any time a Rose Road was mentioned, or a DUI was called in, or Karman's daughter looked a little too long at a family in a restaurant. "Timed out when we were sixteen, pregnant at twenty, and he's dead at twenty-one. Call it bad luck, but now I'm stuck. Online dating is a glorified booty call, and finding a serious partner outside the Clock is a joke. Everybody saves the serious shit for this," she held up her blank thumb where her Clock used to be, "for their *soul mate*. There's support groups, but c'mon, like those'll change a damn thing." Faded lipstick imprinted the martini glass in her hand. She shook her head, took a long sip, and exhaled a raspy breath. "I'm just being sorry for myself." She waved her hand at Barrow and tilted her head to stare at the ceiling. "It was a long time ago, anyway."

Barrow's nose wrinkled. He frowned and stared down at the table. "I never knew that, Karman. I'm sorry."

"Naw, don't be. I'm sorry for being bitter and sappy."

She wasn't sorry; Shannon knew that as well as she did. But Barrow seemed to buy it. "Another round?" Barrow lifted his beer bottle but Shannon shook his head.

"No, I should really get going. I have a file to look over when I get home and I'm exhausted." He tried on a smile.

It worked on Barrow, who shrugged and said, "Suit yourself."

But Karman's narrowed glare dug into him like cat claws. "What file?"

"Aiden Maar," he said the name too quickly, as if it was dying to be said. "Just some guy my landlord wants me to check out for him. It's nothing."

It might be everything.

"You sure you're cool, Wurther?" Karman assessed his face, searching for a crack in his resolve. If she looked close enough, he was sure she'd find it.

"I'm fine," he said, too quickly again, and grabbed his bag. "Thanks for the drink!" He tossed the words over his shoulder, lifted a three-finger wave, and marched toward the door. He felt Karman and Barrow's eyes on him and heard their conversation as he swung the door open.

"Your partner seems off."

"He gets like this," Karman said.

A deep breath shook its way from Shannon's mouth. *He gets like this.* His mind did circles around the statement, dissecting it, disemboweling it, until all he could think about was how often he *didn't* get like this. How thankful he was for a partner like Karman de la Cruz who knew him well enough to keep his secret, even if he hadn't shared it with her.

3

SHANNON GLANCED AT THE TIME on the dash, 1:46 a.m., before he turned on the light above the rearview mirror and flipped open the manila folder.

Aiden Maar had a file as thick as a high-fantasy novel, packed with misdemeanors and a plethora of parking tickets. He was twenty-two with an outstanding lease on an apartment, a well-known reputation on the dark web, and an affinity for skipping town. He always ended up back on the West Coast, though, usually in the southern parts of California: Malibu, San Diego, Pomona.

Laguna Beach.

Shannon covered his face with his hands. He peeked through his fingers, scanning another page in the never-ending file. Aiden was parentless, with an estranged aunt who lived alone somewhere in New York and a brother who lived in Laguna.

"Wonderful," he muttered. He should've told Karman what happened; he should've called for backup instead of trying to stop an art thief who just so happened to be his... Shannon sank his teeth into his bottom lip. His *nothing*. That's what Aiden Maar was; he was Shannon's nothing, and that was that. He tossed the file into the back seat.

Shannon flicked the light off and wrestled with the recliner until the seat leaned back, sprawling out as much as he could.

They should have a choice, shouldn't they? The Camellia Clock doesn't get to make decisions for people. It doesn't get to decide who Shannon would love or cherish or want. He didn't care about its track record, its popularity, or its redefinition of the future. No matter how long Shannon had waited, no matter his excitement, cloaked by nervousness, or his curiosity, masked by pride, Shannon refused to accept *this*.

The Clock was wrong.

The open-aired fifth floor of the parking structure had lamps in each corner of the lot. A gust of October wind stirred outside. A nearby engine clicked off. The passenger door of the not-old but not-new Jeep opened just enough to let a body slip inside—someone tall and lean, wearing torn jeans and a tight gray T-shirt. Shannon jumped and pressed the lock button on the side of his car door. Not that it would help now, not when he'd forgotten—and Shannon never forgot—to lock his doors in the first place.

Shannon's heart leapt into his throat. He stared at Aiden, who looked back with smiling eyes. His buzzed head tilted. He looked like a secret, a dangerous, maddening secret, flaunting himself unashamed—a fox waving his tail in front of a hound.

"What are you doing here?" Shannon chewed up the words and spat them at Aiden.

"I came to see you." Aiden clicked his tongue. "You know, since we're soul mates and all."

"You can't come to see me," Shannon hissed. His eyes bulged. He gaped at the lopsided grin that crawled across Aiden's mouth and the glint in his eyes. "You're a *criminal* and a damn good one at that! Hell, every officer in San Francisco has tried to track you down. I don't need you seeking *me* out, all right?"

"Oh, come on. You don't know that the four paintings that went missing there were exclusively my handiwork." Aiden leaned his head against the seat and chuckled. "I mean, not that they weren't, and not that I'm *not* a damn good criminal, I agree with you there." He stretched out his arms, palms open as if he'd accepted a gift. "But you can't *not* want to get to know me, even a little."

"Even a little!" Shannon sat up. He slammed his hand against the steering wheel. His stomach was knotted, and his face felt flushed. He should lean over and push Aiden right the hell out of his car. Better yet, he should fold Aiden's hands behind his back and cuff him, take him to the station, and book him for the seven suspected burglaries filed under his name.

"The clock was wrong—it had to be wrong." Shannon clutched his hair. "That happens sometimes. The Camellia Clock malfunctions and puts you with the wrong person; it's not common, but it happens..."

Shannon talked with his hands, lost in his own fantasies, fantasies that could sever the ties between him and the sharp-faced, even-sharper-tongued thief occupying the passenger's seat.

Aiden's gaze flicked past Shannon to the lamp on the other end of the parking lot. Two featureless silhouettes ambled closer: the blue of Barrow's uniform, the click of Karman's heels.

"Shut up!" Aiden snarled, swatting at Shannon who continued to talk with his hands. "Shh! You idiot, be—"

Shannon's spine straightened. He pressed himself against the back of his seat, trying to sink inside it, as Aiden swung his legs across the center console and planted himself in Shannon's lap. Long fingers clamped over Shannon's mouth, and Aiden's palm muffled his speech.

Every word he'd been ready to say slipped from him. Aiden's hand was soft. His knuckles smelled like metal and coffee beans and vanilla. Dark, dangerous eyes narrowed at him, and the world around the two of them fell away.

"Quiet," Aiden finished, barely whispering. "You don't want your cop friends to see us, do you?"

Aiden wasn't as light as Shannon expected, but his body was just as he'd thought. Not that Shannon Wurther had spent any time thinking about Aiden Maar's body, because he hadn't. Heat fought its way into Shannon's cheeks, two parts embarrassment, one part curiosity. He hadn't thought about how narrow his hips were, or the expanse of his chest, or the long slope of his neck.

The footsteps that hit the concrete outside the Jeep weren't as loud as Shannon's heartbeat. Neither was Karman's delicate two-martini laugh, nor Deputy Barrow's booming impersonation of the bartender.

Their muffled voices caused Shannon to hold his breath. Aiden tucked his head below the window and hid in Shannon's shoulder.

A truck beeped, unlocking. Two doors opened. Two doors closed.

Shannon tried to take another breath, a longer one, but it stuttered from him when Aiden's nose tapped Shannon's forehead. His knees slid toward the back of the seat and pressed their torsos together.

"Maybe you're right, maybe it was a mistake," Aiden's mouth rounded each syllable. His thin lips brushed Shannon's temple.

Barrow's truck coughed to life and drove away, swallowed by the fourth floor of the parking structure, down the third, the second, until the sound faded into the night. Their absence left an eerie quiet. Aiden peeled his hand away, allowing Shannon to suck in a full breath.

Silence filled the spaces between his body and Aiden, his Rose Road, looming over him. He tried to sit up, but a wide hand on his chest held him in place. Aiden's fingers were long and skeletal. *Fairytale hands. The kind a villain had.*

"You really think our clocks malfunctioned?" Aiden licked his lips. Shannon pretended not to notice. "You *really* think we're not cut from the same cloth, Detective?"

"I don't think it matters to *you* what *I* think."

He leaned, sturdy and warm against Shannon's chest. Aiden's elbows rested on Shannon's shoulders. Aiden's breath was a ghost haunting the top of his cheeks, brushing the bridge of his nose, drifting down to tickle his mouth.

"It matters," Aiden said. Shannon opened his mouth to disagree. Aiden kissed him. Shannon's stomach leapt, his blood rushed fast and his head spun. He swallowed Aiden's gasp, and the kiss escalated from the tentative brush of lips, to a face-gripping, open-mouthed, breathy mess that sent Shannon flying out of himself. Aiden's hips flexed; his spidery fingers tangled in Shannon's hair.

Shannon's resistance crumbled. He reached for Aiden as he would reach for a shot of whiskey or a too-sharp knife or a venomous snake, but he reached all the same. His hands felt good gripping Aiden's waist beneath his shirt and running along the tattoo splayed across Aiden's rib cage. Shannon's back arched. One quivering breath, then another, rushed from Aiden as if he'd been punched. His breath drifted across Shannon's mouth and then his throat and then—

It ended.

As quickly as Aiden had hopped into the passenger seat, slid into his lap, and locked their lips together, as quickly as he was there, in Shannon's gravity, circling him like a predator—

He stopped.

Aiden's eyes weren't as dark brown as Shannon had thought; they were flecked with slivers of amber, a little bit like stars, a little bit like candlelight. He blinked, villain hands resting on Shannon's throat, thumbs making paths on his jaw.

Shannon's tongue was useless now that it wasn't between Aiden's lips. It kept still through a stampede of fragmented thoughts. Aiden's pale face was even paler, shadowed by the car that was shadowed by the night. Excitement battled with fear, and he didn't know if it was Aiden or the enormity of the situation that caused him to tremble.

The Clock wasn't wrong. The Clock *wasn't* wrong. The. Clock. Wasn't. Wrong.

Aiden's pupils dilated. His jaw slackened, and a blotched blush started on the top of his high cheek bones and ended below his Adam's apple. Shannon studied Aiden's expression, bewilderment mingling with disbelief. He felt him shift; the cold was more present when Aiden swung off Shannon's lap and closed the driver's side door behind him.

The fluttering in Shannon's stomach refused to stop. Adrenaline seeped to the top of his skin and soaked him in a feeling that reminded him of fear, but wasn't as tangible. This must be how it felt to be surveyed from above—when an animal ran for its life with a hunter's scope on its hide. He looked right, toward the only vehicle left—a sleek black motorcycle with thick tires, a leather jacket draped over its seat, and a helmet hanging from a handlebar.

Aiden shrugged on the jacket, flicked away a half-smoked cigarette, and straddled the bike much like he'd been straddling Shannon.

The Clock wasn't wrong.

Shannon closed his eyes. Aiden's bike roared past the still-dark Jeep, careened down the parking structure, and disappeared.

A FLASHING LINE BOUNCED IN the search box on Aiden's computer screen. He stared, fingers hovering above the keyboard. One letter at a time, he typed *Detective Wurther*. Enter. The screen loaded and displayed an array of detectives that weren't *the* Detective. He clicked on the search bar and added *Laguna Beach*. Enter. Wurther's face appeared, and below it, listed for all to see, was link after link about *the* Shannon Wurther, youngest detective in Southern California.

A cigarette nursed between his lips, Aiden rolled his eyes. Shannon. It suited him. Aiden mentally sounded it out before he tested it in his mouth.

"Shannon," he said.

One click. Two clicks. An article popped open: "Shannon Wurther—Youth & Success"

"This guy's perfect!" he yelled, startling a seagull from its perch on his balcony wall.

Mercy, a long-haired white cat with a flat face and beady eyes, made a disgruntled noise from the other side of the open sliding door.

"Graduated from a private high school with a 3.9 GPA, has a perfect *driving* record." Aiden laughed. "Who the fuck has a perfect driving record?"

He moved on to the next article. "Of course. Police work runs in the family. Go figure, Mercy."

Mercy yawned.

"Does he do anything wrong? *Anything?* One thing! That's all I'm asking for…" Aiden narrowed his eyes. "Voted Best Study Partner by peers at San Diego State, where he received his degree in criminal law… Okay…" He clicked another link and almost tossed his laptop over the balcony. The same details were repeated. Shannon had a spotless track record. He was known only for his good nature and success as a dedicated police officer. If Google couldn't dig up any demons, Shannon probably didn't have any.

Aiden clicked on a link to Shannon's Facebook profile and rolled his eyes.

He analyzed Shannon's profile picture, all sun-kissed skin and priceless smile. He looked like a guy who shopped at skate shops but didn't skate, wore expensive swim trunks, and reeked of overpriced cologne. "What a *tool*," Aiden hissed.

"Wanna go to the beach, Mercy? I think I might actually throw up if I keep doing this to myself." Aiden was an expert at self-inflicted misery, and Internet-stalking his Rose Road definitely counted as torture.

The cat chirped, rolled on her back, and flicked her tail against the carpet.

It was a Thursday, the Thursday after last Thursday, October ninth. And this Thursday Aiden was at a complete loss, because last Thursday, October second, he'd kissed a man who shouldn't have kissed him back. But as fate would have it, Shannon *had* kissed him back. And it hadn't just been a kiss, no. It couldn't have been that simple—not a chaste taste, or a gentle test. Aiden lit a fire, and Shannon doused it with gasoline. He sensed an echo of Shannon's hands beneath his shirt whenever he thought about it.

"C'mon, Mercy." Aiden slipped a pale pink harness around her front legs. "Let's go."

He tried *not* to think about it and was unsuccessful. In the time it took to step out of his apartment, walk down the cracked cement stairs, and hit the sidewalk, Aiden had imagined Shannon's mouth in eight different ways, from its shape when Shannon's lips tightened to the way it felt pressed against his own. He imagined Shannon's lips gently parted and reddened, his bottom lip shaking around a gasp, his mouth smashed into a snarl or aggressively prying Aiden's lips apart. He imagined the shock last—Shannon's uninhibited surprise after their kiss—open, bitten, and unequivocally beautiful. Aiden thought about all eight different ways Shannon's mouth looked a total of three times before he and Mercy made it to the sand.

"Here's good, yeah?" Aiden glanced over the top of his sunglasses, and Mercy yawned up at him. She flopped in the sand and stretched her front legs out as far as they would go. "Yeah, I thought so."

October in Southern California meant beaches sweltering with leftover summer heat, but not as crowded as true summer days. Some tourists still rushed to the water, wading in the semi-warm Pacific, but most lay on towels and watched from afar. Living in a shitty apartment thirty feet from the sand had its perks: Aiden never needed a towel and he could bring his own food without a cooler. Today's lunch was a peanut butter and apricot jam sandwich, accompanied by a bag of chips and a beer. The beer wasn't usually part of his pre-dinner meals, but the thought of Shannon Wurther's mouth had convinced him it should be.

A couple kids trotted by, giving the normal pause-and-point to the leashed cat that lounged next to him, and then skittered off when they realized who the cat belonged to. In a leather jacket, no shirt, ripped jeans, he wasn't the friendliest sight, but Aiden flashed a smile nonetheless. Those kids wouldn't have run from Detective Shannon Wurther. No, they would've walked right up to him—a gleaming, unsullied example of humankind in its prime.

Aiden decided that he hated Shannon.

"Dreary skies make for dreary days." A man with greasy clumps of string for hair and a worn, weather-beaten face peered at Aiden. He took a seat beside Mercy, paying no mind to Aiden's privacy. His beanie was torn, his clothes were unwashed, and he had long, splintered fingernails. Grime covered his knuckles, and his shoes carried the history of all the places he'd been.

"Makes for sunburns, too," Aiden said.

The man tilted his head. He seemed bird-like and hollow, a man who'd been to war with himself for a lot longer than Aiden had. "It's not every day you see somebody walkin' a cat."

"Today isn't every day."

"How's that sandwich?"

Aiden shrugged. He held his arm out and offered it. Only half was left, but he figured it was better than nothing. "Generic. You hungry?"

The man took it without question. Aiden examined the man's fingerless gloves, covered in sand and dust from his travels. The homeless fellow examined Aiden as well; his gaze lingered on his bare thumbnail. Slanted eyes opened wide, deepening the shallow valleys and dry crevices along his forehead. "Looks like you're on your path already. You're young, too young to have to fight with fate."

"Who says I'm fighting?" Aiden's top lip curled in an exaggerated scoff.

Breathless, raspy laughter sputtered from the man and ended in a coughing fit. He hacked into his palm. A creaky, ancient thing he was, alone and forgotten on a beautiful beach with the world etched in cracked skin. "Boy, you have fighter written all over you! Danger, danger, another wild one born to eat the heart of the world."

Wild one. Aiden smirked. He was far from wild. Born to a mother who wasn't ready for motherhood, given to another mother who was, and raised by two parents in a one-story house with a brother who was better, in a town five miles inland. Nightly homework sessions at Starbucks defined his early teenaged years, marking fourteen and fifteen as the time before. When he was sixteen, fate transformed the after, and continued transforming it as sixteen turned to seventeen, and seventeen turned to eighteen, and every day after.

After, Aiden thought, was what people mistook for wild. He wasn't wild, because that would make him brave. He was profoundly reckless. There was a difference.

Still chomping, the man said, "You know the Clock isn't always a knife in the back, but it isn't always wonderful, either. Some advice for you, wild boy, let what comes, come, and let what goes, go, you understand?"

Stagnancy made a home in this man. It filled the places that were empty with an even-greater emptiness. He waved his hand in Aiden's direction and stared, bulged eyes crusted around the edges. He must have spent his life seeing things, but the way he looked at Aiden was unnerving, as though he'd never seen a thing like him.

Aiden was terrified of being that empty. "Did you let what goes go?"

He gave an enthusiastic nod whilst shoving the rest of the peanut butter and apricot sandwich into his mouth.

"And you don't regret it?"

Empty Man narrowed his eyes and shook his head. "What do you think, wild boy?"

Aiden thought the heart of the world, like fate, was buried in the sea and, despite his hunger, he would never find it. He thought he might be hungrier for Shannon's mouth, anyway. He tossed the unopened bag of chips in Empty Man's lap and stood, scooping Mercy up in one arm and holding his beer in the other. "You can have those," he said. "Nice talk."

Empty Man didn't say anything else, despite his question going unanswered.

Aiden climbed the wooden stairs to a landing where a bench and two trashcans overlooked the beach. He finished his beer and glanced at Empty Man sitting in the sand alone, munching on potato chips, and staring at the ocean. Maybe Empty Man found the heart of the world, maybe he'd been the one to chew it up, and maybe he'd choked on it, too.

Aiden didn't believe in fate. There was no reason to be hungry for it.

Mercy meowed. Aiden tossed his bottle into the green trashcan.

He couldn't help believing in Shannon, though, even if he had decided to hate him.

5

SHANNON RAISED HIS FIST. THE skin stretched across his knuckles paled. He hesitated. The door two inches away was white, with a plain doorknob and a peephole that laughed at his lack of confidence. In his other hand, Shannon clutched a cardboard drink holder stuffed with two large coffee cups. His arm dropped. He leaned forward so the apartment door was cool on his forehead and cursed.

Maybe he's not home. He tugged at the long sleeve of his shirt. *Yeah, he probably isn't even here to answer the door.* Shannon knocked. Once, twice, and on the third knock, the door swung open.

Of course he was home.

The handle of a toothbrush was pinched between Aiden's lips. He quirked a brow and his mouth spread into a peculiar smile with foam bubbling around the edges.

"What the fuck are you doin' here?" Aiden slurred. His bare torso highlighted the massive black-flamed phoenix that covered his side. Unbuttoned jeans hung low on his hips, exposing the blue line of boxer briefs beneath. He left the door ajar and walked away, disappearing inside the shoreside apartment.

Shannon stepped in and shut the door. The first things his eyes had fallen upon were the arc of Aiden's hips, his naked chest, the delicate way his collarbones cast shadows along his shoulders. Now it was his back—the curve of his spine, connecting a long torso to a narrow waist—disappearing around the corner and down the hall.

Aiden Maar's apartment was clean, but not uncomfortably so. The layout was long and rectangular, with an open kitchen to the left and a hallway past the living room to the right. Shannon stood behind a black leather couch, and looked at the wall, which was decorated with framed paintings, evenly spaced photograph collages, and shadow-boxed sculptures.

"Where's your warrant, Detective?" Aiden stood in front of the sliding glass door that led to a miniscule, almost-ocean-facing balcony. He hadn't put a shirt on. Shannon pretended not to notice. "You can't just come barging in here without one, you know."

"It's my day off." Shannon cleared his throat. "I thought I should stop by."

Hooded amber eyes watched Shannon carefully. Aiden was a shark, circling and calculating; his expression was too calm to be dismissed. He tilted his head and jutted his chin toward the cups in Shannon's hand. "You brought me coffee?" There was an edge to his voice, a playful teasing that coaxed heat to pool in Shannon's belly and made him want to leave. Aiden's nostrils flared. One of his brows arched. "What happened to *not even a little?*"

You happened. And it was the truth. He'd been sure his Camellia Clock had malfunctioned. He'd convinced himself that there was something they could do, a way to fix what was broken. But that wasn't the case, and Aiden Maar had been the one to sway Shannon's unshakable opinion. He'd been the one to change it all—a set of dark clouds on Shannon's horizon, a thunderstorm he wanted to play in. Shannon wasn't used to curiosity.

Aiden stepped forward. Shannon stepped back. It was habit.

The pink of Aiden's palms flashed. He offered a crooked smile and sighed. "I won't bite. Is that for me, or what?"

"Yeah, yes. Yes, it is. Sorry, here." Shannon handed Aiden one of the cups and averted his eyes.

"Caramel?" Aiden licked his lips, brow furrowed. He tried to cover his grimace with a smile and chuckled.

Shannon bristled. He rubbed the back of his neck and allowed Aiden to take the cup holder and toss it in the trashcan in the kitchen. "I didn't know what you like," he said. The nervous energy in the room began to relax. Blood rushed back into his hands as he uncurled his fists. "Not a fan of sweet coffee?"

"Hazelnut," Aiden said. One shoulder rolled. "You?"

"Black. Three sugars."

Waves crashed on the beach a few yards away. Two screeching seagulls perched on the chipped balcony. He glanced over his shoulder and shooed them with a wave of his arm.

"I'm gonna let Mercy eat you!" Aiden scowled. The birds didn't pay him any mind. "They always fly up here and mess up my plants," Aiden mumbled as though he was talking to an old friend. He kept his narrowed eyes fixed on the seagulls.

Shannon kept his eyes fixed on Aiden. "Who's Mercy?"

A grin lit Aiden's face. He held up his index finger, signaling Shannon to wait.

"Mercy! Hey, fatass, come out here..." Aiden's feet were silent against the beige carpet. Shannon took shy steps to the edge of the wall where the hallway started and looked down it. Aiden's voice sounded from the bedroom. "There you are! Come here."

Aiden returned with a cat slouched in his arms—and not just any cat. Mercy was all long tufts of cream fur sticking out from her well-fed body. Her eyes were tiny slits set deep in a smashed face. The tip of her tongue stuck out below a fan of bent white whiskers. She meowed, grating and low, and her frizzled tail swished back and forth. "Mercy, Detective Wurther—Detective Wurther, Mercy."

"Shannon," he corrected. He couldn't help but smirk at such a ridiculous creature, especially when it was held in Aiden Maar's arms. "It's Shannon Wurther. You don't have to call me detective."

"Oh, so you really *aren't* here to arrest me?" Aiden teased. He set the cat on the floor. Mercy waddled to the couch and jumped on the middle cushion. "It's Saturday. You're at my apartment. I'm not even going to ask how you got my address…" Aiden paused to sip his too-sweet coffee. "And you brought me a caramel macchiato. What can I do for you, Shannon?"

The way Aiden said his name, drawn out between his teeth as if it meant something, pulled Shannon's gut into his throat. He glanced at his feet, unable to come up with a good reason to be there. He'd looked up Aiden's address, followed his instincts downtown, turned right on Ocean Avenue and parked in the lot by the liquor store, across from Bluebird Beach Apartments. He didn't know why he'd searched for Aiden or why he kept thinking about the gallery, about the parking structure, and about how warm Aiden had felt pressed against him in the driver's seat.

Aiden cleared his throat.

"I wanted to see you." Shannon closed his eyes. He hadn't meant to say that. He hadn't meant to say a damn thing. "To talk," he added quickly. "And get to know you."

"Really?" Aiden drew out the word, letting it linger for far too long. Shannon gnashed his teeth. "Well, all right then." Aiden slid the balcony door open and gestured to a small round table and a pair of chairs. "We'll talk."

They sat for too long staring at each other. Well, not quite staring. Shannon tried to look elsewhere, while Aiden didn't bother. A salty breeze kicked up, tossing around Laguna Beach scents—coffee, wildflowers, aloe, cologne, sun block. The distant sound of laughter mingled with buzzing honey bees and rustling palm trees.

"I'll go first." Aiden leaned back in the woven wicker chair. "How old are you?"

"Twenty-five." Shannon's gaze darted from the edge of balcony to the man sitting across from him. "You're twenty-two. What's your favorite type of food?"

"Thai or Japanese; yours?"

He was tempted to say Southern comfort: Mom's fried chicken, baked macaroni and cheese, and sweet, almost-burnt cornbread. But Shannon skirted it, because he didn't want to get into his family, or his hometown, or let the accent he'd worked to cover over the years slip out. "I'm not picky. A burger and fries will do, or spaghetti. I'm easy to please."

Birds squawked and sang. Mercy sauntered over and meowed from the doorway. She flopped on her back on a patch of sun-warmed carpet.

"Your turn," Aiden said. Held up by his elbow propped on the armrest, his fingers were splayed over his face and his thumb rested beneath his jaw.

"Why'd you drop out of high school?"

"You have my file. You should be able to figure that out, *Detective*. Why'd you decide to be a cop?"

Shannon rolled his bottom lip between his teeth. "I wanted to help people."

"So, it had nothing to do with your daddy being a detective, too? That's convenient coming from the youngest cop on the force with passing scores on the agency exam."

"How do you know about my father?" Shannon scoffed and sipped his lukewarm coffee. "That's not my question. Why do you steal shit?" He winced at the cold bite in his voice. He hadn't meant to be brash— which was ridiculous since it was the truth. Aiden Maar was a thief, a proud one at that. It shouldn't be a hard question to answer.

Aiden's eyes narrowed. He sucked the inside of his cheek between his teeth and chewed on it, much as Shannon was chewing on his lip. His glare was a challenge, *how dare you* rang loud in the tense silence. He snorted; a wry smile crossed his lips. "Why'd you kiss me back?"

Great. Shannon's chest tightened. He deserved that. He should've seen it coming. He looked at the floor and then settled on the phoenix. Its feathers curved over Aiden's hip and its widespread wings stretched up his side and his back to touch the very tip of his shoulder. He was lean: the body of a scrapper. Toned muscles were carved across his abdomen, faded scars littered his skin, and his arms were slender, but capable.

Aiden cleared his throat. "Did you hear me, Detective Wurther?"

"I don't know," Shannon blurted. He looked up and saw Aiden's eyebrows pulling toward the bridge of his nose. His lips parted, he shook his head, and finally he looked away.

On some level, Shannon did know.

He knew that his expectations didn't match the outcome. He'd expected a sweet-tempered school teacher, a mild-mannered botanist, someone safe. He'd prepared for that, he'd settled on that. But buried under what he'd expected, was what he wanted: an undefinable, monumental something.

Deep down, where no one could see it, Shannon had wished for magic. And he thought he might be looking at it now.

Mercy hopped on Aiden's lap. He scratched behind her ears and stared at the skyline; his eyes focused on the glittering seam where blue met blue, air met ocean. "You should go enjoy your Saturday. I'm sure you've got better things to do than spend your time with a high school dropout who steals shit."

"Aiden, c'mon—"

"Don't say my name like that, all right?"

"Like what?"

"Like it's something important," Aiden muttered. "You were probably right. The Camellia Clock made a mistake. We should go back to you trying to bust me, and me getting away. Sound good? Wonderful."

Bitterness turned Aiden into stone. He didn't look at Shannon, not once. His flexed jaw hollowed the space below his cheek, and he rubbed his fingers against his thumb. Shannon thought there was something terrifyingly beautiful about him, like a poisonous flower, or the view on the edge of a cliff. The sun was on his face, and he was something Shannon wanted to touch.

But he didn't. Shannon stood up, grabbed his coffee, and walked away.

Aiden didn't say a word when Shannon opened the door. He didn't turn away from the horizon, or rise from his chair. He cooed at Mercy and stroked her head—such a loving thing for those villain hands to do.

Shannon scolded himself all the way down the stairs.

A WEEK AND A HALF passed. Aiden didn't know whether he was relieved or anxious.

Shannon hadn't been back. They hadn't run into each other at the beach, or in a coffee shop, or at the grocery store. It made him ponder fate and its ridiculous ins and outs—how a clock beneath his thumbnail could define the rest of his life and make the executive decision to tie him and Shannon Wurther together.

Handcuff them, actually.

Not that they had to listen; they certainly didn't. Stories surfaced from all over the world—*Rose Road blatantly ignored*—*Couple defies fate*—*Camellia Clock strikes out*—but Aiden knew he wasn't in one of those stories. There was no getting around it, not after Shannon pressed invisible marks all over his body and left Aiden's mouth impossibly empty. The Camellia Clock *could* be wrong. It happened sometimes; he was aware of that.

But this time it wasn't.

Mercy purred, rolling around on his chest as he lay in bed contemplating what came next. Whose move was it after the terrible-coffee date? Was the ball in his court? Was there even a fucking court to play in? Aiden scooped Mercy up and walked into the living room. Sunlight poured through the sliding glass door. Gray masked the sky's usual blue, broken up by thin, low hanging clouds, hovering just above the ocean.

"Hey!" He dropped Mercy, wrenched the glass door open, and waved his arm at a seagull. "Go to hell!" The seagull perched on the balcony screeched. "Don't eat my ferns!"

He inspected a basket planter in the corner. A few long arms of his wilting greenery were torn off. Aiden swiped at the air until the seagull squawked and flew off. He turned his bitterness to the mound of white fur sprawled on one of the chairs.

"You're a cat, you know. It's in your blood to hunt birds. Ever consider helping me out?"

Mercy yawned and rolled over onto her back. She was talented at dismissing Aiden and she wasn't the only one who could effortlessly ignore him.

Okay, he wasn't relieved. He was anxious. Despite his erratic sleep schedule and pitiful eating habits, Aiden was confident in his ability to stay sane. He was only plagued by thoughts of Detective Shannon Wurther nineteen out of the twenty-four hours in his day—perfectly manageable.

"Mercy, tell me what to do. Should I make an account and message him on Facebook, or is that weird?"

Mercy licked her nose and lent a polite, "Mrow?"

"Okay, what if I try to find him? He showed up here without any warning. That means I can show up at his house, right?" He fumbled with his lighter and cursed.

Mercy purred. Her tail swung to and fro.

He pinched the butt of a cigarette between his teeth. "You're right, that's a terrible idea."

Mercy chirped.

It was torture going to bed, and it was torture waking up. When Aiden woke, Shannon was there, the imprint of his lips was sugar on Aiden's mouth. When he slept, Shannon was a voice that Aiden couldn't discern, another ghost, another nightmare, another dream that shook him awake. Consciousness put him back together in the witching hours, the twos and threes and fours, when the rest of the world slept, but Aiden couldn't. He hadn't expected Shannon to grow inside him, tangle in his ribs, sprout between his vertebrae.

Aiden dropped into the chair across from Mercy and ignored the nagging scrape in the back of his mind. He was plagued by thoughts, assumptions, and daydreams: sometimes Shannon looking at him on the other side of a bed, sometimes bare feet and the smell of freshly brewed coffee, sometimes a smile and the brush of fingertips across his shoulders, sometimes an almost-kiss and *how was work*. But every time, Aiden was stitching together a scene he'd never live out, not in this life, not in the next.

The daydreams about Shannon Wurther were nothing but daydreams and, in the end, that's what they'd continue to be, images mirroring a fresh memory.

Mercy meowed again. She stretched her paws from the chair to the tabletop and rubbed her head against his wrist. Aiden stared at the horizon.

Daydreams. Nightmares. Dreams. Shannon was all around him.

Aiden stubbed out the cigarette and trudged inside. He dressed: black pants, white shirt, leather jacket, boots, and helmet. He kissed Mercy on the head.

A strong buzz prompted him to scramble for his phone. Hoping it might be Shannon, he almost tripped down the last couple stairs. It wasn't, and Aiden couldn't hide the disappointment from himself.

Marcus Maar 10/5 3:22 p.m.
Hey, we should get dinner soon.
Marcus Maar 10/10 6:09 p.m.
How's the new job?
Marcus Maar 10/12 11:46 a.m.
Where are you? I wired you this month's rent.

Marcus Maar 10/14 7:05 a.m.
Aiden answer me

His fingers hovered above the keyboard. Another buzz. Another text.

Marcus Maar 10/14 7:08 a.m.
Fine. When you want to talk about it call me.

Aiden gritted his teeth. He shoved his phone into his pocket without responding to his brother. He tugged his helmet on, fastened the chin strap, gripped the handlebars, and took solace in the smell of gasoline and the powerful growl of the bike as it surged beneath him.

FOG HELD THE HEAT IN, which was inconvenient. It was misleading for the weather to play tricks. Shannon shrugged off his heavy pea-coat and slung it over his shoulder. Karman stomped beside him. Her polished black flats beat the sidewalk.

"Warm for October," Shannon said. He glanced over just as Karman shoved the corner of a supersized burrito into her mouth.

"Always is." She smacked her lips, and her face suddenly lit, as if she'd remembered something important. Shannon was sure a look like that meant she'd figured out his secret-not-secret. "Wasn't there something you had planned this month? Birthday? Deadline?"

He closed his fist around his thumb. She hadn't figured it out, which was a relief as much as it was a burden. A part of him was on the edge of his seat, waiting for her to put two and two together, but another, larger, deeper part of him wasn't sure of his readiness for that. She shrugged and tilted her head, fitting more of the burrito into her mouth. That was that.

What happened at Aiden's apartment wasn't *all* his fault, was it? Aiden was as violently hostile as he was handsome—an unsettling observation, but one that made the situation difficult. Parts of their brief interaction left a shameful taste in his mouth: the leaving part, the bickering part, the being-too-guarded part. Everything else left him wanting: the coffee part, the Aiden's smile part, the him-being-a-cat-person part. Those parts were only fragments of what stole Shannon's focus throughout the day. The rest was like the weather: foggy and too hot to be considered anything but inconvenient.

"So, first things first. Warrant for the drug bust at the house in the Hills comes through today, right?" Karman wiped salsa off her chin as they waited for the crosswalk to change from the flashing red hand to the fluorescent white *GO*. "Then we've got the inside job for the boutique downtown, you know, that one real expensive place that sells the abalone jewelry? Owner thinks she's got someone on her team that's stealing, been recording 'em for weeks now."

"First things first, we stop by my place. I need to ditch this jacket and I forgot my bag."

"You? Forget something?" Karman hooted. "What's with you? Been sleepin' all right?"

Shannon shook his head. "No, actually, I haven't been." It came out brittle, a snap of his teeth.

Karman's head lurched back, and she smiled thinly. "Whoever put salt on your lollipop, I don't wanna meet 'em." She held up her hands in surrender, dropping the conversation where it started. "But let's take your jolly ass to your apartment and then grab your car. I don't feel like walking the Hills today."

They turned right on Fourth and headed inland. Two blocks up, parallel to Main, and five blocks from Aiden's apartment, was Shannon's loft. It was situated over a seasonally-staffed bakery. During summer, June through September, they made smoothies, cupcakes, juices, and pastries. The rest of the year was quiet, and Shannon appreciated the privacy. Even during the busy months, the only bother was heat that rose through the vents from the bakery's ovens, and living in a building on a main road. Traffic was terrible, so was parking. Summer in general was obnoxious.

Two flights of cement stairs led to an entryway with one door. He opened it, darted inside, ignored Karman's noise of disapproval, and grabbed his bag.

"You need a maid."

"No," Shannon growled. He tossed his coat onto a medium-sized couch he'd picked up at the swap meet. "I need to do laundry. It looks messy because I haven't picked up my clothes."

"It looks messy because it is messy, Wurther. You sure you're okay?" She slapped the back of her hand against his forehead, checking for a fever. "The Wurther I know doesn't do messy."

He ducked away from her and rolled his eyes. "Just a weird couple of weeks, Cruz. C'mon let's go." He locked the door behind him and followed Karman down the stairs.

They hit the sidewalk. A horn blared. Shannon looked up and froze.

At the green light across from him, a bike idled: thick tires, sleek black body, engine revving hot. Its rider had his head turned, observing Shannon. He knew that leather jacket, those combat boots. The car behind Aiden Maar honked again, but he didn't budge. Finally, when Shannon thought his chest might burst from holding his breath, the bike's engine roared, and Aiden sped off.

Shannon swallowed. He forced his legs to move, walking after Karman as she continued down the sidewalk without him.

Just like that, in the blink of an eye, Shannon's day was wrecked. His thoughts would consist of nothing but Aiden Maar: the smell of gasoline; the hesitant brush of his lips, long fingers on Shannon's face; the depth of that damn kiss; his helmet, black as night; the twist of his smile, distracting and vicious and too perfect to be real.

"Hey, you good, Wurther? Cindy's got the warrant for us at the station; let's get a move on."

He tried to nod. His throat was scratchy and dry. "I'm good, yeah. Let's go."

Aiden Maar kept him awake, and Aiden Maar kept him on edge, and Aiden Maar was everywhere.

7

OKAY, MAYBE HE DIDN'T MAKE the greatest decisions in the world. Nobody's perfect.

Aiden stumbled against the concrete stairs that led to what he assumed was Shannon's front door. He dug the heel of his palm into the wet, warm spot above his hip. The knife hadn't been a big one— well, it hadn't been big enough. But that didn't stop it from hurting like a bitch when it was rammed through Aiden's jacket.

He probably shouldn't have made a bet with the drunken out-of-towner from Vegas, nor should he have "accidentally" spilled his entire beer on said out-of-towner's date. He hadn't been looking for a Friday night bar fight, but he'd been looking for something—a distraction, a lullaby.

He squeezed his eyes shut and panted, then took more painful steps to the landing that led to Shannon's door. Judging by the amount of blood and the fact that he wasn't dizzy, he probably didn't need stitches. No hospital, no hospital bills, which meant he didn't have to deal with Marcus or insurance companies. But no hospital also meant there was no one to help him get this shit taken care of—this shit being the hole in his abdomen and the blood soaking through his jacket.

Aiden huffed a laugh. Good thing Detective Wurther lived down the street. Convenience had the potential to be ironic, almost as ironic as two days ago when Shannon had walked down these cement stairs. Aiden thought back to that day, to the shared surprise they'd both tried to cover, and the fake disregard at the sight of each other. Maybe it wasn't convenience at all; maybe it was exclusively ironic.

The door didn't open when he knocked the first time, but he didn't expect it to. It was almost one in the morning, and it was the weekend. Shannon probably wasn't home.

Aiden pounded on the door with the side of his fist. Just when a wave of uncertainty started to swell in Aiden's chest, the lock clicked. Shannon was home. Aiden didn't need to call Marcus. Everything was fine.

"What're you doin' here?" Shannon pawed at his eyes with the back of his hands. His short hair, which Aiden assumed was usually groomed to look messy, was actually messy. Sleepiness hung around him in a cloud, becoming visible as he yawned and strained to blink. Black gym shorts hung low on his waist, and his socks were mismatched. Aiden smiled despite himself and the pain biting into his side. Shannon clearly noticed the blood quicker than Aiden wanted him to. He jolted from asleep to awake, quiet and curious, to angry and worried. Aiden hadn't expected the worry.

"What'd you do to yourself?" Shannon scolded. He hauled Aiden in by the arm that wasn't smashed over the wet spot on his jacket.

"Why do you jump to what *I* did to *myself*? Someone else could've done this, you know."

Shannon wasn't gentle. He shoved Aiden against the nearest wall and wrenched his bloody hand away from the wound. "Because you're an idiot," he hissed. "Take this off." He stripped away Aiden's leather jacket and threw it to the floor. Shannon tried to fold his shirt up from the bottom.

"Fuck you—ow! Shannon, that hurts! God... dammit." Aiden swatted Shannon's shoulder, then braced himself against the wall as his ratty T-shirt was peeled away from the wound. Okay, maybe it hurt. Aiden lifted his fist to his mouth and bit his knuckle. Heat grew in his cheeks. His throat felt like sandpaper. "I didn't do this to myself, by the way."

"Jesus…" Shannon turned on the light, leaving Aiden long enough to let him slide down the wall. There was more blood than Aiden had realized. He watched Shannon move through the loft, past a kitchenette, and into the bathroom. A cabinet door slammed.

His legs stretched in front of him on the tile floor and his hand sealed over the wound again. *Stop shaking.* Aiden willed his body to calm down. It didn't work.

"Hey, stop that." Shannon crouched beside him. "You're gonna make it worse if you keep putting your filthy hands on it. Who did this to you?"

Aiden's mouth pinched. He straightened his back and winced when the puncture coughed blood. "Some stupid dick at a dive up the road. I lost a bet, and he stabbed me with a switchblade."

"You're telling me that you did nothing to this guy? He just decided that tonight was a good night to stab you?" Shannon's focus was on the wound.

He batted Aiden's hand away and wiped the blood smeared across his stomach. The tips of his fingers, covered by a damp cloth, brushed the gash. Aiden yelped, scrambling against the wall.

Shannon held him in place. "Almost done…"

"I didn't do anything to him! I mean, I lost a bet and I spilled my drink, but it wasn't a big deal. Some of my beer might've splashed his date."

"Did you *spill* your drink or did you *pour* it?"

A sheepish grin pulled at Aiden's lips. "Is there a difference?"

"So, you *are* an idiot." Shannon drew a deep breath, the way an impatient parent would.

Shannon's nimble fingers placed antiseptic on the cut, which was embarrassingly small now that it was clean. His face was hard in rapt concentration.

He had dimples. Aiden stored their image for his fleeting daydreams and nightly stints of sleeplessness. Shannon was also graced with prominent cheekbones, straight from a magazine—Boy Scout handsome, Ivy League handsome, stereotypical *cop* handsome. He wrapped a bandage around Aiden's side and taped it down.

"An idiot who is covered in blood," Shannon noted while he analyzed the state Aiden was in. Aiden wasn't fond of being analyzed. "And you *reek*."

"I smell bad?" Aiden looked down at himself.

"Like alcohol."

"Obviously. I told you I'd been at a bar." Aiden was thankful for said alcohol. It dulled his anxiety and smothered the panic whispering behind his thoughts. *Stop breathing. Stop talking.*

Shannon sat cross-legged in front of him. Aiden didn't understand his ease. If he was a cop, he should've been assertive. If he was the cop those articles were written about, he should've been overbearing. It seemed he was neither. Shannon sighed and very quietly asked, "How'd you know about my dad?"

Aiden laughed, one single *ha,* and said, "I Googled you! How else would I know? They wrote an article about your promotion, youngest detective on the force and all. Several articles. What'd you think I did? It's not like I can pull your file, Shannon."

He nodded, expressionless. "And why'd you come here?"

It was difficult to choose between being hurt and being pissed. But he didn't have an answer. Not one that made any sense. He'd dragged his bleeding, sorry self all the way to Shannon's loft because it was either that or Marcus, and calling Marcus wasn't an option.

"Nowhere else to go," Aiden said. That was the truth, wasn't it? Aiden didn't have anybody else. Aiden didn't even have Shannon. "Guess I just followed my Rose Road," he added under his breath, glancing at his hands, stained red. He was drunk. He shouldn't have said that.

Shannon exhaled Aiden's name.

"What'd I tell you about saying my name like that?" Aiden snapped. He stood, stumbling to catch himself when pain burned his side. "I'm sorry I came here, all right? I'm just gonna go."

"No, you're not." Shannon's broad chest blocked the door. "You've been drinking, you're hurt, and it's too far for you to walk. You can stay here—"

Aiden tried to push past him. "I don't want to stay here." He was being irrational and he was well aware of that, but he hadn't thought this through—not the Shannon part, not the Rose Road part, not the spending the night part. He hadn't thought about anything except the blood and the pain and the potential hospital bills. Aiden wouldn't admit that dreams of Shannon caused him to go look for trouble in the first place. "And *you* don't want me to stay here."

Two hands, the same hands that'd found their way beneath his shirt in the parking structure, gripped his shoulders, and forced Aiden backward. "You're staying," Shannon said. His voice was too stern to argue with. Not when Aiden, for once, wasn't in the mood to fight. "Couch or bed?"

"Where are you sleeping?" Aiden's face was extremely hot. He looked past the couch to an old wooden trunk that served as a coffee table. Behind it, pressed against the brick wall next to window after window, sat a rumpled, over-sized bed.

"Wherever you're not."

That hurt—not the kind of hurt radiating beneath the bandage. It was a hollow ache, a bee sting on his vocal cords. The same jolt of recognition came before being punched: adrenaline, and then anxiety, and then nothing. Aiden should've braced himself. He should've let it go and never expected Shannon to consider sharing a space with him, especially his own bed. He should've never shown up at Shannon's door.

Shannon watched the adrenaline, the anxiety, the nothing cross his face. Shannon did it again. He said, "Aiden, wait..." And it sounded like screeching tires.

"How about you just don't say my name anymore at all." He eased onto the couch and curled up facing the cushions, aware that Shannon stood over him. Aiden closed his eyes. His lashes were wet.

00:00

SHANNON LIKED TO LEAVE THE blinds open. That's the first thing Aiden realized on the bright October morning. Light beamed through the four windows on the street-facing wall, tugging him from hazy sleep. His eyelids might have been tied to cinder blocks. Pain throbbed in his abdomen. He was still covered in blood—dried on his hands, caked under his fingernails, and smeared on his chest. A water bottle sat atop the table-trunk in front of the couch, and across from it the entertainment stand housed a clawed-foot flat screen and rows of DVDs. The walls were blank, but somehow the space still felt warm. Maybe it was the mismatched couch, the exposed brick and hardwood floors, or the lingering scent of Shannon's cologne.

Sitting up felt like being stabbed all over again. Aiden looked at the bandage on his stomach and the blood on his jeans and laughed. "I *am* an idiot," he whispered.

"Yep."

Aiden bolted to his feet and turned around, wincing as the flesh beneath the bandage stretched.

Shannon glared at him from the bed. He sat up on his elbow, looking annoyed and very cop-like. Judgment circled like vultures. "You *are* an idiot. I'm glad to hear you finally admit it."

Aiden opened his mouth. He narrowed his eyes, collected a slingshot of curses and insults on the tip of his tongue, and then choked on them. Fragments of their argument the night before flashed through his mind: Shannon saying his name, a chorus of compassion and affection, trying to leave, tears.

He'd cried. In front of Shannon Wurther. *No.*

"Wait! No, you don't get to—Aiden!" Somehow Shannon managed to get in front of the door before Aiden could grab his jacket and get out. "You don't get to walk out of here like nothing happened."

Aiden's head pounded. His heartbeat drummed in his knuckles. "Move."

"I'm not moving."

"Move, or I'll knock your teeth in." Aiden seethed. He didn't mean that, but it felt good to say it. He gasped; a strangled breath was knocked from him as Shannon gripped his wrists and shoved his bare back against the wall. "*Shannon,*" he warned, forcing his name through a tight, clenched jaw. The wound on his hip throbbed. Red spots dampened the bandage. Within him bubbled a witch's cauldron filled with hostility.

"Look at me." Shannon let go of Aiden's right wrist and grasped his jaw, forcing his attention. It was too intimate. It was too much of everything. Aiden's reservations dropped. He tried to breathe. "Why don't you want me to say your name?"

He could disappear in Shannon's eyes: blue like stepping off the shelf at the beach or deep sea diving on a clear day.

"Aiden, tell me."

"Because!" Aiden blurted. "I've been waiting for this, too, okay? But when my Clock ran out, it was *you* in front of me. *Detective* Shannon Wurther." He shoved Shannon aside and picked up his jacket, fighting the grating in his throat. "I waited my whole fucking life for you, my *Rose Road*..." Sarcasm filled Aiden's mouth, but he was deflated, even a little defeated. He turned toward the front door, away from Shannon's slack jaw and wide eyes. "Every time you say my name, you say it like it means something, and I know for a fact that you don't want it to."

The door slammed. Aiden rushed down the stairs. His trembling hands searched his jacket until he found the cigarettes hidden in the inside pocket. He bit down on the filter and flicked his lighter until it produced a flame. Smoke filled his lungs.

It was an exhausting, painful, disingenuous thing, trying to hate Shannon Wurther.

SHANNON WURTHER 10/27 11:14 A.M.
are you doing okay?
Aiden Maar 10/27 11:15 a.m.
who the fuck
Shannon Wurther 10/27 11: 17 a.m.
shannon
Aiden Maar 10/27 11:21 a.m.
i dont remember giving you my number detective
Shannon Wurther 10/27 11:22 a.m.
you didn't

Shannon stared at his phone for five minutes while the image of three dots undulated where Aiden was supposedly typing. The straw in his massive 7-Eleven plastic cup swirled through ice cubes as he searched out any remaining soda. Karman's acrylic fingernails clacked against her keyboard on the other side of their conjoined desk. Those three dots kept undulating.

"Did you finish the paperwork for that traffic accident from yesterday? The one in the canyon?" Karman asked.

Shannon stared at his phone. "Yeah, I got that done this morning. Any leads on the campus drug bust from last week? Our informant should have something for us by now."

"Nada."

Aiden Maar 10/27 11:38 a.m.
creep

Shannon battled with himself over what to say. He'd been ready for a long string of words, an exaggerated bit of Aiden that would surprise him. But no. A one-word text was all he got.

Shannon Wurther 10/27 11:39 a.m.
how are you doing? Is that cut healing?
Aiden Maar 10/27 11:43 a.m.
im fine
Shannon Wurther 10/27 11:45 a.m.
did you go see a doctor?
Aiden Maar 10/27 11:47 a.m.
no

Shannon dropped his phone and it clattered against the desk. What kind of irrational, stubborn, negligent person would let that go? Aiden should've gone to urgent care—at least for a few stitches—or to the hospital, to a doctor who would tell him how to take care of the wound. Not that it was *that* bad, but still.

"What's up with you? Got a salty-ass look on your face, Wurther."

"Nothing," he mumbled, glancing at Karman.

"Oh." She dragged the word out the way she always did when she didn't believe him. She watched him with her brows raised. "Okay then. Well, when you want help pulling that stick out, I'm here. In the meantime, we should do a sweep of the high school. The three-month mark is coming up, right?"

He glared. Shannon thoroughly disliked being a cactus, especially when it was Karman who had to deal with him. He tried to smile an apology. "Yeah, we'll need to call a couple canine units and get them ready for it. I'll contact the school and schedule it for tomorrow."

Karman nodded and shuffled through papers on her desk. She held up a manila file and examined it with her head tilted. Her lips pursed. "Maar? Why is this on my desk? I didn't ask for a file on... Aiden Maar?"

Shannon scrambled to his feet and reached for the file. "It's mine. I asked for it. I thought I gave it back to Cindy but I must've left it out. It's nothing."

Karman lifted it away and kept flipping through the mess of papers. "This is that dude you checked out for your landlord, right? Oh, avian tattoo on his side, assault charges, attempted burglary—"

He snatched the file and wrinkled his nose. "He's just some stupid kid, Karman. I should get this back to Cindy."

His phone lit up and buzzed.

Aiden Maar 10/27 12:10 p.m.
how are you
Shannon Wurther 10/27 12:12 p.m.
working, but i'm alright
Aiden Maar 10/27 12:13 p.m.
thanks for patching me up
Shannon Wurther 10/27 12:15 p.m.
i'm sorry things happened the way they did
Aiden Maar 10/27 12:15 p.m.
don't
Shannon Wurther 10/27 12:16 p.m.
i am though, i want you to know that
Aiden Maar 10/27 12:17 p.m.
i gotta go.
Shannon Wurther 10/27 12:19 p.m.
ok?

And that was that. No more undulating dots. No more texts. Silence. He stared at his phone waiting for another message. Nothing. He shoved his phone in the front pocket of his jeans and tried to keep the rising anxiety from showing on his face. Fate sure knew how to pick them. Unruly, volatile, and self-absorbed wasn't Shannon's type, but apparently he was supposed to look past the defects of Aiden Maar and find the parts that might be acceptable. He was going to try. He had to.

Shannon retraced every memory of Aiden that he had stored away: the curve of his lips when he smiled; the singular points of his cheekbones; his small chin; his eyes, always too invasive, always piqued with interest; his warm, ashy breath; his mouth, soft and demanding, pulling the darkest parts of Shannon to the surface when they kissed.

Shannon returned to his desk after he gave Aiden's file to Cindy at the front of the station. He chewed on the straw of his empty soda cup and let the thought of Aiden's legs around his waist and the tangle of his fingers through his hair take him back—back to the first night when he thought the Clock was wrong, back to being a fool, letting his pride win and watching Aiden leave when all he'd wanted was for him to stay.

Karman talked softly on her cell phone, sighed, and rubbed her temples with one hand stretched across her forehead. "Yeah, I'll be right there. Is she okay?"

Karman hung up. She grabbed her purse and shot him a pitiful smile. "Fae has a fever. I have to pick her up and take her to the doctor. You gonna be okay here?"

"It's been quiet. I'm sure I can handle everything. I'll get the canine units ready for tomorrow and check on the highway patrol."

She nodded and fished in her purse for her keys.

"Car been okay?"

"Eh, it's running. Should be good for another two months before something else goes wrong," Karman said through a laugh. She gave a halfhearted wave over her shoulder as she left.

Shannon's pocket vibrated.

Aiden Maar 10/27 1:30 p.m.
dont be sorry

The image of Aiden's eyes misted over, his lips drawn into a thin line, blinking at the ground, forced its way to the front of Shannon's mind. He almost winced.

Shannon Wurther 10/27 1:32 p.m.
dont ask me not to be sorry. i was an asshole
Aiden Maar 10/27 1:33 p.m.
i was an idiot
Shannon Wurther 10/27 1:35 p.m.
fair enough

Once again, Aiden stopped typing, and Shannon remembered the way he looked—pained and soft and everything that Shannon didn't realize he was. The rose, who was usually all thorns and no petals, had wilted.

Shannon looked at the paneled ceiling and wheeled back and forth in his chair.

Summer had faded. It happened every year. Tourists flocked to the beaches to soak up the little bit of heat that clung to the Southern California coast. At night, flames licked the cold from inside concrete fire pits, and locals scoured vintage bars in search of seasonal drinks. The town wasn't transformed. The same palm trees swayed in the wind, but instead of warmth and sunlight, a cool, haunting breeze whipped through the streets and a few more stars littered the sky.

October let the beach-goers soak up the trailing dog days until Halloween. That night was always the death of summer. The last bit of heat was swept away, gobbled up by the ocean, and in an instant, autumn was in full swing. Leaves skittered over Shannon's shoes as he walked past the pizza parlor on Third. Most of the kids dressed as goblins and angels and dinosaurs had retired for the evening. Now, streets echoed with the sounds of taxis, too-loud music, and the distant growl of waves breaking on the shore.

Aiden Maar 10/31 12:05 a.m.
the saloon dumbass. its a bar
Shannon Wurther 10/31 12:07 a.m.
are you with friends?

Aiden Maar 10/31 12:08 a.m.
no

Shannon knew the Saloon, an old bar downtown next to Main Beach, but he didn't frequent it. Every venue in town, up the coast, and inland was doing something for Halloween. There were rooftop parties at resorts, a horror movie marathon at the theater, and events at every watering hole he could think of. He stepped around a stumbling group of undead brides, shared the sidewalk with vampires, and darted out of the way of scantily clad superheroes, as he made his way to the fanciest dive in town—and to Aiden. That was his real destination, wasn't it? They'd shared a few texts, but Shannon hadn't seen him since he left his loft the morning after their argument-not-argument.

It hadn't dawned on him, not until after Aiden's emotional exit, that Shannon might be able to hurt him. He didn't think it was possible. Aiden was... *Aiden was Aiden.* He was cold and jagged and walled-up. He was a stranger.

The streetlight outside the Saloon illuminated a group of smokers standing by the door. Shannon wove through them and slid inside. A mahogany bar stretched down the side of a narrow corridor packed with people in costume. A couple straight out of the Roaring Twenties made room for him at the bar, where he ordered a whiskey, neat. It was hard to make out faces in the dim lighting, and it was even harder when everyone wore a different personality. He caught the eye of a bedazzled blonde dressed as a Playboy bunny, smiled at a man wearing yellow contacts, who was covered in fake blood, pieced together by latex wounds.

It took a few minutes for Shannon to find him, but he did. Aiden was in the back, lurking in a shadowed corner. A wide grin split his face, which was painted like a skeleton, and he talked against a girl's ear. His hand hovered on her lower back, and he smirked when she threw her head back in an exaggerated laugh. His dark eyes locked onto Shannon.

Aiden watched as Shannon side stepped one way and dipped another and he straightened his back when they were close enough to speak.

The girl beamed. She stared at Aiden as if he was exactly what she thought he was—the boy her parents told her to stay away from, with an aura that said *danger, danger* and a devious smile. Shannon rolled his eyes when she placed a hand on Aiden's chest and asked, "Oh, is this your friend?"

"'Friend' is a strong word." Aiden lifted a glass of amber liquid to his lips.

Shannon's mouth twitched. Jealousy? No, that wasn't it. Not at all. Not even a little.

He tugged the bottom of his jacket to the side, flashing the badge attached to his belt. "Detective Wurther, ma'am." The petite brunette shot Aiden a withering look. "May I have a word with your date?"

"He's not my date," she stammered, and offered Aiden another pitiful, apologetic smile. Her faerie wings bounced on her back as she slipped away.

"Wow…" Aiden sighed, laughing through it. "That was mean, Detective." The bar was too loud. Aiden had to shout over the music. "And look at you! I should've guessed you wouldn't dress up."

"Costumes aren't my thing." His gaze wandered the black paint covering Aiden's face. It hollowed his eyes and cheeks and slashed his mouth into segments of flesh, black, flesh, black, flesh. "All you did was paint yourself," Shannon mumbled, gesturing at the rest of him, dressed in a pair of blue jeans with a tear in the knee and a black long-sleeved shirt. "How's that cut of yours doing?"

"I superglued it." Long fingers spread over the place where the bandage had been.

"You what?" Shannon leaned forward. His eyebrows bunched together. He couldn't have heard that right.

"I superglued it! They do it all the time at the hospital!"

"Seriously?" Shannon barked a laugh. He wanted to be surprised, he really did. He leaned his shoulder against the wall and took another, longer sip of his drink. It burned his throat, reminding him to look away once in a while, not to stare at the tendon flexing in Aiden's throat, and especially not at his mouth, which tilted in a coy smile.

"So." Aiden set his empty glass on a round table cluttered with other empty glasses. "What'd you wanna do?"

Shannon's stomach jumped. He crossed one foot over the other. It was Halloween. Talking about anything important was out of the question, and so was going somewhere quiet and less crowded, seeing as everywhere else was just as crowded and just as loud. He shrugged. "I didn't have anything in mind. I just wanted to see you after—"

"Yeah, let's not talk about that." Aiden said it through an endearing smile, honest and distant. "I don't exactly know what we're doing here." He waved his hands between them. "But I'm going out for a smoke."

Shannon stood in the back of the bar while Aiden walked past him. Shannon might have felt his fingertips brush the top of his hand, his waist, but he couldn't be sure. He took a long sip.

He didn't know what they were doing, either, but they had to do *something*.

00:00

HALLOWEEN USED TO BE AIDEN'S favorite holiday. He could dress up as an astronaut, or a dragon, or a knight, and no one would question it. But he was twenty-two now. He couldn't pretend to be something noble or fantastic or important anymore.

He inhaled deeply, enduring the burn the tobacco left behind in his throat. It was cold, finally. The air rolled off the backs of crashing waves and chilled the streets. He rested his back against the wall of the bar. Bass from the music playing inside vibrated along his spine.

The alley beside the Saloon faced the boardwalk that paralleled the sand. A couple played at the tideline. Aiden watched their shadows as they kicked up water with their bare feet and grabbed each other. Were they walking their Rose Road, too? Or did they stray, find love with another, and defy fate? Maybe those shadows playing catch me if you can on the first cold night in fall were two people hoping they could redefine their futures. Maybe their Clocks had stopped, and maybe they'd fallen into each other the way they were supposed to.

Maybe it was all a sham.

Maybe he wanted to be them.

The paper sparked on the end of his cigarette. He pinched it between his teeth and took another drag. Footsteps echoed from the mouth of the alley, treading closer. *Took him long enough.*

"That's a disgusting habit," Shannon said. He stood in front of Aiden with his hands shoved in the front pockets of his perfectly pressed tan pants. His face was all nice angles: a sloped nose, square chin, incredible eyes—eyes like rain. "When'd you pick it up?"

"When I was a teenager." Aiden inhaled again. Shannon stepped closer. "Why does it matter?"

His skin tingled, and his stomach fluttered. A delicious pull started below his belly button. Shannon put his hand on the wall beside Aiden's head. They were about the same height, but Aiden's chunky combat boots gave him an extra inch.

"It doesn't." He lifted his eyes, and his lashes swept across his cheeks. Shannon sighed and asked, "Why'd you get out of my car so fast that first night?"

There was tenderness in his voice and a raw curiosity that pulled harder on Aiden's gut. He looked away from Shannon and his fucking eyes. Aiden had a nice buzz going, his body was loose, he was in a good mood, and now it was all fucked up. He didn't want to talk about the first night. He didn't want to talk about *any* night involving Shannon. Couldn't they just be here? In this night? At this bar? Couldn't moments be fleeting and easy?

Aiden let the alcohol talk. "Because you kissed me back. You surprised me, I guess. I wasn't expecting that you'd be all..." Okay, maybe he shouldn't let the alcohol talk. "All over me. I thought you'd throw me out of your car." He chuckled over the last few words. "I didn't think you'd want anything to do with me."

"Because I'm a cop, is that it?"

Because I'm a mess. Aiden shook his head.

"Then why?" Shannon almost sounded breathless. He almost sounded shocked. The drawl at the end might've been an accent.

Aiden flicked the cigarette butt away and swiped the back of his hand across his mouth, removing flaky black paint. "You're fucking ridiculous, Shannon." Hoping none of it got in Shannon's face, Aiden blew the tail end of smoke at the ground. He heard the wobble in his own voice, the uncertainty, and flicked his wrist up and down. "C'mon, look at you…"

Shannon made an offended noise, a short *ha* that sounded like disbelief rather than mockery. But Aiden wasn't looking at him; he couldn't tell if it was the *ha* of someone who agreed, or the *ha* of someone who was blindsided. Shannon stepped closer, and Aiden stepped back, but there was nowhere for him to go.

"Yeah, look at me." They were rough, calloused words, forced between his teeth like something he shouldn't have to say. Shannon gripped Aiden's face and pulled.

Their lips clashed. They kissed as though they were waging wars and winning them. Aiden tried to steady his breathing. He pushed into Shannon, into his hands, his chest, his mouth, and everywhere else. The back of his head lolled against the concrete wall as Shannon crowded him against it. Smooth hands skirted beneath his shirt, and Aiden tensed, his flesh squirming away from near-frozen fingertips. He didn't know what Shannon was searching for on his skin, his rib cage, the curve of his lower back, but Aiden hoped he never found it—until Shannon's thumb dug into the hollow of his hip.

"Careful, careful." Aiden winced, gripping Shannon's wrist. "Superglue isn't magic—still sore."

Aiden chased his lips, but Shannon examined the messy superglue stitches. Shannon's thumb flicked across the skin above the wound.

The flat of his palm disappeared under Aiden's shirt and stepped over his ribs. The fabric bunched around Shannon's wrist and left a sliver of flesh uncovered to welcome the brisk night air. Shannon's other hand curled around Aiden's neck, and his thumb guided his chin to the side.

Shannon went back to digging his nails into Aiden's side. Warm breath on his throat. Feather light brush of lips against his ear. Pain. Teeth sinking in above his pulse. Aiden faltered, stumbling to speak. He managed a whimper. He gripped the short hairs on the back of Shannon's head, which forced him to stay where he was, to bite harder, to leave marks.

He wanted to wake up with bruises on his neck. He wanted proof.

Aiden had been kissed before. He'd been kissed many times before. But none of the befores were anything like this now. Every before had seemed like stealing, seized adrenaline, mastered and then discarded. This kiss was suspended high above the others: a losing track of, and making sure to, an unfinished statement going on and on. Shannon's teeth in his throat became Shannon's mouth on his mouth, again and again.

This kiss was *it's you* and *impossible* and *you're real*.

They stayed pinned against the wall until whispers from the door of the Saloon turned into laughs and laughs turned into shouts.

"We're drawing a crowd," Shannon mumbled. His thigh pressed between Aiden's legs.

"Good." Aiden clenched his hand on the front of Shannon's shirt and pulled him back.

A raspy laugh was all of Shannon's protest. It was thrilling to hear him laugh, genuine and playful and confident. The smell of bourbon and whiskey mingled in their shared breath. Shannon dragged his lips against Aiden's jaw, his cheek, the bridge of his nose, but stopped a fraction of an inch from Aiden's mouth, just to breathe, just to look.

He couldn't imagine what Shannon saw. Aiden's face was hot beneath the paint, his bottom lip tingled where it'd been bitten, and his stomach was somersaulting. He couldn't catch his breath. He turned his face away in search of cold air. Shannon's forehead rested against his temple. His hands crawled from beneath Aiden's shirt. "Come over?"

"To your place?" Aiden arched a brow.

Shannon shifted and took a half step back. "Yes, to my place."

Someone smoking by the door yelled, "Done already?" Aiden smiled, sheepish and a little embarrassed. He averted his eyes, staring at the scuffed tops of his boots.

"Let's go to the beach first," Aiden said.

Shannon tilted his head, lips barely parted. He gave a curt nod. "All right."

There it was again, the long "ah" in the way he said "all" and the crisp "igh" in his "right." Aiden didn't mention it.

They walked to the beach. Not hand in hand, but close enough. Aiden smoked another cigarette even though Shannon wrinkled his nose and shot him a deadly glare.

The sound of bargoers hailing taxis and skyscraper heels tapping the concrete were the backdrop to Halloween. Add his own heart beating a mile a minute and Shannon Wurther's breathing, relaxed but not, a steady hum by his side. The waves were their only witnesses, lapping at the shore, crashing on the sand and eating the echo of anything else, even Aiden's heartbeat, even Shannon's breathing.

There was stillness under the blanket of darkness on the last night in October, where summer shouted its final hurrah. The moon hid behind dark cliffs. Aiden looked up, his focus drawn to the pinholes that littered the sky. Stars didn't twinkle as people said they did, but he saw them shine, tiny bits of light, like far-away drops of paint scattered above them. Shannon's breath was on his neck again. *Steady, stay steady.* He took Shannon's lips in his own: a hard kiss, a kiss he hoped said, *there's no going back.*

Aiden was a shadow on the beach. His hands were inside Shannon's jacket; his fingertips ran along his chest, his waist. He felt the edge of his golden badge against his pinky. Shannon was the other.

SHANNON WANTED A CAMERA—A DISPOSABLE film camera—a way to capture what happened to Aiden Maar when he slept. The edges that Aiden kept sharp softened in the morning light. His parted lips calmed, became still, as he drew slow, long breaths. One of his arms was above his head and his face was turned away. His shoulders, usually rigid, dipped into the white sheets. The sweep of his eyelashes might have been the gentlest thing about him, even then, even in the stillness.

Muddled violet bruises spanned his throat, starting below the shell of his ear, fading into rings of purple and scarlet as they snaked over his collarbones. Shannon was unnerved. He'd never tried to devour someone like he'd tried to devour Aiden last night. His gaze flicked back to Aiden's face, taking in the straight line of his nose and the arch of his dusty eyebrows, which were a shade or two darker than his fair buzzed hair. Remnants of black paint stained his eyelids.

They'd left the beach a tangle of limbs and lips and heated intentions. As the night lingered, they'd mapped out chests and shoulders and stomachs and each other. Bringing Aiden home wasn't the problem. Neither was falling asleep beside him. It was waking up. It was Aiden being there, picture-worthy in his bed, that Shannon didn't know how to handle. He swallowed the dryness in his throat and shifted, uncomfortable in the tan pants that still clung to his hips. His belt was gone, lying next to Aiden's rumpled shirt. Light shined off the top of his badge.

When Shannon turned back to Aiden, his eyes were open.

Again, somewhere far away inside of them, Shannon saw candlelight.

Aiden's head lolled and pushed into the pillow. His nostrils flared. All the sleepy soft edges sharpened. He turned into a cluster of knives, a shark's mouth.

"What is it?" Aiden rasped. He cleared the sleep from his voice and inhaled, quick as a startled animal.

Shannon eased back into the comforter. "Nothing. Good morning."

That was the simplest way to put it. *Nothing* masked his thoughts: *You're beautiful. I've never been scared of anything until you. I might love you, someday.*

Aiden's vicious smile reminded Shannon of everything illegal he'd ever done: drinking in a park on his sixteenth birthday, stealing a soda from the gas station down the street from his middle school, sneaking into a concert during his freshman year of college. Aiden was new, and still he waded between distant and here, gone and now. He didn't move until Shannon placed an arm across his torso and leaned over.

It was such a tragic thing, holding a cluster of knives, and realizing how painless the risk could be.

Sunlight picked up the lines of Aiden's tattoo, and Shannon traced it with his fingertips. His pulse skittered against Shannon's lips. "What does it mean?"

It took Aiden a moment to answer. Maybe because he didn't want to, maybe because he was too wrapped up in Shannon to notice the question. Shannon liked to think it was the latter.

"What?"

"The phoenix, your tattoo, what does it mean?"

Aiden rolled away, untangling their legs and arms. He watched Shannon's fingers walk up his rib cage, outlining the black ink. "Have you ever felt like you were dying?"

Shannon locked onto Aiden's face. He narrowed his eyes and shook his head. "No," he said, "I haven't." Those were strong words—words that weren't thrown around often—not by people like Aiden, not by people with nothing to prove.

"I have. I figured if I felt like I was dying, I'd probably die, but I never did. So, I got this. The tattoo artist said the ribs hurt the most, so that's where I had him put it." Aiden looked at his tattoo and then back up at Shannon.

Simplicity wrapped around every word. He said *I felt like I was dying* the same way someone said *I had a good day today*, and that made Shannon's stomach turn.

"Phoenixes rise from their ashes. I figured if I was going to die, I might as well be a phoenix, you know? Rise out of all the bullshit after," Aiden said.

"Did you?"

Aiden's brow lifted. "Did I what?"

"Did you die?" Shannon didn't like how heavy the words were on his tongue. He wanted to go back to two minutes ago when he was busy with Aiden's neck.

They stayed like that for too long—Aiden looking at Shannon, searching his face for recognition, wearing an expression that was calm enough to soothe a storm. He craned up, and Shannon sighed against his mouth. "I have to go feed my cat," Aiden whispered. He pressed his lips against Shannon's. "I'll see you, though."

The question went unanswered. Shannon let it go. "Yeah, okay."

After another quick kiss, Aiden left before Shannon could get a better look at his black phoenix, and before he could say *I lied, I've felt like dying too*, and before he could ask if Aiden would stay.

Just stay a little longer.

00:00

"HOLY FUCK, MERCY, HE MAULED me," Aiden whispered.

He spoke to the mirror and to Mercy, who lounged in the sink, peering up at him. She meowed and swatted at his elbow. He stared at his reflection with one hand splayed over his throat where sprawling marks bloomed.

"How am I supposed to...?" He squinted, eyeing the bruises carefully. Each one resembled the next: circular, mouth shaped, and the color of crushed berries. Rows of smaller dark spots hid inside them. *Half-moons. Shannon's teeth.*

Chills ran down his back. He grinned at the sink, and at Mercy, and then at himself. Yeah, it happened, last night really did happen.

But he still didn't know how to cover the monstrosities on his neck before he had to go to work. The bar manager wouldn't be too pleased when Aiden showed up to bar-back sporting enough hickeys to break a Guinness record. He poked a hickey and flinched.

After pacing around his apartment, considering calling Marcus, pricing cheap foundation, and searching for natural remedies on the Internet, Aiden went back to the source.

Shannon Wurther 11/1 12:18 p.m.
what do you mean? youve never had to get rid of a hickey before?
Aiden Maar 11/1 12:22 p.m.
normal hickey, yes. hickeys like this, no
Shannon Wurther 11/1 12:23 p.m.
ice it
Aiden Maar 11/1 12:28 p.m.
its not working
Shannon Wurther 11/1 12:29 p.m.
thats because its only been five minutes

The Internet said to use a frozen spoon, or banana peels, or to scrape the bruises with pennies. Aiden tried all of them, and after another fifteen minutes went back to a cold compress. He stomped into the bathroom and gritted his teeth. His neck looked a little better, but not good enough for work. His phone vibrated on the toilet seat.

Shannon Wurther 11/1 1:05 p.m.
wait. what kind of work are we talking about?
Aiden Maar 11/1 1:06 p.m.
don't worry detective i'm being good
Shannon Wurther 11/1 1:11 p.m.
don't get arrested

A pack of ice snug on his throat, Aiden grinned at his phone and ran his hand along Mercy's back.

11

No one noticed the bruises on Aiden's neck, or if they did, they decided not to comment on them. He did his best to entertain customers, even though his boss only allowed him to pour beers and bus tables, but he couldn't focus enough to keep a conversation going.

His mind drifted to last night on the beach and in Shannon's loft: the way his hands walked over Aiden's body; the drag of his lips and pinch of his teeth; his curious gaze, the sweep of it down his torso, the steady way he drank in every bit of Aiden's face; how he'd taken his time, paused to breathe against Aiden's mouth.

That shared breath held a language Aiden didn't speak, but he sensed it. He felt it everywhere.

The images played like clockwork: Shannon's hands on his face; the lazy kissing deep in each other's mouths; even the shared words, few and far between. Once Shannon's mouth had rested on Aiden's jaw and he'd whispered, "What were you planning to take that night?"

Had they been in a different situation, Aiden would've reacted bitterly. But he'd sighed and said, "*Fortitude Smashed*. It's a contemporary piece made from crushed flowers and accented with pollen to look like paint."

"Why?" Shannon's lips had trailed over his cheek and hovered over the bow of Aiden's top lip. There was no malicious undertone or judgmental gaze, just Shannon looking down at him with a patient half-smile.

"Reminds me of myself," Aiden had admitted. *Smashed up and spread out, not ruined, but a little bit of a mess. A lot of a mess.* Shannon got lost in Aiden's mouth again, and Aiden forgot how much of a mess he was.

Snapping fingers tore him from his thoughts. "Maar, hey, get out of your head, man. Can you wipe down the rest of the back tables? We're closing in five."

Aiden nodded. "Yeah, sorry." He rubbed the back of his neck. "I've got a lot on my mind. Do you need any help with the kegs?"

His boss, Carver, was a short Irish man with a full beard and a get-it-done attitude that Aiden appreciated. Carver was to the point in a way that made work easy, but never pushed harder than he had to. "No, we're good. Everything okay with you?"

"I'm…" Aiden couldn't think of the word. He cleared his throat. "I'm fine, yeah. Sorry."

"Don't be sorry." Carver clasped a hand over Aiden's shoulder. "Your check is on my desk; don't forget to grab it on your way out. You're here tomorrow, right?"

He nodded. "All week."

"Need any time?"

Aiden narrowed his eyes and gave a quick shake of his head. "No, why would I need time?"

Carver's gaze darted to Aiden's hands, and he offered a knowing smile. "I get how it is when the timer goes off. I don't mean to pry into your personal shit, but if you need a couple days off let me know."

His cheeks burned, but Aiden tried not to look surprised and tucked his now-blank thumb into his fist. Sometimes the Camellia Clock was more than a bitch to deal with on his own; sometimes it was publicly embarrassing, too. Empty Man from the beach was one thing, but Carver catching on was an entirely different story.

"Yeah," Aiden said, voice clipped. "I think I'd rather be here. Working takes the edge off."

Working didn't take the edge off whatsoever, but he needed the money. Without having deals set up for jewelry or paintings, he was without a steady income, and touching the funds his parents had left for him was out of the question. Even if he did want to, and he didn't, Marcus wouldn't allow it. He was given enough money to pay his rent and utilities from their joint account, but, other than that, he was on his own.

"Thanks, though. I appreciate it." Aiden finished wiping the tables, took his check, and clocked out.

As soon as he closed the thick wooden door, November wind hit his face. Autumn was delicious, scented of maple and salt and smashed pumpkins, and Aiden loved it. Fall was a whisper spoken before the silence of winter. A cacophony of emotions and colors swirled around the beach; dried leaves crinkled beneath his boots; and along the sidewalk shadows danced, playing tricks on his eyes.

He fumbled in the pockets of the long wool trench coat Marcus bought him last year for Christmas and then lit a cigarette.

He tapped the screen of his phone and almost tripped on a crack in the sidewalk.

Marcus Maar 11/1 9:46 p.m.
Yes, I'm up. Swing by.
Aiden Maar 11/1 9:48 p.m.
hungry ☹
Marcus Maar 11/1 9:51 p.m.
Fine. Diner downtown?
Aiden Maar 11/1 9:52 p.m.
☺ *5 mins*

"THANKS." AIDEN SQUIRTED KETCHUP INTO a cup with a ketchup smiley face drawn into its bottom.

The waitress smiled and touched his shoulder. "You stayin' out of trouble, honey?"

Aiden plucked a French fry from the basket, swiped it through the ketchup, and popped it into his mouth.

"Of course not," he said with a wink. His gaze flicked past the waitress, with whom he'd become acquainted over the years, and he waved his hand toward a shabby man sitting alone at a booth. "Get him something to eat, all right? It's on me."

Kelly, the waitress, smiled. Her skin sagged around her eyes and on her chin, but she still had beauty that Aiden admired. She seemed like a person who kept secrets and didn't make promises. She nodded and tapped her pen against her notepad. "He likes milkshakes, I think. He comes in here all the time and gets water and soup, but he's always talkin' about milkshakes."

"Get him one then, whatever he wants." Aiden didn't like to see hungry people. It was a problem, being generous, but he couldn't help it. Laguna didn't have a large population of homeless people, but at night and in the early mornings, shadows stirred on park benches and individuals dug through garbage cans for food.

A few minutes later, Marcus arrived. Aiden sat with his knees pulled to his chest and his heels on the edge of the seat. He glanced up and offered a feeble smile. Marcus's mahogany eyes slanted as he slid into the other side of the booth. Wire-rimmed glasses perched on his wide nostrils, and his full mouth twisted, a sign he was speculating.

"So?" Marcus arched a brow. "You gonna tell me about it yet or what?"

Aiden growled at him before he slid his phone over. On the screen, lit up for Marcus to see, was Shannon Wurther's Facebook profile picture. Bright smile, full rows of white teeth, tanned skin, beach in the background, hair sticking up from the salt water, sunglasses hiding the blue of his eyes, it was all there—the Shannon Wurther that everyone else saw.

Marcus held up the phone, adjusted his glasses, and grinned. Eyeing Aiden carefully, he gave a couple deep chuckles. "I've been waiting for you to tell me about it. This is him? This is your Rose Road?"

He nodded and shoved another French fry into his mouth. "Yep. He's a cop."

At that, laughter rolled from Marcus in steady waves. It was a good laugh, the contagious kind, and it pulled a smile to Aiden's face.

Aiden snorted. "Yeah, okay, enough," he mumbled, consoling himself with another fry.

"Does he know that I've had to bail you out of jail twice?"

"Yes, Marcus. Hence the cop part."

"Does he know that you steal things for fun?"

"Oh, no, he has no idea. He's just a *detective*." Aiden glared at his brother from across the table. "He… That's how we met, actually."

"Aiden!"

He cowered and showed his palms. "No lectures! I know, I shouldn't steal shit. I get it. I've heard it. Mom and Dad would be upset with me; you're upset with me, just… Skip it, all right? He caught me before I could take what I wanted, but he let me go. That was three weeks ago."

"I know how long ago it was. I knew this October was your month. When you stopped responding to my phone calls, I assumed it was because you'd found your Rose Road."

Kelly walked up to the table and set down two baskets, one with a burger and fries, the other with strips of fried chicken. Aiden picked his entree into small bits and stared at his food. He didn't look up when Marcus cleared his throat, nor when he said, "Do you like him?"

Aiden chewed on a piece of fried chicken, wondering what answer he could give that would be simple enough. "Like" was a word used for food and colors and movies, not Rose Roads. It was used for meaningless somethings. *I like him* or *I like her* was easy to say about someone who didn't matter.

Shannon mattered, and that made *like* an unknowable thing for Aiden.

"Yeah." Aiden breathed the word: a confession more than anything else. "I do."

Marcus wore a pleasant, prideful smile. He tapped Aiden's nose. Face crinkled in a scowl, Aiden swatted Marcus' hand. His brother was the better of them, the truer of the two. He was an art teacher, a gifted painter, older, and wiser. If Aiden was a wildfire, Marcus was a cool breeze.

"Oh, *what*," Marcus dragged the word out as he turned Aiden's chin and stared at his throat. "Did the cop do *that* to you?"

"No, I let someone else suck on me all night." Cheeks darkening, Aiden seethed. "Yes, dumbass, he did."

"So, you two are getting along, then?" Marcus slurped on his cherry Coke and arched his brows.

Aiden shook his head. "We hadn't been getting along until last night. It was... unexpected."

"Why? Everyone likes you," Marcus scrunched his face. Apparently, Aiden's popularity was painfully obvious, and he hadn't caught on in the last twenty-two years. "You're like a six-month-old tiger; people wanna pet you but they're also scared you might kill them. That's the best way to be."

Aiden threw his hands in the air and leaned back. "Why a *six*-month-old tiger?"

"Because they're not totally grown yet. Still fluffy and cute, but big enough to eat you. Teenaged tiger. Emotionally constipated, brooding tiger."

Aiden gaped at his brother. "I'm not a teenaged tiger, you asshole," he said, fighting to sound serious.

Full-bodied, open-mouthed, even a little misty-eyed laughter broke out between them—the kind of laughing that chased away anxiety and made sadness seem secondary. It went on too long, with Aiden wiping his eyes and Marcus crunching ice cubes in his mouth.

"Maybe I am." Aiden sighed. He shook his head and poked at his fries. "I don't know what I'm doing, Marcus. I don't know how to do any of this."

"You like him, right?"

Aiden nodded.

Marcus shrugged and rubbed a dark hand over his shaved head, the only part about them that matched. "You're obviously attracted to him."

Aiden narrowed his eyes, but he nodded. "Attracted" wasn't the term he'd use. A gravitational pull would be more accurate. A head-on collision, an absolute, that's what Aiden felt when he looked at Shannon. Not attraction, but something raw and unobstructed. Necessity. Oxygen. An explosion of unwarranted actions, an eclipse of his control. Aiden wanted to crack Shannon open just to see if he would fit inside.

Attracted was in the same pool as like, surpassed, but not an inappropriate term.

"He's obviously attracted to you."

Aiden waved his hand. "Get on with it."

"Fate doesn't make it easy, Aiden. It put you two together. It's your job to figure out the rest. Do you want to be with him?" Marcus shrugged on his coat and scooted out of the booth. He wasn't going to wait for an answer, probably because he knew Aiden couldn't give one. "Come over for dinner tomorrow. I'll make chow mein."

"Yeah?" Aiden grinned and tossed enough cash onto the table to pay for the homeless man sipping on an Oreo milkshake in the corner booth.

Marcus nodded and smoothed the collar of Aiden's trench coat: a very brotherly gesture, which Aiden had grown fond of in the last six years.

"Yeah, we'll watch a movie. Bring Mercy," Marcus said.

Kelly waved goodbye as they left. Frigid air bit Aiden's cheeks. Marcus turned to him and smiled, but when Aiden tried to say he'd see his brother tomorrow, he said, "Do you think I'm good enough?"

The sound of his own voice sent a chill squirming between his vertebrae. Aiden struggled to breathe. He struggled harder to feign subdued interest. He hadn't meant to bare himself like that. But he would pretend he had, if only to keep his pride intact and Marcus' worry in the shadows.

Marcus' smile deepened, the same knowing smile he'd seen since he was a baby. Marcus slapped a hand on Aiden's cheek. "Course you are. See you tomorrow?"

Aiden tried to smile, but his lips barely twitched. "Yeah, see you tomorrow."

Marcus patted his cheek again and walked to an old VW Bus.

Aiden chewed on the inside of his cheek and glanced at his phone. Shannon's name flashed across the screen.

Shannon Wurther 11/1 11:23 p.m.
when can i see you again

The phone weighed like a brick. He dug in his pocket, lit a cigarette, and read the text over and over.

Aiden Maar 11/1 11:27 p.m.
tomorrow. late
Shannon Wurther 11/1 11:28 p.m.
late?
Aiden Maar 11/1 11:29 p.m.
yeah late
Shannon Wurther 11/1 11:31 p.m.
i'll leave the door unlocked

Aiden smiled around the filter of his cigarette and took a long drag.

12

"HE GOT STABBED, *REALLY?*" KARMAN gasped and shook her head at Shannon from across the table at Mozambique.

"It wasn't that bad," Shannon groaned. He picked at a piece of calamari. "But, yeah, he got stabbed a couple weeks back by some guy at a bar. I tried to find whoever it was, but they were long gone. I don't think Aiden would press charges anyway."

Karman waved her hand. "Okay, but your boyfriend got stabbed, Shannon."

Fae's head shot up; her attention was pulled from her coloring sheet to Shannon. "Shannon's got a boyfriend? Where'd you find him?"

"No, Shannon doesn't have a boyfriend," Shannon said.

"Yeah, honey, Shannon has a boyfriend. He found him in an art gallery; it was real cute. Let's keep coloring, though." Karman scribbled with a crayon on Fae's sheet and then handed it to her. Her flawless brows raised and her crimson lips spread into a wicked smile. "I mean, how did he pull that off? Who gets stabbed in Orange County?"

"Aiden does. Aiden pulls off getting stabbed in Orange County." He inhaled sharply and shook his head. "He could've used some stitches, but he came to me instead of going to a doctor."

"Makes sense, you being his Rose Road and all."

"It doesn't though… A few weeks ago we were in a different place. We weren't in any sort of place, actually. I don't know." He ran his hand over his face and stuffed a piece of fried squid into his mouth. "I don't know if we're in a place *now*. I just—I can't find a reason to be with him or not to be with him, and I've tried. I've made lists. But, I can't stop, I just—"

"God, chill out, Wurther. You want him. He's your Rose Road, soul mate, life partner. He's the whole enchilada. Whether you think there should be a reason or not, this is it. He's it."

"I know that," Shannon growled, cramming another two pieces of calamari into his mouth. "That's my point. I know he's my Rose Road; I can feel it. I get it. But I need to know *why*. Why him? Why us? It doesn't make any sense."

"Who knows?" Karman brushed crumbs off her long-sleeved paisley dress. "Shit, I didn't know. Granted, it's easier when you're sixteen, but come on. Stop being…" She batted the air and her nose scrunched. "Controlling and stuffy."

"Quarter, Mommy."

"Sorry, baby," Karman winced and patted Fae's head. She glimpsed at the drawing of a bouquet on her coloring sheet and whipped back to get a better look. "That's real good! Look at all those colors, Fae. Where'd you learn how to draw like that? Show Shannon!"

"My teacher, Marcus." Fae held up her sheet.

Shannon grinned. "Look at that," he said, eyes wide as he scanned the bent edges of purple stems and smudged bits of navy petals. Even that, a child's drawing of wildflowers, reminded Shannon of Aiden. "It's really pretty."

A waiter swung by the table and served a salad for Karman, pasta for Shannon, and rice for Fae.

"Should've told me when it happened," Karman said. Her eyes flicked from her dinner to Shannon. "Or when I found his file on our desk."

He nodded. "I know. I just didn't know what it was or what to do with it, with *him*. I was still trying to get myself to accept it." He didn't say *I know how you feel about Rose Roads,* because he knew she would try to get around it.

Aiden—everything and nothing at all—was the sensation of being home in a place Shannon had never been. The thought of going through what Karman had, of losing him, was incomprehensible, a computer malfunctioning. Now that Shannon had his Rose Road, he wondered how Karman lived without hers.

"Stop it, Shannon. Stop thinking about whatever you're thinking about and eat your dinner." Karman winked at him.

Fae giggled, watching him. "Yeah, I'm sure he likes you if he's your boyfriend."

Children were irritatingly perceptive.

"I bet you're right," he said and tried to smile, all the while thinking of Aiden, who was on the right side of falling to pieces, while Shannon was on the wrong side of falling into him.

00:00

THE FRONT DOOR OF THE loft was indeed unlocked. Aiden turned the knob, pushed it open, and locked it once he stepped inside. A program played on the television, but the volume was turned down. A couple empty beer bottles were on the coffee table. Shannon's shirt was on the back of the couch; his jeans made a wrinkled pile on the floor. Aiden spotted the long shape of Shannon buried under the comforter. The flashing light from the TV threw disorienting shadows, causing Aiden to trip over himself as he kicked off one of his boots.

So, he was at Shannon's loft in the middle of the night and he had no idea what to do.

Aiden watched the line of Shannon's torso rise and fall; his face was hidden by the bottom edge of the pillow halfway under the white sheets. He put his helmet on the coffee table and bounced on one foot as he tugged off his other boot. A soft purr came from the bed, and

Shannon turned over. He pawed at drowsy half-lidded eyes with the backs of his hands.

"I heard you come in," Shannon mumbled, voice rough with sleep. He ran his hand through his hair and sat up on his elbows. "What time is it?"

Now that his jacket was gone, Aiden fidgeted with his shirt. "Close to eleven. I can go if you're tired."

"You can stay if I'm tired, too." Shannon sank into the bed and swatted the place beside him, inching away to make room for Aiden.

"Yeah, I can do that." His nose twitched, and he glanced over his shoulder at the empty beer bottles. "Can I have a beer?"

"Go for it. Hope you like IPA."

Aiden winced at the light inside the fridge. He snatched a bottle and twisted the cap off. He was still unsure of the protocol of sleepovers and what happened during them—if anything happened at all. Thoughts raced, memories from two nights ago and how he'd never considered it happening again. Not actually. Not like this.

Hoppy bittersweet liquid warmed his throat. He sat on the edge of the bed just out of reach with the lip of the bottle balanced against his mouth. The press of fingertips started at the base of his spine. Aiden closed his eyes. His mother used to pluck leaves from the tree in their backyard and tickle his back with them. Shannon's fingers felt like those leaves. The side of his hand ran between Aiden's shoulders, his thumb brushing Aiden's nape. Eyeing him carefully in the dark, he sat up, tugged the bottle from Aiden's grasp, and took a sip.

Aiden wanted to spread Shannon out on top of the covers and take his time, drink him in, memorize. Aiden wanted to know him, carnally, viscerally, blindingly.

"How's your cat?" Shannon handed the bottle back.

Aiden smirked. "Mercy's fine. She's at my brother's for the night. That's why I said I'd be late. I was having dinner with him."

"Your brother watches her?"

"Sometimes, yeah. We've had her for seventeen years, and when I got my own place I took her with me. My brother makes me bring her to his house so he can spend time with her."

Shannon's forehead rested on his shoulder. He sighed out a laugh as his hands crept beneath Aiden's shirt. "Do cats even live that long?"

Aiden nodded and swallowed another mouthful of beer. Shannon's hands brushed across his stomach, along his sides, over his chest. He leaned into them, unaware that he'd stopped breathing until his lungs started to ache. Shannon took the bottle and set it beside the bed. Aiden wanted to touch him.

"Thought you were tired?" he whispered.

"Exhausted." Shannon pressed the word into Aiden's throat where bruises had faded into muted yellow circles. Lips hovered beneath his ear. "Tell me about your job."

Aiden wanted to consume him, impossibly.

"I'm a bar-back at 101, the dive uptown. Tips are nice; hourly is, too. Why?" Aiden lifted his arms and helped Shannon tug his black shirt away to toss it into the dark.

"Curious. Favorite cocktail?"

His hands settled on Shannon's waist and gripped. "Manhattan. Yours?"

Shannon's back hit the sheets, and Aiden followed. His palms traced Aiden's spine to his nape. "Whiskey anything. Last concert you went to?"

He grinned, shifting when Shannon's legs squeezed around his waist and tugged him down. "Some punk show in Long Beach."

"Punk show?" Shannon's hands found Aiden's throat. Fingers tapped along his jaw. Aiden felt them in places they weren't. Shannon's waist stirred. "I shouldn't be surprised."

The drag of Shannon's index finger on his brow coaxed Aiden to close his eyes. He pressed their foreheads together. *What is this*, Aiden asked the mess in his head, *what is happening to me?*

Aiden chewed on his bottom lip. His arms tensed; one hand was still wrapped around Shannon's hip, the other gripped the pillow near his head. A clipped breath ghosted Aiden's mouth, and he opened his eyes. Shannon's gaze drifted around Aiden's face. He didn't smile or frown. It was an in-between, a tiny curve at the edges of his lips and nothing more.

Aiden swallowed, unsure of the words building in his throat. "I dropped out of high school because my parents died in a car accident when I was sixteen. I didn't know how to deal with it."

Shannon blinked and tilted his head. Aiden slid his eyes away, unwilling to observe even the smallest bit of sympathy. Aiden could've said more, used the proper terminology, told the whole story—the diagnosis his doctor had said with a smile, dissociative dysthymia, the story people cringed at and responded to with *I'm sorry* or *that's terrible* or *it wasn't your fault*—but the last thing he wanted was Shannon's pity.

Quiet surfaced between them. Shannon's hands gripped Aiden's face; his thumb tugged gently on Aiden's bottom lip.

"I always wanted to be like my dad. He was a good cop and he's a good man," Shannon whispered.

Aiden wanted to snatch his thumb between his teeth, but he refrained.

"But he got hurt when he was on duty. He'll walk with a limp for the rest of his life because of it. That's what made me take the exam as early as I did."

Relief surfaced in a sigh. There, they'd said it; what they'd refused to say in the beginning was being said now, and it was enough.

"I steal shit because I like to," Aiden teased and snapped his teeth down on Shannon's thumb. He smiled around the digit, arching an eyebrow. Shannon glowered up at him. "Only art though." He let Shannon's thumb go. "Sometimes jewelry depending on how it's made. I hadn't stolen anything in a while before I met you, since San Francisco, actually."

"Oh?" Shannon narrowed his eyes. "And why's that?"

"The last piece I sold made me ten grand," Aiden whispered smugly. "That's how I bought my bike."

Shannon squirmed. "These are the type of things we shouldn't talk about."

"Then don't talk."

Aiden wanted to kiss him, but he didn't know how. The culprit of prior kisses was long gone. In his place was this Aiden, this thief, this man, and this Aiden didn't know how to kiss.

Aiden gripped harder. His short nails dug into flesh and pillow. Half-lidded blue eyes stared at Aiden from under dark lashes. Shannon's waist arched up to meet the slow grind of hips between legs, legs around hips. There was entirely too much clothing between them—his jeans, Shannon's briefs—but Aiden wasn't brave enough to do a damn thing about it. His lips caressed the high point of Shannon's cheek. Shannon's breathing changed, and Aiden inhaled what Shannon exhaled as his mouth hovered above Shannon's mouth.

Shannon's hands, one on the back of his head, the other resting on his shoulder, buckled down and held Aiden. His lips parted and all at once it was teeth nipping lips, tongues sliding together, and the awkward dance of learning when to breathe and when not to.

He couldn't open his eyes, his chest ached, and his hands wandered on their own accord. They dipped between Shannon's hipbones, and climbed the stairs of his spine. Shoulder blades shifted—tectonic plates beneath his skin. Shannon's hands gripped Aiden's thighs, played in the dip of his lower back, dug into ribs until pain whispered under skin. Aiden pressed into them, hands meant for guns and cuffs and gloves. Aiden related to pain; it reminded him that Shannon was more than someone to kiss.

Shannon steered away and buried the side of his face in the pillow. The tendon in his throat flexed, and Aiden latched his teeth around it, tasting the tremble that coursed through Shannon's body.

Fate had never taken mercy on him; nevertheless, Aiden silently begged, *don't let me destroy this.*

"That night you were in my car, I kissed you back because I wanted to," Shannon blurted. The words skidded off his tongue. "Because you were right there, and I couldn't help myself, and I didn't *want* to help myself. I didn't want to stop. I didn't want you to go."

Aiden stared at him, worrying his lip with his teeth. Caution flashed from Shannon's eyes. He searched Aiden for an answer to a question he hadn't asked.

Is it the same for you? Do you feel this, too?

Shannon shook his head and something caught in his throat, stuttering out before he brought the words to fruition. "I've never wanted anything like I want you."

Shannon pulled, and Aiden fell. They kissed, and if they stopped the sun wouldn't rise, or the stars would blink out, or the ocean swells would cease to roll in. If they stopped, the world would stop, Aiden was sure of it.

He felt Shannon's heart drum, heard the low hum of a moan, the whisper of a curse in the air between them. He opened his eyes and caught deep-seated hunger on Shannon's face as he tossed Aiden onto his back.

When does it end?

Shannon's hand gripped his cheek, and their lips fell together.

Aiden wondered if someday the fire churning in his veins would burn out, if the lack of control tangled in his chest would unwind, and if the wilderness growing within him would ever become civilized again. He wondered if his feelings for Shannon Wurther would become manageable, or if he would always be this, ripped open, clawing at Shannon as if he was something to conquer or something to love.

Something to love. The notion was as sudden as jolting awake.

Aiden kissed him harder.

13

"DO YOU *HAVE TO PAINT* me?" Aiden scrunched his face. He was positive he didn't make for the best canvas, but Marcus kept painting anyway.

"You let me paint you for Halloween! Relax," the older Maar said. "It'll wash off before you have to go to work. It's for the kids."

Aiden rolled his eyes. "I know," he muttered, glancing sideways at a little girl who stood by the tall chair where Marcus had forced him to sit. The side of his mouth quirked to mimic the shy smile she swore. "Hi," he said and arched a brow. "Want my brother to paint your face, too?"

The girl was a pair of short arms and shorter legs. Wild curls bunched under her ears and flowed around her shoulders. She tilted her head, curious and unafraid. "He promised he would in class," she teased. Her shy smile turned bright, showcasing a missing front tooth.

"I have no idea why kids like you." Marcus dabbed a blob of paint on Aiden's eyelid.

He flinched. "I have no idea why anyone likes me. I don't know why *you* like me, Marcus."

"I don't." Marcus sighed. His full lips spread into a smile, and he winked. "I mildly tolerate you."

Aiden mocked a frown and said to the little girl, "My brother's not very nice." She nodded.

"I'm kidding," Marcus groaned and flashed a playful grin at the girl. "How does he look, Fae? Good, right?"

"He's a tiger," she said matter-of-factly.

Aiden's mouth fell open, his eyes rolled, and his head lolled back against the chair. "Am I?" He steered his look from the sky to the girl and from the girl to his brother. "A tiger? Really?"

Marcus grinned at him, smug and impish. "Look, you're even brooding." Marcus couldn't get the statement out before it was run over by deep, belly shaking laughter.

Aiden tried to smother the urge to laugh, too, but it was no use. Like a sneeze, Marcus' laughter brought laughter from everyone around him, and Aiden covered his mouth with his hand to hide it.

"Do you think he's a mean tiger?" Marcus asked Fae.

"No, he looks nice."

"Not scary?" Marcus gawked at Aiden. Residual chuckles hiccupped in his throat.

Aiden pressed his lips together and narrowed his eyes. Marcus had made his point—he'd actually made his point a week ago at their late dinner—but he was making it again, as he tended to do. *Aiden, please. Aiden, don't. Aiden, again? Aiden, you're better than that. Aiden, oh my god.*

Once, twice, sometimes three times, Marcus reminded him of his potential. His remark about being a teenaged tiger was being made for the second time. The hundredth remark about his tendency to take things that didn't belong to him would surface soon, Aiden was sure. *Aiden, Mom and Dad raised you better. Aiden, I'm not bailing you out this time. Aiden, you can get a real job.* He'd heard it all, and even though he *had* found a real job, and *hadn't* successfully stolen anything substantial in months, it would still be thrown in his face.

"No," she said and shook her head, "not scary. Can you make me a butterfly? My mom will be back in a second."

"I sure can," Marcus said. He swatted Aiden's leg and waved him away. "Let me get this adorable tiger out of here and then—" He blocked the punch Aiden aimed at his arm and grinned through more rich, bubbling laughter. "Oh, be nice, you brute. Don't be like that in front of my student."

"You can hit him, too," Aiden said to Fae. She gave a curt nod, but stayed quiet.

Children responded well to honesty, and, although Aiden was a criminal, he wasn't a liar. Honesty, Aiden thought, was the longest lasting piece of someone that could be left behind. Polite niceties and forced interactions bored Aiden into a fury. Rather than put on a show, he opted to be reserved instead. Despite his brashness and attitude, children seemed to understand.

"Go—do something," Marcus waved a dark hand at Aiden, and went to work cleaning his brushes. He smiled at Fae. "And you, Miss Butterfly, hop up here."

"You want a drink or anything?" Aiden asked. He searched the pockets of his black trench coat for his half-empty pack of cigarettes. "I'm going to the coffee place real quick."

"Muffin," Marcus said.

"What kind of muffin, Marcus?" Aiden heaved a sigh.

Marcus waved his hand dismissively, flicked his wrist at Aiden again, and shot him a sour glare. He glanced at the pack of American Spirits and snorted. "Doesn't matter; go do that somewhere else."

He wasn't planning to light a cigarette in the middle of a crowded Saturday Art Walk, but Marcus made his point—again. Aiden wanted to flip him off, but the little girl was watching. She bounced in the seat and called, "Bye, tiger," as Aiden took long strides away from the boardwalk.

Art Walk was the first Saturday of every month, and this was the first Saturday in November. Artists from in town and out of town exhibited their work in the center of Main Beach's boardwalk. Sculptures displayed on foldout tables sat next to handmade jewelry, large canvas paintings propped on easels stood beside framed photographs, and delicately carved wooden wind chimes hung from the hooks of a canopy tent. A path wound through the plethora of cluttered knickknack tables, leading potential buyers through a loop that ended at Marcus' face-painting station and a booth sponsored by the local metaphysical shop.

Aiden cursed under his breath and flicked the lighter again and again. Finally, once his thumb was raw, a flame sparked to life. He leaned against a tall palm tree and watched the streetlight turn from red to green, green to yellow, yellow to red.

Gray winter skies battled with the sun, causing the cloud cover to glow ethereal white on the horizon. Shadows lingered, threads stretched between the ocean and the sky. Laguna Beach, Aiden thought, wasn't the heart of the world, but a knot of its nerves. He didn't hear its pulse beneath the concrete or as a distant drum carried on the backs of crashing waves, but he did feel it. Spikes of energy shot from the ground, and the air was a constant swirl of if's and when's and but's. Laguna Beach seemed like a question—the complex, distasteful, unnerving one that everyone refused to ask—dramatic and timeless, the sensory overload of Southern California.

Perhaps that complexity was what drove the rich to nest here. It was most certainly what kept Aiden around.

Distracted by a buzzing in his pocket, he flicked the cigarette at the ground and stomped on it. Before he could reach his phone, a pair of heeled boots clicked in front of him.

"Pick that up!" The heeled boots belonged to a woman with a lion's mane. Her dark curls framed her face in a twisty arc that fell past her elbows. Aiden's chin jerked, and his eyes widened. People rarely startled him, but she was vaguely familiar. "Do you think it's cool to litter? Polluting our beaches, trashin' our city, c'mon, pick up your garbage, kid."

She narrowed her eyes so her fierce eyebrows became sharp lines. Her plump lips were pursed, painted mauve, and overly glossed. Aiden clawed through his memories. He knew her face.

"You done?" Aiden snapped.

The woman shook her head. "Use an ashtray, asshole."

She pointed one last glare at Aiden and flew off toward the Art Walk.

Aiden watched her go, seeming less and less familiar the farther away she got. Tall black boots, black tights, vibrant purple long-sleeved sweaterdress, all were dwarfed by the amount of hair on her head. Maybe he didn't know her after all.

Aiden picked up the cigarette butt and tossed it in the trashcan. He was inclined to leave it where it was, but the woman was right. He shouldn't leave his bad habits lying around for other people to clean.

His phone buzzed again, and he swiped his thumb across it, then glanced up to make sure he wasn't walking into traffic as he crossed the street.

Shannon Wurther 11/7 12:16 p.m.
hi
Shannon Wurther 11/7 12:20 p.m.
are you working?
Aiden Maar 11/7 12:21 p.m.
yeah i close the bar tonight
Shannon Wurther 11/7 12:22 p.m.
beach tomorrow?
Aiden Maar 11/7 12:24 p.m.
sure. but you can come over tonight if you want
Shannon Wurther 11/7 12:25 p.m.
what time?
Aiden Maar 11/7 12:27 p.m.
i'll be home at 2 probably
Shannon Wurther 11/7 12:29 p.m.
aiden im not an owl

At that, Aiden laughed, out loud and abruptly. The barista, plastic cup in one hand and sharpie in the other, slanted an eyebrow. She cleared her throat, obviously unamused.

"Sorry, yeah, can I get a large—"

"Venti?"

"No, a fucking large—cold-pressed, two shots of hazelnut." He glanced up from his phone and caught the barista rolling her eyes. "And a muffin."

She sighed. "What kind of muffin?"

"What's *your* favorite?" Aiden cooed sarcastically. He arched his brows, and the side of his mouth quirked in an impatient half-smile.

The barista wasn't fazed. "Pumpkin."

"Pumpkin it is." Aiden focused on his phone.

Aiden Maar 11/7 12:35 p.m.
yeah i know that but then we could sleep in
Shannon Wurther 11/7 12:36 p.m.
cant you just come over to my place
Aiden Maar 11/7 12:36 p.m.
i have to feed the cat
Shannon Wurther 11/7 12:38 p.m.
can you leave a key for me
Aiden Maar 11/7 12:40 p.m.
you are an old man. come by 101 and ill give it to you
Shannon Wurther 11/7 12:42 p.m.
fine

"Muffin and cold pressed for the tiger!"

Aiden shoved his phone in his pocket. He'd forgotten about the face paint.

"Thank you." He snarled a grin at the barista. She snarled one back.

14

101 WAS PACKED. ALL SORTS of people struggled to hold conversations over the thrum of seductive music and the clank of glasses. The crack of pool sticks against cue balls ricocheted off the back walls. Lights from low-hanging lamps flickered, sending shadows skittering across the sleek black bartop. Ragged, red-upholstered booths lined the wall across from the bar.

It wasn't the dive of dives, but it made the short list—not dangerous, but sordid; not filthy, but incriminating. It was a place people went to find things: not drugs or crime, but maybe infidelity, another self. 101 sang *you shouldn't be here*, and Shannon found it eerily sexy.

Aiden stood at the far end of the bar with his elbows propped up, eyebrows raised, lips stretched in one of his predatory smiles. Shannon stayed in the corner and watched, engrossed in selfish curiosity. He'd memorized the line of Aiden's jaw, caught glimpses of tenderness between shared breaths, but he'd never studied him—not like this, from afar, cloaked in darkness. It was like turning pages in a diary that didn't belong to him, and the thrill made him smile.

Aiden slapped the bar, grabbed a glass, and filled it from a tap. All straight teeth and narrowed eyes, he spoke over his shoulder as his fingers tapped lazily against the handle. He slid one beer to a woman with a dark pixie cut, then filled another and slid it to her friend.

Both women smiled, their lashes batted, and their manicured fingertips danced along the bartop. Aiden arched a brow at something one of them said and placed a bill in front of pixie cut. Shannon saw it clear as day: their pretty mouths smiling at Aiden, at each other, at the bill. Those two wanted Aiden to chew them up, and Shannon was amused.

They slid off the barstools and waved—the pixie cut first, her platinum friend second. Aiden nodded, leaned across the bar, and accepted a folded twenty-dollar bill between two fingers. He winked. The pixie cut winked back. Shannon fought back a laugh. Aiden rolled his eyes, his predatory grin fell away, and he shoved the bill in his back pocket. One mask was gone, replaced with another.

Shannon took the space the women left vacant and knocked his fist on the bar. "Hey!"

Aiden's head jerked. His granite expression relaxed, and he smiled, a true smile, still as sharp, but not quite as deliberate. "Isn't it past your bedtime?"

"Shut up," Shannon said through a groan. "I've been busy watching you flirt your way to a fat tip. You always charm your way to what you want?"

"Pays the bills." Aiden shrugged and reached across the bar to flick Shannon's nose. "Does it bother you?"

He flinched away. "Not unless you're using it on me."

"Of course I am, Detective. How do you think I talked you into not arresting me?" He grinned, cocking his head. "Here." Aiden pushed a frosted glass filled with dark beer in front of him. "It's on the house."

Shannon slid onto a barstool and watched Aiden go about his night. He worked hard and he laughed more than Shannon had expected. He spoke when spoken to and said only what was necessary: a very Aiden thing. Sometimes he gave a fanged grin, other times his lips twisted into a smirk, but every time it earned him extra cash.

Aiden was good at feigning interest; he wasn't good at trying to hide it, though. As the hour went by he stole side-eyed glances at Shannon.

After a shake of his head or the hint of a bashful smile, he would turn away, engrossed in another customer who thought he might give them the time of day if they tipped him well enough.

Shannon was skimming a text from Karman when a set of keys clattered against the bar.

"Shannon, go home—go to my place." Aiden closed his eyes after the words rushed from his mouth. Shannon had heard him correctly, but he chose to stay quiet. *Home.* What a strange word for them to use with each other. "There's beer in the fridge, but that's about it. Might be some leftover Chinese."

"I can wait for you."

"It's almost midnight. Go." He nodded toward the door. "You're tired. I'll try not to wake you up when I come in."

"No, wake me up," Shannon said.

"Yeah, okay."

Shannon leaned across the bar and asked, "So, should I stick the twenty in your hand or in your pants—"

Aiden's ears turned pink and he palmed Shannon's face, shoving him backward. "*Go* away."

00:00

"HI, MERCY," AIDEN SAID SOFTLY. He shut and locked the door, tossed his jacket on the couch, set his helmet on the kitchen counter, and kicked off his boots. "You hungry?"

Mercy meowed. Her plump, white body wound around his ankles.

The clock above the microwave read 2:14 a.m.

Aiden sighed, preparing himself for the sleep he wasn't going to get. It happened from time to time. His mind buzzed in a body that ached for rest. He could feel nights like these in the hours before, in the pulses of restlessness that caused his hands to twitch, in the midday exhaustion that ambushed him with unwarranted naps. His doctor called it dysthymia; Aiden called it life.

His doctor, the one Marcus had forced him to see since he was seventeen, said he'd be fine in a few years. A steady job would help, therapy would help, friends would help, and even Shannon—before Aiden knew Shannon was Shannon—would help.

"Your Rose Road is due in the next year, right?" the doctor had asked. Aiden had said yes, despite being convinced there wasn't one for him. "People react differently, but I think it'll be good for you to have someone." His doctor was a round Indian man with an Eastern accent. "No pills, Mister Maar. But for your sleeping, I'll prescribe something else."

Unfortunately, Aiden was out of said prescription. He shook the blue bottle and opened it, holding the lip below his nostrils.

"Mercy, how the fuck did I forget..." He inhaled—sweet, sharp, and tangy—the remnants of his last run to the clinic. Strong indica was his saving grace on nights like this. "Do I at least—of course not," he whispered, eyeing the empty bottle of bourbon on the counter.

He'd polished that off three days ago.

Aiden fed Mercy, kissed her between the ears, and left her to eat. Showering would make the insomnia worse. Instead he crept into his bedroom and watched Shannon sleep.

Shannon was on his stomach with his face smashed on the mattress below the pillow and his hands tucked under it. Gently parted lips pressed together as he took a deep breath; his eyes moving beneath their lids. Aiden had never watched someone sleep; he'd never witnessed a dreamer dream. It was private, murky, like looking through tinted glass. He couldn't tell what, but he'd stolen something from Shannon then—a bit of his unknown.

He tossed his shirt on the floor, almost tripped getting out of his pants, and crawled under the covers. Shannon didn't stir, but he sighed. Aiden continued to watch. His eyelids were heavy enough to close, but his mind was too busy. Shannon moved again; his elbow knocked Aiden's shoulder.

"Sorry," Shannon slurred. The movement behind his eyelids ceased, and he opened them. They were blue even in the darkness. "You're home—you're here." Shannon's brow furrowed. His words were sticky and quick. Aiden had said it before, now Shannon was the one calling their *together* a home.

"I'm here," Aiden said.

"How was work?"

He turned to lie on his side. "Work was work. Go back to sleep; you're tired."

"Aren't you?" Shannon blinked. He tapped Aiden's jaw; his fingertips played a gentle rhythm against his skin.

"Sometimes I can't sleep."

"Why?"

"Bad dreams," Aiden whispered. It wasn't the whole truth, but it was enough.

"About?"

"My parents." That was the whole truth.

Alertness sparked in Shannon. Aiden thought he heard the beginning of *I'm sorry*, but it faded into silence quickly. Shannon didn't move closer, which was disappointing, but he nodded. "Sometimes I have nightmares about my dad getting shot, what could've happened instead of what did. I wasn't there. My mind imagines it for me."

Aiden nodded back. "You get it, then."

"I get it."

Shannon's fingertips stopped drumming. They ran up the side of Aiden's face, over the top of his cheek, the bridge of his nose. He closed his eyes, and Shannon touched his eyelids.

Such delicacy, Aiden thought. *Isn't he scared it might hurt?*

That was what most assumed when they looked at Aiden, that he would prick their fingers if they reached for him. On his good days he didn't know why; on his bad days he made up reasons.

"I know I made fun of you for it at the bar," Shannon said. Somehow he'd inched his way into Aiden's space. A welcomed warmth, his breath gusted Aiden's chin. "But you're something, you know that?"

Aiden opened his eyes. "Something?"

"Yes." Shannon sighed. "I don't know how else to say it. I don't want to sound like everyone else."

"You won't."

"You're handsome. Maybe beautiful, I'm not sure."

"You aren't sure?" Aiden lifted his brows. Shannon traced the line of his smile.

"No, I am sure," he admitted and huffed. "I'm sure that you're someone everyone wants to touch," Shannon mumbled. He pushed his head farther into the pillow. "I'm glad you let me."

The witching hours were beehives full of turbulent honesty. Aiden had always been awake and alone during them, left to sort through the truth himself. It was different sharing it with Shannon. Honesty was a lonesome thing. Involving another made it unpredictable.

"I'm glad I let you, too."

It was quiet except for Mercy's chomps echoing from the kitchen. The blinds trembled against a breeze, and, far off in the distance, waves dragged against the sand. Their skin on the sheets, toes curling against the comforter, the mattress whining when either of them moved—Aiden had never noticed any of it. He'd never noticed how alone he'd been until he wasn't.

Shannon's thumb touched Aiden's top lip. "I wish it'd been sooner. I wish I could've been there."

Aiden narrowed his eyes. All at once he was an animal backed into a corner, unable to process what Shannon meant. Timing out as teenagers would've been the end of them. No. He meant something else. Aiden blinked, questioning.

"Our Clocks, I wish they'd timed out earlier in our lives," Shannon said.

Honesty during the witching hours was not a beehive, Aiden decided. It was jet black arachnids with curved teeth and eight eyes, watching, and biting, and crawling.

"It wouldn't have changed anything, Shannon." Aiden nearly choked, but managed to get the words out. His mouth tightened. "My parents would have still gone to Big Bear. They would've still died coming home. I didn't need you; I needed them."

"Yeah, but maybe I needed you," Shannon snapped. His face hardened, and his fingers stilled. He looked away, at the crumpled sheets. Two animals, Aiden realized, backed into opposite corners, hiding from the same spiders. Aiden's mouth went dry. He should reach for him; he should apologize. "Look at us," Shannon whispered bitterly, "already arguing over who needs who."

Frustration festered in Aiden's chest. He was terrible at controlling his tongue when he was tired. "There's no argument," he said. "Do that thing to my face again."

Shannon's fingertips went back to outlining Aiden's face. He trailed them across his lips, his eyelids, dusted the fan of his lashes. "You don't have to bite my head off," he whispered meekly, vowels lingering and merging, another indication of an accent.

Aiden sighed. No, he didn't have to bite his head off. He didn't have to do a lot of what he did, like bristle at any mention of his parents, or turn cold when someone tried to comfort him.

Not someone.

Shannon.

He draped his arm over Shannon's waist, testing a touch.

"No, I don't," Aiden mumbled, defeated.

Maybe I needed you.

It was impossible to imagine Shannon needing anything, especially Aiden.

"I'm not good at this either, you know." Shannon's hand splayed on his cheek; his thumb stroked his brow. "But I'm tryin'."

Aiden wanted to ask where Shannon was from, because he was from somewhere. He wanted to ask why—what would the Clock have changed? Why would Shannon Wurther stoop so low as to need Aiden Maar? He wanted to ask what it felt like to *almost* lose a parent, what relief was like in the moments after. But he didn't.

He curled into Shannon's chest. The hand on his face wrapped around the back of his head, and fingers resumed their dance on barely there hairs. Shannon's knee nudged between Aiden's legs. Aiden tucked his face below Shannon's chin and stayed there, eyes closed, wishing he could sleep.

"You're good at it," Aiden said against his skin. He pressed his lips against the hollow of Shannon's throat. "Better than you think."

Shannon's fingertips drew patterns on Aiden's nape until he fell asleep. Aiden listened to him breathe; constant and lulling, the sound of his heartbeat rippled from his sternum.

Aiden fell asleep sometime after 3:30 a.m. with Shannon's arms tight around him. He'd imagined this weeks ago, in the time between their first kiss and their second. He'd imagined what it might feel like to be wanted by Shannon Wurther.

All the time he'd spent wondering, all the weeks he'd convinced himself it would hurt, and in the end it was this: fingertips on his face and proclamations of beauty, secrets that weren't secrets, and fears that weren't fears, in the hours when Laguna Beach slept, but they didn't.

Aiden didn't dream or, if he did, he didn't remember it. Maybe he didn't need to.

 **15**

Disheveled sheets. Rumpled pillow. Comforter tossed up at the corner. Empty space.

Shannon's nostrils flared. One hand lifted to paw at his eyes; the other braced against the bed. Aiden wasn't next to him. Mercy was, though. She rolled on her back on the cold spot where Aiden had slept for most of the night; her tail flicked Shannon's face.

"Where'd he go, Mercy?"

She meowed at him, yawned, and continued to flick the tip of her tail against his cheek.

Aiden's room was almost bare. Shannon sat up on the bed—cheap frame, too-soft mattress, and stock white trimmings. The nightstand matched a six-sectioned dresser and was home to a lamp with a burnt-out bulb and a well-read tattoo magazine. Light tried to crawl through the cracks in the blinds; clothes in all shades of black, gray, and white were scattered everywhere; and the walls were blank but for one large picture above the bed. Shannon tilted his head and smiled.

He saw a panoramic photograph of crashing waves and golden sand; smiling faces blurred behind sunglasses; volleyball nets in the distance on one end, booths and vendors on the other, and a neon yellow sign in the very center displaying in thick block letters: Welcome to Venice

Beach, all backdropped by a cloudless sky. The palette was muted, the perfect representation of hazy summer days.

Venice Beach, like Aiden Maar, was unrefined. It fit.

In the bathroom, Shannon brushed his teeth with the toothbrush he'd left on the sink last night and ran wet fingers through his hair. He toed the door shut, buttoned his jeans, and followed Aiden's soft cooing to the balcony.

"Mercy," Aiden whispered, singing her name. He grinned at her as she flopped by his feet.

Smoke coiled from Aiden's nostrils. His arms hung over the side of the balcony, a snapback was flipped backward on his head, and he was barefooted and wearing sweatpants. A coffee mug was in one hand, a half-smoked cigarette in the other. He turned back to the horizon, which was painted hues of gray and white. Autumn chill made its presence known in the steam billowing from Aiden's coffee and the fog that hugged the shoreline and pinched Shannon's skin.

"Get any sleep?" Shannon murmured. He stepped behind Aiden. His hands brushed the line of his waist.

Aiden met Shannon's eyes. "A few hours."

He settled his lips on the curve of Aiden's shoulder, avoiding the straight brim of his ridiculous white hat. "That's it? What time is it?"

"Noon, I think. I've been up for a little while."

"Why didn't you wake me up?" Shannon pressed tighter against Aiden's back. It was cold, and he was warm, and Shannon was thoroughly enjoying how uncomplicated their morning was. Well, afternoon. He hoped the rest of the day would stay as uncomplicated, leaving their conversations from last night buried in darkness.

Aiden turned away to exhale a lungful of smoke. "Because I'm not an asshole," he said. His mouth quirked and he tilted his head farther, nudging Shannon's temple with his nose. "There's coffee if you want. I left a mug out for you."

How was it possible that the man from last night was the same man standing on the balcony? Soft eyes, softer skin, calm and patient and unraveled. Anyone who'd imagined playing on the jagged expanse of Aiden's bravado would be disappointed by his lack of consistent smoldering. Mornings when Aiden was too tired to care and nights when he was too energized to worry were the cracks in time that made for unequivocal truth. There was nothing heated about him besides his skin. The razor-edge of his smile was tame and gentle.

Shannon's fingertips traced the line of the phoenix. "I'll get some. What should we do today?"

"You mentioned the beach." Aiden lifted his brows.

"All day?" Shannon rested his chin on Aiden's shoulder.

Aiden shrugged. "I can take you somewhere after," he said hesitantly. "Somewhere I haven't taken anyone in a long time."

"If we go, will we get arrested?"

Aiden laughed through his teeth. "No, Detective," he breathed, voice low and playful. "It's just a place. Nothing for me to steal there."

There were things Aiden was more than capable of stealing, no matter where they went. Shannon said, "All right then. We'll go to your somewhere after the beach."

"And after we eat," Aiden added. He bent his head forward and snatched Shannon's lips in a quick kiss; he had bitter coffee on his tongue and smoke on his breath. He pulled back, lips grazing Shannon's mouth. "You like sushi?"

"If I told you I'd never tried it, would you laugh at me?"

"Yes!" Aiden's bright eyes crinkled around an open-mouthed grin and he did just that. His laugh was an exclamation: a bark followed by a shake of his head. He'd never seen Aiden jump into laughter like that, unexpected and foolish and young. It was mesmerizing.

"How? You live here." Aiden gestured to the city with a wave of his arm. "In Laguna—*right* next to the ocean—and you've never had sushi?"

Aiden reached past him to drop his cigarette butt in the ashtray.

"It freaks me out. Shouldn't fish be cooked when you eat it?" Shannon scratched the back of his head, trailing Aiden inside.

"Do you *want* to try it? Because it's like top five for me, maybe top three."

"Top five?"

"Favorite foods," Aiden clarified.

He'd said that, hadn't he? Yes, he had, during the atrocious out-of-the-blue coffee date that they'd both managed to butcher. Japanese and Thai food, Shannon remembered. He grabbed the empty mug, filled it with coffee, and added an excessive amount of sugar.

"I'll try it," Shannon said. He took a sip and added more sugar. "Where's this place you're taking me after?"

"You'll see." Aiden walked down the hall, leaving Shannon alone in the kitchen. The pipes clanked and groaned as the shower turned on. Shannon caught a glimpse of his back, thumbs tugging at the waistband of his sweats, before Aiden kicked the door shut.

00:00

"THE WAITRESS CAN GIVE YOU the little—" Holding back a laugh, Aiden clacked his chop sticks together. "—rubber band things kids use. It'll make it easier."

Shannon narrowed his eyes.

"I'm serious!" Aiden pinched a piece of avocado roll between his chopsticks, dunked it in a bowl of chili paste, and popped it in his mouth. It was effortless, delicate, and embarrassed Shannon further. "Here..." Aiden put down his chopsticks and reached across the tiny table. "Like this."

Shannon frowned, trying to keep up with Aiden's lesson in chopstick holding. He angled one stick on the crease of his thumb.

"That balances there," Aiden said. He took the other and tapped Shannon's index finger. "This one does all the work. Use your knuckle and the tip of your finger to pick shit up."

"Can't I use my hands?"

"Rude," Aiden teased, squeezing Shannon's fingers together to make the appropriate motion. "See? Easy, now grab one."

The chopsticks slipped right out of Shannon's hands.

"This is stupid," Shannon mumbled. A hot blush darkened his face. "I'm not cut out for sushi eating."

Aiden snatched up one chopstick with his own chopsticks and handed it to him, then picked up the other. "Stop being a baby. Try again."

Again, Shannon dropped the chopsticks. But the third time he tried, he managed to squeeze a piece of avocado roll long enough to get it into his mouth.

Aiden lifted his brows. "See, it's easy."

"Not easy."

"Is it good?"

"It's avocado and rice. This doesn't even count as sushi."

"That isn't what I asked, asshole."

Shannon glowered at him. "Yes, it's good. What else did you order?"

A few minutes later, once the avocado roll was gone and the pot of hot tea they'd shared was empty, the waitress set down an extravagant-looking second serving. A colorful roll curved across a white plate; bright translucent red fish covered the top of the rice alongside slivers of green avocado. Crunchy shrimp stuck out either end, tempura crumbs were scattered everywhere, and pink sauce was drizzled over all of it. Sushi was artwork made of food. No wonder Aiden enjoyed it.

"Salmon, shrimp, some other stuff." Aiden waved his chopsticks over the roll before he snatched an end piece. "Try it."

Shannon wrinkled his nose.

"*Try it*," Aiden hissed.

Shannon grumbled, but managed to sloppily pick up a piece and put it in his mouth. The texture was strange. He chewed, swallowed, winced. Spicy at first, sweet on the end, and cold—not food he'd choose to eat, but it wasn't terrible.

Aiden chewed on the side of his lip, looking very young and very curious in his stupid white snapback and black zip-up sweatshirt. "Good?"

"Weird."

"Okay, but is it good?" Aiden grinned and clicked his chopsticks, waiting for an answer.

"Yes, Aiden, it's good. I like it."

Aiden beamed, grin clamping down into a smug smile.

The waitress brought more tea. Shannon listened to Aiden describe the ingredients in the next roll, which was stranger than the last. They ate quietly, with Aiden stopping to help Shannon with his chopsticks and Shannon stopping to watch Aiden pick at his fingernails. Aiden's foot bumped against Shannon's shin.

This is what it's like to fall, Shannon thought. Really fall.

Aiden cradled his chin, elbow on the table, fingers tapping the side of his face. He looked at Shannon and smiled, the comfortable kind of smile that came from life making sense.

This is what it's like.

It was cold enough at the beach to send them back to the car before they made it to the cliffs or the tide pools. But Shannon didn't mind, and neither did Aiden.

Shannon wore ridiculous sunglasses. They were gigantic, with gold frames and a white 'o' etched into the temple that probably stood for an expensive brand Aiden had never heard of. He laughed when Shannon put them on, and, in defense, Shannon made fun of his hat, which led to Aiden making fun of Shannon's Facebook profile and Shannon growling about Aiden's lack of know-how when it came to style. It concluded in laughter, at each other, at the situation, at the fact that they were blissfully taken with one another and neither was brave enough to admit it.

It was a disaster in the making, because Aiden didn't like people, not the way he liked Shannon. And like was still such a faulty word for what it was.

It, their Rose Road, was not *like* or *love* or *lust*, but some concoction of the three. Love seemed far off, and lust oppressive, and like too tame. Two drops of this, one scoop of that, sprinkles of whatever. What was the recipe? How and when did they fall in love? Did it happen as it did to any other couple? Was it avoidable? Did he *want* to avoid it?

Aiden looked out the passenger window and calmed his fluttering stomach.

He'd never had a crush. He'd assumed that Rose Roads were immune to the crippling effects of one.

He was wrong.

Aiden was just as susceptible to crushes as anyone else. Shannon being his Rose Road didn't change the pace of things, and Aiden was under a spell. After the nights spent working through twenty-something years of pent-up passion and discussing their individual tragedies, it was nice to feel the way he felt now—nervous, melodramatic, and excited—all the makings of a disaster.

"Park here?" Shannon pulled up outside an apartment complex in Laguna Canyon.

Aiden slid his foot off the dash and craned his head. He looked at the other side of the street, crowded with overgrown foliage. "Yeah," he said. "We have to walk from here. You're not wearing gold sandals to match those god-awful sunglasses are you?"

Shannon snorted and pulled the keys from the ignition. "Where are we going? There's nothing out here except hiking trails and the wilderness park."

"That way," Aiden pointed across the road. "There's a hole in the fence along that trail. Once we get through, I think I can navigate us the rest of the way."

"Oh, you think?"

Aiden lit a cigarette and jogged across the street. Shannon cursed at him, but dodged oncoming traffic and followed.

"Yeah." Aiden pushed up his black-on-black sunglasses and shoved his free hand into the pocket of well-worn dark jeans. "I haven't been here in…" He paused to take a drag and glanced at Shannon as he kept pace next to him. "I don't know—eight months? Give or take."

"What is *here*?"

"Calm down, Detective. It's around here somewhere…"

Just as Aiden thought, there was a hole big enough to squeeze through past the stop sign that led to the interstate. He dropped his cigarette and smothered it beneath his shoe. "I told you. Come on; it's back there."

"You're not gonna murder me, are you?"

"No, not yet," Aiden teased.

They were swallowed whole by the winding canyon road. Hills rose all around them, dwarfing cars and apartment complexes. On the other side of the fence was lush forest. Tall, golden grass swayed in chilly, almost-winter breezes. Huge expanses of jagged rocks formed cliffs and miniature mountains, which were overrun by copper vines and thorny cactus. Bright yellow flowers bloomed here and there, fighting to stay alive through the cold.

Aiden followed his feet—they remembered which way to go—down a long-forgotten trail, around a patch of overgrown cacti, and through a break in the tree line.

Sycamores and oaks and willows towered, home to the birds that'd flown south for winter. Sunlight peeked through dense cloud cover and lit up the sky. The trees grew larger the farther in they went, glowing gold and maroon and copper. Aiden was reassured they were headed in the right direction by ancient beer cans, smashed and half-eaten by the earth. Empty cigarette packs, or remnants of them, were home to ants, beetles, and lizards.

All at once the trees cleared, and Aiden smiled.

Shannon's footsteps behind him dwindled. A gasp, bewildered and small, came from him, before he said, "How long has this been here?"

The Hollow hidden in the wilderness park was constructed from wooden planks, zip ties, colored ropes, and a massive amount of dedication. A ladder propped against the largest tree in the center of the makeshift tree house led to a landing with an attached rope bridge. That rope bridge connected with another tree branch, where wooden planks were nailed side by side, spanning four branches. A tire hung in the second tree with a half-assed sign on it that read *Chris's Place*. Below it was the frame of an old car, rusted and tireless, without a passenger seat or a steering wheel, sitting pretty while the weather gnawed on it season after season.

Aiden didn't know who Chris was. He didn't know how the tree forts had come to be, but they were still here, and that was all that mattered. He turned to Shannon and said, "I have no idea. I found it when I was in high school while I was hiking. I'd come down here with my friends, and we'd stay until it got dark. Sometimes we'd sleep here in summer—get drunk, get high, do stupid shit. Cool, huh?"

Shannon's lips parted in a smile. "Yeah, it's cool. It's really fucking cool."

"We called it the Hollow." He glanced at Shannon who looked up at the levels of the fort. Hazy topaz light bounced off his sunglasses. "You wanna go up?"

Aiden climbed the ladder first. Across the rope bridge he tiptoed, arms outstretched, balancing with one foot in front of the other. Shannon followed. Aiden whacked the rope and almost sent Shannon toppling.

"Don't!" Shannon hissed, shoving Aiden's shoulder when he made it across.

Aiden jumped on the tire. He swung one way and then the other, with his eyes settled on Shannon, who sat on the deck with his back against the tree trunk.

Light played tricks in the Hollow. Aiden swung on the tire, a freshly lit cigarette between his lips, and watched as sunlight danced across Shannon's face. His head was tipped back; his long-sleeved shirt clung to his torso. They were both younger, playing in a tree house in the middle of the woods.

Time wasn't real. Shannon wasn't a cop. Aiden wasn't a thief.

Aiden wanted to take this ease with him, back to his apartment, to Marcus, to 101, to Shannon's loft. He wanted to bottle it up and drink it—an elixir that granted everlasting youthfulness, a potion that would keep him here, enamored and nervous and looking at Shannon as if he was just as magical as this place was.

"We should've picked up a six-pack," Shannon said.

Aiden hopped off the tire and landed on the deck. He feigned a dramatic gasp. "Shannon Wurther!" He slapped a hand over his chest. "That's illegal."

"Shut up. I'm still allowed to have fun."

Aiden took off his hat, pushed his sunglasses on top of his head, and then rearranged his snapback, brim facing backward. He plopped down in front of Shannon, stubbed his cigarette out, and situated his ankles over the top of Shannon's thighs.

"Tell me something."

Shannon pushed his sunglasses to the top of his head, messing up his made-to-look-messy hair. "Like?"

"Something, anything."

"Your hat is stupid."

Aiden rolled his eyes, but Shannon laughed and shook his head. "I'm kidding. What do you want me to tell you?"

"Tell me something true," Aiden said and scooted forward.

Shannon hummed. He grabbed Aiden's hips and pulled, sliding him across the wooden planks until Aiden's knees were over top of his legs. His fingertips played with the bottom of Aiden's sweatshirt. "You're not what I expected."

"Okay," Aiden smirked, glancing at the sliver of space between them. "Now tell me a lie."

"I..." Shannon paused and swallowed. His hands drifted under Aiden's sweatshirt; they were cold and jarring on his skin. "I don't get nervous around you."

"Why would you?" Aiden tilted his head.

Shannon's brow furrowed; his lips parted and closed. His tongue darted out to wet them, and his eyes went every which way around Aiden's face. "Either you have no idea what you look like, or you have every idea and you enjoy making people squirm."

He frowned, hands fidgeting against the rough wooden planks. Aiden never had been fond of what people had to say about his looks. He'd gone through school a shock-and-awe kind of kid and grown into an even greater shock and an even breathier awe. Aiden knew what he was. He knew what people thought about what he was. "I know what I look like. What does that have to do with it?"

"What does that...?" Shannon laughed. One hand slid across Aiden's thigh. The dumbfounded expression he wore made Aiden tense.

Suddenly uncomfortable, Aiden steered his gaze to the deck again. "People think I'm dangerous, that's why they're attracted to me. I'm every honor roll student's wet dream when it comes to pissing off their parents."

"'Dangerous' is a strong word." Shannon sighed. The hand resting on Aiden's thigh moved to his face. Shannon studied him and thumbed his cheekbone. His index finger dragged along Aiden's jaw. "You're impossible to read. No one knows what you're thinking when you're thinking it—a perfect poker face. All these angles and bones..." He traced his nose, his brows, his Cupid's bow. "They're in all the right spots."

Aiden braved looking up. Shannon looked back.

"A secret," Shannon added. His thumb brushed Aiden's mouth. "Everyone's always dying to know everything, and you don't give it to them. That's why people think you're dangerous." Shannon flicked his wrist in a circle, gesturing at Aiden's face, "And you're also beautiful, which helps."

He laughed, and so did Aiden, hoping the heat in his face subsided before Shannon noticed. The hand inside his sweatshirt swiped up his side, down to his hip, over and over.

"Your turn. Tell me something true," Shannon said.

"I like you."

"I hope so; you're stuck with me. Now tell me a lie."

Before he could answer, he drew Aiden into a kiss lighter than any they'd shared before. Aiden thought it might count as their first, despite how many times they'd kissed already. Their lips fell together, pushing and pulling in slow fluid motions. There was no urgency. Aiden felt Shannon smile as his lips slid up and away.

"I'm totally used to this. People make me feel like this all the time."

"What does this feel like?" Shannon asked.

"Déjà vu," Aiden said. Shannon tugged Aiden farther into his lap. "It feels like I've known you forever, but I don't know you at all—the feeling you get when you're driving to a new place but you swear you know the way, a directionless path that's easy to navigate. What does it feel like for you?"

Aiden kissed him, longer and deeper. The sound of their lips meeting and parting was accompanied by rustling leaves and cawing crows.

"More intense than I'd like it to," Shannon admitted. "But you summed it up, honestly. At first it felt like I was sucked into your orbit. Now that we've..." Shannon couldn't say slept together, because they hadn't technically slept together, and that, beyond anything else, terrified Aiden. "Tried to eat each other—"

Shannon stopped when Aiden threw his head back and laughed.

They laughed a lot together. Aiden had been right about the smile lines, and he adored them.

Shannon pressed his grin into Aiden's throat. "It's the truth," he said through a sigh. "But now that we've gotten past that, it feels new, but not."

"Are we past it?" Aiden leaned back to catch Shannon's mouth. "I'm not past it," he rasped, unsure of the person inhabiting his body. Aiden Maar would never say something like that. He would never paint himself as sexy or deserving. And that was what he became, wrapped up in Shannon Wurther, fooling around in a tree house like teenagers, pushing every doubt to the far reaches of his mind.

The youthful elixir of The Hollow turned him wild.

Shannon's hand crept farther up his back; the other settled on his thigh. Aiden took the chance to run his hands along Shannon's chest. His fingers found the grooves beneath his collarbones, the toned divots and hard planes he hadn't yet felt. All the time they'd spent in Shannon's bed was blurred; fragments of both nights watermarked the inside of Aiden's skull. They'd been a different version of themselves, discovering each other like wounded, hungry, desperate things. This was real, he thought. This didn't leave him begging; it left him yearning.

"Why do you do that?" Aiden asked. He hadn't meant to say anything, but the words slipped out.

"Do what?"

"Put your hands under my shirt. You've done it since the first night we met."

Shannon immediately tried to retract his hand, but Aiden stopped him.

"I didn't say stop, did I? I was just curious," Aiden blurted.

"I..." The side of Shannon's mouth pulled down and he shrugged. "I don't know. I enjoy touching you. Would you rather I touch you elsewhere?"

Shannon's hand slid across Aiden's belly button. He gripped the front of Aiden's jeans, dipped fingers beneath the denim, and tugged. Aiden's stomach lurched into his throat. His heartbeat escalated. He hoped none of the surprise showed on his face or in the way he trembled into the kiss Shannon planted on him. He squirmed, hips canting up, and drew a ragged breath. No, Aiden wasn't going to have this conversation in a tree house, not the one where he explained his lack of sexual history. *Virgin*. Aiden hated the word, but it was the only one there was.

"Yes," he said against Shannon's mouth, "but not here."

Shannon arched a brow. He pressed his palm between Aiden's legs. "Not here?"

Aiden hissed through his teeth. His face was warm. Everywhere else was warm. "I hate you," he whispered, but didn't move. "But no, not *here*, in this tree house."

"All right." Shannon snaked his hand up Aiden's torso and teased at the zipper on his sweatshirt. He pulled it down, inch by inch. "What about here?"

"Fuck off," Aiden said. Shannon fastened his mouth between Aiden's collarbones. Aiden's lashes fluttered; his breath caught in his throat. "We're gonna fall out of the tree, Shannon."

"We're gonna fall out of the tree," Shannon mocked, high-pitched and teasing.

Aiden swatted the back of his head and squirmed away, zipping up his jacket as he went. He fished for his pack of cigarettes and dug out his lighter, all the while glaring at Shannon, who watched from his place against the tree.

Aiden fell back on the wooden planks with an arm dangling off the edge. He inhaled smoke, exhaled his anxiety, inhaled smoke again, and exhaled embarrassment. Shannon's foot kicked the side of Aiden's foot, and Aiden kicked back, which resulted in their feet steadily knocking together.

Just as Aiden was Shannon's secret, and Shannon was Aiden's secret, the Hollow was their secret now.

"Did you ever carve anything into the tree?" Shannon craned his head over the edge of the deck, looking intently at all the letters etched into the tree's trunk. Names in different shapes and sizes, phrases, quotes, curses, and lyrics covered the tree from six feet above the deck to the very bottom.

"No." Aiden sat up on his elbows, took one last drag, and twirled the lit end of the cigarette against the deck. "Some of my friends did, though. They're probably down by the bottom, Vance, Daisy, Jonathan. Daisy spent three hours carving *Brand New* lyrics into it."

"Daisy?"

"Yeah."

"You smiled when you said her name." Shannon sat up straighter, at ease and comfortable, the way Aiden liked to see him. "Do you guys still talk?"

"She's off at college doing things with her life." Aiden waved his hand nonchalantly. "We were really close until she graduated, took photography together, hung out every day. She's the first person I told after I found this place."

"Were you guys like together, or...?"

"Why?" Aiden snorted.

"I'm allowed to be curious." Shannon scratched the wood; his fingers stretched toward Aiden, who sat just out of reach. "I dated someone for five years, eighth grade to senior year. Chelsea Cavanaugh."

"Daisy was my best friend. I didn't date anyone, ever, actually. But it's good to know you shacked up with someone before I got ahold of you." He grinned, but the words were sticky in his throat.

So, Shannon *had* dated someone. Of course he had, what was Aiden thinking? They'd find each other, fresh and untouched, ready to conquer the world together? No, that was a childish fantasy, and he knew better. Shannon Wurther had dated, he'd been in a dedicated relationship, and that made perfect sense. And yet, Aiden's chest tightened. "What was she like?"

"Chelsea?" Shannon's eyes widened and then rolled, which was satisfying to watch. "We still talk sometimes, but not as much as we should. She was a great student, top of our class, Homecoming queen. We danced at prom. It was high school," he scoffed and pinned his gaze on Aiden. "It was a long time ago. She wouldn't approve of who I am now."

"And who's that? Youngest detective in SoCal, living in Laguna Beach, already nailed down a career, and all before he turned twenty-six? Yeah, who *would* approve?" Aiden squinted at Shannon. "I'm sure she'd approve of the dangerous thief this so-called detective hangs out with all the time. Think she'd like me?"

Shannon offered a pained smile. "You'd give that poor girl a heart attack, Aiden."

Once again it was laughter, belly-aching, booming, chest-rattling laughter. Aiden crawled into Shannon's space and kissed him, tasting the impossibility.

"You think so?" Aiden said against his lips, setting his knees on either side of Shannon's waist and his hands on Shannon's face.

"You're everything she'd try to contain, all the best parts of the world that she's scared of, that's you."

Aiden's jaw slackened. His heart raced. Shannon's eyes were half-closed, his cheeks were tinted pink. His honesty was a raw, open thing. Aiden was a sucker for candor and blue, blue, *blue* eyes.

The impossibility of Shannon and Aiden, two separate beings, becoming Shannon and Aiden, an intricate something, was a wild, wonderful, magical thing. And Aiden loved the way it tasted. He kissed him again. And again, and again, and again.

17

"YEAH, YES... NO, SHANNON—DON'T RUSH or anything. I just texted you to let you know I'm heading home..." Aiden perched his phone between his shoulder and ear as he pulled his arms through the sleeves of his coat. "I'm still at my brother's—probably like, twenty minutes. Oh, *yeah*," Aiden hummed pleasantly and dug in his pocket for his cigarettes, "bring ice cream. Vanilla's fine... it's pie, Shannon, not a fancy ass... Okay, yeah, all right, whatever. Twenty minutes. Bye."

Marcus watched him, head cocked, a condescending smile plastered on his face. "That was adorable."

"Fuck off," Aiden mumbled around the butt of an unlit cigarette.

He pulled the slider open and walked into the small fenced-in space that served as Marcus' backyard. It was a rectangle, half cement, half grass. A barbeque was stationed under the bay window. Aiden plopped down in a chair and kicked his boots up on the table.

Marcus sat across from him and made a point of grabbing Aiden's ankles and shoving his feet off. "You ever consider being polite?"

"I'm polite," Aiden hissed. He lit his cigarette and took a drag. "Thanks for dinner. You still shock me every year by not burning your house down."

"You're welcome; thanks for stopping by the store for me." Marcus pointed at Aiden's mouth. "You need to quit those. Mom would slap the shit out of you if she saw you smoking."

"Don't use Mom on me. It's my New Year's resolution."

"Wasn't it last year's resolution?"

"Last year I didn't have you *and* Shannon climbing down my throat about it. So, yeah, this year it's my resolution."

"Am I ever going to meet this guy?" Marcus adjusted his long-sleeved brown shirt. He pushed his glasses up on the bridge of his nose. "You pretend you're not in deep, but you are. I can see it." A wide dark finger waved around Aiden's face. "I'm your brother; I know these things."

"Am I ever going to meet this chick?" Aiden arched a brow.

"Don't deflect."

"I'm not…" Aiden chewed on the end of his cigarette. "I mean, you'll like him, that's for sure. He'll like you. But I'm not in deep or whatever, I just…" He tried to look at his brother, but Marcus wouldn't drop the wide grin. Laughter crept up Marcus' throat. "Okay, whatever, asshole. So what if I am?"

Marcus closed his eyes, shook his head, and laughed into the night air, which made Aiden laugh, too. "It's not a bad thing," Marcus said. "You're always pretending you don't feel things. It's pretty amazing to see you like this."

"Like what?"

"Bambi-eyed, checking your phone constantly, *not* stealing, the list goes on. Mom and Dad would get a kick out of it."

Aiden rolled his eyes. "You don't know I'm not stealing."

"You're not reselling expensive jewelry and artwork, Aiden. That much I do know," Marcus said matter-of-factly. "I check your listings. You think I didn't keep tabs on you after the second time I had to bail you out of jail?"

Aiden made an extended *ppsshh* noise with his lips. He stared up at the white Christmas lights Marcus had strung from the roof to the fence.

He wasn't going to argue.

It was Thanksgiving. He didn't want to fight with his brother and he didn't have any ground to stand on. Through all the screaming matches, stints in jail, teenage drug use, and excessive partying, to the adulthood thievery, callous attitude, and lackluster bartending job, Marcus never told Aiden he was hard to love, even though Aiden knew he was.

He hadn't known Marcus checked his listings, though, and that meant Marcus had acquired a separate router, done plenty of research on the dark web, and probably seen Aiden's listings queried by more than a few unsavory buyers.

"Mom and Dad would love him," Aiden mumbled, taking a short drag off what was left of his cigarette. "They'd want him to come over all the time. Dad would take him to those weird theater performances he went to. Mom would ask if she could paint him. They'd embarrass the hell out of me."

Marcus chuckled and stayed quiet, waiting to see if Aiden would continue.

Aiden didn't. He couldn't. His words got stuck behind his teeth where he pushed them around with his tongue and chewed on them until they disintegrated. He cleared his throat. "Yeah, they'd really love Shannon," he said.

"Why don't we do dinner sometime before Christmas? Holidays make for awkward introductions, anyway. Next Thursday?" Marcus stood and pulled Aiden up into a tight embrace.

"That's the eighth, right? I should be able to. I'll ask Shannon tonight and get back to you. You should bring your new girlfriend-not-girlfriend." Aiden leaned his cheek against Marcus' shoulder and sighed. He'd worn the same cologne since Aiden was in middle school; it was full-bodied cinnamon, the one their Dad wore. "Thanks again for dinner." *And everything else.*

"Don't forget the pie," Marcus said and patted Aiden on the cheek.

AIDEN WALKED UP THE STAIRS to find Shannon leaning against his front door with a quart of vanilla ice cream in one hand and his cell phone in the other. It'd taken Aiden twenty-five minutes instead of twenty to get to his apartment, which meant Shannon had beaten him there.

Shannon flicked the kitchen lights on. Aiden fed Mercy. They didn't bother with plates, but piled ice cream on top of the pie that was left in the tin and took it into the bedroom. Aiden listened to Shannon ramble about Karman's delicious tamales and the cases they'd been working on. Shannon listened to Aiden talk about Marcus' fiasco with the yams, how the marshmallows caught fire in the oven and almost burnt the house down. They laughed and laughed and laughed, sitting in bed half-dressed and barely awake.

"I don't let people feed me, Wurther. You should know that," Aiden said, opening his mouth for another forkful of apple pie. "This is a disgrace. I'm ashamed of myself."

Shannon poked Aiden in the chin before he gathered a bite for himself. "I'm scared you might bite my hand if I'm not careful."

Aiden bared his teeth.

"This is taboo for us to talk about, but have you been *out* lately...? I haven't heard of any artwork going missing—"

"No," Aiden said, teeth snapping down. "I picked up more hours at 101 to make up for it. You assume you'd know if I'd taken anything, Shannon? There's a reason I haven't been caught."

"It's because you're good at avoiding security cameras," Shannon slurred around a mouthful of pie. "You also weren't dating a cop at the time, which probably made things easier."

"Yeah," Aiden scoffed. "It did, actually. Why are we even discussing this?"

"I have to know these things for when I arrest you." He held another forkful of pie in front of Aiden's mouth. "Obviously, that's still the plan. Feed you pie, cuff you in your sleep, haul you down to the station, and charge you for the seven open cases you're a suspect in."

"Seven?" Aiden blurted, covering his grin, mouth stuffed full of food. "That's all they got in my file? *Seven?*"

Deep-set blue eyes slanted into two slits. The playfulness dissipated. Sarcasm faded into surprise and then into anger. Shannon stared; his mouth squirmed before it pressed down and flattened. A hot blush burned his cheeks. His knuckles whitened around the pie tin as he set it on the nightstand atop a growing pile of tattoo magazines.

"Don't," Shannon warned, holding up his index finger. Aiden opened his mouth, and Shannon hissed, "Don't say one word."

Shannon flopped on the mattress near the foot of the bed. Aiden tried to stifle his laughter and dropped his hands into his lap, watching Shannon's jaw move side to side. The hollow points on his face were sculpted, shadowed by the miniscule lighting. Aiden saw the dark spaces below his cheeks, the tension that cut grooves between his brows, and lips twitching along syllables he couldn't put together.

"Sixteen," Aiden whispered.

"Shut up!" Shannon hit the bed with a closed fist. "Aiden, don't tell me. Do not."

He pushed off the wall and crawled over the length of Shannon's body. Aiden's hands rested on either side of his head; one knee pressed between his legs. "Sixteen," he said again, nose brushing a dimple. "Three of them are in my living room."

Shannon's lips parted. He closed his eyes, slow and deliberate. "I should report you."

"You should." Aiden nosed at Shannon's jaw; light evening stubble scraped his lips.

"Technically, I should *arrest* you. You're not making my job any easier."

"I'm not the one who brought it up, Detective. I'm just being honest."

"No, you're being smug," Shannon snapped. His hands ran up Aiden's spine until they rested on the sharp wings of his shoulder blades. "You're proud and cocky and fearless, and that's not a combination of qualities most people would throw around as carelessly as you do."

"I'm not most people."

Shannon hummed in response. Cheek cushioned against the comforter, he glanced past Aiden's shoulder. Aiden didn't know what captured Shannon's attention. His own hungry focus was on the flexed tendon that curved from his earlobe to the inside of his collar bone. He traced it with his lips. Shannon's breath changed from even and quick, to labored and weak.

"Where'd you get that one?" Shannon mumbled. He tilted his head back, giving Aiden more room.

Aiden's brow furrowed. "What?"

Shannon touched the back of his head, a gentle encouragement.

"That one, the photograph above your bed. I'm assuming you stole it from somewhere."

"You and your assumptions." Despite a wave of exhaustion, Aiden traversed every path between Shannon's chin and sternum. He paid mind to his shoulders, and the tip of his tongue played lazily with an earlobe. Shannon gripped the back of Aiden's neck and craned into his mouth. Once Aiden was sure he'd left more than a couple lingering marks, he slid next to Shannon and draped his arm across his chest. "I took that in high school for a photography project. Daisy drove us to Venice one day, and I had my camera, so," he gestured lazily at the wall, "that's where it came from. Marcus had it printed on a matte canvas a couple years ago for my birthday."

Shannon sat up, and Aiden grumbled as his cheek slid off Shannon's chest to land on the bed. He blinked, too tired to convince his arms or legs to move.

"You took that?" Shannon cocked his head. "That picture right there?"

"No, the other giant photograph of Venice Beach."

Shannon swatted him. "That's really good, Aiden. People would pay a ton of money for photos like this."

"It's not that good."

"It is, though!" Shannon poked him in the thigh and then in the arm. "You should be a photographer. People would love it, especially the people out here. I mean, look at where you live—Laguna Beach, tourist haven, beach city, wedding destination. You have a perfect opportunity."

"It's a class I took in high school; it's not a big deal. It was fun, but I'm not serious about it."

"You should *get* serious about it."

Aiden grunted and scooted to the top of the bed. He reached for the lamp, missed, reached again, missed. He cursed under his breath and stretched until his finger finally swiped at the switch. He snaked around Shannon and arranged his arms this way, pushed his legs that way, until they were properly tangled. Shannon's restless fingertips played on Aiden's nape.

"You should buy a nice camera."

"Shannon."

"You *should*, Aiden. You should invest in your skill set."

"Shannon, be quiet."

"I'm serious."

"And I'm tired," Aiden snapped, shoving his face in Shannon's chest. "This is probably the only time I'll ask you to stop talking about how gifted I am, so please. Sleep. Now."

Shannon's breath was warm on Aiden's temple. "You can get a nice one cheap at one of—"

"Shannon!" Aiden curled around him and squeezed. "For the love of god, be quiet. You know I have a fucked-up sleep schedule, just..." He finished his statement with a whine and covered Shannon's mouth with his palm.

Shannon licked his hand.

Aiden bit his chest.

"Fine," Shannon grumbled, tossing Aiden's wrist away. "But you should do it; you should be a photographer."

Aiden closed his eyes, focused on the rise and fall of Shannon's chest against his cheek, and felt Mercy curl up against his foot.

He remembered the click of the camera the moment he'd taken the picture: Daisy's graceful twirls down the boardwalk; Vance hot on her heels; Jonathan's skateboard, its wheels on the asphalt, an iconic sound; and Aiden's camera, solid in his hands—one, two, three, a half-circle, and that was all it took.

Aiden fell asleep with his thigh thrown over Shannon's waist, thinking of what it used to feel like, capturing moments.

How would this one look?

18

CARVER CLASPED HIS HAND OVER Aiden's shoulder. "New girl needs to train up front; you good for the night?"

"Yeah, I need to pull some glasses from the back, but other than that everything should be stocked. I'll probably stick around for a while after I clock out."

"Sounds good. First drink's on the house. You're gin, right?"

"Bourbon."

"Ah, gentleman's drink, that's right."

Aiden liked his job. He was good at it, Carver now let him bartend when it was busy, and 101's atmosphere—bouncing between a sense of urgency and general fluidity—felt comfortable. The bar was crowded for a Sunday: two bodies deep along the bar, booths overflowing, music blaring from the speakers overhead. Aiden glanced around the corner to see if the pool table in the back was being used, and to his surprise it was unattended.

He tidied the shelves in a hurry, restocked the open cabinets below the bar with glassware, and then clocked out. Carver slid a short glass down the bar to him; amber liquid sloshed up the sides. Aiden tipped his head, slipped around the corner, and snatched a pool stick off the rack.

December was carefree and expensive and rich in forgery. People pretended that shopping for gifts was a pleasantry rather than a chore; they filled out Hallmark cards; drew hearts over the 'i' in Merry Christmas; doodled on Starbucks' seasonal red cups. But somehow, under all the falsities and manufactured kindness, December felt like coming home.

"Need a partner?"

Aiden glanced up as he was taking a sip of his drink. A man watched him. Dark green eyes scanned Aiden's face and traveled down his chest, then settled too long on his waist. The man wasn't shy, and Aiden wasn't in the mood to play games. He wasn't behind the bar and he wasn't trying to get something from someone, so there was no need to acknowledge whoever he was.

"No," Aiden said curtly, curling his hand around the pool stick to show the blank square of his thumbnail: no numbers, no Clock, an obvious denial to whatever invitation the tan-skinned, green-eyed Laguna Beach local was handing out.

"You sure? We could have fun."

"I'm sure."

He finished his drink, placed his pool stick across the table, retrieved a second drink, and then played a game of pool by himself. The stranger was with his friends out of Aiden's direct line of sight, which was appreciated.

Once, Aiden would have bypassed introductions and answered that man with a kiss. But that was months ago, and Aiden wasn't the same Aiden. He was Aiden Maar who belonged to Shannon Wurther, and this Aiden was satisfied. No more teasing people he had no intention of going home with; no more fishing for compliments from wide-eyed women and flirting roughly with men outside concert halls; no more bloody knuckles and bloody make-outs and bloody nothings. Aiden had something. And that something was a good something.

He finished his second drink too quickly. His head spun.

"Okay," Aiden mumbled, a little embarrassed by his lack of stability after a meager two drinks.

He reached for his phone.

Shannon Wurther 12/5 8:08 p.m.
im not off for another hour, gotta file some paperwork and take karman home. whats up?
Aiden Maar 12/5 8:09 p.m.
nothing just saying hi

He'd been hoping for a ride, since December was a cold, cold month. But he wasn't going to say that, because if he did, Shannon would stop whatever he was doing and rush over. Aiden would walk. He racked his pool stick, grabbed his empty glass, turned, and gasped.

Warm, slick lips smacked against his. Aiden jolted back. He was hyperaware of his surroundings. His heart thudded. He shook his head, looking the green-eyed man up and down.

"You just don't take a fucking hint, do you?" Aiden wiped his mouth with the back of his hand.

"You look like fun," the man said. One thick brow quirked, and his smile was lopsided.

Aiden shoved his index finger at the man's chest. "You're lucky I fucking work here, or I'd break your jaw."

"Come on, don't be like that." The stranger sighed; his eyes were far away. He was drunk, piss drunk. Aiden almost felt sorry for him.

"Where are your handlers?"

"What?"

Aiden rolled his eyes. "Hey!" He stood on tiptoe and scanned the room. "Who does this belong to?" He picked up the man's wrist and forced him to wave his arm, a noodle of a limb.

Within seconds, a stunning woman with midnight skin and long braids was hauling him away to a group of blushing hipsters at a high table by the restrooms. She apologized profusely, using words like 'breakup' and 'heartbroken' and 'fucked up' to describe her drunken friend.

Aiden didn't say a word. He ordered a Manhattan to wash away the taste of whatever fruity drink that uninvited kiss had left in his mouth. "Extra bitters," Aiden said.

Carver gave him extra bitters. He also told Aiden it was fine to chain his bike to the back door for the night, for which Aiden was grateful. He finished his drink, put his helmet in the back room, walked outside, and started to lock up his bike.

It didn't happen the way Aiden had thought it would.

When the red and blue lights lit up the asphalt beneath his feet, he ignored them; they weren't for him. When a gruff voice told him to stay where he was, he didn't listen—the command couldn't be for him. He latched the lock around the chain and made sure his bike was under the awning. A heavy hand settled on his shoulder. *A brave and stupid thing to do.*

"Son, we got a call concerning an intoxicated youth. That wouldn't be you, would it?"

"Nope." Aiden yanked away. "I'm going home. I've had a weird enough night as it is. Got kissed by some idiot, long night at work. I'm exhausted, I have to feed my cat, and I don't need this shit. And I'm not a *youth*."

"You sure about that?" The officer was short and round with a bald head and a groomed goatee. He had one hand on his belt, the other stretched in front of him, a warning. "I'm going to have to ask you to take a seat on the curb."

"Am I being detained?"

Aiden didn't wait for an answer. He walked away, disregarding whatever the officer shouted. He hadn't done anything wrong. He was going home.

The officer grabbed his arm and pulled. Aiden turned; his knuckles cracked the edge of the officer's brow. The officer cursed and stumbled. Something long and cold—a black baton—struck Aiden in the mouth.

He saw a white flash. High-pitched ringing blasted in his ears. Handcuffs bit into his wrists.

"Are you fucking kidding me?" Aiden shouted, spitting blood on the ground and stumbling as he was tossed against the car.

Deputy Barrow shoved him into the back seat. "You're going to jail, punk."

"Not the first time, asshole."

00:00

SHANNON GOT THE CALL WHILE he was driving home from Karman's.

It went something like: Wurther, we've got an Aiden Maar here who says he knows you. Assaulted Barrow. Description matches an open case.

Rage simmered in his veins, sudden and blinding. It turned to shards of glass, splintering in every direction. His heart plummeted into his stomach. He tried to put his finger on it, on the feeling itself—anger with the volume turned up, worry flipped inside out. Shannon was completely unsure of his ability to keep it together.

He stormed into the station, unaware that his anger and topsy-turvy worry played on his face like light glinted off a sharpened knife. He didn't acknowledge Cindy at the front desk, nor did he stop when Barrow tried to step in front of him. He walked straight to the holding room, where a thick glass window allowed him to watch Aiden pace back and forth like a caged tiger.

"What'd he do?" Shannon spat out.

Barrow stammered. "He... He was outside a bar, angry, violent. I was responding to a call about some teenagers and found him, thought he was messing with someone's bike."

"Bring him out here."

"Wurther, that's—"

"Now."

In the cell, Aiden locked onto Shannon. He swiped at his mouth and walked back and forth, shoulders poised, ready for battle. Shannon was reminded of Aiden's potential. He was a dark, thundering, aggressive force, barely contained by the frayed shreds of his self-control. He surged against Barrow's arm when the officer gripped his shoulder. Shannon heard the snap of Aiden's teeth when he said, "get the fuck off me," saw the glint in his eyes that said *if I could get my teeth in you I would; if I could rip your throat out I would,* and Shannon believed it.

A wide red bruise encircled Barrow's swollen left eye socket. Broken capillaries dusted his temple and the bridge of his nose.

"I didn't do anything," Aiden said, jerking away from Barrow. "Shannon, I didn't fucking do anything. Ask him what I was doing!"

"Barrow, what was he doing?"

Officer Barrow's face darkened. He trembled, huffing in frustrated breaths. "He was messing with someone's bike, drunk outside of a bar—"

"Which bar?" Aiden asked.

"Shut up," Barrow snapped.

"Which bar?" Shannon took a step forward.

"That grimy one up north, 101."

"Yeah, the place I work!" Aiden exclaimed. Wide eyes pleaded with Shannon from across the room.

"He says he works there," Barrow mumbled.

"He does work there," Shannon said icily, "and let me guess, the bike you saw him messing with was a black Triumph, right?"

Aiden's lips quirked one way and then the other in a contented smirk.

Barrow's red face turned white. He narrowed his eyes. "Yes, it was. He claims it's his."

Shannon pulled his teeth apart, forcing his jaw to unclench. "That's because it *is* his."

"Wurther, how do you know this kid?"

"He's not a kid."

Shannon sighed, and at the same time Aiden snarled, "I'm his Rose Road."

Fingers tapping on keyboards halted. File cabinets stopped squeaking. Chatter stopped chattering. It was as if the entire room gave the tiniest gasp, and then followed it with absolute silence. Heads lifted from desks. Barrow's wide eyes widened even farther, and he immediately stepped out of Aiden's space.

Piper, head of the Homicide department, laughed outright. "Oh, Wurther, fate's a magical thing, isn't it? Landed yourself a stick of dynamite if I've ever seen one."

"Fuck off, bitch," Aiden snapped.

She whistled, ruby lips curving into a grin. "Oh, yeah, about ready to pop, too. Problem is," she lifted a slender, tan finger, "he matches your description from the night of the gallery mishap. Is this him?"

Careful to keep his back straight and his breathing even, Shannon bit the side of his tongue. *Yes. It was.* Staring at him from across the room—a ferocious, deadly thing—was the mishap from the gallery.

"Tattoo matches and everything," she added. Her hand carded through a waterfall of black hair.

Aiden exhaled a soft breath, and Shannon watched something inside him crack. He mouthed Shannon's name, almost as if he hadn't meant to.

"No, it isn't. Lift up your shirt, show them your tattoo," Shannon said, waving his hand.

Aiden did as he was told.

"The burglar wasn't as pale, and his tattoo was an Asian design, not this; eyes were darker."

Lies. Lies. Lies.

"That's convenient, Wurther. This Aiden Maar is a suspect in multiple other incidents, but we have nothing on him. You're sure it wasn't him?" Piper asked. She flared her nostrils; the gold stud on the left side protruded.

"I'm sure." Shannon didn't look away from Aiden.

Barrow shook his head, his hands settled on his hips below his slouching belly. "Well, he's still under arrest for assaulting an officer."

Aiden gaped, but Shannon flashed his palm, signaling him to be quiet.

"Did you have reason to detain him, Deputy Barrow? As it turns out, Aiden does work at 101, the bike you thought he was tampering with belongs to him, and you had no reason to question him. Was excessive force used?"

"Wurther!" Barrow bellowed. He coughed; his cheeks turned from white to cherry. "He hit me. I have proof." He pointed to his battered eye. "And, in turn, I detained him."

"He grabbed me," Aiden hissed, "pulled on my shoulder, and shoved me backward. That's why he got hit."

Shannon turned to Barrow. "And then what? You hit him back?"

"Yeah, with his fucking baton," Aiden mumbled, licking across the wound on his lip.

The silence wound tight enough to snap. Barrow withered under Shannon's unusually sharp gaze.

Piper snorted pleasantly. "Careful, Barrow. Looks to me like you've made a big mistake."

"Don't you have a case to solve, Piper?" Barrow snapped. "Dead body to analyze? Fingerprints to match?"

Piper arched her thick brows. She glanced from Barrow to Shannon and back again. "Release Maar. He's free to go."

"You don't have the authority—"

Piper's head fell back and she laughed, silencing any protest from Barrow. She waved at another deputy and flicked her hand at Aiden's cuffs. "Go on, get those off him."

Barrow slammed a notepad against Shannon's chest. "Your Rose over there said something before he did this to me." He pointed at his eye again. "You should probably know." He stared at Shannon; anger blistered his face with red splotches. "I won't press charges this time," he said, too low for anyone else to hear.

Shannon's stomach flipped. He looked at Barrow, who was a good man, but a stupid one, and opened the notepad. One statement jumped out. Shannon read it twice. *Mentioned having a weird night and being kissed. Drunk. Slurred words.* He read it again—*and being kissed*—then he tossed the notepad onto his desk.

Aiden brushed past him, an unlit cigarette already pressed between his lips. He was a wildfire, scorching whatever stood in his path. Dark eyes were glassy. His chest heaved. Shannon thought Aiden might cry, but then he realized he'd mistaken his expression.

Aiden Maar wasn't upset; he was a Molotov cocktail on the verge of exploding.

Shannon glanced at Piper. To thank her without words, he gave a gentle nod. She nodded back and waved three fingers toward the door, telling him to go.

By the time Shannon caught up to Aiden, he was leaning against the Jeep. His hands trembled, fumbling to light his cigarette.

"Get in the car," Shannon said.

Aiden rolled his eyes.

"Now," Shannon snapped.

Aiden shoved the cigarette back in his pack and slid into the passenger seat. "Someone's mad."

"I'm mad." Shannon stomped on the gas pedal.

19

THEY DIDN'T TALK ON THE way to Shannon's apartment. They walked up the stairs, and Shannon closed the door behind them, then shoved Aiden against the wall. Shannon waited. His mouth hovered close to Aiden's, expecting an apology, a clarification, *something*.

Aiden's top lip curled in a daring snarl. "What is it, Detective?"

Shannon gripped his jaw. "That's all you have to say?"

Aiden's short laugh gusted against Shannon's chin before their lips collided, all heat and anger and frustration.

Aiden shoved his jacket off. It fell at their feet. "You still mad at me?"

Yes. Shannon's was mad at Aiden. And mad—he scoffed, gripping Aiden's throat—mad was an understatement. Shannon blistered with rage. It churned his stomach. But the way Aiden said it, *you still mad at me,* with a smile on his face and a blush staining the tops of his cheeks infuriated him further.

Shannon flipped him around, stripped Aiden's shirt, tossed it, and forced Aiden's palms against the wall. He leaned into Shannon's torso; the back of his head rested on Shannon's shoulder.

"What were you thinking?" Shannon rasped.

"I was chaining up my bike. I didn't do anything illegal!" Aiden's eyelashes fluttered when Shannon bit his shoulder. "I don't even know what you're pissed about."

Shannon bit harder. "You kissed someone."

"Oh, my god, you're jealous," he teased.

"Yeah, and you told everyone I work with about us. Thanks for that."

Aiden turned. A smile, cunning and cruel, lingered on his face.

"Thanks for that?" Aiden parroted. He clicked his tongue against his teeth. He was an unlit firework, capable of beautiful, destructive things, but only when lit. Controlled and smoldering, Shannon watched as Aiden sparked. "Sorry I embarrassed you. But about that guy…" He ducked toward the couch. "He kissed me; I didn't kiss him. If it matters any."

"You didn't—" Shannon made a sound between a sigh and a growl. He pulled air in through his teeth and hummed on the exhale. Aiden was sensitive. Aiden was also a razorblade. Those two qualities didn't make for the easiest discussions, especially when Shannon's patience was capped. "You didn't embarrass me," he said, trying to hold back the snap of his teeth.

"Oh!" Aiden barked a laugh. "Okay. The look on your face was just relief, then."

"I didn't want the entire station knowing what goes on in my personal life, all right? And are you forgetting that I saved your ass back there? You were under arrest, Aiden. Barrow could've pressed charges!"

Aiden's tongue darted to lick his teeth. Shannon imagined they might grow into fangs. "That shithead deserved it," Aiden cooed, a singing bird, a cawing vulture. "I should've hit him harder."

"Why do you do this? Why do you act like a child, rather than just admit that what you did was stupid? I don't understand. I don't get why you, of all people, would hit a cop, no matter the circumstance!" Shannon paced. Clouds of bitterness and unease swirled above them. Aiden sat on the couch, with his elbows on his knees.

"Fuck off, Shannon." Aiden refused to look up. He didn't have to shout to get his point across. "You're pissed because some other guy put his mouth on me. You wanna talk about that, let's talk. You wanna talk about me punching a cop, I'll go."

Being laid bare was daunting. Shannon wasn't used to the way Aiden slithered into his chest, scooped his heart into his palm, and squeezed. He echoed inside; his breathing rattled his rib cage. Shannon forced his throat to tighten and swallowed, resisting the urge to raise his voice.

Control—that belonged to him—Aiden couldn't have that.

"Why'd he kiss you?"

"How would I know?" Aiden snapped. "I was playing pool by myself, having a drink, and this weird guy tried to talk to me. I blew him off. When I was about to leave, I turned around to put my pool stick away, and he was right there." He waved his hand in front of his face, gesturing from the open air to his lips. "He kissed me."

Shannon's jaw hurt. "And?"

"And nothing!" Aiden laughed—full and exasperated; his mouth was a line of barbed wire. "He was wasted, so, instead of knocking his teeth in, I found his friends. They apologized, and then I bought another drink."

There wasn't anything to say, was there? Aiden still hadn't looked up at him. Shannon opened his mouth, grappled for words, and clamped his lips shut. The moon peeked through the clouds, lighting up the fog. He sat on the edge of the bed. Aiden stood in front of him; the waistband of his worn black pants blocked Shannon's view out the window.

"Why does it matter?" Aiden's voice cracked on the last word, which turned his frustration into something else.

Shannon shied from his hands, but Aiden followed. He crawled on top of him, pressed against Shannon's chest, and shoved him into the comforter.

"Tell me," Aiden reiterated.

It was natural to grab Aiden's waist, to run his hands up his sides, but Aiden didn't allow it. He snatched Shannon's wrists and pinned them above his head. "What? I went to a bar, got drunk, fucked around with someone else. Is that what you think I'd do?"

"I don't know what you'd do, Aiden." Shannon flexed his hands. Aiden's grip tightened.

"Don't give me that shit. You honestly think I'd do that? Really?"

Aiden's thumbs swiped back and forth along the sides of Shannon's hands. He hovered over him, burning Shannon to a crisp. The cut that curved over the ridge of his bottom lip was red around the edges. His knees parted farther around Shannon's waist. One by one, Aiden's fingers slid into the palms of Shannon's hands.

"I don't like it." Shannon fought with his words, trying to catch them as they tumbled out. "I don't like the idea of someone putting their hands on you, much less their mouth. The fact that Barrow hit you was enough; I didn't need to know about the guy from the bar, too."

"You don't think Barrow should've hit me? And how'd you even know about that, anyway?" Aiden smiled, and it was a relief.

Shannon's engine was still red hot; unrequited anger vibrated beneath his skin. He turned away and stared at the front door. The tip of Aiden's nose tickled his cheek. His breath was smoky and familiar.

"Shannon." Aiden unlaced their hands and sat up. "You either talk to me, or I leave. I'm not going to sit here and try to figure out what the hell is wrong with you if your plan is to pout."

Shannon sat up. His hands latched onto Aden's hips, he pulled him close, and hid his face in Aiden's throat. "I wanted to kill Barrow for hitting you. I wanted to strangle the life out of him. You'd mentioned a kiss, and he wrote it down in the paperwork, that's how I knew about it. I don't want anyone touching you but me, and I don't want anyone touching me but you, all right?"

"Why didn't you just say that?" Aiden mumbled. His hands drifted over Shannon's shoulders.

"Because I'm scared to death of you, Aiden!" Shannon stared at the ceiling. His voice escalated and the long-lost Georgia accent surfaced. He swallowed, trying to keep his wits about him, as Aiden's lips dusted the curve of his collarbone, the line of his throat, his jaw. "You're the first person who's ever done this to me, and I don't like it. I don't like feeling like this."

"And you think I do?" Aiden laughed against his ear. "You think I enjoy being all fucked up by you?"

Shannon turned to look at Aiden. Aiden carried an undeniable calm, a regal knowledge of himself, of his own venom, that was impossibly attractive. He wore his faults as a crown of glass and steel. His arms drew back from Shannon's shoulders, and he began unclasping the buttons on Shannon's shirt.

"I'm sorry—" Aiden sounded a little annoyed, a little true. "—for getting arrested and for punching your cop friend, but it's probably not the last time it'll happen."

"I'm sorry for assuming the worst and overreacting." Shannon stared at Aiden's fingers as they flicked each button open. "But can you at least *try* not to get arrested again?"

A smirk was all he got. Aiden pawed the shirt from his shoulders and tossed it to the floor. "No promises," he mumbled.

The sensation of Aiden's smooth palms, the tips of his fingers, and the brush of his knuckles ended their argument. He swayed against Shannon's clumsy hands and pushed into them as he tried to unfasten the button on Aiden's pants. Shannon felt shaking hands, one on the back of his neck, the other dancing across his chest, and he faltered. Aiden's eyes squeezed shut, painfully so, his lips were cinched. Shannon grasped his wrist. Aiden's nostrils flared.

"What's a matter?" Shannon's accent stuck to the walls of his throat.

Aiden shook his head. "I've never done this." His gaze fell away, and he chewed on his already busted lip. He seemed less a viper, more a man, and Shannon wasn't sure how to process that. "Neither have I, but we can stop if you want." Shannon rested his hands on Aiden's waist. Shannon wasn't sure what Aiden meant, but Shannon wasn't lying when he said he hadn't done it. He'd never had someone like Aiden to do anything with.

"No, Shannon," Aiden hissed, "I've *never* done this."

Shannon cocked his head, unaware that Aiden's hostility wasn't pointed at him, but at something else entirely. Aiden turned away, hiding the glowing blush that lit his cheeks. His hands fell from Shannon's face to his own lap, where they fidgeted.

Understanding came to Shannon in waves. First he was embarrassed: pondering what he'd done wrong, wondering how they'd gone from so ridiculously angry with each other to where they were now. Then the last wave crashed.

Shannon narrowed his eyes, grabbed Aiden's chin, and tugged. "Are you..." Shannon smirked, watching Aiden's jaw grind back and forth. "Are you a virgin?"

Aiden rolled his eyes and snorted. He leaned back on Shannon's thighs and worried his bottom lip between his teeth. He didn't say anything, but he didn't have to. Aiden wore the truth like war paint across his tense brow and clenched jaw. Shannon didn't mean to, but he almost laughed. It came out as a haughty breath that earned him a cold, vicious glare.

"You're serious?" Shannon tilted his head to find Aiden's reluctant, sour gaze. "You've never... Not even to try it?"

"No, asshole, I didn't. I've hooked up with people, but it never went further than hickeys and ass-grabbing. Happy?"

A sense of awe fell over Shannon. *How?* How could the man draped over his lap, the dangerous, sharp-tongued Aiden Maar, make it out of his youth without being someone's conquest? He was wild and insufferable and everything a teenager would want: a perfect storm, a practice run before they found their Rose Road. That's what Shannon had done. He'd had a high school girlfriend, fooled around in college dorms, and met people at bars and clubs. That's what everyone he knew had done. Except for *his* Rose Road—except for Aiden.

He grasped Aiden's cheek and ran his thumb along his mouth. Aiden flinched when he brushed the reddened cut. "Do you want to?"

"That's a stupid question," Aiden seethed. He tried to look away, but Shannon pinched his chin, commanding his attention.

"Do you want me to show you?"

Aiden's parted lips clasped together. He searched Shannon's face and his nostrils flared around quick inhales and even quicker exhales. They picked each other apart in the silence. Still trembling, Aiden tried to nod. He swallowed once, twice. His hands fidgeted in twitches and jerks. Unkempt ferocity glowed behind his eyes. He nodded and kissed Shannon.

"We'll take it slow," Shannon whispered against his lips, "one thing at a time."

Until ten minutes ago, Shannon had been sure Aiden had more experience with intimacies than he did. He welcomed the newfound power and the tiniest bit of authority. He felt the drag of Aiden's tongue between his lips, the labored gasp, and the uncertain roll of his hips in Shannon's lap. His hands continued to quiver as they threaded through his hair.

Shannon pulled and Aiden kicked until his jeans were gone, leaving him looking very bashful, and very bare. Black briefs displayed the angled cut of his hipbones. Shannon watched the lean muscles below his skin tighten and relax. A tiny scar to the right of his belly button was all that was left of his makeshift superglue stitches.

The blinds on the far windows were open, sending rich black and navy shadows across Aiden's skin.

"Shannon…" Aiden swallowed his name. It was a question, Shannon thought. Aiden's eyes, honey and coal and sparking flames hidden beneath dark blond lashes, darted this way and that, across Shannon's waist, down his legs.

Spread out on the bed with a blush creeping from his chest to his face, Aiden was still a cluster of knives. Shannon's willingness to bleed defied every shred of control he had left.

Shannon took his time crawling up Aiden's body. He counted each set of ribs with his teeth, drawing soundless breath from Aiden's lungs.

He chewed on the arcs of his collarbones, left blooming marks on his chest. The long slope of Aiden's neck extended, he dug his nails into Shannon's scalp, and held him down. The indentions from Shannon's incisors could spell out their love story, if they had one at all.

"You all right?" Shannon asked.

Aiden pulled Shannon's face down, craned forward, and sealed their lips together. They stayed in that kiss for as long as they could and stole gulps of air between interludes of teeth and lips and tongue. It wasn't until Aiden made a sound in the back of his throat, a growl or a moan or a little bit of both, that Shannon finally broke away. He started at Aiden's jaw, placed his lips there, and trailed them down his neck, over his chest. Aiden squirmed when his teeth scraped the top of Aiden's hipbones, then latched onto the smooth flesh on the inside of his thigh.

According to Shannon Wurther, Aiden Maar was the best kept secret in the universe. Being in his orbit was like being pulled toward the sun, melting away, falling back to Earth, and slamming against the ground without any complaint. Aiden's chest heaved. Instead of placing his hands on Shannon's shoulders, or the back of his head, or his jaw, or anywhere Shannon wanted to feel them, he buried them in the sheets. His neck was a long line of white, stretched back. His lips were red and bitten where he pressed them down in attempt to mute himself. Shannon crawled back up Aiden's body. Aiden's eyes squeezed shut, and whimpers, barely under his breath, fluttered from him.

"Stop being quiet," Shannon said against his mouth, trying to catch his breath. Aiden grasped his face and kissed him. It tasted like smoke, and salt, and copper. Shannon reeled back and found the cut on Aiden's mouth torn open. Drops of blood left cherry streaks on his lips and darkened his mouth. Shannon swiped it with his thumb, licked it clean. "I mean it," he said.

Wide, defiant eyes scanned him in the dark and watched Shannon disappear down the length of his body. Aiden listened, reluctantly, but he listened. His legs tightened around Shannon's ears, and he gasped, low, throaty groans turned tender and shaken. His hips rose off the bed and Shannon forced them back down, gripped Aiden's waist hard, watched his bloody mouth tremble.

Aiden's back arched. He said Shannon's name as if it might have been a prayer or a plea or the only name he knew, and Shannon swore he'd never heard it spoken until then, until Aiden let it slip past his lips.

20

THE SHOWER IN SHANNON'S APARTMENT was small. He had a shallow tub and a shower head that sprayed a little too hard for Aiden's liking.

Hot water scorched his back as Aiden rested his forehead against the white wall with his eyes closed, trying to coax his body to stop reacting to phantom touches. Tremors danced on his skin. His knees wobbled. Shannon's fingertips were ghosts, their bruising grip on his waist a whisper, and the way his voice rasped—*Stop being quiet*—was the tumbling of dry, autumn leaves.

He hadn't expected it to happen like that. He hadn't expected to be torn up, to be cracked open.

Memories flashed behind his eyelids. He saw Shannon's wide baby blues in the gallery and the disbelief that honed his face into the personification of skepticism. Aiden remembered the first night. He remembered losing the battle against his better judgment and testing a kiss. That could've proved the Clock was wrong, that fate was just another fad. But when Aiden stepped off the ledge, he'd forgotten how long the fall could be. He'd made the mistake of being sure Detective Wurther wouldn't kiss him back.

That was months ago, and it seemed as if it'd only been a week.

His tongue darted along the edge of the small gash on the side of his mouth. Aiden squeezed his eyes shut tighter, but all he saw in the darkness was shadowed skin, wet lips, and Shannon hovering over him, sucking blood off his thumb. *I mean it.*

"Fucking hell, Wurther..." Aiden whispered. He swallowed, freeing his mind of the repetitive memories, and grabbed a bottle of shower gel off the shelf.

The door opened. He heard Shannon's bare feet against the tile. Jeans hit the floor. The shower curtain crinkled as it was pulled away. He glanced at Shannon, ran a soapy hand over the back of his neck, and struggled to keep his composure. A part of him was embarrassed, unsure of what to do, how to act, what to say, and another part of him, a larger part of him, was itching to reach out and touch. Shannon did that for him. He stepped in and blocked the water, then ran his hands through the soap lingering on Aiden's shoulders.

"Gardenia?" Warmth pooled in Aiden's abdomen, spreading out into the rest of him like unruly vines. "They don't give you cop-scented soap with your uniform?"

Aiden felt Shannon's smile pressed between his shoulder blades at the top of his spine. "You don't like it?"

"That's not what I said."

"What do you use? Ice Pick? Eagle Screech?"

Laughter punched from him, abrupt enough that his lip stung. Water made for slick bodies, and Aiden liked the way his skin felt against Shannon's. "Organic vanilla," he admitted and laughed again, at himself mostly, "and sandalwood. I get it at the crystal shop downtown."

"Here you are buying organic bath products and you have the nerve to question my gardenia body wash." Shannon snorted, nosing along Aiden's neck.

There it was again: the length of his vowels, the drop of his "ing" and the top-heavy beginning of "gardenia." Aiden glanced over his shoulder before he turned around to lean against Shannon's broad chest. He fought the urge to let his eyes wander and focused on his face, the tilt of his nose, the water that clung to his lashes. Shannon Wurther wasn't just cop-handsome, Aiden decided. He was the kind of handsome people swooned over, the kind of handsome other men envied. Not rough, but lacking finesse, he fit somewhere in-between, walking the line that separated hard and soft.

"Thank you for covering for me with the whole gallery-case thing," Aiden whispered. "For a second there I thought you might not."

Shannon hummed and kissed Aiden's shoulder. "You think I'd let them take you?"

"I don't know."

"You should know by now," Shannon said.

"You ever gonna tell me where you're from?"

Shannon tensed. His jaw fell slack and he gave a subtle shake of his head.

"Oh, come on." Aiden squeezed shampoo into the palm of his hand and threaded his fingers through Shannon's hair, which was something he thought he would never do, not in this life, at least. He scraped his nails against Shannon's scalp. "Criminals have to be smart to be criminals. And we aren't deaf. You gonna tell me, or what?"

A shared shower was an intimacy Aiden never imagined he'd experience. Shannon's forehead rested on his shoulder, and his fingers made patterns through the water low on Aiden's back. Aiden couldn't dissect the peacefulness, an occupying of space and skin and being that dulled his senses.

Aiden thought he could breathe, and maybe he didn't have to be a phoenix, because here, relaxing in a cloud of steam with Shannon sighing against his ear, he didn't feel like dying.

Shannon sucked in a breath and paused, obviously resisting the answer. Finally, he said, "Georgia."

Ah, he knew it.

It had to be somewhere in the south, but Aiden hadn't been able to place just *how* south. It wasn't the gentlemanly drawl of Virginia or the gruff clip of Texas. It was willowy and round and small-town. Georgia made sense.

"Why do you hide it?" Aiden set his hands on Shannon's chest and gave him a little push, forcing him to stop hiding in the slope between Aiden's shoulder and neck.

"I moved to Laguna when I was seventeen and I was afraid of sounding stupid. I wanted people to take me seriously at the police academy, so I learned how to hide it. Kept getting better at it as time went on; sometimes I forget I have it at all."

"Why would you sound stupid?" Aiden's eyebrows pinched together. "That's a ridiculous thing to be afraid of."

Aiden's gaze finally darted away to creep across the contours of Shannon's body. He was typical Laguna Beach, with cliché shadows beneath his hipbones and a long torso where the skin was stretched over tight muscle.

You'll ruin this. Aiden heard himself, a rasped whisper in the back of his mind. *You know you will.*

Looking at Shannon brought an eerie sense of his own vulnerability, and he tensed. The sudden urge to shrink away was almost as strong as the urge to curl his hands into fists.

Shannon's lips pressed together in a gentle smile, as if he might be looking at a loaded gun, or a wounded coyote, or something beautiful. Aiden wasn't sure which.

"It is a ridiculous thing to be afraid of, isn't it?" Shannon said. The water was going cold. He twisted the knob, and the water trickled to a stop.

Shannon's remembered words were a crack of thunder in Aiden's mind—*Because I'm scared to death of you, Aiden!*

Before Shannon could step out of the tub, Aiden snatched his arms and closed the space between them. Their lips were wet and slick, sliding together in smooth, quick motions. The water was off, but Aiden pressed Shannon against the still-warm wall.

Shannon, pulled in by the tide, licking the sand. Aiden, crashing against the shoreline, sinking ships at sea.

It was a ridiculous thing to be afraid of, Aiden thought. But all the while, even as he tried to catch his breath, it was apparent that what Shannon Wurther was afraid of most was Aiden Maar.

And Aiden was just as scared of him, and his eyes, and his power, and everything about him that made Aiden feel alive—as though he might not need to rise from his own ashes after all.

21

CITRINE WAS AIDEN'S FAVORITE STONE. Variations of yellow beams went every which way when he twirled the jagged crystal in the light. He'd fished this stone from a black-bottomed dish at a store he rarely visited. It was a little smaller than the tip of his thumb, a tiny mountain range of ridges in the shape of a teardrop. Transparent gold hues shot from its center—a firework miniaturized and contained in crystal.

His hand twitched, and he scooped it into his palm, flicking the citrine under the sleeve of his leather jacket. He picked up a similar stone and dropped it into the pile; the sound masked his thievery. In an identical bowl was a pile of purples. Shades upon shades of amethyst were balanced in a heap. Some had gray spines and violet teeth; others were spherical, fading from deep eggplant on one side to watery lilac on the other.

The sign above the bowl read: *Amethyst—for clarity, detoxification, and spiritual protection.*

Perfect. He grabbed a piece like his citrine, jagged and raw, slipped it into the sleeve of his jacket, and moved on.

On the other side of the store, next to a display of Himalayan salt lamps, an assortment of chains, some long, some short, some gold, and most silver, dangled from hooks. Aiden plucked a dainty medium-length chain from one hook, and a shorter, thicker chain from another.

These, he would buy. The stones themselves were less expensive than the chains, but it wasn't the need to steal that drove him to it. It was the itch under his skin, the act in itself: hiding something and walking out with it, a mediocre little secret. The crystals were not paintings or rare jewelry. He wasn't fascinated with them as he was with the other things he stole, and the two tiny stones pressed against his wrist weren't going to a rich buyer in Costa Rica, either. Money or no money, Aiden loved the tension that bloomed in his abdomen and the heat that swelled around his wrist where the stones dug into his skin.

"Will that be all?" The woman behind the counter had a hawk nose and small eyes. She squinted at him from behind gigantic round glasses.

Aiden nodded and used the hand concealing the stones to give her his debit card. They bit into his wrist, and he smiled. "Yeah, that's it."

She sighed through her nose and gave Aiden another once over. He wasn't their typical flashy, suburban customer. A woman who did fit that description walked around analyzing massive hunks of stone, pieces of amethyst the size of his head and black tourmaline carved in the shape of lotus flowers.

He rolled his eyes when the clerk refused to hand him his card and instead placed it on the counter in front of him. He slid it into his wallet, which was kept together by ample amounts of duct tape.

"Thank you," he cooed.

The shopkeeper ignored him completely, and Aiden laughed all the way out the door.

00:00

LAGUNA BEACH CANVAS & SCULPT was different during the day.

Shannon hadn't given it a look since the night he'd timed out, but he'd driven past it at least a hundred times. It never ceased to tease at his attention; he was curious about Aiden's treasure. He thought of the name again and again.

Fortitude Smashed—how contemporary.

It sounded urban and chic and expensive, which was fitting since the painting had space in an esteemed gallery in the middle of a tourist town. He circled the staircase toward the far wall. Sketches of sleeping wildlife spanned each massive space: a lion drawn with smudged charcoal, a koala whose fur was dark fingerprints, an elephant with black handprints for ears. Lining the right wall, where the backdoor was closed and locked, a collection of photographs showed scenery from Laguna Beach via helicopter, wide expanses of beach after beach, opaque summer sunsets over the water, glittering lights from downtown, and streets packed with the blurred lines of fast-moving cars.

He glanced at the door. Aiden's stuttering breath filled his mind, and he remembered his cocky introduction. *Aiden Maar.* Shannon thought about that moment more than he should have. It filled the spaces where rational thought would be.

"Sir," a tidy woman said, as she leaned across a black desk just inside the double glass front doors. Her silver hair was arranged in a tight bun on her nape. Wrinkles spanned her face, edging from the sides of her eyes and the corners of her lips. "May I be of any assistance?"

"I'm looking for a piece called *Fortitude Smashed.*" Shannon sounded out the title with as much delicacy as he could muster. He'd never browsed through artwork of this caliber. "Is it still featured here?"

The gallery associate clucked her tongue and smiled. "Oh, yes, what a fantastic little piece it is! We have it, but only for a few more days. It's been purchased."

Shannon frowned. The thought of buying it hadn't occurred to him until she mentioned it was no longer available. As soon as it wasn't within reach, Shannon wanted it. *Typical.*

"You're welcome to take a look, though. It's right this way."

He followed her around the back of the black metal staircase. She gestured to a four by four canvas, if it was a canvas, hanging on the wall in a thin glass box.

"Beautiful, isn't it?" She crossed her arms over her chest and sighed.

It was, in the oddest way, beautiful. Fanned across the middle of the canvas, a lily burst open; petals exploded from its center. Bright tangerine and sunshine yellow pollen stained the spaces between each pink and white petal. A green stem, dried and withered, curved down alongside pressed baby's breath and uncanny magenta dandelions. It was violently expressive, a containment of life and death in one place.

"Gorgeous," Shannon agreed. "Does the artist have any more pieces like this?"

"Yes, in fact, she does. We'll be getting a few close to Christmas. Would you like to give me your information? I'd be happy to call you as soon as we begin showing them."

Shannon, focus stolen by the flowers, nodded. "What's something like this cost?"

"*Fortitude Smashed* was set at a comfortable twenty-five hundred, sir. Most of Miss Scott's work is priced in that area, some climbing into the three's and four's."

Aiden had taste, Shannon gave him that.

"Is it for your home? Office?"

Shannon handed her his card and shook his head. "No, ma'am, it's for someone else."

"A Rose Road, then?" Her eyes creased around a smile.

"Yes, ma'am."

"Lucky," she cooed, patting Shannon's shoulder as she walked back to her desk and filed his information.

Reminds me of myself.

The lily's stem was snapped from the rest of the petals, which gave the flower a sense of detachment. It was nature's grenade in the midst of detonating, a slow-motion explosion blasting out from the center. Pollen sprayed, blood and fire, the very moment bottled and pressed, torn limb from limb and arranged to make a peculiar brand of beautiful.

No wonder Aiden was reminded of himself, Shannon thought, scanning the piece again.

They were one and the same.

00:00

"MERCY, WILL HE EVEN WEAR this?"

Mercy rolled over with a corner of the sheet stuffed in her mouth. She scrambled to scratch at the bed with all four paws.

"Don't—hey! Don't do that; you'll ruin my comforter. I asked you a question."

Mercy's tongue stuck out between her teeth; her fur bunched up around her ears. She meowed, short and to the point.

"Yeah, well, I don't exactly know what else to get him," Aiden said. He wrapped a bit of wire around the slender tip of the amethyst and looped it through a bundled piece of silver that slid along the medium-length chain. "So, he's getting a necklace."

The pile of fur beside him batted at the swaying crystal. Aiden leaned across the bed and plucked a half-smoked joint from the ashtray. He lit it, inhaled, exhaled, and watched the afternoon light bounce off the amethyst, sending lilac shards dancing across his bedroom walls.

Aiden's phone buzzed on the pillow.

Daisy Yuen 12/7 5:03 p.m.
Guess who landed an internship with mothafuckin Blizzard?
Aiden Maar 12/7 5:03 p.m.
daisy did
Daisy Yuen 12/7 5:04 p.m.
Guess who needs a place to stay after the first of the year?
Aiden Maar 12/7 5:05 p.m.
daisy does
Daisy Yuen 12/7 5:05 p.m.
☺
Aiden Maar 12/7 5:06 p.m.
i have a couch and a kitchen and a working shower
Daisy Yuen 12/7 5:07 p.m.
That's all I need in life

Aiden Maar 12/7 5:07 p.m.
its been a minute
Daisy Yuen 12/7 5:08 p.m.
Only four years. See you in a month. Thanks for saving my ass.
Aiden Maar 12/7 5:09 p.m.
anytime

He hadn't seen Daisy's name flash across his phone in a long time. They followed each other on Instagram. She checked in on holidays and birthdays and sometimes sent him pictures of kittens, but he hadn't heard her voice in months. He puffed on the joint and stared at the exchange of texts. He scrolled up, down. Read them, reread them.

Aiden often jumped before he looked, especially when it came to the few people he cared about, but he probably should've thought a bit longer before offering Daisy his living room. *What was there to think about, though? It was Daisy.* It was his best friend, returning from her stint in college, and he had the chance to live with her. He had the chance to remedy the loneliness he pretended he didn't suffer from.

He swiped across the screen and clicked on Shannon's name.

Aiden Maar 12/7 5:14 p.m.
so daisy is gonna live with me

Three dots. Bounce. Bounce. Bounce. Buzz.

Shannon Wurther 12/7 5:15 p.m.
yay?
Aiden Maar 12/7 5:15 p.m.
yes yay. she got a badass internship in irvine
Shannon Wurther 12/7 5:17 p.m.
smart cookie. is this a good time to ask you to come to milford with me for new years?

Aiden stared at his phone. The weed made his thoughts fuzzy and his limbs slow-moving.

"Mercy." Aiden swatted the bed. She yawned. "Shannon wants me to meet his parents."

She meowed.

Aiden Maar 12/7 5:20 p.m.
you sure?
Shannon Wurther 12/7 5:21 p.m.
yep.
Aiden Maar 12/7 5:22 p.m.
alright yeah
Shannon Wurther 12/7 5:23 p.m.
okay

He sank into the comforter and hauled Mercy against his chest. She let him squeeze her, meowing contently when he nuzzled his face against her head.

"Well, this'll be interesting," Aiden mumbled.

Interesting was the easiest thing he could come up with. It was bound to happen. He knew that; he understood that. But the thought of meeting a household of Wurthers was overwhelming. Shannon was enough; he was more than enough. The idea of his mother *and* father, retired cop father no less, opened a pit in Aiden's stomach. He barely knew how to behave as it was. How was he supposed to act around Shannon's family? Aiden didn't know how to be anything other than himself, and he was well aware of the effect he had on people.

Everyone's always dying to know everything, and you don't give it to them. That's why people think you're dangerous.

Aiden took a deep breath.

Mercy acknowledged him with a quiet, "Mrow."

22

THERE WAS NOTHING ABOUT THIS conversation that Shannon wanted to have.

Sex wasn't an uncomfortable topic—he was an adult—however, talking about sex with Karman was all-inclusive, no detail left unsaid. She could go on for hours, days even, rambling about which position was best for who, what to start with, which foods to eat before and after, down to the music that should be playing in the background.

Now, she was going on and on about preparation. What to do—and Shannon knew what to do—when it came to Aiden Maar's virginity.

"I don't need a play-by-play; I can handle that part. I need advice on how to talk about it, not what to do."

Karman lounged on the worn purple loveseat against the front window of the Koffee Klatch, while Shannon sat across from her on an egg-shaped futon. She said, "You're the one who texted me, sweetheart. I'm just surprised you went this long without finding out."

"It's only been two months, Cruz."

"Yeah, but still, I would've knocked that shit out in the beginning. That's just me though. So, what now, where are you with this situation?"

Shannon's brows pushed together, deepening the two lines that appeared between them when he was nervous or confused or deep in concentration. "What do you mean, where are we?"

Karman twirled her hand and fluttered her lashes. "C'mon, spill. Are we talkin' dry as a desert here, or have you at least ventured down south for *something?*"

"Karman." Shannon groaned. His head lolled back. The coffee cup in his hands burned hotter the tighter he held it.

"So, who went down on who?"

Shannon's mouth tightened. "We're talking about my virgin boyfriend, who do you think?"

Karman grinned. She waved her hand as if she was beckoning an animal. "You totally went down on him first. Details, c'mon."

"We're not children, Cruz. Can we get back to the point, please? I told him we'd take it slow, and that's my intention, but how slow do I take it? How am I supposed to bring this up with him? He's nervous as it is. I don't want to freak him out."

"Ask!" She sipped her cappuccino. "Ask him about it, you idiot. Talk to him about what he likes and what he doesn't. It's not that hard; you guys are fated. The more you think about it, the worse it'll be."

"I can't just ask him."

"Why not?"

"You don't know him. He'll clam up, shut down, get angry. I don't know. It was fine when we sort of talked about it before because we didn't do much talking."

"What's the problem, then?" Karman kicked one leg over the other and smoothed her black pants. A stark white coat was draped around her and tied at her waist. "Continue with the not-talking and you'll be fine. It's obvious you two are physically communicative rather than emotionally. Some Rose Roads vary between the two, some lean one way more than the other. Over time it'll balance out."

"I think we're more than physically communicative. We're emotionally... I mean, we talk, Karman. We talk a lot, we just... Wait, how do you know all this terminology?"

"High School Camellia Clock Therapy," she said, as if it was nothing. Shannon hadn't attended that; he hadn't had to. It made sense, though.

Karman was young when she timed out, and schools all the way from middle school to college had therapeutic options, classes, counseling, the works, in case a couple needed help.

It was too bad Shannon and Aiden were two grown men who couldn't communicate. If they wanted help, they'd need to sign up for couples counseling—absolutely not—or organized group exercises—no—or better yet, spend a month taking compassion classes—*hell*, no.

"How do you solve problems together?" Karman leaned forward with a sly smile curving her lips. "Do you sit down and talk? Find a solution step-by-step?"

"No, absolutely not. We're terrible at speaking to one another about anything serious. I get mad, he gets mad, I get upset, he gets upset. We usually just—"

"Work it out physically?"

As always, Karman was right. He stared at his lap while his thumbs picked at the lid atop his coffee cup. His mind kept rushing back to Aiden's trembling hands, one on the back of his neck, the other on his chest, and apprehension showing on his face like flashing lights. *Stop. Halt. Slow down.*

He thought about Aiden's nervousness, and he thought about how they'd solved every situation through physical affection. Upset with each other? Physical. Pleased with each other? Physical. Confused with each other? Physical.

From the first night when Aiden had kissed him to yesterday after he'd been arrested, all Shannon and Aiden had done to work through their differences was attempt to devour or smother each other.

"It won't work forever," Karman piped up.

Obviously, the look on his face was as good as a teleprompter. Words scrolled by that displayed his every thought and worry and curiosity.

He inhaled sharply and shrugged. "We'll figure it out. Is that your advice, though, to ask him what he likes? You think he'll respond well to that?"

"I don't know him, remember? That's all you, Wurther. He responded well to it before, didn't he? Don't be scared of him. Don't hold back; that'll just make things worse. You said he's high-strung, right?"

Shannon's eyes bulged and he scoffed, "That's an understatement."

"Then let him come to you," Karman said. "Let him call the shots."

"You're probably right."

"I'm always right," Karman chirped.

00:00

AIDEN FIDGETED IN THE PASSENGER seat. Shannon turned up the radio.

They hadn't talked about it—the dinner. Aiden wondered if they should've.

He had terminology lined up, a way to describe Marcus that would alleviate some of the pressure. But it was all wrong, and he knew it. Marcus wasn't stuck-up; he wasn't bitter or high-and-mighty or overwhelming. He was just better, and Aiden didn't know how to say that without sounding as though he was searching for pity.

"What if he doesn't like me?" Shannon blurted, flicking his left blinker on as they idled at a red light.

"He'll like you," Aiden assured.

"Okay, but what if he doesn't?"

Aiden rolled his eyes. He raked his gaze from Shannon's standard blue jeans, to the tight knit white sweater with large oval buttons left open at the collar, to hair groomed into whipping waves on his head, messy and inviting and handsome. Marcus would adore him, the way he did everything that was traditional and good-natured. He would take one look at Shannon and understand why Aiden felt inadequate.

"Aiden, is there anything I should know? Anything I shouldn't say?"

"He's an art teacher; we like pineapple on our pizza; don't bring up our parents. That's it."

"Does he know about... Does he know how we met?" Shannon parked the car. He offered Aiden an apologetic look, lips drawn into a frown. He'd been aware of his offense as soon as he'd said it.

"Yes, he knows I'm a fuckup; don't worry. Get out of the car," Aiden snapped, unfastening his seat belt.

They walked through the front door of the pizza parlor. Its walls were plastered with sports placards and team flags. Claw machines, a photo booth, sticker dispensers, and an assortment of video games crowded the back room. Tables spread out in front of the counter, which had a pale yellow menu lit above it.

Aiden nudged Shannon with his shoulder. "C'mon, he's over here."

He stalked toward a round table. Bats fluttered around inside him. Beer bottle dangling from his hand, glasses on the tip of his nose, Marcus watched a basketball game on one of the many big screens attached to the right wall. He glanced up when Aiden slapped the table with his palm.

"Hi." Aiden nodded at Shannon. "This is Shannon. Shannon, this is my brother, Marcus."

Marcus offered a smile and extended his hand to Shannon. "Nice to finally meet you, Shannon."

Aiden stepped around the back of Marcus' chair and curled his fingers over his brother's shoulders. He rested his chin on the top of Marcus' head and watched as Shannon grasped his hand and gave a polite shake.

There, it was over.

Marcus cracked his neck, but Aiden didn't move, just slid his cheek to rest on top of Marcus' head. This, he realized, as he stared at Shannon across the table, might *not* be a disaster.

"Pineapple and jalapeño?" Aiden eyed Marcus down the slope of his nose.

Marcus nodded, lifting Aiden's head along with his own. "That's fine with me. Shannon, do you like pineapple and jalapeño? It's kind of a weird combination, we know."

Shannon shrugged; his hands were folded in his lap and his back was straight as an arrow against the wooden chair. Aiden smirked, pleased with the scratch of Marcus' shaved head against his cheek and the sight of Shannon's confused little smile.

"That's fine. Get ranch, though," he said, glancing from Marcus to Aiden and back again.

"Blue Moon sound good?" Aiden straightened up.

Shannon nodded. "Yeah, sure, whatever you're having."

"Make the pizza an extra-large!" Marcus said before Aiden could walk away. "I invited someone. She should be here any minute."

Aiden's lips slipped into a surprised 'O' and then parted into an open-mouthed grin. "You brought the mystery girl?"

"Go order the pizza, Aiden."

"I actually get to meet this woman?" Aiden cooed snidely.

"And her daughter, which means you have to be on good behavior. Can you handle not being an asshole for an hour?" Marcus snapped his fingers. "Go get the pizza."

Shannon watched Aiden. He gave a dismissive shrug, but his gaze lingered until Marcus leaned forward and engaged him in conversation. Good, they could talk, and Aiden could escape, which had been the plan the whole time. Shannon didn't look too excited about being left alone with Marcus, but Aiden was sure they'd get along just fine.

He pretended he didn't know what he wanted until the cashier looked sufficiently annoyed. Once two chilled blue bottles were in his hands and a table number clasped between his fingers, Aiden turned from the counter. As he was staring at his feet he heard a squeaky voice yell, "Shannon!"

Aiden snapped to attention. He moved out of the way of another family waiting to order and watched a woman walk up to their table. A smaller version of her sprang into Shannon's lap: baby pink sneakers, big curls around her shoulders, and ruddy-tan skin. Shannon also looked up, just as the blood was draining from his face, and locked eyes with Aiden.

Aiden had a sinking feeling, followed by an unintentional scowl when he realized that the woman sitting beside Marcus was the woman from the beach, and the woman from the beach was the woman from the parking structure—a cop, a friend of Shannon. Last, anxiety bubbled to the surface, masked as stubborn, irrational annoyance.

He forced his legs to move, put one foot in front of the other, and handed Shannon a beer before he sat. He stared at the woman next to Marcus. Her lips were heavily painted plum, her lashes were dark, and bronzer glittered on her cheeks. Her wild hair was swept back in a ponytail, thick ringlets bursting from the back of her head.

Shannon squeezed Aiden's knee beneath the table.

"Small world," Karman snapped. "Turns out you're more than a littering ass, after all. You happen to be dating my partner." She extended her hand. "Detective Cruz," she said smoothly, "you can call me Karman. It's a pleasure to officially meet you."

"You've met?" Shannon croaked.

"Quarter," Fae said, playing with the buttons on Shannon's shirt from her place on his lap. "Hi, tiger."

"Aiden Maar." Aiden took her hand. She squeezed; his knuckles popped in her grip. "You happen to be dating my brother. Don't worry, we're nothing alike." He growled a smile, and she growled one back. Growl tamed to a pleasant grin, he shifted his eyes. "Hi, butterfly, do you wanna play video games with me?"

"I'm Fae now, but you can still call me butterfly if you want. Are you Shannon's boyfriend? He talks about you."

"He does?" Aiden's gaze flicked to Shannon. "Yeah, I guess I am his boyfriend. Does he say nice things?"

"Yeah, I guess. He says he found you in an art place which means you must be art, which is cool. Marcus teaches me about art."

Aiden chewed on his bottom lip to suppress a smile. "Well, Fae, do you wanna play with me? I'm bored."

Marcus heaved a sigh.

Fae nodded. "I guess so, yeah. They are kinda boring, huh?"

"They're totally boring,"

Shannon's thumb stroked Aiden's thigh, and when Aiden looked up, Shannon smiled at him.

Aiden took Fae's hand and glanced at Karman, who analyzed his every move, a bird of prey surveying a mouse. "I'll bring her back when the pizza comes out." Aiden arched a brow.

Karman nodded. "I know," she said sharply and turned to Fae. "Be good, baby. Don't let that tiger bite you, okay?"

Aiden narrowed his eyes.

Fae tugged on Aiden's hand. "Do you bite, tiger?"

"Ask Shannon," Aiden cooed innocently.

00:00

Shannon knew the gradations of Karman's anger. Tonight she was a solid furious, but Shannon couldn't figure out why.

She stared at him across the table. He chewed on his bottom lip. Marcus shifted his arm around the back of her chair and tapped on her shoulder. She eyed his dark fingertips, turned, and eyed him. He eyed her right back.

"This is interesting," Marcus said, deep voice a rumble in his throat.

Shannon sipped his beer. Interesting was an understatement.

"This is very interesting, actually," Karman said, pointing her words at Shannon.

"Where'd you two meet?" Shannon asked.

"I'm Fae's teacher. We met at the school a few months back." Marcus grinned.

Karman shook her head. "Oh, no. He meant me and his raptor of a boyfriend. Which reminds me, he smokes? You're dating someone who smokes? That's disgusting, Shannon. And you," she shoved her index finger at Marcus, "you didn't tell me *that* was your brother. You just said he was harmless."

"He's not harmless," Shannon groaned.

"He's *totally* harmless," Marcus retorted, tipping his head back to laugh. "It's just the way he carries himself. He looks threatening, but he's not. He's a good kid."

"He's not a kid, Marcus. He's a criminal and he doesn't look like a threat, he looks like a vampire." Karman rolled her eyes.

"He doesn't look like a vampire," Shannon hissed.

Karman nodded. "He does. I bet you anything he's been to that weird fetish bar in L.A. The sin bar or whatever it is."

"Bar Sinister?" Shannon scoffed. "He's never been there."

Marcus dipped his head as if to say, *yes he has,* and nodded along, keeping quiet.

"Let's ask him when he gets back." Her lips thinned into a forced smile.

"He's made bad choices, but he's not a bad guy," Marcus said, softer this time. She glanced away. "You shouldn't judge."

"I'm a cop, Marcus," she bit.

"Doesn't mean you need to be like this," Shannon said. The toe of his shoe whacked her shin under the table. "You're the one who's kept on about me being accepting, and now when you meet him this is how you act? Get off your high horse, and stop embarrassing yourself. Did you forget that you're here with his brother *and* his boyfriend?"

Shannon settled for smoldering at Karman rather than admonishing her in front of her date. She stared at him, face hardened into bitterness and defeat. She was wrong. He knew she was wrong, Marcus knew she was wrong, and she knew she was wrong. But pride was Karman's downfall, and even though she'd been caught, she wasn't going to back down. Instead she blushed, huffed, and stood up.

"Fine. I'm getting a beer," she said. Embarrassment blinked across her face before she stifled it. "And French fries. You guys will eat some, right?"

Marcus and Shannon nodded.

"Will Aiden eat any?" she muttered.

"I'm sure he will," Shannon said. He tried to meet her eyes, but she looked at the floor.

Marcus nodded again. "Yeah, he'll eat anything; get ketchup."

Karman walked away. Her heels smacked the floor on each step.

Shannon stared at his hands nestled together in his lap. He glanced up when Marcus cleared his throat. "This is awkward," he said, taking the honest route rather than the polite one. He offered a feeble smile, but it faded quickly.

Marcus shrugged, unfazed. "Our parents adopted Aiden when I was five years old. They carried him in, balled up in a blue blanket, a little white glowworm…" He laughed, and so did Shannon. "I knew right then, right when mom handed him to me and said, 'you're his big brother, he's gonna need you,' I knew that I would love him more than anything. And I do. He's my own terrible wonderful, you know?"

What a beautiful way to put it, Shannon thought, and he nodded. "I do know."

"Where are you from, Shannon?" Marcus smiled through his words; his hands were laced around the knee that was kicked over his thigh. "You hide it well, but I heard it come through."

"Milford, a small town about an hour east of Savannah. I made my way to California for college and ended up staying. Joined the police force and got partnered with Karman. She's my best friend, believe it or not."

"I believe it," Marcus assured. "You two bicker like Aiden and I, which means you're close. It's a good thing."

The conversation paused while a waiter dropped off their pizza and three large cups of ranch dressing. Karman followed, munching on French fries, with a beer bottle pinched between her middle and index finger. Moments later, Fae appeared and bounced into a chair next to Karman. Aiden sat beside Shannon with a shiny fluorescent caterpillar sticker stuck to his cheek.

"We shot zombies," Fae said. She gave one heavy nod. "Lots of them. We got stickers, too. He's a bug; I'm a monkey." She pointed to the shiny monkey sticker on her forehead.

"Oh, yeah? That's good. Did you thank him for the sticker and for playing with you?" Karman asked, but her eyes stayed glued to Aiden. They stared at each other, an unnerving sight, until Aiden tilted his head.

"She did," Aiden said. "Did you guys have a nice talk?"

"Oh, it was great. Hey, by the way, have you ever been to that goth bar... you know the one, it's in Hollywood, Bar Sinister?"

If Shannon could've scrambled across the top of the table and strangled her, he would've.

"Yeah, I used to go all the time. What's it to you, Detective?" Aiden hummed. One eye closed around a coy wink.

Wearing a smug grin, Karman swirled back in her seat. Both brows shot up, and she held her hands against her chest, mock surrender. "Nothing, hot stuff. Just curious. So, what do you do, Aiden? Shannon says you work at 101—sorry about Barrow, by the way, and that whole situation." She circled her fingers around her mouth, in the same place Aiden's was still healing. "Shannon told me what happened. He's a complete moron."

"It's fine," Aiden said and coughed, flicking his eyes to Shannon.

"What happened?" Marcus asked.

"I got arrested—for nothing this time—ask Shannon."

"It was for nothing," Shannon confirmed.

Marcus narrowed his eyes and pushed his glasses up the bridge of his nose. "And you got out of it because he is who he is?" He gestured loosely to Shannon.

"That's exactly how, that and the fact that he hadn't done anything wrong," Shannon said, dulling his tone from sharp to stern. He flicked his gaze to his partner. "Karman, you didn't tell me you were dating."

Karman tensed. Marcus chewed a mouthful of pizza. Aiden snatched a fry. Shannon hadn't been in such an awkward situation in years. He couldn't remember when he was so fully strung between resentment and amusement. Surely he'd never been witnessed a web of lives as tangled as this table was.

"Surprise," she sang, lifting her beer bottle.

Shannon lifted his, too.

Marcus gave a bold, loud laugh. Aiden followed suit. Shannon fought the urge to join in, so Karman beat him to it. Suddenly there was a cacophony of laughter. Karman shook her head and covered her mouth with her hand. Aiden played with Shannon's fingertips under the table. Even Fae giggled, picking jalapeños off her pizza and replacing them with French fries.

"You've got a good laugh, Karman." Aiden rested his elbows on the table. He sipped his beer. Something in the way he said, *you've got a good laugh,* sounded more like, *we're even,* and it was a relief.

"Wurther told me you were good-looking; he used the word 'gorgeous,' actually. He wasn't lying," Karman said.

Aiden's gaze drifted from Karman to Shannon, who ate his pizza and pretended he hadn't heard a word.

"He gets it from his brother." Marcus sighed playfully.

"Gorgeous, huh?" Aiden whispered, fingers crawling across Shannon's leg.

Shannon's eyes swept sideways. Cheeks tinted, Aiden smiled at his plate. Moments like this, quiet and secret, were gentle rarities. Shannon couldn't get enough of them.

He didn't say anything; he didn't have to.

"I think he is, too," Fae whispered.

Shannon bit back his grin, shook his head, and snatched Aiden's hand under the table.

**23**

DECEMBER WAS A FRACTION OF a breath—fogged and brief. As quickly as it came, it left.

The day after their night out at Papa's Pizza Parlor, Karman called to apologize for being what she flavorfully labeled a *crusty bitch*, and Shannon forgave her. She explained in vivid detail how angry she'd been over nothing and burst into tears on the phone. "Shannon," she'd said, "I'm so fucking happy for you." And Shannon had listened while she talked about her lost Rose Road; the echo of her voice told him she was locked in her bathroom, hiding from Fae. Shannon didn't know what to say, so he said, "I love you, you crazy bitch." And they laughed, and laughed, and laughed.

Midway through the month, Shannon received a call from *Laguna Beach Canvas & Sculpt*. He stopped by one night after work and inspected the collection. Canvases large and small covered the wall behind the staircase, and the same silver-haired woman who'd assisted him before helped him pick one. "Good choice," she'd said, eyeing him carefully. "I'm guessing this Rose Road of yours is a collector?"

And Shannon had laughed, startling her, before he'd said, "Something like that."

However, the piece wouldn't be available until the collection had served its time in the gallery. Shannon agreed to pay for it and pick it up in March. But he was left without a Christmas gift, and that was unacceptable. So, he did his research and found the highest rated photography supply store in Laguna, and he went there.

December always shot by, but this year, on this Christmas Eve, Shannon hoped it would slow down. He opened the door to Aiden's apartment, and Mercy greeted him by winding around his feet. On the other side of the room, standing on bare tiptoes, Aiden hung ornaments on a withered clearance Christmas tree.

"How much did you spend on it? Five dollars? Four?" Shannon laughed. He set a bottle of spiced rum on the counter and put a carton of eggnog in the fridge.

Aiden shrugged; an unlit cigarette dangled from his mouth. "It's all they had left." He grinned. "But it'll work. It looked even more pathetic strapped to the roof of Marcus' van." He flicked one of the glittering orbs. "I got ornaments from the dollar store, too. Aren't they great?"

"That tree is hideous."

Aiden plucked the cigarette from his lips so he could laugh in agreement. "Oh, c'mon, it's doing its best."

While Aiden smoked on the balcony, Shannon made drinks. He took them outside, where the bitter air sent goose bumps across his arms. The sleeve of Aiden's blue sweatshirt slid off one shoulder; his sweats hung low on his hips. He angled his mouth and blew a gust of gray smoke over the balcony.

"You've only got a few more days of that," Shannon said, gesturing at the glowing orange tip of the cigarette.

"I know. That's why I'm smoking twice as much."

Shannon handed him an eggnog.

"Tomorrow should be interesting." Aiden sipped his drink and rolled his lips together. "I haven't done anything for Christmas in years. Me and Marcus usually just make food and watch Hallmark specials."

"It'll be fun. Karman's a great cook."

Aiden stubbed out his cigarette in the ashtray. "Do you want your gift now or in the morning?"

"Depends on what it is."

"It's not edible, it doesn't make any noise, and it's not wrapped."

"In the morning." Shannon grinned. "You don't get yours until the morning anyway because I left it in my car by accident."

"Oh." Aiden's brow furrowed. "Smooth move, Detective."

They drank two cocktails each, enough to warm them up and settle them in, but not enough to do much else. They decorated the tree with Aiden's bargain ornaments, strung tinsel around its cracked, near-brown branches, and chased Mercy off when she tried to climb it. After they both stood back and took a good look at it, Aiden snapped a picture with his phone. Shannon noticed him fiddling with it, swiping one way, then another.

"What're you doing?"

"Posting on my Instagram," Aiden mumbled.

Shannon snatched Aiden's phone, which catapulted them to the floor, arms and legs and hands everywhere. Aiden scrambled for his phone, hissing and biting curses under his breath.

"You have an Instagram? Of all the social media, you choose the one I don't have. Why?"

"Because you *don't* have it." Aiden seethed. He maneuvered his phone from Shannon's grip and flashed the screen. "There, look, see it? Just an Instagram. You told me I should take pictures, so I have been."

"Look at that..." Shannon glanced from each square picture to the next. One was of a coffee cup with the beach in the background. Another was of Mercy, sprawled in one of the chairs on the porch. Cocktails lined up on 101's bar. "Hey!" Shannon tried to grab the phone, but Aiden pulled it away. "That was me, wasn't it?"

Aiden's eyes narrowed, and he sat up, crossing his legs beneath him on the beige carpet beside their scrawny Christmas tree. He showed Shannon the picture, which was softly lit by early morning light, Shannon's eyes half-open, on white sheets. Aiden's hand rested on his cheek, and gave viewers the sense that they were the ones reaching out to touch him.

"What does the caption say?" Shannon asked.

Aiden's mouth tightened. He shook his head and said, "Nothing."

When Aiden tried to stand, Shannon snatched his ankles, knocking him back to the ground. "Show me!"

Aiden thrashed in his grip, finagled his way out, and darted down the hall. Shannon's hands caught Aiden's waist before he made it through the bedroom door.

"Show me." Shannon laughed against Aiden's neck, who heaved in breath after breath with a bashful grin.

"It says *what a view,*" Aiden whispered. He scrolled down to display the caption. Low and behold it said: *what a view.* Below it a comment from an account named "creatureflower" said: *damn boy who is that? why didn't you tell me?*

"Who is creatureflower?" Shannon laughed through his nose, which was embarrassing.

"Daisy," Aiden said, gentle and warm. He clicked on her profile, scrolled, brought up a picture. "That's us in high school. Way back when."

Shannon leaned over Aiden's shoulder with his arms wrapped around his middle. In the photo, Aiden had one eye closed, mouth open, tongue out, and he was flipping off the camera. His head was closely shaved, and he wore a faded band T-shirt. Daisy was thrown over his back with her arms around his shoulders and her legs around his waist. She had shoulder-length, jet-black hair; a narrow face; pretty, small eyes; and black lipstick. They both had silver hoops dangling from their septums.

"You had a piercing?"

"Have," Aiden said playfully. He reached up with his thumb and index finger, sniffed once, wrinkled his nose, and pulled the two silver spikes from his nostrils. "We did them ourselves at a party one night." He snickered under his breath. "We were idiots."

Shannon craned his head, moving one hand to Aiden's cheek. "Let me see." Shannon pushed Aiden's jaw until he turned to look at him.

The dainty silver spikes diving from Aiden's nostrils didn't look as obscene as Shannon had thought they would. He quirked a brow. "It looks good. Why'd you hide it?"

"Why'd you hide your accent?"

"Fair enough."

Aiden turned around in Shannon's arm and his fingers curled around Shannon's wrist. He tossed his phone on the floor near the closet, unzipped his sweatshirt, and let it fall off his shoulders.

Shannon watched, trailing his gaze across Aiden's bare torso as though he'd never seen it before. He saw it often, practically every day. But he didn't often see Aiden with this confidence. Shannon watched a fire eat away at Aiden's composure. Aiden flicked Shannon's belt loose and slid it from his jeans.

"Done with Instagram already?" Shannon said. He stepped closer, and Aiden nodded.

"Done with a few things."

"Like?"

Aiden dropped Shannon's belt and hooked his fingers through the two belt loops below his hips.

"Taking it slow," Aiden said.

Shannon touched the top of Aiden's hands and guided them away from his jeans. He laced their fingers, and Aiden's hands flexed. Shannon glanced from their busy hands to Aiden's mouth and his red and bitten lips.

Aiden pulled on Shannon's wrists. He stumbled over a pair of Vans. Aiden's back hit the bed first. He pulled, and Shannon fell, to be granted a flurry of warm lips on his mouth, his neck, his temples.

Taking it slow consisted of doing exactly what Karman had suggested—letting Aiden do what he pleased, when he pleased. Shannon had never said it, but he didn't know what Aiden had been worried about. So far, Aiden had been careful, timid at times, but nothing shy of a superb lover.

Now it was Shannon who was nervous.

"You sure?"

"Are you?" Aiden said, pulling Shannon's shirt over his head. His eyes flashed in the darkness, holding Shannon's attention.

Shannon shoved Aiden's sweats down until they were kicked away; his mouth was on Aiden's throat and his hands were around his thighs, picking his hips up off the bed.

00:00

Aiden had planned it.

He would *never* tell Shannon, but it was the truth. He'd made the decision last week. Since then, he hadn't been able to focus on anything else.

It wasn't some magical, monumental moment; Aiden prevented it from being that by fooling around with Shannon as much as possible. He'd put his hands where he wanted and his mouth where he wanted; he'd made sure to familiarize himself with Shannon's body and encouraged Shannon to become familiar with his. This was different, though. This was what they'd been putting off, the line they'd never crossed, the point in their foolery where they'd always eased away from each other.

Virgin was such a juvenile word, when Aiden thought about it. After everything they'd done together, Aiden was sure he wasn't considered one, but still, he'd planned Christmas Eve as the last night he'd ever use the label.

"How do you want to do this?" Shannon asked breathlessly against Aiden's sternum.

Aiden shook his head. "Doesn't matter."

"You have to tell me."

"Whatever you want, I don't care."

"Aiden—"

Aiden lifted his hips, annoyed. He'd planned it all until this point: the kissing, the stripping, the hands between legs and lips down stomachs, and everything in-between. But he hadn't planned a conversation. "Shannon, shut the fuck up and get on with it."

Shannon mumbled into Aiden's shoulder with his hands skidding up his sides. Aiden squeaked—embarrassing—and his heart kicked when his face was suddenly pressed against the comforter. Shannon's mouth climbed his spine, and his arms caged Aiden's shoulders.

It wasn't that Aiden didn't thoroughly enjoy being thrown around— he did—but he hadn't imagined it happening the way it was. He hadn't prepared for Shannon's praises, the soft *you're incredible* that Shannon whispered at the nape of his neck, or the quick *breathe, don't stop, let me hear you*, or the possessive, shaken rasp when Shannon gasped his name.

Aiden hadn't known he could feel the things Shannon made him feel. He'd assumed it would be like a movie, either rough and fast and needy or tender and affectionate and slow. Not once had he entertained the idea that sex with Shannon could be both, that sex with anyone could be anything but typical.

It scared him how typical it *wasn't*.

Shannon bit Aiden's shoulder and his fingers clenched tight around Aiden's hips.

Aiden didn't know why he'd ever bothered trying to imagine this. The details were too fine-tuned. Everything was too this or that, too much and too little: the heat from Shannon's breath and hands making paths across Aiden's stomach, fingertips against thighs and hips straining to stay put, the weight of Shannon's chest pressed against his back, white sheets between Aiden's knuckles, stark and permanent and grounding, replaced by Shannon's fingers when he grasped Aiden's hands.

There wasn't anything explicitly beautiful about it.

It was tumbling and laughter. It was messy, overdue, and long-awaited, electrified by sounds Aiden wasn't sure he'd conjured. It was disorienting, with intermissions of heated kisses and in-betweens of stillness. It was *is this okay* and *yes, god, yes*, and fingernails on backs, and teeth in flesh, and soft lips on cheeks.

It wasn't explicitly beautiful, but Aiden wasn't sure if anything was, and this was a more fitting experience than any he'd encountered.

Aiden didn't know what to say afterward. He'd said quite a lot during, which would've been embarrassing if Shannon hadn't been encouraging him. He laughed against Shannon's mouth while they tried to catch their breath, and Shannon smiled through a slow, lazy kiss.

Music drifted from the living room—Christmas covers by gritty punk bands—and Mercy sat in the doorway of the bedroom with an ornament hanging from her mouth. Aiden glanced at her, and then back at Shannon.

"She totally fucked up our Christmas tree, I guarantee it," Aiden said, swallowing a slow breath.

Shannon choked on a laugh before he said, "We would've heard it."

Aiden furrowed his brows. "Sure we would've," he teased and rolled his eyes. As he was sitting up, Shannon's arm curled around his side and pulled him back down. Aiden hardly resisted.

"If she knocked it down, she knocked it down." Shannon tugged Aiden to his chest.

"It's a fire hazard."

"There aren't any lights on it." Shannon laughed. "You're one of those guys, huh? Come up with any excuse to run off before we even take a shower."

"Fuck off, Shannon." The curse sounded sweet despite its nature. "Start the shower; I'll be right there."

Aiden slithered from Shannon's arms, slid on a pair of sweatpants, and walked into the living room, where he found the Christmas tree toppled over. He stared at Mercy as she trotted by, ornament swinging from her mouth.

"How dare you," he hissed.

Mercy didn't hiss back. She hopped on the couch and ignored him.

Instead of picking up the fallen tree, Aiden stepped over it and onto the porch. Frigid winter air attacked his exposed torso, making the pack of cigarettes resting on the balcony seem less and less enticing. Aiden cursed under his breath as shaking hands fumbled with the lighter. Once he had the cigarette lit, he looked toward the horizon. Smoke curled from his lips and from his nostrils. He touched the silver piercing in his nose.

It'd been a long time since an after was tolerable. Since anything that came after was worth celebrating. His afters were always painful: after sixteen, after his parents died, after he was arrested. Every after was a consequence of something cruel that Aiden inflicted on himself.

This after with Shannon wasn't a mistake.

The pipes groaned. Aiden put the half-smoked cigarette out carefully, saving the rest for later.

No, this after was something else.

"Oh my god, Mercy! You *did* knock the tree over!" Shannon yelled from inside, voice strained around weak laughter.

Wild, and wonderful, and magical.

Aiden smiled.

24

Shannon woke to Aiden straddling his hips.

"Wake up," Aiden said. He tugged on Shannon's chin and kissed his sleep-lazy lips. Something cold and rough scraped Shannon's chest. "It's Christmas, Shannon. Wake up."

His fingertips brushed Aiden's thighs, his waist. He cracked open his eyes, burdened with the weight of foggy sleep. "Merry Christmas," he slurred, yawning.

"I made this for you."

That pulled Shannon's attention to whatever dangled from a chain in Aiden's hand. Shannon pawed at his eyes and blinked, looking at Aiden hovering over him with a quizzical look on his face, then at the necklace he swung above Shannon's chest.

"What is it?" Shannon grasped the stone, which was violet merged with transparent lilac, fading in and out between plum and lavender. Around its top coiled a thin silver wire, braided into a nest that fastened the stone to a hoop. "You made this? It's beautiful."

"Amethyst. It's supposed to help clear your thoughts, increase your intuition." He paused, winked, and added, "and shield you from thieves."

Shannon smirked.

"It's for protection." Aiden touched a similar fiery yellow and orange stone hanging around his neck. "I have one, too."

"What's yours for?"

"Mine's citrine. It's for livelihood, stability, and happiness."

"I can't believe you *crafted* me something." Shannon grinned at the purple stone as he twirled it back and forth. Aiden nodded, legs parting farther around his waist. He craned down and folded his arms over Shannon's shoulders. "Thank you," Shannon whispered.

He set the necklace on the bed beside them and kissed Aiden once, quickly and gently, before he tried to sit up. Aiden shoved his shoulders down.

Shannon frowned. "Yours is in my car."

"I can wait," Aiden said. A smile twitched on his mouth and he sighed, swooping down to bump their noses together, coaxing Shannon to kiss him properly.

This morning, properly meant deep and slow and long to pull a low hum from Shannon's throat. He sat up with one arm curled around Aiden's waist. Aiden's legs tightened around him. He pulled back and slipped the necklace over Shannon's head before he slid his arms over Shannon's shoulders and pulled him close again.

Amethyst against his sternum, citrine between his collarbones, raw stones and cold silver scraped Shannon's chest. He opened his eyes and caught a glimpse of Aiden lost in the movement of their lips. His lashes swept over his cheeks, his brow was relaxed, his face was as serene as Shannon had ever seen it.

Aiden fingernails scraped the back of Shannon's neck, wound through his hair, and tugged. "I'm glad you like it," he said, eyes half-drawn curtains, heavy and enticing.

Shannon nodded absently and closed his eyes. Aiden's shoulders wore bruises from the night before. Shannon kissed them. His throat was peppered with marks from Shannon's teeth. He kissed those, too. He gripped Aiden's hips as they rolled in his lap and listened as Aiden's breath quickened. Shannon glanced at Aiden's waist, where he saw bruises shaped like fingertips and teeth and mouth and hipbone. He kissed those as well.

00:00

IT WAS LIGHTER THAN THE last one Aiden had held.

He danced it between his hands, sleek silver, digital, with a wrist strap and a lanyard. His skin was still damp from the shower. Aiden swallowed, glanced at the photograph above his bed, back at the camera in his hands.

Shannon hadn't listened to him. He'd done exactly what Aiden said he wouldn't do himself: invested in his skill set.

And for that, Aiden was grateful.

"You bought me a camera?" He sat cross-legged in the middle of the bed.

Shannon nodded shyly. "I did, yeah. That's what that is."

"I know that's what it is, asshole," Aiden mumbled, lips splitting into a grin.

"Coffee?"

Aiden nodded, staring at the camera in his lap. He fiddled with some of the settings. Excitement crawled under his skin. Shannon pinched Aiden's chin, lifted it, and pressed their lips together.

"Thanks," Aiden said against his mouth.

Shannon nodded. "I'll get you some coffee."

Aiden pointed the camera at Shannon's bare back, where sweats were low on his hips, and clicked the capture button just as he walked out of the bedroom. How Shannon didn't wear stripes from Aiden's fingernails was beyond him.

This camera was lighter than the last one, but it felt just as solid, filled with purpose and life and substance.

00:00

"THAT'S A GOOD ONE," SHANNON said. He watched Aiden pan through a slideshow of photos he'd taken at Karman's house on Christmas.

The screen on the back of the digital camera was small, but the images were crystal clear. He paused on a photo of Fae perched on Marcus' knee as she ripped wrapping paper in a blur of greens and reds. Marcus, head cocked, glasses resting on the tip of his nose, smiled at her. Arms crossed over her chest and a gentle tilt to her lips, Karman stood in the background. Aiden hit the button and the screen changed to show Shannon shielding his face with one hand, the other outstretched, attempting to cover the camera. The next photo was the same shot, just more of Shannon's hand and less of his face. The one after that was a picture of Aiden and Shannon smiling at each other, post kiss, out of focus and badly lit.

"That's my favorite one you took of us," Shannon said.

Aiden's mouth scrunched. "There are ones like it that aren't blurry."

"I know, but I like that one."

The plane jolted. Aiden fumbled with his camera and gripped Shannon's knee. His chest heaved, and he rolled his lips together. He hadn't told Shannon he was afraid of flying, and Shannon was sure that, if he asked him, Aiden would still say he wasn't.

"We've got ten minutes left. This is just landing turbulence; we'll be on the ground soon."

"I'm fine," Aiden snapped. His nostrils flared and he chewed on his lip; his knuckles were white around Shannon's knee.

Shannon's parents would be waiting for them in the old Cadillac outside Milford's tiny airport. His mother would be wearing something floral, and his father would be sporting a new fancy cane to carry the weight of his bad right side. They'd ask Aiden a million and two questions, and Shannon would panic. He loved his parents, he did, but sometimes they pried.

They always pried.

"Sir, please fasten your seat belt for landing." A stewardess gestured at Aiden's lap.

Aiden looped the dark brown lanyard around his neck. The camera dangled against his chest. He clicked the seat belt into place and clasped his hands in his lap. Aiden, who was almost always still and observant, was restless. He adjusted his septum ring, tugged on the sleeves of his leather jacket—which he'd refused to take off when they boarded—and played with the frayed hole on his knee, making his jeans look less manufactured-tattered and more tattered-tattered.

Shannon swatted his hand. Aiden swatted back and grumbled. Shannon tugged at his wrist, and Aiden turned, lips parted, armed to reprimand him for being bothersome. But he stopped before he could say anything and glanced down as Shannon's fingers slipped between his knuckles. Shannon squeezed and let his thumb swipe back and forth along Aiden's hand.

The plane dipped. Aiden's back straightened. He chewed harder on his lip. "Your parents are going to hate me," he blurted.

"They're going to love you."

THE AIRPORT WAS FILLED WITH people coming and going.

It was New Year's Eve, and Shannon should've expected as much. After they landed, Aiden made as many detours as he could: first the bathroom, then the gift shop, and last a snack stand where he pondered over which soda to buy until Shannon snapped at him to keep moving. Aiden settled on iced tea, the sweet kind that Georgia was famous for.

Shannon checked his phone.

Mama 12/31 4:05 p.m.
Did you land?
Shannon Wurther 12/31 4:06 p.m.
heading out now

"C'mon, they're outside." Shannon tugged on Aiden's wrist. Boots practically dragging against the carpet, Aiden stumbled as he walked forward. "My mom's name is Loraine, my dad is Lloyd. Just be yourself, okay?"

"You sure you want that?" Aiden sneered.

"Be yourself, but be good."

Aiden shrugged. "Impossible, but I'll give it a go."

The automatic doors slid open, and Shannon walked out with Aiden trailing behind. At the curb, a weather-beaten white 1966 Cadillac idled, and leaning against it was his mom. She wore a cream jacket and beneath it a pink and orange floral dress that hit the ground, where gardening boots were strapped to her feet. Long strands of chestnut hair whipped around her face, which was round to match her plump body.

"Hi, Mama," Shannon said with a sigh, accepting Loraine's arms as they wrapped around him.

She clutched him far too long, squeezed, and patted, and kissed. "Oh, sugar, why don't you come home more? You know we all miss you 'round here. And I didn't even get Christmas this year! Now, that I understand, seeing as you've finally got yourself someone to spend it with. Where are they, show 'em to me!"

Shannon glanced over his shoulder, where Aiden stood a few feet away.

Aiden lifted his chin, eyeing Loraine curiously. He looked as he always did, pensive and striking and unusual. His lips parted, and he waited.

"This is Aiden Maar," Shannon said slowly. He swallowed, watching his mother watch Aiden. "My Rose Road."

Loraine blinked. Her eyes widened and her brows lifted high. She had big almond-shaped eyes and a nose like Shannon's, upturned and small. People had always told Shannon that they looked alike. They had the same olive skin, dark hair, and strong features.

"Well, holy shit," Loraine said through a laugh. "Lloyd! Lloyd, get your ass out here. You won the damn bet." She waved. "Come here, sweetie. Let me get a look at you."

Aiden glanced at Shannon. Shannon nodded. Aiden stepped forward, allowing Loraine to put her hands on the tops of his arms and look him up and down.

"Aiden, then?" She winked, taking in the entirety of him. "Nice jaw," she said gently. Aiden flinched when she put her hands on his face. "And look at those." Her thumb touched just below his left eye. "You've got a pretty pair of lookers, honey."

"Mama, stop being invasive."

The car door slammed.

"Handsome," Loraine continued, ignoring Shannon. "Oh, a little rebellious." She dragged her index finger down Aiden's nose. "He treatin' you good, sweetie?"

Aiden glanced at Shannon.

"No, I'm talkin' to you, Aiden. Is my son treatin' you as he should?"

"Of course he is," Aiden said softly. Confusion played across his face, but Aiden let Loraine do as she pleased. "I wouldn't be here otherwise."

"Good!" Loraine patted his cheeks with both her hands. "Lloyd, look at this boy, looks like he crawled right out of a music video."

"Mom, please!" Shannon's mouth hung open in silent aggravation. "Can we go now? Aren't we doing dinner at the house?"

His father's raspy laugh announced him. He walked forward, using his redwood cane to carry some of the weight on his right side. Shannon tried to smile, but every time he saw his father, Lloyd had aged. His once-ash-blond hair was gray, and his face was raddled with thick wrinkles. He was groomed, dressed in a button-up shirt tucked into tan pants that were a little too tight for his growing belly. He grinned when he reached Shannon.

"Hey, Dad." Shannon accepted a heavy pat on the back.

"This is him, huh? I knew it. You owe me ten bucks, Loraine."

"Oh, hush, you old coot. Aiden, this is Lloyd." Loraine stepped back and made room for Lloyd.

They didn't shake hands; his father didn't like being touched. He'd maybe hugged his father three times in his life—once at his graduation from SDSU, a second after his father retired, a third when Shannon made detective.

"What'd you bet on?" Shannon tried to swallow his accent, but it tickled his throat.

"I said girl; your father said guy," Loraine said. "That damn bet's been goin' since you were four."

"Aiden, is it?" Lloyd's voice was as deep as it'd always been. Aiden nodded. "Good name. Different. I like it." Lloyd swatted Aiden on the back and nodded. Aiden's lips tightened into a pale line. "Your mother's right, Shannon," he said as he glanced over his shoulder, "this boy looks like trouble."

"He is." Shannon motioned at the car. "Can we go now? Are you two done?"

They piled into the car: Shannon and Aiden in the back, Loraine and Lloyd in the front. Shannon watched Aiden wring his hands and pick at his nails. He tried to keep up with a conversation filled with questions shot at him from both his mother and his father. Some he answered; others he steered in a different direction.

Shannon's phone buzzed in his pocket.

Aiden Maar 12/31 4:23 p.m.
that was the weirdest shit ever
Shannon Wurther 12/31 4:23 p.m.
i know im sorry
Aiden Maar 12/31 4:24 p.m.
you look like your mom

Shannon smiled at his phone and then at Aiden, who refused to look up.

Shannon Wurther 12/31 4:25 p.m.
they like you
Aiden Maar 12/31 4:25 p.m.
i guess

"Aiden, do you like fried chicken?" Loraine glanced in the rearview mirror.

Aiden nodded. "Yeah, I do."

"Good, I was hoping you'd say that. You can help me make dinner while Lloyd takes Shannon to pick up ice cream for the turnovers."

Aiden's jaw slackened. He stared at Shannon, wide-eyed, a frantic animal in search of an emergency exit. Shannon thought Aiden might leap out of the car, so he placed his hand delicately on his thigh. Aiden swiped it away.

"No arguin' now," Loraine added.

Shannon tried to offer a smile, but it came out a grimace. Aiden typed viciously.

Shannon's phone vibrated.

Aiden Maar 12/31 4:30 p.m.
you owe me
Shannon Wurther 12/31 4:31 p.m.
you'll have fun

25

THE HOUSE SHANNON HAD GROWN up in was much like the one where Aiden had grown up. Framed photos of Shannon's high school graduation hung on the walls, next to old Christmas cards and memorabilia from Shannon's college days. His yearbooks were stacked in the living room above the fireplace, along with Lloyd's framed Medal of Honor. Usually people had to die to get one of those, Aiden noted.

No wonder Shannon was such a go-getter; he wasn't just living in his father's shadow. He was chasing familial valor. The thought wasn't a pleasant one.

Aiden dipped a piece of chicken into a glass bowl filled with spiced batter and then coated it with a layer of flour. Loraine tossed the salad with her hands, mixing in crumbles of feta cheese and slices of avocado. They hadn't spoken much. Aiden was terrified to break the silence.

"So," Loraine began, taking the chicken from the cutting board. She put it in a skillet popping with hot oil. "My son says you're a bartender, but bartenders usually have to speak to make good money."

"I don't want to make a bad impression," he said.

"Doesn't matter if you do, sweetheart. Won't change a damn thing, will it?"

"I don't know if it will, that's why I'm opting not to get myself in trouble."

"That bad, huh? You're so sure I'm not gonna like you?"

Aiden coated another piece of chicken in flour. "Shannon and I met while I was trying to steal a painting from an art gallery. We timed out that night, right before he could handcuff me."

Loraine gave an easy laugh as she worked her way around the kitchen, peppering this, salting that. She adjusted her apron and pulled her pony tail tight. "Mmmhm, and…? You think I'm perfect?"

"No, but your son might as well be."

"My husband might as well be, too. That doesn't mean anything, though. I'm not an angel; got myself in plenty of trouble when I was your age. Did Shannon end up turning you in?"

Aiden considered his answer. "No," he said quietly and put the chicken leg in the skillet.

"Then you aren't as bad as you think. Hand me that." Aiden handed her a serving plate. "What else? You killed someone? Grand theft auto? What is it?"

"No." Aiden laughed. He shook his head and handed Loraine a beer when she asked for one. "I think I'm past that part of my life. I'm a bartender, yeah, and I, uh…" He glanced at his camera, sitting on the kitchen table beside his backpack. "I'm trying to get into photography. Shannon bought me a camera for Christmas."

"Well, look at you." Loraine leaned her hip against the island in the center of the kitchen. Yellow cabinets lined the paisley walls. Aiden glanced around, avoiding her eyes, but he couldn't stay away for long. She took him in from the tops of his boots to his black tank top; a glint of color nestled between his collar bones where the citrine necklace hung. He looked back at her, and she smiled. "We all make mistakes. Sometimes they're worse than others, and sometimes they're not. You seem pretty wholesome, Aiden, and you've got honest eyes."

"You think I'm wholesome?"

"I can read a person well by how they act around me. You don't."

"I don't what?"

"You don't act," she said. She opened another beer and handed it to him. "You don't lie. You aren't an open book, but you don't mind if someone has a problem with what you've got to offer. I respect that." Loraine licked salad dressing off her pinky finger, and Aiden thought it was something Shannon might do. "And you're damn cute," she added, clanking the necks of their beer bottles together. "Help me set the table."

Aiden smiled at his feet. He'd never been called wholesome, not once. It was a word used for people like Marcus and Karman and Shannon and Daisy, but not him. Aiden had always lived up to everyone's assumption that he was the exact opposite.

Whatever Loraine saw in him, Aiden wished he could see it, too.

00:00

SHANNON SAT BEHIND THE WHEEL of his first vehicle, a blue Chevy pickup, and listened to the nothing that occupied the space between him and his father. Their relationship had always been a quiet one. Sometimes, when a hollow place would emerge that was vast and deep enough to warrant unrest, his father would ask how he was doing—not the standard inquiry, but a real question.

He hadn't asked anything real for years, not since Shannon took the agency exam, not until now, when Lloyd fixed his eyes on Shannon. "You all right, Shannon? You doin' okay?"

Shannon's hands tightened around the wheel. "I'm scared. What happens if I lose him?"

"What makes you think you will?"

"We're different." The words tasted foreign. He'd been used to saying it, but Shannon was starting to question whether it made sense. Different wasn't a term he'd use to describe the two of them, their *together* so to speak; it was more than that. They weren't different; they were something else entirely. But Shannon didn't know how to explain it, and *different* was the only word he could muster.

"You two are different? Or you're different as an item?"

"Both, I think."

"It can be both." Lloyd pointed left at a grocery store attached to a strip mall. They'd added a few stores since last year. "He reminds me of someone I saw a long time ago, this Aiden of yours. A man was standing against a wall outside one of those night clubs in Atlanta. He was the type you didn't approach, but wanted to. I looked at him and thought, 'what an empty, solitary person.' I said it to your mother, actually. I said, 'Loraine, look at that guy; doesn't he look lonely?' And your mother said, 'no, he looks like he's ready to conquer the world.'"

Shannon pulled into a space and shoved the gearshift into park. "So, what? Aiden looks like he wants to conquer the world? What does that mean?"

"Be his world; let him conquer you." Lloyd shrugged. "That's how I got your mother to fall in love with me. I let her eat me alive."

His father slid from the truck and the cane smacked the concrete as he got his bearings. Shannon sifted through his father's wisdom, if that's what it was. He'd never been sure.

Shannon closed his door and followed Lloyd inside. They talked about ordinary things—his job, how he liked the loft, Laguna Beach, how the Jeep was running—but all Shannon could think about was the little bit of his father that surfaced in those hollow places. He smiled when Lloyd grinned at him. He had a chipped front tooth and the skin around his mouth sagged. Shannon remembered when that tooth wasn't chipped, when Lloyd's mouth was a straight line, when his father was a man made for brave, honorable things, and he remembered the sacrifice he'd made when he gave them up.

What would Shannon's sacrifice be? When would he have to make it?

Lloyd tapped his cane and pointed it toward the frozen food aisle. "C'mon, kid, ice cream's this way." Resting on the handle of his cane, Lloyd looked over his shoulder. Deep blue eyes stared back at him, lighter than Shannon's, but just as bright. "What does Aiden like?"

"He'll eat anything, but I'm pretty sure strawberry is his favorite. Or any weird berry flavor."

"Ah, then berry it is," Lloyd said and swatted Shannon on the back. *Let him conquer you.*

Shannon should listen to his father. He knew that all too well, and yet somehow the idea of being conquered felt distant, as if it'd already been done.

00:00

THEY ATE AT THE DINING room table. Shannon sat across from Aiden, while Lloyd sat at one end and Loraine sat at the other. He kicked Aiden gently under the table, and Aiden kicked him back harder. The conversation stayed light. Shannon did most of the talking, steering the direction one way and then another. There was no need to get into anything heavy, which is what would happen if he let his mother get her two cents in.

Loraine did manage to ask, "So, when are you two moving in together? Lloyd and I found our own place six months after we timed out. I bet there are some great little houses on the coast, extra room for kids and all."

Aiden's mouth fell open.

Shannon forced a smile and waved toward the kitchen. "Those turnovers sound good. Mama, why don't we—"

The three knocks were perfectly spaced out, light enough to be considered polite and firm enough to steal attention. Shannon looked at the door. Loraine plucked the napkin off her lap and flicked one wrist from Aiden to the kitchen.

"Go on and get dessert," she said, and Aiden nodded. "I'll get the door."

Shannon cocked his head and his brows pinched together. He followed his mother from the dining room to the entryway. Loraine unlocked the door and pulled it open. Two joyful gasps and giddy laughter fluttered through the house.

Shannon didn't laugh. He didn't do much except stare.

"Oh my god, oh my god, oh my *god*," Chelsea exclaimed. She stood on the porch, one hand perched on her hip, the other holding a pie. Blonde hair swayed around her shoulders, down to her elbows, longer than he'd ever seen it. She gave one stomp of a heeled foot. "Shannon! What're you doin' here? You didn't tell me you were visitin' this year. I assumed you'd come and gone already, fly in Christmas morning, and fly out twenty-four hours later. That's how you do it, right?"

"Usually." Shannon cleared his throat. "I was here an extra day last year, but you were skiing in Aspen, remember?"

Chelsea feigned a dramatic gasp. "That's right, you texted me, huh?"

"Oh, Chelsea, it's so good to see you." Loraine took the pie and patted Shannon on the shoulder. "Shannon, she comes by every New Year's Eve and brings us a sweet something or other, you know that. She hasn't missed a single year, not since you two were sophomores."

Chelsea's pleasant smile pushed dimples into her cheeks. She had a heart-shaped face, unchanged in the three years since he'd seen her. A pair of blue jeans hugged her small figure, and a delicate pink top flowed over her shoulders. He'd seen her on Facebook from time to time, checking in at medical conferences, posting pictures of her horses, but he wasn't prepared for how unchanged she'd be. The Southern belle of Milford, Georgia, grown up and still the same. Shannon couldn't help but feel a twinge of pity.

"Well, give me a hug!" Chelsea swung her willowy arms around Shannon's neck and squeezed. He circled an arm around her middle; his fingertips hovered over her waist. "What're you doin' here, Shannon? It's been so long; tell me you're stayin' for a while, please. I'd love to catch up."

"Just tonight and tomorrow, but you can always call me, you know. Or take a vacation in Laguna."

"Oh," she said as she swatted his shoulder, "come on, stay a week or so. It's about that time, isn't it?" Chelsea flashed her right hand, showcasing the glowing white numbers beneath a French manicure. Her eyebrows shot up, and she waggled her shoulders. "You never know, it might…"

Chelsea's voice trailed off, a very un-Chelsea thing, and her gaze swept past Shannon. Long golden strands of hair dipped as Chelsea's head twitched to the side. The sound of heavy boots against tile explained Chelsea's faltering. Her lips parted, and Shannon watched as she carefully put the pieces in their right places. Once, her gaze fell to his hand, and Shannon unraveled his thumb from his fist.

"This shit is delicious," Aiden mumbled around a forkful of raspberry turnover. He bumped his shoulder against Shannon's, paying no mind to Chelsea. "How'd your mom even make these?"

"Aiden," Shannon growled.

Aiden glanced up questioningly, before he caught on to Chelsea's hardened jaw and forced grin. There was no dismissing the woman's sudden bristle, and Shannon knew that one of Aiden's many skills was sniffing out hostility. He hoped he wouldn't encourage any more of it.

"This is Chelsea Cavanaugh." Shannon gestured from Chelsea to Aiden. "And Chelsea, this is Aiden Maar, my Rose Road."

"Hi," Aiden said. He straightened his back, arched one eyebrow, and looked Chelsea up and down.

Chelsea was busy doing the same, raking her gaze from Aiden's feet to his pierced nose.

"This…" Chelsea swallowed. "He's your Rose…?"

"Surprise." Aiden's teeth clanked together. "This is your ex? The one you told me about?"

If Shannon could've crawled across the lawn and ripped open a trench, he would've happily buried himself. Chelsea and Aiden sized each other up, testing how sharp their teeth were. Aiden, his Rose Road, as polite as a rabid coyote, and Chelsea, his ex-girlfriend, who'd been convinced since they were thirteen that they would be together forever. Though Shannon had moved across the country, it seemed she'd held on to that memory.

"You talk about me?" Chelsea asked.

Aiden's eyes blazed.

"We dated for five years. You were my best friend. Of course I talk about you." Shannon shifted from one foot to the other.

"Well, Aiden." Chelsea cleared her throat and clasped her hands in front of her waist. "I bet you're just so happy to be here in Milford with Shannon this year."

Aiden took another bite of the turnover. "Thrilled."

Shannon inhaled sharply.

"You two should come to my party tonight. I mean, I don't know if that's your *scene*, Aiden." She shrugged, petite nose wrinkling. "It would be all of mine and Shannon's old friends. My sorority sisters will be there, too. You remember them, Shannon? Dorothy and Jesse... Oh, you know." Chelsea stopped to sigh. "I understand if you two can't make it, but do stop by if you can. I'm sure everyone would love to see you."

"Your parents' place?" Shannon asked and instantly regretted keeping the conversation alive.

"What exactly is my scene?" Aiden interrupted.

Chelsea's gaze bounced between the two of them. "Yeah, it's my house now. They bought a one-story once I graduated. I've been helping them with the practice. Never can have too many doctors, right?" Chelsea laughed, and Aiden's eyes widened; a sarcastic smile stretched across his face. "I didn't mean any offense, sweetie. You just don't look like the type that would be in our social circle."

Shannon braced for impact. His muscles seized and he bit the inside of his cheek. Chelsea wasn't good with words, she never had been, but Aiden was a master with them. Shannon waited for whatever string of curses he would throw at her, but, to his surprise, Aiden was silent. He walked away, leaving Shannon to be offended for him, which he most certainly was.

"Why would you say that?" Shannon stepped away when Chelsea stepped forward.

"I didn't mean any harm, Shannon. I bet he's real nice. You should come by." Chelsea had to force the words out. Her smile was fake and distant. She waved to Loraine and Lloyd. "Bye, y'all!"

Loraine and Lloyd shouted pleasant goodbyes.

Chelsea stepped back and tried to smile again; this time it was real, far away but painful to look at, stitched together with regret and memories and disintegrating hope.

Reality had always been hard for Chelsea; the sheer volume of it when it fell upon her crippled her intentions. When Shannon had told her he was leaving, she'd pretended not to hear. When he'd told her he wasn't coming back, she'd laughed. But he did leave, and he didn't come back, and somehow she still thought they might be something in the end.

Chelsea wasn't good with words, but she was good at hurting the things that hurt her.

That's why it was less than impressive when she looked at Shannon and said, "That's what California gave you? *Him?*"

Chelsea always had been good at hurting what hurt her, especially when it came to Shannon. Unfortunately for Chelsea, Shannon was not the same Shannon who left.

"Goodnight, Chelsea." Shannon shut the door.

SHANNON'S PHONE BUZZED. HE GLANCED at the screen.

Chelsea Cavanaugh 12/31 7:58 p.m.
I'm so sorry, Shannon. Please forgive me, I was taken off guard and I didn't know how to react. Obviously I reacted poorly. That was extremely rude. Please apologize to Aiden for me and come by the party. It's going to be a lot of fun! Happy New Years! ☺ ☺

Loraine hollered up the stairs where Shannon and Aiden were changing clothes. "What're you two doin' tonight? You takin' him out to our old spot?"

"Yeah, Mama, that's the plan!"

Aiden zipped up his leather jacket. "We can go to that party if you want," he said, eyeing Shannon from under his lashes. "All your friends will be there; it isn't like we have anything else to do."

"Chelsea does throw good parties. You sure you want to? She was a bitch, but—" Shannon turned the screen so Aiden could read the text, "—she says she's sorry."

"What was up her ass, anyway? Is she still into you?"

"Chelsea and I always knew we'd time out this year. She was convinced we'd time out together, had this master plan throughout high school about what we would do with our lives. She'd be a doctor; I'd be an officer. We'd stay here in our hometown forever, and that would be that. Once I grew up, I realized that I wanted more and decided to move away. She didn't come with me. End of story."

Aiden snorted. "But you're still friends?"

"Why wouldn't we be? Chelsea's got her own issues to work out, but that doesn't mean I don't care about her. We were really close for a huge chunk of my life. I can't make that go away."

"How many people will be there?"

"Enough for us to get lost," Shannon said, glancing at Aiden. "We're only here for tonight, anyway. It's not like we'll see any of these people for another year, if at all."

Aiden shrugged. "Fine, but I get to pick the booze."

"Fine." Shannon grabbed the truck keys.

26

GEORGIA WAS A JUNGLE. REGAL trees lined the two-lane highway like
sentinels guarding the forest. The darkness wasn't as dark, and the moon
wasn't as bright, but the stars—Aiden couldn't get enough of them. He
watched the night sky whirl past the open window in the passenger's
seat of Shannon's old beater. *The 1975* played on the radio—a song
about heartbreak, or maybe not, maybe it was about breaking hearts.
Aiden didn't know, but it didn't matter. He listened to the keyboard
and watched the stars pass by, streams of light that dipped in and out
of mossy tree branches. He leaned his foot to the side as it balanced
on the dash. Shannon sat beside him with both hands on the wheel,
staring at the empty road.

"Where are we going?"

"Someplace I used to go when I was little," Shannon said, glancing
at Aiden, whose attention was still captured by the stars.

"Your parents are nice."

"They do their best."

Aiden turned and rested his head against the seat. Shannon didn't
look away from the road, which gave Aiden a moment to watch him.
His face was relaxed, and his skin gleamed from the obnoxious winter
humidity. A black beanie—Aiden's beanie, actually—fit snugly over

his head. He drummed his thumbs against the steering wheel, and his eyes shifted to the passenger's seat where Aiden openly stared.

"What?" Shannon mumbled, glancing down in an attempt to find the purpose behind Aiden's staring. "Stop that."

"I'm allowed to look at you." He took in the Shannon Wurther who wasn't Detective Shannon Wurther: the one wearing his beanie, and a ridiculous red scarf, and an expensive jet-black peacoat, the embodiment of early morning coffee and a summer breeze, someone who had an entire page dedicated to him in his high school yearbook, and went home early from college parties, and never thought he would be driving through his hometown with Aiden Maar riding shotgun.

"Yeah," Shannon spat, flustered, "but stop."

Aiden lifted his camera and took a picture.

"Why?" Aiden choked on a laugh. His brows drooped, and a grin twitched on his mouth. "You don't like it when I look at you?"

Keen blue eyes narrowed, and Shannon's lips flattened. He shook his head; his gaze wobbled between Aiden, who was shrouded in shadows, and the road, illuminated by two bright headlights. "That isn't what I said, and you know it."

"Then why do you want me to stop?"

Aiden's foot fell off the dash, and he glanced from Shannon to the empty space between them. The bench seat was obstructed by the gearshift, but Aiden slid around it to take up the area along Shannon's right leg.

"Aiden," Shannon made a noise like a wounded animal as he breathed his name. Whether it was a warning or a plea, Aiden didn't know, but he liked the sound of it.

"Chelsea seems awesome, too," Aiden growled, which earned him a pitifully wilted look. Aiden walked his fingers across the top of his knee. Shannon swatted his hand. "I bet you two were the pick of the patch."

"I'm driving."

Denim was rough against the tip of Aiden's fingers. He ignored Shannon's whining, slid between his legs, and gripped the inside of his thigh. "No shit."

Shannon squirmed. One hand locked around Aiden's wrist, the other kept steady on the steering wheel. Aiden bit back his smile and watched Shannon's cheeks tint and his mouth loosen.

"Aiden, I will crash the car. Don't."

"Live a little." He dragged his lips across Shannon's jaw.

"I'm trying to by *not* crashing the car, which you will most definitely make me do if you don't *quit*—"

He grasped Shannon's chin and pulled just enough to steal a kiss. Wide eyes blinking at the highway, Shannon tore his face away. The distraction hadn't lasted long enough to veer them off the road, but the truck did accelerate, and that distracted Shannon enough to allow Aiden to slide his hand up another inch.

"What's wrong with you?" Shannon snapped. His knuckles whitened on the wheel.

But Shannon lacked assertiveness, and Aiden returned to his ministrations. Skeletal fingers skipped over Shannon's waist and tugged at the button of his jeans—not unfastening, but putting pressure where it shouldn't be. Shannon's Adam's apple bobbed, and he chewed on his lip; his gaze was fixed on the darkness ahead.

"Why don't you like me looking at you?" Aiden leaned close to Shannon, until his mouth was inches from the scarf protecting his throat. Shannon's obsession with control gave Aiden the chance to play far too many games with his reservations.

"Fuck you," Shannon whispered. His clenched jaw hollowed the space below his cheek bones. "I like you looking at me, but you don't just look at me. That's the problem."

Shannon Wurther was too reserved to acknowledge that his cracked composure was an engine revving. Watching Shannon's restraint come apart was unconventionally sexy. Aiden pressed his palm down, and Shannon gasped, lashes fluttering.

Aiden's tongue darted across his lips. "You're right, I don't want to just look, I—"

His statement was cut off when Shannon wrenched the wheel to the right, sending him tumbling into the passenger's seat. The back of his head smacked the door. His camera whacked him in the chin. He yelped—one foot on the floor, the other on the seat, knee crooked and body bent. He caught a cruel smile curl Shannon's lips.

"You're an asshole!" Aiden tried to sound serious but he laughed.

The tires gripped the dirt road, tossing pebbles and mud behind them as the truck lumbered deeper into the woods. Trees stood all around them, covered in shadowed green moss and winter ferns. Huddled together at the base of bulkier trees, courageous flowers fought the cold. Aiden sat up, looked out the window, and rubbed the sore spot on the back of his head. His brow furrowed, and he sneered at Shannon, who said, very simply, "Stay over there."

00:00

SHANNON COULD'VE KILLED HIM. IT was hard not to, almost as hard as it was to stop him.

He glanced at Aiden, whose long limbs were covered in familiar dark clothing and whose attention was held by the trees that rushed past the window. Shannon could've let him—he could've stayed still and tried to focus on the road. The thought twisted low in his stomach. No, he would've crashed the truck. He most certainly, without a doubt, would've gotten in a wreck.

"A lake?" Fingers tapping impatiently on his cheek, Aiden cradled his face in his palm. He sat up straighter and peered out the window. "Is that where we're going?"

"Yeah, it's tradition."

"Are we going *in* the lake?" Aiden's eyebrows shot up. He turned and cast an unsure glance at Shannon. His top lip twitched, and he chewed on one side of his mouth.

"Yeah, we're going swimming in freezing cold water in the middle of the night." He couldn't help it; he laughed. "No, Aiden. We're not going in the lake; calm down." Shannon pulled up in front of the large body of water, grabbed the gearshift, and gave it a couple shoves before it clicked into park. The lake's edge was overgrown, riddled with unearthed roots and thick vines. Branches swooped low over black water. Dusty moonlight reflected from ripples. "We're here to find lightning bugs."

"That was the most Georgia thing you've ever said to me."

"My mama fries the best catfish in town."

"Never mind," Aiden sighed, snapped his fingers, and pointed them at Shannon in the shape of a gun. "You win, *that* was the most Georgia thing you've ever said to me. But I'm sure it's true."

"You just wait until tomorrow. The only place you'll hear people sound more southern than at church is at a barbeque or a football game." Shannon cleared his throat, shoving his accent back. Being home thickened it in his mouth and made it nearly impossible to avoid.

"We're actually going to church?" Aiden laughed.

"Mama says we're goin', we're goin.'"

"You're a professional with that voice. I see that, now that I'm hearing it," Aiden said. He stood at the edge of the lake with his hands tucked in his pockets. "I like it when you don't hide it."

Shannon stood beside him, overlooking the water. "Why?"

"I feel like I'm witnessing a part of you that you don't show everyone else. Usually the things people hide about themselves are the best parts."

"Or the worst."

Aiden smirked. "Or the worst."

Shannon nudged Aiden's shoulder and pointed toward a path that led into the woods. "If they're out here, they'll be in that clearing. C'mon, we'll have to stand still for a few minutes once we get there or else they won't light up."

"I've never actually went looking for bugs before. Usually I avoid them."

"We've done it since I was little." Shannon bumped his shoulder against Aiden's as they walked down the path, through long grass, around two giant trees, and under a low-hanging formation of knotted branches. Aiden held his phone out to light their way, but as soon as they came into the clearing, a small oval patch of grass surrounded by bushy ferns and mossy stumps, Shannon put his hand over it. "Put it away; our eyes will adjust in a minute."

Aiden blinked at him and slid his phone into his pocket. They stood, staring up at the stars. Shannon listened to Aiden's impatient sigh and took a step closer when he started to fidget. Shannon took his fingertips, touching each one reverently, from Aiden's thumb that jutted from his palm, his crooked index finger—broken one too many times—to his middle finger, long and sloped beneath his second knuckle.

"What are you—"

"Shh," Shannon hushed, "you'll scare the bugs."

"I'll scare the bugs," Aiden repeated, snorting a laugh. He spread out his hand for Shannon to play with. "My hands have seen some things," he added, "probably too much."

"Like?"

"Artwork that wasn't meant for them," Aiden said gently. He rested his head on Shannon's shoulder. "Jewelry that wasn't meant for them, people that weren't meant for them. An excessive amount of alcohol over the years." He paused. "Blood," he rasped, "some that was mine, some that wasn't. Years ago they saw drugs, some expensive, some not." He laughed at that and leaned back. "My hands can attest to my recklessness."

Shannon laced their fingers together. "What people?"

Aiden chewed on his lip. He stared at Shannon, and Shannon watched him battle between answering or staying quiet. Silence won. Aiden flipped Shannon's hand in his own, bringing the tips of Shannon's fingers to his mouth.

"What have these seen?" Aiden traced Shannon's knuckles. They looked dark against Aiden's chin; spidery shadows crawled over his face.

"Not enough." Shannon swallowed. His index finger tapped the tip of Aiden's nose. "Lakes and streams and rivers, the ocean, blood, some mine and some not." He glanced at Aiden, but Aiden was staring at his hand. "People I barely remember; places I don't want to go back to."

"What places?"

Shannon thought of his father. He thought of gunshots, and red and blue lights, and sirens. He thought of the background noise of his childhood, a symphony of cicadas—and Lloyd's stern voice when he was twenty years old. *It comes with the job, son. One day you'll pull that trigger.*

Aiden's lips parted. "Shannon," he whispered. Dots of light were reflected in his eyes.

Shannon followed Aiden's gaze to a handful of fireflies hovering above their heads. A couple of them blinked, surrounded by an effervescent glow, hazing the darkness like steady, frozen flames. Shannon found a few more and one settled close to Aiden's cheek.

"What do we do now?" Aiden whispered.

"We're supposed to ask them something. Don't ask it out loud, but just ask. You should have an answer before next winter."

"So we're wishing on lightning bugs?"

"Basically, yeah."

Aiden slid Shannon's hand to his cheek and held it there. Shannon cupped his face, and looked around as more and more winter fireflies lit up the darkness.

Magic. That's what he'd always assumed they were.

He looked at Aiden, whose lips curved and whose eyes darted around.

"What'd you wish for?" Aiden tilted his head back to look at the whirling specks of light above them.

"I can't tell you."

Shannon didn't wish for anything, that was the truth. He'd been in the same spot last year, catching fireflies in his hands and whispering questions to them through the slots in his fingers. Alone and curious and hopeful, he'd asked them about his Rose Road: *Will they be as magical as this? Will they be extraordinary? Will they change me?*

They'd answered him in October, three resounding one-syllable words, *yes, yes, yes,* and Shannon didn't need to ask anything else.

27

THEY ARRIVED AT CHELSEA'S PARTY carrying a bottle of champagne in each hand, a case of beer under Shannon's arm, and a bottle of bourbon under Aiden's. Her house was exactly what Aiden assumed it would be, a castle fit for farm royalty: Craftsman style, too big to live in comfortably, high-gloss painted white picket fence around the property, perfectly trimmed suburbia-chic lawn, and cars of all shapes and price tags parked in and around the driveway. Music thrummed from inside, where lights flashed and balloons tapped against the ceiling.

Chelsea swung the door open with a pleasant, unmistakably Ivy League smile plastered on her face. "Oh—" And there it went, fading right along with her practiced excitement. "Shannon." His name was a question, and Aiden arched a brow. "You came? You guys came! Wow, yeah, please come in." She stepped to the side; her square wedges wobbled against the polished tile of the entryway. A strapless cream dress hugged the slight curves that accentuated her thin figure. "That's... quite a bit of alcohol."

"It's New Year's," Aiden said matter-of-factly. Of course they brought *quite a bit* of alcohol. It was a gift, a pleasantry, a proper way to say "nice to meet you," even if the pleasantries were faked and the niceties were forced.

"Well, thanks for bringing stuff. You guys totally didn't have to." White and pink nails waved at Aiden. Her over-plucked eyebrows were a chemical shade of blond. "Are you ready to have some fun? God, it's been so long! It's so good to have you back in town." This, she said to Shannon.

"It's nice to see you too, Chels. Thanks for the invite. Kitchen?" Shannon started walking before she said yes and bumped his shoulder against Aiden's as they wound their way through the crowded house.

Shannon Wurther's hometown was filled with the spirit of what he left behind, that was easy for Aiden to see. He watched conversations pick up between groups of people huddled near the couch and caught several hawk-eyed folks looking Shannon up and down before they inspected Aiden—searching for his pedigree, he assumed, or scanning him for weapons.

Chelsea's home was just as put together on the inside as it was on the outside, and even with the clutter of red plastic cups, beer bottles, and shot glasses littering every near-flat surface, Aiden could tell it was the space of an organizer. The floor was covered with throw rugs, which he assumed she'd purchased for the sole purpose of protecting the ivory carpet from the party. A DJ played music from a top-of-the-line paper-thin laptop hooked up to three bulky speakers. Empty picture-hangers dotted the walls where she'd removed family pictures, paintings, or other hanging décor that could be broken, or stolen.

"Cups? Glasses?" Shannon craned to look in the cupboards—which were labeled with white stickers: Cups, Plates, Tupperware, Stemware down to Spoons and Forks. Aiden fought not to peel them off and rearrange them. Poor Chelsea might have a panic attack if he did.

"What about them?" He looked at Shannon and popped open one of the champagne bottles.

The cork hit the ceiling and sped back at him. He ducked and winced when it knocked an empty plastic cup off the counter. Shannon shot him a tired, but patient, smile. Aiden tilted the foaming neck of the bottle over the sink, put his open mouth under it, and hummed around the taste of sparkling dry champagne.

Shannon laughed, finally, and it was louder than anything else in the room. He took the bottle for himself and tilted it against his lips in silent agreement that using a glass was a ridiculous idea.

"See?" Aiden said, trying not to growl at the people still watching them from the other side of the crowded room. "We'll lose our cups or break the glasses; this is better."

"You'll lose your cup. And you're absolutely right; I don't know why I thought I could hand you something breakable without you breaking it."

Aiden scoffed and reached for the bottle. Shannon held it behind him at arm's length.

Narrowed eyes glared at Shannon's Cupid's bow. The counter bit into Aiden's lower back as he leaned against it. Shannon set the bottle beside Aiden with his fingers latched around its green neck; his free hand settled on Aiden's waist.

"Your friends are confused." Aiden tilted his head. "They have no idea who I am or why I'm here with you. My money's on them thinking I'm an arrest-in-progress."

"Oh, no. I'm sure Chelsea told *everyone*." One side of Shannon's mouth lifted. "I doubt they think I'm arresting you." He gripped Aiden's waist a little harder. His fingertips curled under the bottom of Aiden's tank top and tapped on his exposed hip, right above the black line of his jeans.

"I don't know, Detective. Take a look around. All eyes have been on you since we walked in. You must've been a pretty big deal around these parts." His voice dropped into a mock Southern accent.

"Don't make fun." Shannon unmasked the boyish Georgia drawl that he fought to keep at bay in Laguna.

A short, clipped laugh burst from Aiden.

"And I don't think they've been looking at me, by the way." Shannon looked around the room. "They're definitely looking at the most interesting thing in the room, which is you."

"I'm not interesting."

"You've got California written all over you." Shannon tugged on the front of his jacket. "Looks like you might bite 'em if they get too close."

Out of the corner of his eye, Aiden spotted Chelsea's silky blond hair. Her mildly irritating voice whined out the lyrics to whatever bullshit song was playing.

He pushed off the counter and into Shannon's chest, grasping his face with both hands. Their lips fell together; the taste of champagne mingled between them. Aiden gripped the hair on the back of his head; Shannon's arms wrapped around his middle. He opened his eyes to peek at Chelsea, who watched from the doorway.

Aiden felt Shannon smile. "Don't be petty," Shannon said against his lips.

"Petty's written on my birth certificate right next to 'Might Bite You.'"

"Of course it is." Shannon rolled his eyes, snatched the champagne bottle, and untangled himself from Aiden's arms.

Even over the boom of music and the ever-present shouting between rooms, Aiden flinched at the ring of Chelsea's shrill voice. "I have to admit, I didn't believe it until right now," she exclaimed, looking impeccably dishonest and manufactured. She crossed her arms over her chest. "How'd you meet?"

Shannon opened his mouth, but no words followed.

"He tried to arrest me," Aiden piped up. Chelsea's humoring expression fell. Shannon tilted his head to stare at the balloon-covered ceiling. "It was super-romantic, threw me against a wall and everything," he added, lips pulled back, showing his teeth in either a smile or a snarl.

Chelsea's gaze skittered between Aiden and Shannon. Her pink lips rounded in a silent 'O' that Aiden thought was her default expression. She laughed, obviously attempting to go along with a joke that wasn't a joke at all. "Wow, he's funny too, Shannon. The Clock did a good job." She turned to Aiden. "You know, Aiden." She sounded out his name as if it was foreign. "I wanted to tell you before, you totally remind me of like, a singer, or a guitar player, or you know, a musician."

"Oh? Yeah, no, I'm none of those things. I'm a retired burglar and I pour beers for a living, and you know what? I'm gonna go smoke." He patted Shannon on the back, right between his shoulder blades. "You two have fun. Make sure you tell her all about our first sleepover. You remember that? When I got stabbed? Good times." Aiden took the champagne from Shannon, whose lips were squirming, snuffing out laughter—and surely a bit of anger.

Aiden heard Chelsea say, "He smokes?"

Shannon sighed, a familiar sound, but Aiden was around the corner, bottle against his lips, weaving through pulsing bodies in the living room before he heard Shannon's response.

00:00

THAT WENT AS WELL AS Shannon could've hoped for.

Chelsea thought everything was a joke, which kept his throat strained around contained laughter through the entire conversation and made it easy to sneak away after she'd finished her long-winded college success story.

He popped open another bottle of champagne and tried to get through the living room without being interrupted. He should've known better. As soon as Aiden wasn't by his side, every face he recognized, and even some he didn't, had something to say.

"Hey, buddy!"

Shannon waved.

"Wow, so what was it like?" Shannon shrugged and gave a half-assed answer.

"Is California pretty?" Yes, to that he gave a resounding yes.

"It's been ages! Who was that you were with? Chelsea said he's your Rose Road." A nod. Multiple nods. "He's really hot." That was a girl he'd taken chemistry with. He remembered her. He nodded again.

"Totally." That was Chelsea. Even muffled by the music, her grating sarcasm was a dead giveaway.

A song came on that everyone knew, granting a window of opportunity for an easy escape. Shannon slipped out of the crowd in the living room. He found the back door, which led to the spacious backyard stocked with a couple open coolers, a tented pool, and a bubbling Jacuzzi filled with people—one of whom lifted an arm and hollered, "Wurther! Heard you were here!" Shannon had no idea who the guy was, but he waved back, offered a smile, and followed the smell of cigarette smoke.

Nestled in darkness on the lonely side of the house, Aiden smoked. The dark ivy champagne bottle dangled from Aiden's fingertips. His chest caved as he exhaled, head tilted back, smoke billowing from between his lips. The sole of one boot was propped against the wall. Red glowed at the end of his cigarette and lit his mouth and chin.

Shannon had seen it all, all of Aiden, all of his Rose Road, and all of him reminded Shannon of winter's end, the time before a full bloom, when things thawed, and the sun shone brighter. That's what Aiden was, spring surging to life from beneath a layer of frost—and Shannon loved him.

Thoughts shouldn't come as fast as that one had. It knocked Shannon backward, dried his throat, and sent his head spinning.

The world turned, second by second, and, for once, Shannon couldn't keep up.

One breath at a time, one thought at a time, one thing at a time. Shannon chewed on the realization. Alcohol simmered in his veins.

Aiden turned his head, the same handsome face from the gallery, the same soft smile from inside his car, and the same sharp eyes that watched him tangled in the sheets of his bed. Shannon's tongue stuck to the roof of his mouth. It was as clear as the day was long that Shannon Wurther was aggressively in love with Aiden Maar. However, that clarity hadn't surfaced until right then, on New Year's Eve, at his ex-girlfriend's house, drinking champagne in a dog run. Like everything else Aiden Maar, falling in love with him happened in pieces: recognition, dismantlement, and then the haunting presence, a cold whisper in Shannon's chest.

"You got your own bottle?" Aiden chuckled, pleased.

"I figured you'd finish that one."

He flipped the bottle upside down. Shannon was correct. Aiden had finished the bottle on his own.

"Yeah, thought so." Shannon leaned against the wall next to him. "Retired, huh?"

The dog run spanned the length of the house and was closed off by a gate attached to the driveway. Aiden heaved a sigh and flicked his cigarette into the dark.

"Bet you're excited, Detective."

"I am." He turned to meet Aiden's eyes. "I'm glad I won't have to arrest you."

"You were actually going to?" A sly curl at the edges of Aiden's lips matched the tone of his voice, playful and teasing, a part of Aiden that wasn't covered in thorns.

"No, I wasn't."

"Yeah," Aiden mumbled, turning his gaze to the night sky. "Thought so."

The back door swung open and Chelsea yelled, "Two minutes!"

What it would be like to love him, Shannon wondered. Would it hurt? He was sure it would. Would there come a time when he wouldn't love him? Shannon watched Aiden watch the sky. No, he thought, there would never be a time when he wouldn't. Why now? Shannon touched Aiden's hand.

Aiden grabbed his wrist and pulled, cutting off Shannon's silent questions. "C'mon, we should go in for the countdown."

"Yeah, okay," Shannon said around the lip of the champagne bottle. Aiden's hand uncurled from around his wrist, and his fingers laced between Shannon's knuckles—warm hands, fairytale hands.

The living room was a mess of people, dancing, singing, and throwing confetti in the air. The music was louder, a song Shannon remembered from the ride to the lake, a song he knew and Aiden knew, too. In an instant they were singing, mashed in the middle of an ocean of people, some familiar and some not, one more familiar than the others. Voices singing about breaking hearts and finding them fought over the chorus of people yelling ten, nine, eight, seven…

Another countdown. Another year. Another winter gone. Another spring ahead.

Aiden slipped his arms over Shannon's shoulders and a smile lit his face, bright and true and merciless, stirring a wave of heat to whip against Shannon's bones. They sang along, grinned around each word, and stared at each other as streamers and glitter rained on the crowd.

Champagne bottles popped, the DJ cranked the volume up, and the whole room shouted, "Happy New Year!"

Shannon sipped from the bottle of champagne and then held it over Aiden's mouth, tipping it against his lips. He should have said it. He should have leaned over and pressed his lips against Aiden's ear and said, "I fucking love you." But he didn't. The words were there, spinning in him, knocking against his insides, sending his heart ricocheting in his chest.

Aiden grabbed the back of his neck and pulled him close. They kissed, messy and overwhelmed and honest, the kind of kiss that told a story—incomplete—but a story all the same. Spilt champagne dripped from Aiden's chin. Shannon dropped the empty bottle at their feet and put his hands to better use. He pressed them low on Aiden's spine and drew him in, sealing their bodies together.

Aiden laughed, and Shannon thought it was exquisite to watch Aiden sing about falling out of love while Shannon was falling irreparably in love. Aiden's eyes cracked open, molten and alive and a little bit like candlelight.

He was a wolf and he was beautiful and he was everything.

And god, Shannon loved him. He did, he did, he did.

"AIDEN..."

No.

"Aiden."

No.

"Aiden!"

"No." He wasn't sure whether he'd responded to any of the earlier mentions of his name. They started slurred, whispered into the pillow by his head, and then repeated, stern and drowsy; the third was an aggravated shout. "What the fuck is wrong with you, Shannon? Go back to sleep."

Did people get up on New Year's Day? Aiden didn't. His plan was to stay right where he was, in the dark, sprawled on someone else's bed, enduring a nasty, champagne-flavored headache. He shoved his head in the pillow and turned away from Shannon, who stood by the side of the bed, buttoning his jeans.

An open palm swatted the bed next to Aiden's face. No, Aiden had absolutely no intention of moving until sundown. Once it was dark he would shower, dress, and seek out the nearest place that served everything dipped in batter and fried. They were in Georgia, which meant fried food wouldn't be tough to come across.

"Get up." This time it was a growl, urgent and panicked. Aiden cracked one eye open and shifted, his stomach pressed against the mattress with his arms under the pillow.

"Why are you freaking out?"

"It's ten. We have to be at church at twelve, our flight is three hours after that, *and* we're still at Chelsea's."

"I haven't sinned enough for church." Of course he had.

His brow furrowed and lips pursed, Shannon responded with a clipped laugh.

Aiden blinked. A light from the connected bathroom illuminated the pearl white carpet. He blinked again. A mirrored closet faced the bed, and its reflection showed all of the room they'd stumbled into hours ago, a room they'd been sure was a guest room—not that Aiden had paid any attention to the room or anything other than Shannon. It hurt to lift his head. It hurt worse to look around.

Baby pink curtains tied back with lace strings let in the dusty morning light. A silver lamp stood on a black nightstand, which was home to the half-empty bottle of bourbon they'd shared after the champagne, the countdown, and the four cigarettes that came after the countdown.

It was entirely Shannon's fault they'd landed in any room. Almost screwing against the side of Chelsea's house wasn't the best idea, but, during Aiden's fourth cigarette, with both of them drunk and unable to escape each other, Shannon plucked the half-smoked cigarette from Aiden's mouth and took its place—initiating the loss of their self-control. So, Aiden steered them up a flight of stairs, down a hallway, and into a dark room. Shannon stretched out beneath him with Aiden's fingers in his mouth. Words, not words, rough, not rough. Shannon saying, "You taste like champagne." Aiden's teeth breaking skin on Shannon's shoulder. Shannon saying, "You taste like me." Aiden's head spinning, heart pounding. Shannon's uninhibited desires, and Aiden being surprised he knew how to fulfill them.

They'd been sure the dark room was a guest room. He sat up on his elbows and squinted at a framed certificate hanging prettily above a fully stocked vintage vanity.

The Degree of Bachelor of Science

Chelsea Renee Cavanaugh

Aiden couldn't help it. His face hit the pillow and sharp, vicious laughter shook his whole body. It made his headache worse to laugh, but there was no stopping it.

They were not in a guest room. The bed they'd practically destroyed was not for visiting relatives or for decoration.

"Get. Up." Shannon grabbed Aiden's ankles and pulled. "I know you think this is funny, because you're petty and terrible, but it's not. I am a horrible friend, I am a horrible ex, and worst of all—"

The bedroom door swung open. In the doorway, arms crossed, a sickening smile stretched across her face, Chelsea stared at them. She leaned over to scan Aiden's bare form. She took in the tattoo first and then the low dip of his back and thigh scarcely covered by her Egyptian cotton sheets. A thin eyebrow lifted. Her lips twitched.

"Y'all have a good time last night? I sure did, sleeping on the couch and all." Chelsea's accent was thick as honey. She pushed daggers into Aiden with her eyes, one foot rapidly tapped the carpet. "Thanks for leaving your cancer sticks all over my backyard, Aiden, and for your consideration in general." Her smile faded. "I sure love cleaning up after other people." The last of her speech was directed at Shannon.

Her gaze was poisonous; Aiden was impressed.

"I'll pick them up." Aiden tried a smile, but her lips tightened at the sight of it. "We're sorry." His teeth sank into his bottom lip, stifling another laugh.

"Chels…" Shannon's face darkened. He shook his head and stammered, "I'm so sorry. I had no idea this was your room, we just found it, and we were drunk, and—"

"No idea? Nice try, Shannon, but five years together is a little too long a time to conveniently forget." She glanced at Aiden, and her face hardened. "You know that bed just as well as I do."

Shannon's mouth closed. He exhaled, sharp and indignant.

"Leave the sheets in the laundry basket," she snapped. Chelsea turned and left. The door didn't slam, but it might as well have.

Confrontation wasn't one of Aiden's strengths, but at least he hadn't said anything too horrible. Shannon repeated his own atrocities over and over as he paced around the room and threw Aiden's clothes at him.

"I'm horrible, absolutely horrible. How could I not *remember*…?" A wrinkled black tank hit Aiden's chest. "She'll never forgive me for this, Aiden. We were friends, you know? We have history." Jeans smacked him in the face. "Horrible friend, horrible ex, horrible drunken mess." Boxers next, then jacket, one sock.

"The title of 'horrible, drunken mess' is mine. I'm the longstanding champion of drunken messes and being horrible. Pretty sure someone gave me a trophy for it once." Aiden flashed his teeth.

Shannon stopped pacing and hung his head back, a very Shannon thing to do. His hands covered his face. "We're horrible," he whined. "We have to apologize. A real apology."

"Oh, okay." Aiden snorted. He zipped his jeans. His tank top was perfumed with spilt champagne, and the smell turned his stomach. "'Sorry for fucking in your bed, Chelsea. Come visit sometime.'"

Shannon groaned and threw one of Aiden's black combat boots, which whacked him in the shin.

"I'm kidding! We'll say we're sorry again, okay? Fucking relax. I guarantee you it'll go over better if you do the apologizing. She loves you too much not to forgive you, anyway."

The anger making waves on Shannon's face gave way to sadness, or perhaps pity. He ran a hand through his hair and sighed. "She does, doesn't she?"

"Yeah," Aiden said quickly. He smiled, forced and thin. It was difficult trying to fabricate sympathy for a woman who was the human embodiment of everything Aiden despised.

"I don't want to hurt her, Aiden." Shannon wrung his hands. His tenderness for other people, even people like Chelsea, was one of the traits Aiden loved most about him and envied. "What do I say? 'I'll always care for you as a friend? Your Rose Road will change everything?'"

"You're asking me to help you with sentiment?"

"*Horrible*," Shannon repeated. The soreness faded from his voice. He sighed and prodded Aiden in the chest with his index finger. "You, me, we're horrible." Aiden smiled, and pressed his lips back against Shannon's when he stole a kiss. "And gross. Help me with this."

They piled the sheets, comforter, and frilly pillows into a laundry basket that Chelsea had left outside the door. They made their way down the stairs. Hissed chatter died as they walked through the living room to the front door. Chelsea and her three-piece squad of plastic friends eyed them as they crossed the open entryway that led to the kitchen. They all had different shades of yellow hair, Chelsea's being the least offensive, and they looked Aiden up and down with their noses high in the air.

"Leaving?" Chelsea asked.

"Yeah, we have to get to church, actually."

"I bet you do," she said and gave one enthusiastic nod. Her mouth smiled, but her eyes were glaciers.

Aiden cleared his throat. He touched Shannon's wrist and murmured, "I'll be in the truck." It was best he left, he knew that. But Shannon's face dropped, and he snatched Aiden's hand, wordlessly asking him to stay. Aiden shook his head. "Shannon," he flicked his gaze to Chelsea, "go talk to your friend. I'll wait."

Chelsea also cleared her throat. A resounding hum from her trio of pet vultures followed.

Aiden opened the door.

"Oh, Aiden!" Chelsea called. The cheeky tone of her voice cracked through her forged smile. He glanced over his shoulder. An unlit cigarette drooped from his lips. "It was *such* a pleasure meeting you! I'm sure we'll see each other again real soon."

Aiden winked. "It was a pleasure, wasn't it?"

He heard Shannon curse as the door shut behind him.

Aiden laughed all the way to the truck.

00:00

SHANNON RUBBED A HAND OVER his freshly shaven face. The reflection was someone he faintly recognized, someone he'd left behind. His eyes were deeper, mouth quieter, brow tenser, older and younger at once.

"You could've tried being nice, Aiden! We desecrated her safe space; you littered in her backyard. We deserved her... temper, I guess," he said, loud enough that Aiden would hear him across the hall.

"How did you ever stand dating her?" Aiden called from the bedroom.

Shannon rolled his eyes. "It was high school. We had classes together and shared a group of friends. She was sweet and kind and classic, I guess. Still is, you know. She has her faults, but Chelsea's a good girl." He buttoned his cuffs, smoothed the front of his shirt, and centered his necklace. Tan pants, pressed and hemmed, felt strange without the weight of his badge.

"I *was* nice, by the way. Sorry your shitty ex is a hyena, but it's not my fault she's still got it bad for you. Her jealousy isn't my fucking problem."

"I never said it was!" Shannon stomped across the hall. "But I think you could've at least..."

Aiden stood by the bed. He glanced over his shoulder. A crimson shirt covered his upper half, fitted and tucked into black pants—no holes in the knees, no muscle tee or tank. A black tie was knotted intricately in a way that unearthed one of Aiden's secrets: He knew how to properly wear a tie. Another revealed secret was a decent pair of shoes. But his greatest secret was in the angles of his face, the nooks and crevices that could nick a finger. Aiden sharpened further in elegance than he did in comfort, transforming from a cluster of knives into an intricate collection of stealth weapons, unsheathed, black-handled, and poised—as much a work of art as blood was paint at a murder scene.

He shoved his hands into his pockets. All sarcasm and impatience, he sighed. "I could've what, Shannon?"

"You could've nothing. You're right. She was jealous, and I don't blame her. You're a frightening thing for her, Aiden Maar."

Thin lips spread into a smile. Its gentleness betrayed his claws and darkness, rare and poignant. He either believed Shannon, or he didn't. Perhaps that was his greatest secret. "Why's that, Wurther?"

Shannon closed the distance between them in two long strides. He flicked Aiden's black tie, caught a glimpse of silver chain beneath his collar, and tugged on a belt loop. Aiden stared at Shannon as his gentle smile turned clever and coy. He lifted his head when Shannon brushed his jaw with the tips of his fingers.

"Because you're one thing she will never compare to," he mumbled. Aiden's eyebrows rose. His tongue darted out to taste the pad of Shannon's thumb before he snatched it between his teeth.

"Eleven forty-five," Aiden said around his thumb.

Shannon wanted to feel the warmth of Aiden's mouth. "What?"

"It's eleven forty-five. Church, dumbass."

He pulled his hand back. Amusement ran rampant on Aiden's face. Shannon floundered to regain his composure, stepped away, and grabbed the truck keys off the dresser. "Church, yes, yeah. Let's try not to be horrible, all right?"

A laugh, as gentle as his fleeting smile, and Aiden said, "All right."

"All right," Shannon echoed.

Six years.

Aiden hadn't stepped inside a church in six years.

Forcing his legs to move, counting each step, he followed Shannon, Loraine, and Lloyd. It was a dark building, with stereotypically high ceilings, stained glass, and tall steeples. Four steps led to the two front doors. Six rows in, right in the middle of the pews, flowers, crosses, and holy water, they sat down. The pew was cold against Aiden's legs. Vulnerability gnawed on his thoughts and nibbled the back of his neck.

Six years. Six years. Six years.

Marcus' arm around his shoulder; his voice, soft and waterlogged.

We're gonna be okay, me and you.

The smell of lilies and baby's breath, salt and burnt out candles.

I'm gonna take care of you, and you're gonna take care of me. We're gonna make them proud.

Hands on Aiden's face, his shoulders, his arms; people he hadn't seen in years, shadows he didn't recognize.

If you need anything at all, Aiden, you let us know.

A priest making the sign of the cross over two beautifully crafted closed caskets.

They will be missed.

Marcus tugging Aiden's face into his shoulder, a shield.

You can cry, you can cry, you can cry.

"Aiden?" Shannon set his hand gently on Aiden's thigh. He flinched. "Hey, what's wrong?"

Aiden put one word in front of the next. He counted the syllables before they slipped through his lips. Breathe, inhale, hold it. "Nothing, I'm fine," he whispered, exhaling.

"You're not."

"I am," Aiden snapped. He didn't brush Shannon away. He slid closer and took Shannon's hand in his own.

Shannon's thumb swept across his wrist and pressed down. "Your heart's racing."

"I'll be fine."

"We can go outside."

The pastor adjusted the microphone. He said, "Happy New Year, everyone."

Now in the kingdom of Heaven.

"We're gathered here today to celebrate a new spring, a new summer, a new fall and winter, the turning of the clock, a new beginning."

A celebration of life.

"God has a plan for every one of us, and this year it's up to us as a community to see our plans to fruition. We must allow his guiding light to illuminate our path, and take shelter in the protection he provides."

Sasha and Christopher haven't left us behind; they've moved on to greater things and together they will look down upon us and smile.

Aiden's phone vibrated in his pocket. He jolted, finding his hand empty and shaking against his thigh. He pulled out his phone and glanced at the screen.

Shannon Wurther 1/1 12:10 p.m.
Deep breaths
Aiden Maar 1/1 12:10 p.m.
i cant breathe

Shannon Wurther 1/1 12:12 p.m.
Yes you can. Count them

One. Aiden inhaled. Two. It burned his lungs. Three. Aiden exhaled.

Shannon Wurther 1/1 12:13 p.m.
you should have told me
Aiden Maar 1/1 12:15 p.m.
I didnt know
Shannon Wurther 1/1 12:16 p.m.
Im sorry
Aiden Maar 1/1 12:17 p.m.
its not your fault

After another set of three breaths, Aiden's foot started to tap. He chewed on his lip. The next breath came easier. But the heaviness pressed on his collarbones again, slithered between his ribs, and clawed at his lungs. He hadn't felt such breathlessness in a long time.

Aiden couldn't remember the last time he'd lost control, the last time he'd fallen apart. Once it happened, it happened. Once it was over, it was over. Last April. April before last. All six April's before this coming April. And all the Aprils after.

Aiden wanted to ask the pastor, "Have you ever felt like you were dying?" Just to see if he said yes. And if he did, Aiden would ask, "How do you make it stop? How do you live?" Just to see if there was an answer, if there was an after.

"Please stand and show your love for your neighbor with a handshake or a hug," the pastor said.

Everyone except Aiden rose from their seats. His body was cemented to the pew. A sensation of weightlessness swelled in his gut, overwhelmed by the oppressive anchor sitting atop his chest.

Make it stop. Aiden tried to catch his breath.

"C'mon." Shannon's voice. "Aiden." His hand curled around Aiden's wrist. "We'll be outside." This he said to Loraine. Aiden caught a brisk nod from her before they slipped past.

Say something, Aiden scolded.

One. Two. A third step. The fourth. His shoes hit the dirt parking lot, and Shannon steadied him with hands on his waist, then his shoulders.

"Lean back," Shannon said, and Aiden did.

He felt warm wood against the back of his head, sunlight on his face, and Shannon's hands. Aiden leaned against the side of the church and listened to tires crunch against pebbles in the lot and cicadas hiss from the trees a few yards away. He told his lungs to do what they were supposed to do. *Inhale, hold, exhale.*

"I don't know what happened," Aiden croaked and he hated how pitiful it sounded.

Shannon touched the base of his neck with one hand and held onto his right wrist with the other. "You had a panic attack."

"I don't have panic attacks."

"Sure looked like one to me, sugar."

"Sugar?" Aiden laughed, but it was broken and small. "How would you know what a panic attack looks like?"

"I've had them."

Aiden's eyes cracked open. Now was as good a time as ever, he thought, and forced the words out before he lost the courage to say them. "I have dysthymia. It's a form of depression, but I'm not like..." He circled his hand, embarrassed. "I'm not *depressed.* I just fall apart sometimes because I'm a fucking disaster, and that's what my doctor calls it. Anxiety comes with it. I guess panic attacks, too."

"You're not a disaster," Shannon said. A crooked smile dimpled his cheeks. "We all fall apart sometimes."

"Yeah, but I don't know how to put myself back together; that's the dysthymia shit I was talking about."

Shannon nodded. "Can you breathe?"

Aiden inhaled. The weight was gone. The emptiness in his stomach filled again and roiled last night's alcohol. He nodded. "You didn't have to do that—take me out—you didn't have to leave your parents in there."

"I know."

He leaned against Shannon's chest and caught the sweet scent of floral cologne. Shannon's hand played on the back of Aiden's neck; his fingers drew circles above his collar. They stayed like that, leaning against an old church beside a stained-glass window, with Shannon not saying a word and Aiden still counting his breaths, until the doors opened and the New Year's service was over.

In the fleeting time between—Shannon's thumb was below Aiden's left ear, Aiden was inhaling his eleventh breath, and everything was still—Aiden realized that there was nothing like being in love with someone. He'd never felt it, not until that eleventh breath, and Shannon's thumb, and the tender way he held Aiden as if he wasn't something that needed mending, but something that needed validation. During that time, fractured and motionless and silent, Aiden's heart plummeted, because he loved Shannon Wurther, and loving someone meant giving them the tools to destroy you. The things that turned Aiden into a weapon, all the tools Aiden had used on himself year after year after year, how bold and cruel and mistaken they would look clutched between Shannon's fingers.

An accident, the breathlessness, red knuckles, dying.

A smile, the brush of fingertips across his shoulders, an almost-kiss, *how was work.*

"When's our flight?" Aiden inhaled another breath, the last one he counted.

"We need to be at the airport in two hours."

Aiden set his forehead on Shannon's shoulder. "Sorry I'm a mess."

"You're not a mess," Shannon laughed against his ear. "Did you not hear me when I said I have them, too?"

"I figured you'd said it to make me feel better."

"I didn't. So, when I have one, and I will, put me back together all right?"

Aiden nodded. "Yeah, okay."

Loraine's voice carried high over the crowd of Sunday-best churchgoers. "You boys ready for lunch? We're goin' to Becky's before we drop you off at the airport."

"What's a Becky's?" Aiden's stomach turned.

"Lunch place down the road," Shannon said. "We should eat."

Aiden heard Lloyd ask if everything was all right, and Shannon nodded. He saw Loraine's eyebrows ask a silent question. Shannon growled at her. He slid in the back seat next to Shannon; his phone was slick against his palms.

He wanted to say it. He wanted to look at Shannon and say, "I think I love you, but I wouldn't know. I've only ever loved myself." But it would be a lie, half of it at least. He swiped his finger across his phone and typed out a message: *I love you happy new year*

A second later his phone vibrated.

Marcus Maar 1/1 12:45 p.m.
I love you too Aiden. Hope youre having a good time. Happy New Year.
Aiden Maar 1/1 12:46 p.m.
tell mercy i love her
Marcus Maar 1/1 12:47 p.m.
She says she loves you too.

00:00

SHANNON DIDN'T SLEEP ON THE plane, but Aiden did. He tucked his face against Shannon's shoulder and refused to move for the duration of the four-and-half-hour flight.

Karman picked them up from the airport and asked a million questions about their New Year's. Aiden didn't talk much, and Shannon caught him playing with his camera in the rear-view mirror. Shannon answered question after question and listened to Karman ramble about how Marcus and Fae almost burnt the house down with sparklers.

"I swear, your brother is as crazy as you sometimes." Karman glanced over her shoulder.

Aiden raised his middle finger and narrowed his eyes. He'd thrown his cigarettes in the trash on the way out of the airport. Shannon didn't want to imagine what the next few days would be like: Aiden kicking a bad habit, and Shannon being the one who'd convinced him to.

Once she dropped them off at Shannon's loft, they crawled into bed and slept until the next morning. Life went on as it was supposed to. It was a new year, Shannon and Karman were taking on more cases, Aiden was getting a few more hours a week at 101, and slowly but surely Laguna Beach was starting to thaw.

Winter faded, and in its place flowers began to bloom and rain pelted the streets from low-hanging clouds. Spring was on the horizon.

Shannon decided he would tell Aiden he loved him when it was warm and new and bright and great. He would sit him down on the beach and say it as plain as day. He wouldn't crack or lose his words or fall silent. Shannon would say, "I love you, Aiden Maar," and he hoped Aiden might say it back.

Aiden Maar 1/15 2:04 p.m.
i just got a call from daisy. shes here early.
Shannon Wurther 1/15 2:06 p.m.
Yay?
Aiden Maar 1/15 2:06 p.m.
yeah except i gotta cancel tonight, sorry
Shannon Wurther 1/15 2:07 p.m.
its okay. Tomorrow?
Aiden Maar 1/15 2:09 p.m.
I work ☹
Shannon Wurther 1/15 2:10 p.m.

Monday?
Aiden Maar 1/15 2:12 p.m.
okay monday
Shannon Wurther 1/15 2:13 p.m.
spaghetti?
Aiden Maar 1/15 2:14 p.m.
Yeah yum

"Wurther." Karman held up a file. "Piper's on leave for a few months. Homicide needs us to step in; you up to it?"

"Why's Piper on leave? She never misses work."

"Clock shit, apparently. Something happened with her daughter. They're taking an extended vacation because of it."

"Is her daughter okay?" Shannon stared at Karman, unnerved.

Karman was always difficult to read when it came to Camellia Clocks, but sometimes she was more than that. Her tragedy turned her cruel, icing over the part of her that Shannon admired most: her compassion.

"She'll be fine," Karman said. She lifted her eyes, daring him to push further. "As far as I know, Piper's daughter had been with her Rose Road for two years. He left in the middle of the night a week ago and changed his number so no one can find him. Shit happens, people disappear. She'll heal."

Shannon's mouth clenched. *You haven't.* The words were on the tip of his tongue, but he didn't let them past his teeth. He didn't have the energy for what would come after.

"What's the case?"

"Looks like we've got an open domestic abuse charge, felony possession of drugs—methamphetamines, intention to sell—and…" Karman tapped her pen against the open file. "Assault with a deadly weapon. Internal shit, family, extended family, drugs have been in the household for a while. Dude was an informant, got out and missed his court date, now there's a warrant."

"Why is this being handled by homicide?"

"He's wanted for attempted murder in Arizona." Karman squinted at the third page. She handed the file to Shannon. "And there's an unsolved case here, guy gunned down north of Anaheim during a deal gone bad. They think it's him, this, uh…"

Shannon scanned the paperwork. "David Mortez."

"Yeah, him."

"They took someone wanted for attempted murder and offered him a deal as an informant; go team," Shannon whispered sarcastically. Karman nodded.

"You wanna do this?" Shannon asked.

She nodded. "As long as you do."

"All right," Shannon said, but his stomach flipped. "We'll take it on. Let's hope we can make a clean arrest."

"We will." Karman popped a barbecue-flavored chip in her mouth and shook the bag at Shannon.

He took one, and it crunched under his teeth. "We'll see."

30

AIDEN ANSWERED THE DOOR WHILE Daisy was still knocking.

She jumped. Beside her stood a suitcase almost as tall as she was with a backpack strapped to the top of it. She bounced on the toes of her Converse and grinned with lips a little too big for her chin. Her usual dark bob was angled into a stylish cut: shaved in the back, long strands over her ears, straight bangs across her eyebrows. One side of her hair was stark white, the other midnight black.

"Holy shit, Aiden!" Daisy lunged forward and clasped her arms around his neck. She practically climbed him. "Look at you! Look at this!" She lifted his shirt. "You're actually working out now?"

Daisy, a tiny, compact thing, balanced around his waist easily, and Aiden spun her around.

"I quit smoking and started running," he said. He set her down, and she dove for Mercy, who slept soundly on the couch. "I thought I might cough up one of my lungs at first, but I guess it paid off. It's only been two weeks, and you and Shannon both noticed."

Daisy gasped. She held Mercy against her face and went back to bouncing excitedly. "Shannon? Instagram guy! The Abercrombie model! He's your Rose Road, right?"

Mercy, a ragdoll in Daisy's slender arms, yawned.

"Yeah, that's him." Aiden pulled the suitcase inside and closed the door. He smiled at her, and she smiled back, both of them too excited to do anything except stare.

Daisy was the same, but not. She'd grown from an awkward, pretty teenager into a startling, beautiful woman—odd in the best ways, with a curved nose that she always said she would fix with plastic surgery, and small, dark eyes. Her brows were the same, thick and sharp; her ear lobes stretched around fancy crystal plugs. Aiden swore those were the same shoes from junior year, but instead of black-on-black accented with spikes and lace, Daisy wore a striped red and white crop top, high-waisted shorts, and knee-high black socks.

"Daisy Yuen," Aiden whispered.

"Aiden Maar," she whispered back.

"Hungry?"

Daisy nodded and kissed Mercy's face. "Starving."

"Diner?"

Daisy grinned. "Always."

"Okay, wait, wait, back up." Daisy stuffed a fry in her mouth. "You're a professional *burglar*? You steal shit and make money by selling it on the Internet to dealers?"

"Used to," Aiden corrected. "Not anymore, that's just how we met."

"And he has a bombshell ex-chick who hates you."

"Correct."

"And his partner is dating Marcus?"

"She doesn't call it that, but yeah. Karman and Marcus are dating. He's got a toothbrush at her place and everything."

Daisy leaned back in the booth. They sat by the window, their old spot, and ate fries smothered in cheese sauce. Kelly brought Daisy a vanilla Coke, her usual order, and they swooned together over how wonderful it was that Daisy was home. Daisy ordered a veggie burger and Aiden ordered chicken strips. It was as if nothing had changed. They were back in high school, eating late at night, worrying about chemistry exams, and Vance being an asshole, and how they were going to score something fun for a party that weekend.

She tapped the tip of her nose and smirked. "You still have it."

"Yeah, I started wearing it down again. You took yours out?"

"Hell, no!" Daisy plucked down her septum ring, black with silver spikes on the tips. "I hid it when my mom drove me to the airport. She still doesn't know about it."

"Still? We did them freshman year, which means it's been..." Aiden's gaze drifted to the ceiling, and he curled his fingers, counting. "Daisy, it's been eight years. How has she not seen it?"

"I've been at school. The only time she saw me was on break. Speaking of which, she took me to fucking China, did I tell you about that?" Daisy waved her index finger at Aiden while she sipped her soda. "China, Aiden. Told me I had to go visit my grandparents and ask them for guidance since this is my Clock year. I watched them brutalize a goose. Grandma snapped its neck right in front of me. I burst into tears; eyeliner ran everywhere; it was terrible. Pandemonium."

"Did you eat it?"

"Of course I didn't, you monster," she said with a snort and threw a fry at him. "Tell me more about Abercrombie."

"Shannon," Aiden corrected.

"I'm calling him Abercrombie, might as well get used to it. He's a cop, which is hilarious; he's from Georgia, also hilarious; and he's... good in bed, or?"

This time Aiden threw the fry. Daisy tried to catch it with her mouth, but missed, and ended up with cheese sauce smeared on her cheek.

"You need a car," Aiden said matter-of-factly, changing the subject. The diner wasn't the place to discuss his sex life with Daisy; she was too loud, and Aiden was too honest. She would laugh at him, and he would be embarrassed. Not that Aiden had anything to be embarrassed about, but his apartment was more appropriate for that discussion. "How much do you have saved up?"

"Enough. Like twenty something. I have my grad money, my internship pays well, and I was a waitress at the twenty-four-hour café on campus, made a ton of tips. I'm thinking practical, a Toyota or something."

"By practical, you mean fast?"

Daisy rolled her eyes and munched on her burger. There was ketchup on her chin and cheese sauce on her cheek, and she smiled at him around a mouthful of food. Again, it was as if nothing had changed, and Aiden almost wished they were sixteen again.

He'd make better choices. He'd keep in touch. He'd probably go to college. He'd *be* something.

But they weren't sixteen, and Aiden couldn't go back, and he said it loudly in his head, *you'll be fine, you'll be fine, you'll be fine,* no matter how envious he was of everyone else's success.

00:00

SHANNON MET DAISY ON JANUARY eighteenth.

He opened the apartment door and walked inside to be greeted by Aiden, who popped his head out of the kitchen and said, "I just put the noodles in."

Shannon nodded and gestured with his chin at the woman on the couch talking on the phone. She swiveled her head one way and then another; her slender hand perched on her knee.

"*Mom,*" Daisy groaned. She held the phone away from her ear, flashed a curious smile at Shannon, and curled two fingers in a wave. Her conversation switched between Mandarin and English. "Aiden's fine—Aiden, say hi," she shouted, and held the phone over the arm of the couch.

Balancing on one foot, Aiden leaned out of the kitchen. "Hi, Mrs. Yuen!"

Shannon, unsure what to do, squeezed past Aiden and sat on the kitchen counter.

"I start a week from today, next Monday. Yeah—Yes, Mom. I promise. We won't get in trouble, oh, my god—Aiden!" Daisy held the phone out again. "Tell her we won't get in trouble."

Aiden snatched the phone. "Hi, Violet. I'm good, yeah. Yeah," he laughed, holding the phone between his ear and shoulder as he stirred sauce in a skillet. "I'm dating a cop. He'll make sure we don't do anything stupid." Aiden glanced at Shannon and smiled. "That's right, you heard me. Yeah, he willingly dates me. Crazy, I know. Nope, not holding him against his will."

"Mom!" Daisy yelled, as if her mother could hear her from the couch. "Don't be mean!"

"Uh-huh, yeah. Here's Daisy." Aiden handed the phone back.

"Not holding me against my will, huh?" Shannon dipped his finger in the sauce and tasted. "Needs garlic."

"Am I?" Aiden asked, and opened the fridge, shoving a container of minced garlic at Shannon's chest.

"Yeah, it's Stockholm syndrome. I can't bring myself to leave."

"Good." Aiden laughed. He drained the noodles and then caught Shannon's lips in a quick kiss.

Daisy made a noise from the couch as if she was cooing at a baby. "Mom, I have to go. Aiden cooked dinner. Yeah, you heard me right. He cooked. It *is* incredible. No, it won't poison me. I love you." She paused, said something in Mandarin, and hung up.

Daisy flopped on the couch with her elbows on the arm rest and her chin in her palms. She kicked her feet above her rear and grinned. "I'm Daisy." She looked Shannon up and down. "You're Shannon. We'll be friends in no time."

Shannon liked her.

"You dress like an asshole, though."

Maybe Shannon didn't like her.

Taken off guard, Aiden almost fell against the counter laughing.

"He's totally Abercrombie, Aiden." She pointed at Shannon. "What even are those things on your head?" Daisy tried not to laugh and failed.

Shannon's face heated. He tapped the top of his head; the edges of his sunglasses were cold on his fingertips. "These?"

Aiden slid against the fridge until he hit the tile and howled.

The bright kitchen lights gleamed off Shannon's gold sunglasses. He frowned, turning them in his hands. He swung his foot at Aiden, but Aiden caught it, rubbed Shannon's calf, and rested his forehead against his shin. Shannon tugged at the sleeves of his brown knit sweater, adjusted one of the buttons below the collar, and analyzed every stitch in his blue jeans. Aiden and Daisy continued to laugh, pleased with themselves.

It didn't take long before Shannon was laughing, too. "Sorry, I don't buy pre-ripped jeans and Sharpie my fingernails black."

Aiden's mouth rounded. His teeth dove into his bottom lip. Daisy stopped laughing; her mouth hung open in a grin. Shannon glanced between them, suddenly afraid he'd crossed a line.

"We totally did that in high school," Daisy admitted, and started laughing again. "We had punch cards at Hot Topic and everything."

Cheeks red, barely able to breathe, Aiden let go of Shannon's foot and curled in on himself.

"I'm just kidding, Shannon," Daisy said. "Sort of. I'm still gonna call you Abercrombie, and we did have punch cards. But anyway, it's nice to meet you. I'm glad you have a sense of humor."

"You think he would've stuck around this long if he didn't?" Aiden stood up, reigned in lingering chuckles, and patted Shannon's thigh. "Now that Daisy's gotten her initial insult out of the way, we should probably eat."

"Was that what that was?" Shannon tilted his head.

"Yeah, I had to be sure you weren't the bad kind of cop, the pretentious, chased-us-when-we-were-teenagers kind," Daisy said.

Shannon's head jerked back. "You could've told her I wasn't," he said, throwing the words over his shoulder.

Aiden shrugged and piled spaghetti into separate bowls—probably the only three he owned.

"I did; she had to see for herself." Aiden handed one bowl to Shannon, the other to Daisy.

The only table in Aiden's apartment besides the coffee table was on the balcony. It was cramped and a little cold. Still, they decided to sit outside and enjoy the sunset. The sky was all pinks and purples and oranges, too beautiful to miss. Aiden sat in Shannon's lap, and Mercy sat in Daisy's.

They ate their spaghetti over a conversation that consisted mostly of Daisy reminiscing, and Aiden laughing, and Shannon listening. Daisy spoke with her hands: grand gestures and intricate flicks of her wrists. She had a windy voice, and smiled when she spoke, and her slate-colored eyes were bright and alive.

When Daisy asked Shannon question after question, he answered. They talked about his childhood, Aiden chimed in about Loraine's cooking, and Daisy went on and on over nonsense like favorite video games, whether he enjoyed science fiction movies, and what the last book he read was.

Shannon decided, after an argument over *Star Wars* ensued, that he liked Daisy. She was interesting and honest and she made Aiden smile, which was one of her most flattering traits. Aiden wouldn't genuinely smile at someone who didn't deserve it.

Daisy—like everything else Aiden collected—was priceless, beautiful, and Shannon couldn't help being fascinated.

"Blizzard's rumored to be one of the top companies in OC to work for," Shannon said. "Congratulations."

"Thanks, man. I'm still in shock over it. I can't believe they actually took me on." She shrugged and tilted a beer bottle against her lips. "I guess I start with scenery design, and then hopefully in a year or two they'll hire me on permanently, and I can move into weapon creation. That's what I really want to do."

"Go get your sketchbook," Aiden said.

Daisy shot him a nasty glare. "No."

"Yes, go get it."

Daisy didn't move.

Aiden slid off Shannon's lap and stood up, which Shannon appreciated, since his right leg was numb. He returned with a leather-bound black book stuffed with variously sized papers. Daisy didn't bother trying to stop him; it was obvious she'd known him long enough not to put in the effort.

"They aren't that good; the stuff on my laptop is better," Daisy mumbled.

The sun had long since set, and the only source of light was a dim bulb next to the door, but it was enough. Aiden got comfortable in Shannon's lap again and opened the sketchbook. All sorts of creatures, faeries, mermaids, dragons, and elves, filled each page: beautiful, unique pieces, some smudged in pencil, others inked.

Shannon glanced at Daisy and found that she was watching. Something daring sparked behind her eyes. Looking at her reminded him that wolves ran in packs.

"These are incredible," Shannon said.

Daisy nodded as if she'd heard it before. "Thanks, Abercrombie."

And they laughed, and laughed, and laughed.

31

It wasn't warm enough, not yet.

It wasn't new enough, or bright enough, or great enough, and Shannon wished it was.

January spun a web of cold nights that turned into colder mornings, and every stretch of silk that expanded toward the edge brought them closer to spring. Soon January was gone, and with it went the tail end of winter. February was a sigh of relief, waking into blue skies and mid-day rainfall, brave surfers, and iced coffee instead of hot.

Shannon watched his life move, forward and then back, into Aiden's tentative touches in the middle of the night, and out of the case he'd dived into at work. His days were spent convincing himself that the gun on his waist wasn't as heavy as it felt, and his nights were spent being reminded that he was in love.

He was in love and he was too scared to do anything about it.

It wasn't new enough, or bright enough, or great enough, and Shannon wished it was.

He wished, he wished, he wished, and he wondered what the fireflies would've said if he'd asked.

Will he love me back? Will he love me at all?

But some days weren't spent worrying about cases he wasn't sure he could handle, or Karman's overuse of the word *homicide*, or Piper's constant texts to check up on them. Some days Shannon pushed all those thoughts to the back of his mind. Some days, like this day, he spent with Aiden. There was no better way to put Shannon's busy mind on standby than pleasure, and, as fate would have it, pleasure was Aiden's second language.

He learned it quickly, same as someone learning to roll their r's in Spanish and swallow their vowels in French. His hands memorized the places on Shannon's body that tensed beneath them, the hidden jolts and jerks and gasps that left Shannon wondering how Aiden could've ever been nervous about this.

Shannon looked at him, spread out on the loft's floor. Aiden's pale skin was lit with a glowing blush, his eyes were half-open, and his head tilted back. He wrapped his lips around Shannon's index finger; his tongue rubbed sure and slow against it.

Aiden keened, and his hips canted as Shannon rolled his waist between them. His teeth scraped Shannon's knuckles. There was nothing sexier than looking at Aiden, a locked door that everyone wanted to open, and holding the key.

"Get on with it," Aiden rasped. He sucked Shannon's middle finger alongside the other.

"Down, boy," Shannon whispered. He pulled his fingers from Aiden's lips and slithered his hand beneath the fabric of Aiden's black briefs. "We've got all day."

Aiden smiled sheepishly. His eyes slipped shut. "We don't, actually." A soft whine built in his throat. "I have work at five."

"It's not even noon." Shannon smothered his laugh in Aiden's neck, satisfied with the uneven, breathy sounds he made, and the slow, building arch of his spine.

One quick motion and Shannon was on his back, staring at the ceiling and at Aiden who hovered over him. A razor-sharp smile curved Aiden's mouth. He kissed Shannon briefly, before he trailed his lips along the column of his throat, his collarbones. He teased at Shannon's abdomen, sucked light marks next to his belly button, and hooked teeth around his hipbones.

Shannon chewed on his bottom lip. His hands found Aiden's shoulders, then traced his jaw and the tops of his arms. Aiden dug his nails into Shannon's sides, with his open mouth just above the waistband of his boxers. He bit, sucking another blooming bruise on Shannon's pelvis.

Reluctantly, Shannon glanced down, rewarded with dark eyes, pupils blown wide, staring up at him. Aiden was an expert at anticipation. He enjoyed playing games, teasing, taunting, building, and making Shannon lift his hips off the floor, babbling incoherent pleas and curses. It was a shame Shannon loved it as much as he did, because it was terribly embarrassing.

"Tell me," Aiden whispered, tugging at Shannon's boxers to expose more of his hip. He dragged his bottom lip along Shannon's thigh.

Shannon's breath left him and returned in a shaky gasp.

"C'mon," Aiden said. He raked his nails down Shannon's stomach. "Tell me what you want—"

Aiden halted.

Three knocks. One right after the other, evenly spaced, sounded distant and surreal. Shannon's eyes flew open. Brakes screeched in his mind. Aiden huffed, annoyed.

Shannon blinked at the ceiling. His heart hammered in his chest. No, he couldn't have heard that right. Aiden sat up and glared at him.

Again, the sound: three knocks, one right after the other, from the front door. Shannon lifted to his elbows while Aiden rolled his eyes and flopped on his back.

"Well, go." Aiden waved his arm at the door. "It's Valentine's Day. I'd like to actually fuck you at some point."

Shannon nudged him with his foot and smirked. "It's probably just someone selling something. And I resent that statement, by the way. You should want to whether or not it's a holiday."

"Please. Like you don't get laid every day," Aiden snorted, crawling into a patch of light that came through the open windows.

Shannon hunted for his sweats, found them, pulled them on, and ran his hand through his hair.

Three more knocks.

"Oh-fucking-kay!" Aiden shouted.

Shannon kicked him playfully in the leg as he walked by, and noticed the frustrated, dark blush on his cheeks and chest.

He unlocked the door, opened it, and said, "Hey, sorry about that, we didn't…" The words curdled in his throat, sticking together like sap. Shannon's whole body tensed. He swallowed, unsure whether he could take a breath or not. The blood in his face drained. "…hear you. What…are you, what…"

Standing on his porch, wearing a beige pencil skirt and a pearl white blouse accented with blue lace, was Chelsea Cavanaugh. She clasped her hands in front of her waist and grinned; her bright seafoam eyes were wide. She bounced in a pair of navy heels and gave a painfully forced laugh.

"Surprise! You told me to visit anytime, so here I am!"

If there was anything Shannon wasn't expecting, it was Chelsea Cavanaugh.

"I was thinkin' to myself a few days ago—I was thinkin', Chelsea, you've got four months to go, and who says your Rose Road is in Georgia?" She hit the back of one hand against the palm of the other over and over, eyebrows trying to keep up with her speech. "Could be anywhere, right? Why not here?"

And if there was anything Shannon was completely unprepared for, it was Chelsea Cavanaugh.

"You've gotta be fucking joking!" That was Aiden, who cackled from inside. "Is that your hyena, Shannon?"

Chelsea cocked her head, unaware that when Aiden said hyena, he meant ex-girlfriend. Unable to form words, Shannon pulled the door, shielding Chelsea from whatever she would see if she peeked inside.

Her smile dropped, but picked up again, as if she'd caught herself being rude. God forbid Chelsea was intentionally rude, Shannon thought; she might explode if someone accused her of such a thing.

"Is that Aiden I hear?" Chelsea's voice cracked over his name.

"It *is* her!" Aiden yelled from inside. He shuffled around, either getting dressed or getting the rest of the way undressed; one meant he was going to come speak to her, the other meant he was going to harass Shannon until he closed the door. Both scenarios had Shannon sweating.

Aiden was putting his pants on and came to the door with them unbuttoned and barely clinging to his hips. He grabbed the door and wrenched it open. "Chelsea," he cooed, which she smiled at despite the sarcasm, "what the hell are you doing here?"

"Be nice," Shannon said.

Chelsea batted at the air. "My Clock goes off soon, and I decided to take some personal time to handle everything. I'll be staying at Laguna Inn, that nice boutique hotel on the cliffside, until after I find my Rose Road. Mama and Daddy gave me a twelve-month leave."

"Mama and Daddy gave you a twelve-month leave?" Aiden's eyes bulged, and he put on a mock southern accent. "Well, shit, howdy, who's gonna watch the farm?"

Shannon bristled. God forbid Aiden was anything *but* intentionally rude. He palmed Aiden's face and shoved him backward. "Stop it," Shannon snapped under his breath.

"I see he's as pleasant as ever. What a wonderful guy," Chelsea sang.

Aiden's vicious howls echoed through the loft, laughter sharp enough to cut the tension. The bathroom door slammed, and Shannon sighed, relieved. Dealing with Chelsea was enough; dealing with Chelsea *and* Aiden was a deadly cocktail he wasn't brave enough to drink. He tried to smile, but Chelsea's attention got caught in the welts on his abdomen, long red stains from Aiden's fingernails.

"So, hi, you're here," Shannon said, pulling her attention back to his face. "You could've called, Chels."

"I know I could've, but I figured you'd try to talk me out of it."

"What? No, I would never…"

Chelsea's over-plucked eyebrows lifted.

"You're right, I would've." Arms folded across his chest, he leaned against the doorway. "But you're here now, and that's great. And just…" He motioned toward the bathroom. "Sorry," he said through clenched teeth, "about Aiden. You two are oil and water, you know?"

"Oh, honey, don't apologize." She touched his shoulder and jerked her hand back when she realized she'd brushed a violet bruise. "It's not like he has an off button, right?"

"Aiden? No." Shannon closed his eyes and shook his head. "*God* no."

"You two have anything planned for this evening?"

"No, he has to work tonight, unfortunately."

"Well, if you aren't doin' anything, how about dinner, me and you? We can catch up, have a couple drinks; it'll be fun!"

Chelsea dragged out *fun*, all southern belle and magnolias, familiar and beautiful and unexpected. But Shannon glimpsed the genuine excitement in her eyes, the soft smile on her face, and the hopefulness stitched across her brow. She folded her hands; gold bangles jingled around her slender wrists.

"I could really use a friend," she added, the first bit of honesty she'd let past her lips. "And you're about the best one I got."

Shannon's heart sank. He smiled at her, and she smiled back. Their history buzzed around them. The fact that she'd uprooted her life, come all this way, marched up Shannon's stairs, and was asking him for nothing more than dinner, was a sad, sad thing.

His stomach flipped. If he was the best thing she had, she didn't have much.

"Yeah, of course, I'll show you around downtown and everything. It'll be fun." He was a better liar than she was, but a part of him acknowledged that it might not be a lie. Shannon was, on some level, excited to spend time with her.

Chelsea may be annoying and boisterous and difficult, but she was still Chelsea. He owed it to her to be there when she needed him.

She beamed. "Let's say about six?"

"Six," Shannon repeated.

"All right, then."

"All right," he said gently. His accent followed hers, syrup-coating his words.

Shannon shut the door. Chelsea's heels click-clacked on the stairs. He leaned against it and stared at the light bulb above the entryway. The bathroom door cracked open.

"She gone?"

"Yes, Aiden. She's gone. Thank you for being polite, as always."

"I'll apologize later."

"Everyone knows how well your apologies go," Shannon snapped. He glanced at Aiden, who narrowed his eyes. "She's going to be here for a while; you get that, right?"

Aiden rolled his eyes.

"She's my friend. I need you to at least *try*, okay?" Shannon turned his attention back to the light bulb, waiting for Aiden to bark at him or say something horrible. But Aiden did neither.

Instead he said, "I'll tolerate her as long as she tolerates me."

Shannon rubbed a hand over his face and heaved a sigh. "This is going to kill me. Both of you," he groaned, "both of you are going to put me in the ground, I swear."

Wet feet plopped against the floor, trailing water with them. Shannon closed his eyes and inhaled a long steady breath. Aiden stood in front of him, soaking wet. A puddle formed around his feet. He walked his fingers up Shannon's chest.

"You're getting water everywhere."

"I'm standing naked in front of you and 'you're getting water everywhere' is what you say?" Aiden gripped Shannon's cheek and pinched his chin with his thumb.

"You left the shower running." Shannon's gaze trailed the length of Aiden's body. The thought of Chelsea drifted farther and farther away.

"For a reason," Aiden mumbled. His fingernail stabbed Shannon's jaw before he let his arm fall and took Shannon's hand. "You coming or what?"

"Are you going to be corrigible, Aiden Maar?"

"Corrigible? No, probably not. I'll be nice if she's nice, though. Tell her not to be an uppity bitch, and we'll get along just fine."

Aiden let go of Shannon's wrist and took a step back. Water glistened on his skin; droplets curved down his torso and legs, clung to the tops of his collarbones, shone on his shoulders. He was something—Shannon was sure. As he looked at Aiden, lit by the afternoon light that poured in from the windows, he imagined how Chelsea must have felt looking at him, too. Aiden was distinctly beautiful and terribly intimidating, the sensation of doing something deliciously wrong.

"Come here." Shannon bit back a subdued smile.

No wonder she hated Aiden.

He stepped into Shannon's space, gripped his wrists, and forced them against the door. Shannon allowed it, pleased at how hard Aiden kissed him, possessive and dirty and rough. He sealed their bodies together, dropped Shannon's wrists to tug at the waistband of his sweats, pushed them down. Shannon clumsily followed him as they made their way toward the shower. Aiden's hands gripped his face. Shannon pushed him against the bathroom door and slotted his hips between Aiden's legs.

"She's a bitch; I'm an asshole. That's not changing. You get that, right?" Aiden's breath gusted Shannon's mouth.

Shannon nodded. He was aware of that, hypersensitive to it. "You'll grow on each other."

Aiden forced a laugh through his teeth and turned the doorknob, almost tripping backward into the bathroom. Shannon steadied him with hands curled around his back. "Keep telling yourself that," Aiden said.

The bathroom was fogged with steam; the shower still sprayed hot.

"I will," Shannon said matter-of-factly.

No wonder Chelsea hated Aiden, with all his authenticity and un-apologetic attitude and genuine knowing of himself. He was everything she'd always wanted to be, and couldn't.

"Stop talking, just…" Aiden's eyes closed; his hips were flush against Shannon's. Warmth glowed in his cheeks; his jaw slackened. Pleasure, pleasure, pleasure, his second language, spoke to Shannon like a gun going off, an engine revving, a storm raging. "Just get on with it, get on with it."

God, no wonder she hated him.

No wonder Shannon loved him.

 32

AIDEN MAAR 2/14 5:46 P.M.
i cant believe youre taking her to dinner tonight
Shannon Wurther 2/14 5:46 p.m.
you said it was okay
Aiden Maar 2/14 5:47 p.m.
I changed my mind
Shannon Wurther 2/14 5:47 p.m.
aiden
Aiden Maar 2/14 5:50 p.m.
*dont do that. its the universal holiday for romance and youre taking
your ex to dinner? thats weird shannon.*
Shannon Wurther 2/14 5:51 p.m.
because you're so romantic.
Aiden Maar 2/14 5:51 p.m.
wow thats nice
Shannon Wurther 2/14 5:53 p.m.
*omg you had to work! shes all alone. Don't make this a big deal.
Theres no need to be jealous, you know that*
Aiden Maar 2/14 5:54 p.m.
I am not jealous of her
Shannon Wurther 2/14 5:55 p.m.

stop acting like it then. its dinner. thats it.
Aiden Maar 2/14 5:59 p.m.
Im coming over after work
Shannon Wurther 2/14 6:01 p.m.
Good

Daisy's eyebrows lifted. She stared at Aiden's phone where he'd slid it across the bar. "Oh-hoh, wow. He's actually taking this chick to dinner on Valentine's Day?"

"Yes," Aiden snapped.

He hadn't realized how pissed he was until he got to work. Couples and triads and groups of people sauntered around 101, sipping drinks, eating complimentary strawberries, and rubbing up against each other. Aiden hadn't realized how jealous he was until he thought of Chelsea slipping on something tight and whipping her bleached hair in Shannon's face.

"That's kind of fucked-up," Daisy said.

Aiden shook a martini shaker over his shoulder—Carver was letting him bartend for the night—and strained the cocktail into a short glass over ice. The liquid was fluorescent pink, a shitty excuse for a raspberry-vanilla vodka and coconut rum cocktail. He shoved it at Daisy.

"Should I be pissed?" Aiden asked. He rolled his bottom lip between his teeth. "I feel like an asshole for being pissed."

"Would Shannon cheat on you?"

"No, of course he wouldn't."

"Is Chelsea a threat?"

"No, but she's irritating. I would rather chug drain cleaner than be in her presence."

"Then, no, you shouldn't be pissed, but I get why you are." Daisy sipped 101's signature drink and gave a thumbs-up. "This is good; it tastes like I'm not getting laid tonight."

Aiden tried not to laugh, but he did, and Daisy laughed right along with him. She shrugged and shook her head. She had festive pink bows pinned above her ears and a heart-shaped button fastened to the front of her cropped black jacket.

"Heard from Vance or Jonathan?" Aiden tested.

Daisy's eyes snapped forward, a warning. She sipped her drink and shook her head. *Don't go there* rang loud in the silence, a testament to their train-wreck of a youth, before she sighed and said, "Are you going to fight with Shannon over this tonight? Because you shouldn't."

Aiden accepted the swift subject change. "Chelsea is super-hot. She's a fucking Barbie doll, and she's smart, and she made something of herself, she's..." He paused, reigning in his emotions. There was no need to shout about her success. He was sure Chelsea would be doing enough of that for everyone. He finished softly, growling out the words. "She's a *doctor*, Daisy."

"So?" Daisy shrugged. "You're hot, too. Look at you." She flicked her index finger up and down. "You're ridiculous. Don't even get me started; you have nothing to worry about. Who cares if she's a doctor?"

"Yeah, whatever, but I'm not like her, okay?"

Daisy made a dismissive noise. "Do you think Shannon really cares about that? He looks at you like you hung the goddamn sun, Aiden. You guys have a hell of a sex life. You go on dates at least twice a week. He bought you a camera, which means he actually pays attention." Aiden opened his mouth to interrupt, but Daisy flashed her palm, silencing him. "He dresses like an asshole sometimes, but I mean, c'mon, we dress like assholes, too." She sipped her drink, pointed her pinky at him, and said in a voice made raspy by the alcohol. "Don't compare yourself to what *he* left behind."

Aiden shrugged while he dried a batch of freshly washed glassware.

"I want to meet this chick, this *Chelsea*. I bet you anything she isn't all that."

Aiden looked down his nose at Daisy. "She's beautiful, and intelligent, and awful."

Daisy shook her head confidently. "Doesn't matter."

"You want to meet her?"

"I want to meet her," she confirmed through a hard nod.

Aiden walked toward the center of the bar, eyeing Daisy as he went. "Fine," he said, and helped a group of customers that bellied up to the bar for 101's terrible signature cocktail.

00:00

SHANNON TOOK CHELSEA TO THE Whitehouse, a safe restaurant that was half-bar, half-eatery. There was no confusing it for something romantic, he hoped, and Aiden was aware it was a place Shannon went with his friends—Karman's favorite bar, Shannon's favorite appetizer specials, an easy, familiar place and a Laguna Beach staple. Chelsea would enjoy the laid-back, chic atmosphere.

They sat on the restaurant side in a small booth by the window. Chelsea smiled, glancing at the menu. Her hair was arranged in a fancy braid, and she wore a gold necklace he recognized from their childhood. Looking at it, a locket strung around her throat, made Shannon think of all the times he'd caught her reapplying makeup on their cheesy teenage dates. Even now, years later, it looked like a noose.

"Are you getting excited about your month?" Shannon asked.

"Oh, no, I'm terrified," she sang, grinning at her hands folded neatly on top of the menu. "I don't know what I'm doin' here, but it was better than bein' there. I don't know what to expect, and I hate not knowing. What was it like for you? Making yourself love him, how'd you do it?"

"I didn't," Shannon bit. "Loving him just happened."

Shannon's lungs fluttered and tightened. He hadn't told anyone that. Not even Karman. Shannon was suddenly aware of every move he made, every scratch of his nail against the frayed edge of the menu, every clink of the ice cubes in his glass of water. It was such a strange thing, hearing it out loud. He steadied his breathing, glanced up, and met Chelsea's ever-knowing smirk.

"So, you *do* love him. How?"

"You know, you two are a lot alike. I have a type: blunt and cruel."

Chelsea shrugged, batted her lashes, and waited.

"I didn't..." Shannon paused as the waiter stopped by their table. They ordered a platter of fried seafood to start. Chelsea asked about every salad until she narrowed her decision to a classic Caesar, and Shannon ordered linguini.

Chelsea resumed her patient stare, twirling her straw with two fingers.

"I didn't make myself love him, it just happened that way. I knew it would, but I didn't know when, and I haven't told him yet. You can't say anything, Chelsea. You can't use this as ammo in an argument you two get into, you hear me? I'll never forgive you if you do."

"Who says we'll get into an argument?"

Shannon narrowed his eyes.

"I wouldn't do that to you, Shannon. You may think I'm cruel, but I'm not that kind of cruel. Are you going to tell him?"

"Yes." Shannon winced when his voice shook. "Sometime soon, I think."

"How did you make it work...?"

This, Shannon could tell, was an actual question. Chelsea's voice had lowered into something weak, and she pulled her hands into her lap, hiding her nervousness. She stared at the table, thanked the waiter when he served their appetizer, and cleared her throat.

"I mean no offense, so don't get all mad, but you two aren't the typical couple. He's not... He's not what I thought you'd ever want, but somehow you love him. How'd you do it?"

"You keep asking me how, and I don't have an answer, Chels." Shannon laughed. "I always thought the Clock would give me someone safe, someone predictable. Aiden is... He's always there, whether he's in the back of my mind, or sleeping next to me. Things changed when I met him, I stopped thinking about my life and I started thinking about his, and now all I can think about is *our* life. If we'll have one, if we're building one together, what will happen if I ever lose him. And..." Shannon huffed. "You've *seen* him, right?"

Chelsea wore her wounds as badges, and Shannon realized as soon as he'd asked that he'd wounded her. She cut a piece of fried shrimp and dipped it into spicy garlic sauce. She chewed slowly, giving ample time for Shannon to digest what he'd said.

"I meant to ask, did you go on dates? Did you communicate properly? Was there ever a time you had to figure out a problem together? How did you introduce each other to your families? You know—normal things. But I'm glad he makes your world spin the right way, sweetie."

Shannon's cheeks burnt. His lips pinched together. "We're still working on our communication. We're not… Karman says we're more physical than emotional, I guess she's kind of right."

The waiter set their entrees in front of them.

Shannon hadn't imagined dinner conversation with Chelsea going in as many different directions as it was. He hadn't expected her to ask about Aiden, since she clearly wasn't fond of him, and he hadn't expected her to question the Clock. She'd always said she'd let it happen the way it was supposed to, but that was when she'd tried to convince both Shannon and herself that they were destined to be together.

Aiden had thrown a wrench in her plan, and Shannon could see the gears turning as she tried to put together a new one.

"I know what we can do," Chelsea winked, and Shannon instantly regretted agreeing to dinner, because that was a typical Chelsea Cavanaugh gesture, one that said she had a proposition she wasn't going to let him get out of. "I bought two tickets to the Camellia Clock Preparation Panel at a convention in Los Angeles on March first, and I think you should go with me. They'll have all kinds of information, advice, how to's, support groups—"

"Absolutely not."

"Shannon Wurther, you're goin'."

"I am not goin' to some ridiculous Clock convention, Chelsea." Shannon's eyes squeezed shut. Georgia drawl swam in his throat.

"You *are* goin'! You're goin', and it's gonna be fun." She jabbed her finger at him. "And you're gonna be my emotional support," another jab, "and I'm gonna forgive you for sleeping with your boyfriend in my bed at my own party." Her lips pinched together.

Shannon opened his mouth, but stayed silent.

She leaned across the table and whispered, "How's that?"

Shannon's mouth quivered. He fumed, but there was nothing to say. This wasn't a battle he was going to win, not by a long shot.

"Mmhm," Chelsea hummed, drizzling dressing on her salad. She raised her brows; a pleased smile curled her lips. "That's what I thought."

33

SHANNON ENDURED AIDEN AND DAISY'S cackling on Monday, Karman's constant research about the convention on Tuesday, and Chelsea's nonsensical positivity on Wednesday. Throughout the rest of February, he tried to keep the topic of the convention from passing between him and Aiden, but Aiden's teasing was relentless.

On Saturday, Shannon wove through the bustling crowd of convention-goers with Chelsea by his side. The Los Angeles Convention Center was a sea of future Rose Roads, all disconnected, wandering between panels, taking notes in journals, and scoping the exhibitor hall.

After they spent far too long in the exhibitor section, Chelsea dragged him to the Preparation Panel.

"This is what I came for," she whispered.

Shannon nodded. The lights dimmed.

"Just to be ready, you know?"

Shannon nodded again. Chelsea Cavanaugh might have been the only person Shannon knew who was more self-aware than he was. Not only did she pick apart her faults with distinct precision, but she constructed intricate plans to fix herself, whether she needed fixing or not. Like Shannon, who rehearsed even the simplest statements before they left his mouth, Chelsea was a creature constructed of many possibilities. Unlike Shannon who broke them down, Chelsea swallowed them whole.

A woman walked across the stage; her fiery red hair was distinct against the blue backdrop. She wore a simple black dress and smiled behind a cordless microphone. He recognized her from somewhere, TV probably, and wasn't interested in a word she had to say.

"Margot," Chelsea whispered in Shannon's ear. "She's the leading couple's counselor for Rose Road management. You remember her, right? She's written five books and had that television special on Fox last year."

Shannon nodded. No, he didn't remember and he didn't care, but Chelsea wouldn't want to hear that. He pulled out his phone midway through Margot's speech, typed a message, and hit send. Aiden replied immediately.

Shannon Wurther 3/1 2:34 p.m.
what are you doing?
Aiden sent a picture of his running shoes.
Shannon Wurther 3/1 2:35 p.m.
talk to me im bored
Aiden Maar 3/1 2:36 p.m.
I was busy being fit and healthy
Shannon Wurther 3/1 2:36 p.m.
send me another picture
Aiden sent a picture of his bare foot.
Shannon Wurther 3/1 2:38 p.m.
ew put that away
Aiden sent a picture of his bare upper half.
Shannon Wurther 3/1 2:40 p.m.
☺
Aiden Maar 3/1 2:41 p.m.
go speed date
Shannon Wurther 3/1 2:43 p.m.

no
Aiden Maar 3/1 2:45 p.m.
im going for a run
Shannon Wurther 3/1 2:46 p.m.
no
Aiden Maar 3/1 2:47 p.m.
Yes

Shannon shoved his phone in his pocket and glanced at Chelsea. She was transfixed, gaze pinned to Margot. She drew in a slow breath, listening as Margot explained, in vague but exuberant details, the keys to walking a Rose Road without tripping.

"In most cases, the Camellia Clock will make the correct decision. By most cases, I mean ninety-eight percent of them. That's a big percentage, and it's the reason we, as a community, keep using the Camellia Clock today." Margot paused to allow for applause.

Chelsea clapped politely. Shannon did not.

"Divorce rates have declined exponentially."

More applause.

"Families are staying together, guided by energy," Margot held out her arms, "by *fate*."

Applause, and cheers, and whistles. Shannon rolled his eyes.

"It goes without question that fate can change, but it isn't typical, not in the slightest. One in ten thousand Clocks will speed up, changing the original data collected at the time of birth, one in ten thousand will slow down, and, in the rarest cases, Clocks that have timed out once may start counting again. A restarting timer is one in a million."

Shannon thought of Karman, and he hoped.

"Timers can go off for couples; they can go off for triads, too, and even quartets. But what happens after the Clock stops? That's why we're all here, isn't it?"

Chelsea nodded. Shannon couldn't tell if she'd blinked.

"A Rose Road is a beautiful, blooming flower. It needs care. It needs patience and room to grow, but if you give it what it needs, something precious will take root. Several different things can happen, the first being abrupt confusion; that's the typical response."

True, Shannon thought.

"The second being resentment. You did not decide this, and sometimes our hearts and minds don't align. Resenting each other in the beginning is also quite normal."

Shannon lifted a brow, intrigued.

"Third, you both make a choice. That choice is a subconscious one. Physical…" Margot held out one hand, then the other. "Or emotional."

A couple people whistled.

Margot acknowledged them with a nod and a wink. "You'll make this decision without knowing it. From what I've seen, most couples start out as emotionally receptive to one another, which is extremely beneficial to establishing communication. However, physical couples tend to become closer in a shorter amount of time."

Shannon thought back to the Saloon. He remembered looking at Aiden, painted like the dead, dangerous and beautiful, and wondering *how could he think I don't want him*? It was a sudden thing, making the conscious choice to fall into him that night, and it was strange to hear about it now.

You'll make the decision without knowing it.

As if Aiden was a decision Shannon had made long before they met. The idea made sense in an eerie, uncomfortable way.

"Statistics show that physical Rose Roads move in together quicker than their emotional counterparts, but are lacking in the communication department. Over time, these two segments of your relationship will merge," Margot said.

"Which one did Karman say you were again?" Chelsea whispered.

"Physical."

Chelsea's lips flattened and she dipped her chin to giggle at her lap. Chelsea had a nice laugh when it wasn't forced.

Margot continued. "It's theorized that fate has a pattern. We've found that genetically, energy replicates again and again. Usually, the Camellia Clock will make pairings that are much like the pairings before them. A person will be paired with someone like their mother or father, brother or sister."

Shannon watched Chelsea's smile fade.

"However, that is speculative at best. Now, let's answer some questions, shall we?"

Chelsea stared at Margot; her lips were drawn into a frown. Shannon was reminded that Chelsea was capable of being afraid. The frown was gone before he knew it; her fear was replaced by feigned excitement, forged well enough to almost put him at ease. Almost.

"This is something, isn't it?" She clapped along with the crowd. "It's nice to see all these people here, making an effort to be the best Rose they can be for their Rose Roads, you know?"

Shannon nodded. He patted her knee, and Chelsea glanced at his hand.

"I'm still terrified," she admitted.

Shannon nodded again. "Me, too."

00:00

IT HAPPENED AGAIN.

The world turned, but Aiden couldn't feel it. There were sounds, but he couldn't hear them. He told himself to get up, to reach for his phone, to breathe, but he couldn't. There was nothing like it—the inability to gather oxygen. Exhausted after waking, anxious, in a dark room, hoping that no one came looking for him, Aiden curled up under his comforter.

It was too soon, he thought. April eighth was too far off to warrant such complications.

Yet, there he was, complicated.

The bedroom door opened. He pulled the comforter tighter around his face.

"Nope," Daisy chirped. "No, you're not doing this."

Aiden said nothing. The energy it would take to speak wasn't worth sparing.

"Aiden, let me in." She tugged at the comforter. He gripped it between his fingers until his hands shook. "Aiden Maar, you let go of this blanket. We're going to the beach."

"I can't," Aiden said.

He must've sounded weaker than he thought, because Daisy quieted. Seconds went by, all the time it took for Daisy to understand, and the bed dipped. She'd been through this with him before, so many befores that Aiden was embarrassed she had to go through it again. One arm squirmed beneath the comforter, followed by the rest of her. Daisy crowded against him, occupying the space he couldn't find. Everything outside his body was void. The only thing he managed to do was count his breaths, one right after the other.

"I can call Marcus," she said gently.

He shook his head.

"I can call Shannon."

His eyes widened.

"Can you talk?"

He shook his head again. Talking would require movement, and if he tried to make anything except his lungs work he might suffocate.

Daisy rested her palm on his cheek. "This is me," she said slowly. "Daisy Yuen, I'm right here, and so are you."

One breath. Two.

"You're Aiden Maar, and you are my best friend, and you're going to be fine."

Three. A fourth.

"It's a Sunday afternoon in Laguna Beach, the second day in March, and it's beautiful outside. The sun is shining. Birds are singing. You're not dying. You're here with me. You're alive."

Five. Six. Seven.

Daisy nodded.

He nodded back.

"Say your name."

"Aiden Maar," he whispered.

"Say my name."

"Daisy Yuen."

Daisy sighed, and Aiden thought it might've been the first sound he'd heard that day. He stopped counting his breaths and blinked, aware that his hands were occupied by Daisy's, curled in a ball against his sternum. She gripped and he gripped back.

"Aiden, it's been six years," she said. "You have to go see your doctor."

"It doesn't happen often. I don't know why it happened today."

"Does Shannon know?"

"About the dysthymia, yes. About the disassociation, no." Aiden untangled his fingers from Daisy's and rubbed his face. "There was me before my parents died, and there's me after. I guess this is what after looks like; can't do anything about it except deal."

"What happened doesn't define you, you know that. You're more than a before and after."

Aiden pulled her against his chest, and she wrapped her arms around him. This was real. He was alive. He could breathe. "Maybe," he said.

"Not maybe, definitely. Can you eat?"

"I should," he admitted.

"We'll eat then. Are you ready to go outside?"

"Yeah, just not alone."

"You're not alone!" She laughed against his neck and squeezed him tighter.

The anxiety melted, a candle burning out. "Daisy to the rescue."

"You don't need rescuing. You need a Togo's sandwich with extra avocado."

Feelings returned in flashes. He smiled, and there was warmth. He laughed, and it tickled his stomach. He stretched, and the world came back together, turning and turning.

"Good?" Daisy patted his shoulder.

Aiden slid out from the comforter. Mercy meowed from the doorway.

"Good," he said.

You're not dying. You're here with me. You're alive.

Aiden wanted to believe it. God, he wanted to.

34

DAISY HAD LEFT HER PURSE at work. That wouldn't have been a problem, but without her wallet, which was inside her purse, she couldn't show her ID. That was a problem.

"Go with her to Irvine. I'll meet you guys at the outdoor mall in an hour," Shannon said. He resisted the urge to check his phone. It had vibrated, and he'd stashed it away when he saw that it was the saleswoman from *Laguna Beach Canvas & Sculpt* calling. A few minutes later, it'd started ringing again, and now a single buzz alerted him to a new voicemail.

"We don't have to go out tonight, guys. We can always get stuff and drink here." Daisy flopped on the couch and hoisted Mercy into her lap.

"That we can," Aiden said. He shrugged at Shannon. "You can grab some clothes from your place and spend the night?"

Shannon had been waiting for a reason to sneak away. If going to collect clothes was his opportunity, then he would take it. "Yeah, that's fine. I'll go right now."

"Let's all go. We can run by the store on the way home." Aiden reached for his jacket.

"No, no, that's okay." Shannon plucked his keys off the kitchen counter. "You guys go to the store, get whatever you want. I'll only be a few minutes."

"That's stupid. Why drive two cars?" Aiden narrowed his eyes.

Shannon chewed on the inside of his cheek. It wasn't necessary to pick up the Nichole Scott painting, but, if he didn't, it would be all he could think of for the rest of the night. Only one thing would deter Aiden from trying to accompany him.

"I have to meet up with Chelsea. She left her sweater in my car last weekend. I didn't realize it until I dropped her off after the convention, so."

Aiden groaned and rolled his eyes. "Fine, whatever. Daisy, it's you and me. We should probably get some food, too, now that I think about it."

"Pizza," Daisy said.

"And hot wings," Aiden added.

"Lots of ranch." Shannon put his sunglasses on.

Daisy rifled through empty bags of seaweed-chips and wasabi peas until she found her car keys on the coffee table. "Should we get potato wedges, too?"

Aiden said, "Obviously," while Shannon said, "Yes, please."

Shannon descended the stairs first and listened to the two of them bicker as he made his way to the Jeep, parked next to Daisy's shiny new Scion FRS.

They went their separate ways. Daisy and Aiden headed south, a rampage of bass echoing from the open windows. Shannon watched them disappear down the road, turned on his blinker, and headed past his loft into downtown.

"IT'S PRETTY, RIGHT?" SHANNON RAN his hand along the top of a simple black frame; the Nichole Scott painting was mounted in its center.

Chelsea leaned against the back bumper of the Jeep and tilted her head. "That's for Aiden?"

Shannon nodded.

"It's different…" Chelsea looked at it owlishly. "In a good way," she added, waving her hand at him. "Like, a weird, kind of cool way. They're real flowers?"

"Yeah, freeze-dried and clear-coat preserved."

"And to get it you had to lie and say I needed something?"

Shannon sighed, nodded, and offered her a smile. "We're having pizza and drinks tonight at Aiden's place. You're more than welcome to come."

He was sure she would decline. No force on this planet would make Chelsea Cavanaugh want to spend an entire night with Aiden Maar. That, Shannon was certain, would render an absolute and solid "no thank you."

"Oh, yeah? Well, that sounds fun. I'd love to."

Shannon's face must've shown a variety of expressions other than positivity, because Chelsea pursed her lips and reeled back.

"Shannon Wurther, don't pity-invite me places!" She whacked his arm, and he flinched. "If you don't want me to hang out with you, don't bother tryin' to be nice about it!"

"That wasn't it!" He backtracked, shielding the frame under his arm in case she aimed another strike at him. "I just remembered that we ordered a medium pizza. Let me text Aiden and tell him to make it a large. You like buffalo wings, right?"

Nose high in the air, Chelsea folded her arms across her chest. Her long sweater swayed around her ankles as she shifted, adjusting the top of her jeaned shorts. "Honey barbeque if you don't mind," she chimed.

Shannon Wurther 3/7 5:56 p.m.

dont get mad

Aiden Maar 3/7 5:57 p.m.

What

Shannon Wurther 3/7 5:57 p.m.

chelsea is coming over

Aiden Maar 3/7 5:58 p.m.
NO

Chelsea ran her fingers through her hair and shot a stern glare at him.

Shannon Wurther 3/7 5:59 p.m.
please shes all alone out here aiden please dont be a dick right now
Aiden Maar 3/7 6:01 p.m.
omg fine whatever she better be nice
Shannon Wurther 3/7 6:01 p.m.
Honey bbq wings please
Aiden Maar 3/7 6:02 p.m.
wow ok

"It's takin' a while to change that pizza order, Shannon," Chelsea said. Shannon rolled his eyes. "Go grab clothes. We're staying the night." Chelsea's flip-flops smacked the sidewalk.

Shannon Wurther 3/7 6:04 p.m.
extra lg pizza

Aiden sent a crude picture of his middle finger.

SHANNON STEPPED OVER A PAIR of knee-high black boots, and then over a hairbrush, carefully making his way to the TV remote on the other side of the couch.

Daisy had commandeered Aiden's living room. It might as well have been her bedroom. The couch was made up with four different blankets, and the coffee table was now a desk, littered with tea bags and Daisy's laptop, sketchbooks and expensive drawing pens. Her unzipped suitcase was under the table, displaying rumpled articles of clothing shoved this way and that, and hollow in the middle where Daisy had clawed her way through the mess.

Chelsea stood behind the couch staring at the artwork that adorned the walls.

The front door opened, and Daisy gasped, hurrying to set down the two liters of juice.

"Oh, Shannon, I'm sorry." Daisy zipped her suitcase, closed her laptop, snatched up some of the trash on the coffee table, and kicked her shoes into a pile against the entertainment center. She glanced over her shoulder as Aiden toed the front door shut. "Aiden, do you need help?"

Aiden balanced a case of beer under one arm and held a paper bag in the other. Bottles clanked when he set the bag on the kitchen counter. "I'm already inside, so no." He glanced at Chelsea, then at Shannon. "How'd you beat us home?"

Shannon shrugged. "I don't know. What took you guys so long?"

"Aiden couldn't decide on which alcohol to buy," Daisy said.

Shannon nodded. That made sense. "What'd you end up getting?"

Shannon peered at Chelsea and patted the space beside him on the couch. When Chelsea sat, Mercy hopped on her lap, startling her.

"Both!" Aiden pulled a bottle of bourbon out followed by a bottle of tequila. "Hi, Chelsea," he said from the kitchen. It was mildly sarcastic, but Shannon could deal with mild. "Have you met my roommate, Daisy?"

"Hello, Aiden. It's nice to see you again, and no, I haven't had the chance to." Chelsea's eyes widened when Daisy flopped beside her.

Daisy plucked Mercy from Chelsea's lap. "Not a cat person?"

"I enjoy them, but I prefer horses. It's a pleasure to meet you, Miss Daisy."

"*Miss* Daisy," Daisy parroted, brows climbing on her forehead. "I like her, Aiden. She could get a job as a Disney princess."

"Oh, bless your heart," Chelsea cooed, flapping her hand.

Aiden barked a laugh from the kitchen. "That was definitely southern for 'fuck you.'"

"Was it?" Daisy sucked in an exaggerated breath. "Be honest, if it was, I'll be impressed."

"It was," Shannon confirmed.

Daisy tipped her head and grinned.

"Well, it's clear as day that you two have known each other for some time. Friends, I'm guessin'." Chelsea gestured from Daisy to Aiden with a flick of her wrist. "How nice."

"Chelsea," Shannon warned, as if he tugged a leash.

Chelsea and Daisy stared at one another, Daisy wearing an amused smile, and Chelsea trying not to bare her teeth.

"We went to high school together. Speaking of high school, I think I'll start drinking now." Daisy hoisted Mercy into her arms and carried her into the kitchen. "I don't think I've had tequila since senior prom."

Aiden snickered, messing with something on his phone. "You threw up on my shoes."

"You told me tequila went bad if you didn't finish it after it was opened; that was entirely your fault." Daisy hovered close to Aiden, and Shannon caught the hushed movement of their lips, confirming that they were discussing something. That something was Chelsea, Shannon was sure.

Shannon tapped Chelsea's shoulder, and she tensed. Her gaze shot sideways.

"Relax, Chels. They don't bite," he whispered.

"Oh, I know for certain that one of them does; I've seen it." She circled her index finger around Shannon's throat. "Don't be actin' like I'm the one being strange."

"It wouldn't kill you to chill out."

"It wouldn't kill *them* to be polite."

"Pizza's on its way!" Aiden hollered. Two glasses clanked. "Anyone else want a drink?"

Daisy appeared next to Chelsea like a phantom. Neither Shannon nor Chelsea had heard her. Daisy pulled her feet onto the couch and rested her chin on top of her knees.

"Here, Charm School, I made you a drink." Daisy held out a cup filled to the top with a mixture of something that smelled fruity.

"Excuse me?" Chelsea glanced from the drink to Daisy and back again.

"She calls me Abercrombie," Shannon said through a heavy sigh. "Just go with it."

Chelsea frowned, but took the drink.

"You're extremely pretty," Daisy said, eyeing Chelsea as she sipped her apple-tequila-nonsense.

Shannon glanced at Aiden, who leaned against the kitchen counter and watched.

Chelsea hummed pleasantly. Her gaze traveled from Daisy's folded legs to her face in one blink. "Well, thank you very much. You're quite pretty yourself."

Aiden grinned at Shannon.

At least the hard part was over.

00:00

Somewhere between Aiden's second and third drink, the pizza arrived, accompanied by wings and wedges. They'd pushed the coffee table against the wall next to the entertainment stand, and Daisy had stored her suitcase in Aiden's bedroom for the night. Four blankets stretched across the carpet, and pillows from Aiden's bed littered the floor.

Shannon lounged next to Chelsea, since she refused to leave his side, and Daisy occupied the couch with Mercy asleep on her stomach.

Aiden watched Chelsea, more or less annoyed. Chelsea, who wore her pedigree like armor, cast her pompous attitude around the room in less-than-stealthy snickers and eye-rolls. She sat against the side of the couch, close enough to Shannon that Aiden wanted to squeeze between them. There was no reason for him to be jealous, but for some reason Chelsea had that effect on him.

"You don't like olives?" Aiden noted.

Chelsea picked them off her piece of pizza and dabbed it with a napkin.

"No, I don't. You're perceptive, Aiden."

Shannon stared at the ceiling.

Since Chelsea had arrived, she'd been quiet and distant, judging every movement made and word spoken. Even after Daisy tried to slither past Chelsea's defenses, she continued to sneer, whispering to Shannon after Aiden spoke, smirking at anything Daisy said. It was, as Aiden liked to call it, fucking bullshit.

"What happened to you? Like, what messed you up this bad?" Aiden laughed and shook his head.

Chelsea glared.

"You can fucking hate me for the rest of our lives, but that isn't going to change anything." Alcohol boiled encouragingly in his veins. Shannon said his name, but Aiden continued. "I'm not going anywhere, and I don't know what kind of shit you've been through to make you as stuck up as you are, but I don't care."

This time it was Daisy who said his name. Aiden kept going.

"I get that I'm not one of your blue-ribbon champions, but if you plan on staying in Shannon's life you might as well get used to me. I get it, really I do." He held out his arms, waiting for her to interrupt. Chelsea was a silent statue with a pair of icepicks for eyes. "I'm not a cop, or a lawyer, or a doctor like your daddy—"

"Shut up," Chelsea snapped.

"Oh, did I hit a nerve? What? Because I'm not like your Ivy League bloodline, I'm not good enough?"

"You don't know shit about me, Aiden!" Chelsea slammed her hands on the floor.

Daisy bolted to the other side of the couch, away from where Shannon and Chelsea sat on the floor. Mercy darted into Aiden's bedroom.

Shannon shouted something, but Aiden was in the midst of exploding. He barely heard what Shannon said over the sound of his heartbeat in his ears. *Aiden, calm down. Chelsea, that's enough!*

"I know you're in love with my boyfriend, and I know you're a stuck-up bitch, and I know you pretend to have a perfect life, but if you do, then why are you here? Why, Chelsea? What are you scared of?"

Shannon was on his feet, but Chelsea shoved him aside before he could get between them.

Aiden stood. She was tall, but her nose was still a bit lower than his.

She shoved Aiden backward with both hands. "Go ahead, Aiden. You think you can talk to me like that? Go ahead! Act like you know everything in the world. I'm right here; you wanna say somethin', say it. I'm not scared of anything, especially not you."

"You're scared of *something*, and you're angry, and you're a grade-A asshole," Aiden growled. "Don't bother daring me when I'm the one who called you out. Sorry, Shannon hasn't run across the country to escape from me yet, but I can't help what he did to you. I didn't make that decision for him. Do what you need to do to make yourself feel better about it, all right?"

Chelsea's face tightened. Her whole body shook. "You've got a lot of nerve pretending you're on the same level as me. Thief, low life, nothin' but a goddamn waste!"

"At least I know what I am," Aiden hissed.

Shannon grabbed Chelsea's arm, but she yanked it away. "Shannon deserves better," she said slowly. Those words were bullets, aimed and fired.

"Keep it coming, Charm School. Go on, do it. Do it, Chelsea! Whatever it is you need to—"

A loud crack broke around Chelsea's open palm as it struck the side of Aiden's face.

Daisy's hands flew up to cover her mouth.

Shannon's breath caught.

Aiden took a step back. He rubbed the red mark that covered his left cheek. It took seconds for Chelsea to get a proper grasp of her actions. She gasped and stumbled over her words, whispered and then squeaked.

"Aiden... Oh, lord, oh, my god." She stepped toward him, but Aiden flashed his palm. "I am an absolute terror. I didn't mean to—I never, please believe me, that was—"

"Jesus Christ, Chelsea. Ouch," he whimpered, eyeing her carefully. The malice was gone. "I expected you to hit me, but not that hard. You done being pissed now? You feel better?"

Shannon might have been having a heart attack. He stood next to the couch, jaw slack, and stared at the two of them. Daisy tried not to laugh.

Chelsea's chin dipped. Her lips clamped shut, and she took a deep breath. Her eyes were misted over, but the tension was gone.

"Are you all right?" She touched his hand.

"I'm fine." His jaw clenched and unclenched; his eyes narrowed at her under a tense brow. "Don't worry about getting mugged. You could throw a mean right hook if you wanted to."

At that, Daisy did laugh.

"You shouldn't have said those things to me, and I shouldn't have said those things to you," Chelsea said. She shoved him gently, and, for the first time, Aiden was granted a real smile. "But yes, if you must know, I do feel better."

"Now that we've gotten that out of the way, can you stop acting like I'm trying to ruin your life by existing?" Aiden asked, exhaling a long, tired breath.

Chelsea looked hurt. "I'm sure I can manage that, yes."

"Good." He rubbed his cheek and waved toward the blanket fort in front of the television where Shannon stood, flabbergasted. "Back to our scheduled programming."

00:00

THE PIZZA WAS GONE. THE wings were gone, too.

Shannon plucked a cold potato wedge from the cardboard container. He glanced at his phone. 2:56 a.m.

Aiden was curled up against his legs with his head resting in his lap. Shannon stroked his hair, which had grown out over the months, and brushed his thumb along Aiden's cheek. Red outlines of Chelsea's fingers remained.

"He's right, you know." Chelsea sat across from him on the other side of the empty pizza box, playing with the ends of her sweater. "I'm a grade-A asshole."

"You both are," Shannon whispered. "None of that needed to happen."

Daisy shifted on the couch. Her arms were thrown over Mercy, who purred beside her.

Chelsea nodded. "Yes, it did. Aiden had a point to prove and he proved it. He's smarter than I gave him credit for."

"He pushed your buttons, Chels. He started a fight for no reason. It didn't need to happen," he reiterated.

"I said ugly things. I hit him *hard*," she said, sighing.

"Hell yeah, you did. I would've hit him, too." Daisy cracked her eyes open and smiled at Chelsea. "He wouldn't have done what he did if he was unsure of the outcome. He was trying to break you down."

"It worked." Chelsea sipped her fifth drink and winced. "God, how does he drink this stuff?"

"Years of practice," Aiden mumbled, stirring awake. "You intimidate the shit out of me."

"Me?" Chelsea laughed and took another drink. "*I* intimidate *you?*"

Aiden didn't open his eyes, but he craned his head in search of Shannon's hands. "Yes, Chelsea, now it's your turn. Say something true."

"You..." Chelsea paused.

She looked to Shannon, and he nodded.

The witching hours were beehives full of turbulent honesty.

"I'm jealous of you. I envy your ability to be whoever you want without repercussion," Chelsea said.

"Someone else go," Aiden said sleepily.

"I don't think I'll ever be as great as my dad, and I don't think I want to. I don't know if I have it in me to give up what he gave up," Shannon said. He leaned on the end of the couch so the back of his head was propped up by the armrest.

Aiden wrapped his hand around Shannon's thigh.

Daisy cleared her throat. "I ate a piece of salami by accident when I was in college and cried in the middle of the cafeteria."

Shannon tried to swallow his laughter, but Aiden didn't.

It was too late and too early at once, but it didn't matter. They laughed until it hurt, until Chelsea started to cry, and Aiden opened his eyes, and truths turned into confessions. They laughed until Daisy admitted that she'd been lonely for a long time, and they laughed until Chelsea started talking about her father.

Aiden sat up only to crawl between Shannon's legs. He leaned back against Shannon's chest, and Shannon wrapped around him.

"I miss my parents," Aiden whispered.

"I miss them, too." Daisy pulled Mercy closer to her face.

"What happened to them?" Chelsea, blissfully unaware, tilted her head. She took a sip of her drink and blinked, watching Aiden closely, with a blanket pulled around her shoulders.

"They died," Aiden said. Shannon felt Aiden's chest lift, a breath of preparation. "They went to Big Bear for their anniversary. I had a game—I played soccer," he clarified, leaning his head against Shannon's shoulder. "My grades were low so they benched me. The school told my parents. They left the cabin early to talk to one of my guidance counselors. Someone tried to pass in the opposite lane. It was a head-on collision."

Shannon listened, and kept still, making sure not to move suddenly or take long breaths, scared that if he did Aiden might flee, a startled bird, a flighty deer.

"Don't say you're sorry," Aiden said gently.

Chelsea opened her mouth.

"Don't say it wasn't my fault, either."

Chelsea closed her mouth.

Aiden took one of Shannon's hands and it slid it under his tank top. Shannon drew patterns on his stomach and listened to him breathe. He leaned his cheek against Aiden's temple, nosing along his jaw until Aiden tucked forward, taking shelter beneath Shannon's chin.

"It's against the rules of nature for me to like you, Aiden Maar," Chelsea said.

Aiden smirked, but Shannon could tell how close he was to falling back to sleep. His body was loose and pliant, his eyes were closed, and his breathing was slow. After six months, Shannon was still entranced by Aiden like this—too close to dreaming to be anything other than peaceful and uncomplicated.

"But I do." Chelsea sighed. "I'm rather upset at myself for it."

"It's okay, I like you, too." Aiden yawned. He curled up against Shannon's torso, legs kicked over Shannon's thigh. "But let's not get carried away. You're still a bitch. I'm still an asshole."

Shannon closed his eyes. He wasn't comfortable, but he didn't care, because Aiden was almost asleep.

"Cheers to being friends," Daisy said. Her arm dangled over the edge of the couch, holding an almost-empty cup. "And to fighting the good fight."

It was 3:32 a.m. A time full of secrets that weren't secrets and fears that weren't fears.

35

SHANNON SHOULD'VE TEXTED PIPER BEFORE they obtained the warrant. Karman disagreed and repeated as they drove in the I-5 fast lane that everything would go as planned.

Instinct was the first indication that things wouldn't go as planned. It nagged in his stomach, whispered in the back of his mind, *today isn't the day, turn around, wait,* but Shannon didn't listen, because Karman was rarely wrong.

Rarely.

00:00

DAISY YUEN 3/20 4:03 P.M.
Yo can I come kick it at your work tonight?
Aiden Maar 3/20 4:05 p.m.
yeah do it we can play pool when I get off
Daisy Yuen 3/20 4:05 p.m.
Rad. I'll bring you food.

Aiden sent four thumbs-up emojis.

00:00

"We should call for backup, Karman."

"We're here for the wife, not the dude. He wouldn't be stupid enough to stay here. Chill out."

Shannon adjusted his badge, then his gun. "I have a bad feeling."

"You're full of bad feelings. Get out of your head, Wurther."

A dog barked from the house next door. There was a pink Little Tikes tricycle in the driveway next to a beat-up Volkswagen. A rocking chair swayed back and forth on the porch. Someone had been outside moments before their arrival. They'd left their steaming cup of coffee on a dusty square table. The screen door had four locks. The front door behind it had two.

Karman knocked. Shannon kept his hands in front of him and not on his holstered gun.

The front door opened. Karman kept the screen door propped with her foot and flashed her badge.

Hollow eyes belonging to a scrawny woman with tousled dark hair and loose skin stared back at them.

"Mrs. Mortez?" Karman smiled pleasantly.

The woman gave a stiff nod.

"I'm Detective Cruz." Karman gestured to Shannon. "This is my partner, Detective Wurther. We have some questions; may we come inside?"

Mrs. Mortez attempted to slam the door. Karman's palm shot out, followed by the bottom of her boot. She kicked the door open. Mrs. Mortez yelled something in Spanish. Shannon's heartbeat sped up. He stole a glance at Karman, then into the house, back at Karman.

Karman shouted in Spanish. She didn't look back at Shannon. "He's here!" Karman drew her gun. "Get on the ground! You're under arrest!"

Shannon's hands shook. Something crashed in the far room, down the hall, next to the kitchen. Shannon could see the side of a sink on the left and heard muffled voices from a television on the right. Cartoons. The back door slammed.

"Karman, wait!"

00:00

DAISY SHOOK A PAPER BAG at Aiden as she walked up to the bar.

"You like falafel, right?"

Aiden nodded. Dysthymia was a bitch, and despite the years that passed and the fact that Aiden was perfectly capable of feeding himself, Daisy still brought him dinner from time to time. He'd never liked looking back on the extent of his high school wreckage, but Daisy's presence brought it to the forefront of his mind.

When he was sixteen, she'd made sure he ate, hid bottles of alcohol from him, and attempted to get him to graduate. None of her love could've kept him from derailing: not when she flushed the drugs down the toilet, not when they sat in companionable silence during the nights he refused to sleep, not when she cried to him after junior prom, *you're my best friend and you're gonna die if you keep this up! Don't take yourself from me, Aiden, don't you dare.*

But he didn't die, even if he thought he was going to, even if he wanted to.

Daisy went to college. Aiden stayed alive.

"Hey, you all right?" Daisy dipped the edge of her sandwich into a container of tahini sauce.

Aiden blinked the memories away. "Yeah, thanks for the food. What do I owe you?"

Daisy shrugged. "Don't worry about it."

"You sure you wanna hang out for four hours while I work?" Aiden crunched a green pepper.

"I brought my tablet; I'll doodle."

00:00

SHANNON HEARD THE FIRST GUNSHOT.

He didn't hear the second. His heartbeat was too loud.

Karman's voice was a siren, panic rising into high-pitched caution when she shouted, "Put her down!"

A little girl whimpered. Saliva pooled in Shannon's mouth.

"David, we can talk about this," Karman said.

David Mortez was as hollow as his wife. His eyes were sunken, two dull, dark orbs. The skin around his mouth was dry and chapped. His body was made of long arms and longer legs—a skeleton wearing a coat of ashen skin.

Shannon could've made the shot. If he pulled the trigger, he wouldn't hit the child in David's arms, the mess of shaking bones and pink ribbon pigtails. Shannon could've put a bullet between David's rabid eyes. His index finger twitched.

It comes with the job, son. One day you'll pull that trigger.

The little girl rambled in Spanish. David shoved the gun harder against her shoulder.

Karman said something to her gently, Shannon didn't know what.

"Put her down, and we'll work this out." Karman's hand tightened on her own gun. She gasped, holding her ground when David swept the gun out in front of him and aimed at her.

Shannon could've made the shot, but he couldn't pull the trigger.

David let the girl go. She crumbled by his feet. David's hands quaked around his gun, silver and small, pointed at Karman's chest. He stepped toward the back door.

"Stay where you are!" Karman stepped forward.

Another shot.

Shannon knocked Karman to the floor.

The bullet hit the wall behind them. Footsteps echoed off the back stairs, and the little girl crying by the television screamed. A car roared to life. Tires squealed. Karman stirred beneath him, her chest filling and emptying—a rhythm Shannon kept count of while his fingers went slack around his gun.

Shannon could've made the shot.

00:00

AIDEN WORKED BEHIND THE BAR, while Daisy sketched on her tablet in a booth.

Hours went by slowly at first, but steadily speeded up as the night went on. By the time Aiden was about to clock out for the night, 101 was packed. Herds of people came in for drinks after long days at work or for a mid-week meet up with friends. He was used to it and made cocktails two at a time, sometimes three at a time.

Carver had already approached Aiden about a promotion, and now that he could bartend during the week, Aiden was certain he'd be bumped up to lead bartender soon.

"Evening, what can I get you guys?" Aiden leaned over to catch an order of five drinks for a group playing pool. "I'll bring it out to you guys, all right? What's the tab under?" He listened, nodded. "Yeah, sure, no problem."

Aiden took the twenty, stuffed it in his pocket, and made margaritas. It was about time to clock out. After he ran the drinks and unloaded the dishwasher, he'd finally get a minute to sit. His feet hurt, another thing he was used to, and he curled his toes in his boots to alleviate the ache.

"Daisy?" Aiden carried the tray of drinks toward the pool tables, craning his neck to see if she was still doodling in one of the booths.

There was no sign of her.

He dropped the drinks off, thanked the customers for their patience, and went to the back to unload the dishes.

When he walked out, Daisy was nowhere to be found.

"Carver!" Aiden swatted the bar. Carver's green eyes flashed his direction. "Seen Daisy?"

Carver shook his head. "Saw her talking to some guy a few minutes ago. Maybe she's outside?"

Aiden shoved his helmet under his arm and nodded. "Yeah, maybe. See you tomorrow, man."

The back door was heavy. It slammed shut as Aiden looked at his phone, checking to make sure she hadn't texted or called.

"Aiden!"

Aiden dropped his helmet and his phone. His helmet carried more weight, and the crunch of it against the asphalt sent an echo around the empty parking lot. His phone clattered. It sounded like his body felt—brittle noises, bunched and sudden, the sound of his bones wincing.

Daisy hadn't screamed his name. Her voice was a gasp, a whimper, and a shout all at once.

It was an unusual feeling, the kind that came after an abrupt reaction.

Aiden's bones continued to wince.

He'd heard her, and then he'd seen her. He'd heard her, and then he'd gone cold. Emotions drained from him, a puddle beneath his feet. He shot toward the sound of her voice and the man who held her against the wall.

Aiden didn't bother saying *put her down* or *get away from her*. He ripped at the man's arms and kicked his legs out from underneath him. Daisy hit the ground and clutched her neck where fingers had been wrapped. She gasped and choked and crawled out of the way.

"The fuck, man—"

Aiden's fist knocked the rest of whatever the man was going to say out of his mouth.

The man reeked of booze and smoke. He lumbered forward; one of his knees smashed into Aiden's stomach. He was lazy in his intentions, swinging an arm haphazardly at Aiden's head and missing completely. He swung again and knocked Aiden's forehead against the wall. Fighting someone who was drunk wasn't fighting at all, and Aiden was aware of that. Adrenaline kept everything numb. Another weak strike busted Aiden's eyebrow. Aiden slammed the bottom of his boot into the man's kneecap, once, twice, until it snapped.

He heard Daisy call his name. He punched the man in the mouth again. And again. And again.

The man hit the ground. He moaned, clutching his knee. *Could he feel anything at all? Was he in pain? Did he regret it yet?*

Aiden swept his foot back, aimed, landed his laces on the side of the man's face. He kicked him again. And again. And again.

Time passed. He wasn't sure how much. It couldn't have been long.

"Stop! You'll kill him!" Daisy gripped Aiden's arms. He brushed her away.

Another kick. Blood splattered his jeans and he thought, *good thing I wear black.*

Daisy shouted, "You're better than this!" But it sounded as if it was being called across a football field. Aiden at one end, her at the other, the man at his feet, and his intentions solidly mounted in every strike he landed.

The man was almost unconscious. Aiden kicked him in the chest.

The back door opened. Daisy fumbled over an explanation.

"Aiden!" Carver's voice.

Warmth filled his nostrils, dripped over his lip. Aiden wondered if his piercing was still in, or if the man had knocked it out. He slouched against the wall. The sound of tires against asphalt mingled with Daisy's hiccups, and Aiden's heavy breathing, and the man's labored moans.

"Aiden!" Karman's voice.

Daisy sobbed beside him. She tugged at her skirt. Carver opened one arm, a shield, and she crawled under it.

The man stirred, tried to get on his feet. Aiden surged forward. Two hands latched around his forearms.

"Aiden!" Shannon's voice.

00:00

KARMAN AND SHANNON HADN'T SPOKEN, not since they finished giving their descriptions to the deputies. Social services took the child. The Anaheim station would send them any information they found on David Mortez and his wife. Shannon texted Piper once they were off the freeway.

Shannon Wurther 3/20 7:43 p.m.
We're fucking up this case
Piper Kapoor 3/20 7:34 p.m.
it's the beginning don't get discouraged

"We'll get him," Karman said, breaking the silence. "He can only get away so many times."

Shannon didn't say anything.

They got the call while they were on their way home, sitting in silence and defeat, wondering if they'd taken on a case that was too big for them, a case that came with sacrifices Shannon didn't know how to make. The call came in as any other call would. Dispatch read the description of those involved, and then gave the address.

Sexual assault. Female victim. Two men involved. It didn't register at first: not until Shannon repeated it in his head, the description, the address; not until he heard. Black and white hair.

"Daisy…" Shannon didn't know he'd said her name.

Karman asked, "Is Aiden working tonight?"

They looked at each other.

Karman grabbed the radio. "Cruz and Wurther in pursuit."

SHANNON FLIPPED AIDEN AROUND. KARMAN stood beside them.

Aiden's face was covered in blood, most of it his own, but some of it not. His nose poured dark red, and his eyebrow was split. Shannon's chest tightened. His stomach lurched. He stared, unable to tear his gaze away from the marks on Aiden's face, from the dark of his pupils eating away the brown in his eyes.

"Go." Karman pushed Shannon's shoulder. "You can't do this part; go get the assailant."

Shannon stumbled. Aiden swatted Karman's hand away from his face. Karman ushered him inside, and Shannon heard her say, "Let's get you cleaned up."

The man on the floor stood up. Shannon gave him a once-over: his face, mangled by Aiden's fists; his eyes, swollen slits; and his hands, red from where they'd landed on Aiden's eyebrow, his nose, and his mouth. Shannon looked at the man, he grabbed his gun, and before he could think or say anything, he shoved it against the man's temple. The man made a dismissive noise and went limp, probably unaware that the cold, smooth circle on his head was the barrel of a gun. "I should fucking kill you—"

"Wurther!" Karman appeared out of nowhere, as if she'd sensed Shannon's instability. Her fingers latched around his wrist. His index finger twitched on the trigger. "Put it down and get Aiden out of here. Deputies are on their way."

Shannon didn't move.

"Shannon!" Karman's fingernails dug into his wrist. "Don't do this to me tonight. Get your head in the game and get it together. I need to take Daisy to the emergency room. You need to get your Rose out of here, *now*."

Shannon lowered the gun, clicked the safety on, and holstered it. Karman nodded and pointed toward the Jeep.

Aiden was talking to Carver in 101's cluttered back room. He dabbed at his nose with a wet cloth, adjusting his bloodied septum jewelry. It was apparent he hadn't seen what Karman had, and that was a relief. Shannon put his hand low on Aiden's back. "We have to go. Now."

"It was self-defense. I saw it," Carver blurted. "They'll need my statement, yeah?"

"Yeah," Shannon said. "Stay put, Barrow will be here soon. Karman is taking Daisy to get checked out."

"Do I still have a job?" Aiden mumbled, wiping blood off his face.

Carver didn't miss a beat. "Sure do. Take tomorrow off. See you this weekend."

"Let's go." Shannon took Aiden's hand and pulled.

 36

SHANNON DIDN'T KNOW WHAT WAS sore and what wasn't. Aiden wouldn't tell him. He dabbed the cut on his brow and tried to bottle his annoyance when Aiden jerked away. The welt on his cheek was darkening into a bruise, and he licked the dried blood on the edge of his top lip.

"Stay still," Shannon said, keeping his tone as placid as he could.

"I'm fine, Shannon." Aiden looked away.

"Don't..." He breathed out the rest of what he wanted to say. *Don't lie. Don't pretend. Don't turn to stone.* "Let me do this."

Like a tripwire, Aiden snapped, "I said I'm fine!"

"You aren't, Aiden!"

Aiden shook his head. His weapon was silence, and Shannon couldn't stand it. He pressed the damp cloth against his brow, then the top of his lip, following Aiden's movements as he tried to dip one way and lean another. Shannon put his hand on Aiden's waist to keep him still, but Aiden gasped. He yelped, squirmed back on the counter, and shoved Shannon's hand away. Aiden's shaking palm gripped his side; a pained expression twisted his face so fast Shannon almost missed it.

"What is it? What..." Shannon's voice trailed off.

Aiden's nostrils flared. He rolled up the edge of his shirt and displayed a nasty bruise on the left side of his belly button, vibrant reds swirled with blackened violets, blotched and spread out among a city of broken capillaries.

Shannon's breath caught.

"He got a knee in," Aiden mumbled. "It's fine, it'll go away in a few days."

"You should've called me," he whispered, unable to tear his gaze from the mark on Aiden's body.

"Oh, okay," Aiden snarled. He pushed off the counter. His feet hit the floor, first right then left. "As soon as I saw a guy with his hands around Daisy's throat, my first inclination should've been to call you. Sure, Shannon, when hell freezes over."

"What if he had a knife? Or a gun?" Shannon had no idea why he was arguing, or why his voice raised, or why a pit opened in his gut.

Aiden favored his right side as he walked down the hallway. Mercy circled his feet. He paused to hoist her into his arms. Shannon wasn't used to Aiden's slow movements or seeing him bite back a wince.

"I would've taken it from him," Aiden said, glancing at Shannon over the curve of his shoulder. Confidence matched his level of restrained fury. His mouth tightened, and he took a sharp breath, absently stroking Mercy's head. "You see the bad guys from a good guy's perspective. I see them from their own. You have no idea what he would've done to her. The thought of it makes me wish he *had* pulled a knife, because I would've—"

"Killed a man? Or gotten yourself killed?" Shannon's eyes widened. He tore his gaze away from Aiden and pointed it at the ceiling. "Good plan, Aiden. Fantastic."

"Look, I know you think reciting Miranda rights and flashing your badge is the way to get things done, but sometimes shit happens. Sometimes there's no fucking time for playing cop. I watched someone grab Daisy by the throat and shove his hands…" Aiden's voice gave out. Shannon didn't look at him. "I watched my friend get assaulted," he finished stronger than he started, words crisp and even. "I'm not ashamed of beating the shit out of the guy who did it."

"I'm not asking you to be ashamed, I'm asking you—"

Aiden groaned and shouted, "Arrest me, Detective!" He slammed the bathroom door before Shannon could finish.

It took an insurmountable level of control not to follow him into the bathroom. Shannon had more to say, he had more to bitch about, more to throw in Aiden's face. Every rational part of him—and most of Shannon was rational—screamed to leave it alone. Aiden wasn't at fault. He was hurt, but he wasn't *hurt*. He'd done the right thing in a situation that called for drastic measures. Aiden was hurt, Shannon reminded himself, but he wasn't *hurt*. He heaved a sigh, frustrated with himself and with Aiden and with his job. Mercy waddled over and wound through his legs.

"Mercy, why am I like this? Why am I such an asshole?" He looked down, and she looked up, seated in front of his shoes, yawning.

Talking to animals was a habit Shannon picked up from Aiden. He could probably use more of Aiden's habits, now that he thought about it. Not that Aiden was the most level-headed man in the world, but at least he went away to be angry. Shannon shouted it, threw it against the wall, stomped his feet, and laid blame, even when there was no blame to dish out and no reason to be angry. Control was a fixed point in Shannon's line of sight; any blur around the edge and he was whipped into a cacophony of emotions he lacked the software to process.

The top of his hand brushed his holstered gun, and flinched as if he'd touched an open flame.

Aiden wasn't the one Shannon was disappointed with.

Twice he'd pulled his gun, and twice he'd been reminded how easily he could pull the trigger.

He walked past the bathroom and took off his belt. The gun went under the bed with his badge, his shoes, by the foot of the bed, his shirt wherever it landed.

Mercy's bowl was empty; he filled it. Aiden's bed was unmade; he made it. Dishes were in the sink; he washed them. Half an hour went by. The pipes continued to groan, and the water continued to run.

00:00

A<small>IDEN HAD A TOWEL DRAPED</small> over his shoulders and a pair of gray sweats on when Daisy opened the front door. He stopped in the middle of lighting a half-smoked cigarette he'd found in his ashtray and tried to meet her eyes.

Daisy cleared her throat and said, "Miss Cruz is here with me. Can she come in?"

"Cruz?" Aiden stepped inside and leaned on his right foot, peeking past the cracked door. He said her name again, louder. "*Karman?*"

"Yeah, yeah." Karman pushed the door open and closed it behind her. Her head turned one way and then another. She was much more cop than Shannon. Her curiosity was a search, and every item she looked at was a clue.

"He's asleep." He tried to straighten his back, to look confident in his own home. "Everything okay?"

Karman's faded-plum lips pressed in a thin line. She swallowed and jutted her chin toward the patio. "Can we talk?"

"Is there hot water left?" Daisy interrupted meekly. She twisted the sleeves of her sweater around her hands and pushed her knees together. A doll, Aiden thought, but stronger than she looked. He'd seen it, caught the fire in her helplessness. How she'd tried to stop him. *Stop! You'll kill him!* As if Aiden was a better brand of monster. *You're better than this!* Daisy's strength was in her ability to look at tragedy and give it a prettier name, to reign in nightmares and call them dreams.

He nodded. "Yeah, I left towels for you. Are you going to bed right after?"

She went from pulling her sweater down to rolling it up, shoving the sleeves to her elbows. A blue hospital band circled her wrist. "I was going to, yeah. Can I have Mercy tonight?"

"Of course."

Daisy examined the bruise on his side, inches below his rib cage. She lifted her chin and stared at him. Trembling lips clamped together.

She gave a curt nod, a wordless thank you. "He didn't actually... Just so you know, he didn't..." Daisy stopped and swallowed. "I'll see you in the morning?"

He nodded again. Daisy's fingertips trailed across the bruise as she walked by. They felt frozen, the touch of a corpse. A tight smile, soft and sad, accompanied fluttering nonsense. She might have said, "Thank you for everything," or "You're so fucking stupid," or "You didn't have to," but he didn't know. It was probably a mix, everything coming out at once. She stood on the tips of her toes and her arms felt frail around his shoulders.

"He might've killed me if you hadn't," she whispered, and that part he did hear.

Aiden squeezed her, such a tiny thing, and watched her walk down the hall. She took small, quick steps, and glanced into Aiden's bedroom as she went. Once the bathroom door was closed and the pipes started howling, he turned his attention to Karman. She was already fixed on him. Her lashes flicked from his bare feet to the tip of his nose.

He lit the stale half-smoked cigarette and closed the slider. It was an unfamiliar burn now. His lungs shriveled, his muscles relaxed, and his heart beat faster. He gripped the wall and looked out over the horizon where black sky met black water. "If you're here to lecture me, you can skip it. Shannon beat you to it."

"He put his gun to that man's head, Aiden."

Karman stared at him, but he refused to give her the satisfaction of staring back. He looked at the water and chewed on his bottom lip. A fern tickled his shoulder.

It wasn't unbelievable. Shannon was more than capable of letting his anger win. But the image that pieced together in his mind—Shannon's eyes changing from worried to vengeful, Shannon holding the barrel of a gun against the side of someone's head—made his stomach flutter. Aiden was glad he hadn't seen it.

"Why are you telling me this?"

She worked the bottom of a navy blouse out of high-waisted black pants, unfastened her pony tail, and ruffled her mane of curls. "You two are different brands of the same, you know that?"

"Again," Aiden gritted out, "why are you telling me this?"

"Because you need to think about that, Aiden Maar. My partner and I had a hell of a day today. He almost shot a man, rightfully so, but couldn't." She held up her hand, telling him not to interrupt. "Then he almost killed a man tonight because of his feelings for you. And not almost, if I hadn't been there, I'm just about positive he would've. You don't think that's something you should know?"

"If you're trying to make me feel guilty—"

"You're misunderstanding me," Karman muttered impatiently. Her tone dropped, the rough and calloused rasp fell away. "That man loves you," she stressed. A warm hand rested on Aiden's arm. "That's what I'm trying to tell you."

Aiden glanced at her, catching the wide-eyed, slack-jawed face of a woman who protected everything but herself.

"And one more thing, Aiden," she said. He turned, settling his gaze on her. "What you did tonight was brave. I've got a daughter at home waiting for me right now, and I feel safer knowing there's people like you in the world."

Responses built, assurances that he wasn't brave, he wasn't like her, and he wasn't like Shannon. But he couldn't get the words out. Karman's gaze stayed on him for a moment longer. He was a clue that she'd keep, Aiden decided. Karman tilted her head. Maybe she was trying to trust him. Maybe she was trying to scare him.

"Take the compliment," she snapped.

"Thank you, ma'am," Aiden hissed.

Neither one of them excelled at admitting when they were wrong. Aiden was wrong about Shannon. Karman was wrong about Shannon, too. They were both wrong about each other.

00:00

THE BED DIPPED. SHANNON OPENED his eyes, dangling between asleep and awake. Karman was gone; he'd heard her leave. Daisy finished her shower a few minutes ago; around the same time, Aiden had walked into the bedroom and closed the door. He saw the bow of Aiden's spine through the dark, saw his head resting in his hands. The pale expanse of his shoulders lifted around a weary sigh. Shannon knew that sound, exhaustion and nervousness and static energy. He knew when Aiden was too tired to sleep.

"You're awake," Aiden said.

Someday Aiden's observant behavior might be unnerving. But for now, Shannon took comfort in it.

Shannon sighed. "So are you."

Aiden set his hands on the bed and braced, sliding in beside him. A gust of air left him, snuffed out as soon as Aiden realized it was audible. The angry bruise on his side rippled under the strain of his flexed abdomen, and he muffled a long exhale as his body relaxed against the comforter. He was as quiet as a storm that passed in the night—raindrops on the roof, cracks of thunder too far away to rumble.

"Is Daisy all right?"

"No, but I think she will be." His gaze followed the twirling ceiling fan.

"I think so, too."

Quiet drifted over them again. Aiden's chest rose and fell; Shannon turned on his side to face him. All the places on Aiden that Shannon was convinced might hurt to touch, never did. He realized it then, as he examined the bridge of his nose, the round shadows beneath his cheeks, each curve and dip of his mouth, what used to scream *danger, danger* was overshadowed by staunch regality. There were few things in the world that Shannon appreciated in their rawest form, but Aiden was one of them.

Busted fingers stretched across Aiden's stomach. Layers of skin peeled up in patches on his knuckles, marking his hands deadly for all to see. Shannon took one of Aiden's hands, brought it to his mouth, and trailed his lips across the peaks of his knuckles.

The rise and fall of his chest paused, and Aiden lolled his head to the side. He watched Shannon through half-lidded eyes, buoyant gaze hovering around Shannon's mouth.

"I don't think the world will ever forgive you for loving me," Aiden said, hushed and gentle.

Shannon kissed the side of his hand, and then his palm, his wrist. He'd been waiting for the right time, as though there ever would be one, to tell Aiden that he loved him. He was going to make a speech out of it, Shannon decided, a proclamation that Aiden couldn't deny. As they ate sushi on the beach, or walked home from 101, or in bed as they tried to catch their breath. He'd thought about the ways he'd tell him, long-winded, pouring his heart onto the floor and hoping none of it spilled on Aiden's shoes, or straight-forward, saying it just as he should've months ago. A simple *I love you, Aiden Maar, please don't argue with me over it.* That would've done the job.

It wasn't warm, or new, or bright, or great, but it was enough.

"I don't recall ever asking the world's permission," Shannon said.

Aiden laughed. A reverent smile curved his lips. "So, it's true then."

"What is?"

"You love me."

He'd thought of a million ways to say *I love you* without ever saying it. "How could I not?"

Both eyebrows shot up, and Aiden grinned, daring Shannon to let him form a list.

"Yes, Aiden, I love you."

His grin faded, and he dragged the tips of his fingers along Shannon's lips. "That's a reckless thing to do."

"Sometimes I think you want it to be more reckless than it is."

"You're probably right."

Shannon curled over Aiden's torso, avoiding the bruise on his side, and gripped his cheek. Aiden searched for Shannon's lips in the dark.

"The world's never loved me, but I've loved the world. I think I love you more than anything else in it," Aiden said. "Sometimes I think you *are* it, sometimes I'm convinced you're what I loved about the world before I knew you, and now that you're here, I get it. I understand what I loved during all those years it never loved me back."

The barbs of Aiden's words sank in and pulled, anchoring Shannon to the bed, and to Aiden, and to everything else that encompassed the two of them. He sucked Aiden's bottom lip between his teeth, kissed him the way he deserved to be kissed—patient and deep and unhurried.

"The world loves you." Shannon sighed against his mouth. "And if it ever stops loving you, remember that I do."

 **37**

AIDEN SHOOED A SEAGULL AND brushed his fingertips across the wide pink and cerulean leaf of a potted caladium. The succulent in the middle of the table needed water, and the hanging basket of begonias hadn't bloomed yet, but when it came to his makeshift balcony garden, Aiden was pleased. The seagulls had only destroyed one of his ferns, and the rest hung over the balcony wall, fronds of emerald and jungle green.

He watched Daisy shuffle around the living room. They hadn't talked about it yet, but he was sure they would. Daisy was good at deflecting, almost as good as he was, but it'd been a week, and she couldn't keep skirting past the subject.

She cleaned the coffee table with orange oil, folded her mountain of clothes into a decent pile next to her suitcase, and arranged her shoes along the wall. Aiden stepped inside, closing the slider behind him.

"Daisy."

"What?"

"Stop cleaning."

"Why?" She furrowed her brows, glancing at him while she straightened the remote in the center of the coffee table. Her sketchbook was stacked on top of her closed laptop with pens placed perfectly in a row beside it.

"Because you're going crazy."

"I'm not…" She huffed, narrowing her eyes. "I'm not going crazy, Aiden."

"Do you want to talk about it?"

"Do *you?*" she hissed accusingly.

"Don't bring my shit up, that's not for two weeks. I'm talking about you. Do you want to talk about it?"

Daisy spun in a circle and started fluffing the couch cushions. She folded each blanket, and refolded them. "You were there. You beat his ass. What is there left to talk about?"

"There's a lot we need to talk about. Like for one, are you okay?"

Daisy stopped folding the blanket, the fourth one she'd picked up, and squeezed it against her chest. Her gaze fell to the floor, and she shifted from foot to foot. "I'm weak," she said. It was a plain statement, something she'd obviously discussed with herself many times. "I shouldn't be, but I am."

"What can I do to help you fix it?"

"I'm not something that needs fixing, just like you aren't something that needs fixing. We aren't ruined, Aiden. I'll be fine."

"Of course you will be. You aren't a full-blown disaster like me. But in the meantime, while you continue to show signs and traits of being a lesser, more manageable disaster, we should probably figure out a way to handle it."

"I'm… pissed!" Daisy threw the blanket at the couch. "I hate feeling like this! I hate not being able to fight my own battles. Don't you get tired of it?"

"Of what?"

"Not fighting back!"

Aiden tilted his head. "Sometimes. What should we do about it?"

"Fight!"

"Okay, we'll fight. Pick a class and I'll go with you. We'll learn how to fight."

"Our battles aren't the same." She threw her hands above her head and ran her fingers through her hair, merging strands of stark white and charcoal black. "I know what you're doing, okay? I get it, and you're good at it, but I know your game. You can't break me down."

"MMA, jujitsu, karate, what'll it be? Seriously, find a class and we'll go. We'll learn how to fight."

Daisy flopped on the couch. "Aiden... Stop, come on. That's not the kind of fighting you need to learn, all right?"

"It's the kind of fighting *you* need to learn, though."

Aiden's fight was with himself; Daisy's was with a moment.

Aiden leaned against the back of the couch. He looked at her, arms folded across his chest. Daisy gazed up at him. He watched her watching him, her eyes flicking from the almost-healed cut on his brow, to the faded bruise under his hairline. Aiden knew what she was doing, and Daisy knew what he was doing. They couldn't fix each other. They couldn't fight each other's battles.

"Fine, we'll take an MMA class. What're we going to do about you?" Daisy asked.

"That's not for two weeks."

"You don't have to keep punishing yourself, you know? You could let it go one of these years." Daisy covered her face with her arm; her chest rose and fell as she steadied her breathing. "Come here." She extended her arms toward the ceiling.

Aiden walked around the other side of the couch and dropped on top of her, bracing his elbows on the couch beside her shoulders. She wrapped her arms around him and made a small *oof* when he squished her under his dead-weight.

"Your birthday's coming up," Daisy whispered. She touched the back of his head and twirled her finger through inch-long hair, reminding Aiden that he was in desperate need of a haircut.

"Yeah, a lot of things are coming up."

The anniversary of his parents' death was twelve days away, a yearly battle he never won. Not that he fought back; Aiden never really had.

But that didn't stop it from being a war he waged within himself, one version of him screaming at the other. He had two parts—a before and an after. When they collided, Aiden was the outcome. He didn't know how to be anything other than his before and after.

"Don't disappear on me, all right? I'll worry," Daisy said.

"Stop cleaning things excessively; I'm already worried."

"Twenty-three, huh? What should we do to celebrate?"

"Jump off a cliff." Aiden laughed, but Daisy didn't. "I'm kidding, relax."

"It's not funny, Aiden." Her voice was small and far away.

Don't take yourself from me, Aiden, don't you dare.

Aiden's phone vibrated. He rolled off the couch, onto the floor, and felt along the top of the coffee table until it fell off and bounced against his leg. He held it above his head and swiped across the screen with his index finger.

Shannon Wurther 3/27 2:05 p.m.
how is daisy doing? still cleaning everything?
Aiden Maar 3/27 2:07 p.m.
Like a maid. we're going to take mma classes
Shannon Wurther 3/27 2:08 p.m.
Thats a good idea

"Shannon thinks it's a good idea for us to take MMA classes."

"Til I kick his ass!" Daisy exclaimed, mock punching the air with two scrawny arms.

Aiden Maar 3/27 2:09 pm
she says shes gonna kick your ass
Shannon Wurther 3/27 2:10 p.m.
I dont doubt it

Daisy's teasing faded, and the interlude of playfulness ended.

"We'll be okay, right?" Daisy's hand brushed Aiden's forehead, dusting his week-old bruise. "You're okay, right?"

He sighed. "I'm alive. So are you. That means we'll probably be okay at some point."

"Two weeks from now, will you be okay?"

Aiden looked up, and she peered at him. Daisy had seen him at his worst. He hoped she stuck around to see him at his best, if he ever had one. He smiled, but it didn't feel right, like the beginning of a lie.

Aiden didn't answer.

Daisy didn't ask again.

"Shannon told me he loved me," Aiden whispered.

Her fingers tapped the bridge of his nose. "How does it feel?"

"Heavy, like I'm not cut out for it."

"Do you love him?"

His throat clenched. "Yeah, I love him."

"Then it won't be that heavy for long," she said gently.

Aiden stared at the ceiling. Fire churned and simmered in his veins. He thought of Shannon and he thought of Daisy. He thought of his mother's smile. He thought of his father's laugh, and how much Marcus sounded like him. Wilderness grew inside of him.

He thought of Shannon first, and he thought of Shannon last.

Aiden Maar 3/27 2:21 p.m.
do you still mean it?
Shannon Wurther 3/27 2:22 p.m.
Mean what?
Aiden Maar 3/27 2:24 p.m.
that you love me
Shannon Wurther 3/27 2:27 p.m.
Yes

Aiden watched three dots bounce on his phone.

Shannon Wurther 3/27 2:29 p.m.
do you?
Aiden Maar 3/27 2:31 p.m.
yeah. when did you figure it out
Shannon Wurther 3/27 2:35 p.m.
New years
Aiden Maar 3/27 2:36 p.m.
I love you
Shannon Wurther 3/27 2:36 p.m.
I love you too

Maybe Daisy was right, maybe it wouldn't be that heavy for long.

"I found a Groupon for ten mixed martial arts classes, twenty bucks each!" Daisy shoved her phone in his face. "We'd start next week."

"Send it to me," Aiden said.

He wanted to type it out again and again. *I love you* after *I love you* after *I love you*. But he didn't, instead he typed out: *you were so incredible that night. you made me feel like I was worth it*

Shannon Wurther 3/27 2:37 p.m.
thats because you are worth it. I remember how you tasted. you had champagne all over your mouth. I remember how you looked in chelseas bed.

Aiden choked on a laugh.

"What's so funny?" Daisy tried to snatch his phone, but Aiden tucked it in his pocket.

How quickly things could change—from Halloween to New Year's, from New Year's to now.

"Nothing. You hungry? I bet Kelly's working."

Daisy lifted a brow. "Cheese fries?"

"Cheese fries," Aiden agreed.

00:00

SHANNON LOOKED AT CHELSEA OVER the edge of the glass tilted against his lips. The plate of stuffed mushrooms was growing cold between them, and Chelsea stared at him, open-mouthed and wide eyed.

"Someone... Shannon, someone tried to...?"

"Yeah, but Aiden was there. He beat the guy within an inch of his life."

"Well, sure he did! I would've done the same damn thing. Someone put their hands on a little thing like Daisy; I would've hit him over the head with a barstool!" Chelsea's accent thickened when she was angry, her vowels elongated and merged, loud and unabashed. Her presence was a reminder of home, of summer trips to the lake and the smell of homemade barbeque sauce. Somewhere between when Chelsea had made her unexpected arrival and now, Shannon realized he'd missed her.

Karman pulled out a chair and sat. "That was Barrow," she said, tapping her phone. "All charges against Aiden were dropped; it was ruled self-defense. Cindy just filed all the paperwork. The guy he kicked the living shit out of has a broken nose, fractured rib, busted knee, and a bruised ego. He'll do time after he gets out of the hospital."

"Does Daisy have to do anything else?" Shannon asked.

Karman shook her head. "I'm e-mailing her the information right now, but no, as far as Daisy and Aiden are concerned, case closed. Anyway, we aren't on the clock, so." She waved her hand dismissively. "Are you and Aiden doing anything next week?"

"Yeah, probably. Why?" Shannon's brow furrowed. "What's special about next week?"

Karman stopped typing. She flicked her gaze from Shannon to Chelsea and back again, with her bottom lip pinched between her teeth. "He didn't tell you, did he?"

"Tell me what?"

"Yeah, tell him what?" Chelsea leaned forward, a grin plastered across her face.

Karman swallowed. Shannon watched her lips part and her brown eyes soften under The Whitehouse's dim lighting. She cleared her throat and tucked her phone in her purse. "I'm going to the cemetery with Marcus to put flowers down for their parents. The anniversary of their passing is next week, on the eighth."

Shannon sat back. That, he thought, was behind Aiden's restlessness and distance. Not that he'd been distant physically, but sometimes Shannon would catch him gazing at nothing, trapped in daydreams. The reason behind his faraway thought was Aiden's past creeping into his present, and now that Shannon was aware of it, it seemed so blatant, so transparent.

Chelsea, realizing it wasn't gossip they were talking about, busied herself with her phone and the goat-cheese stuffed mushrooms.

It shouldn't have come as a surprise that Aiden wouldn't tell him about it. Shannon was aware that Aiden's twenty-third birthday was at the end of April—on the twenty-ninth—and he knew that Aiden wasn't one for celebrating it, but he'd never put the two together. Spring, as Aiden explained to him weeks ago, was *supposed to* be a time for rebirth. Shannon should've realized that when he said supposed to, he didn't mean would be.

Karman grabbed a mushroom and shoved it in her mouth. "Marcus told me Aiden doesn't do very well. I don't think either of them handles it in a healthy way, but, if I had to guess, I'd say Aiden is the more dramatic of the two."

"He talked about it, though," Chelsea chimed in. Her voice was a little unsteady as she tried to lighten the tone at the table. "We all… I mean, he told us about his parents and… Well, he didn't seem all right, that's for certain. But he did talk about it, which has to mean he's handling it on some level."

"You finally put them in a room together?" Karman mumbled, pointing at Chelsea.

"He was drunk." Shannon ignored Karman's question. He leaned on the back legs of his chair and stared at the ceiling. "He'd never talked to me about it in detail like that, not until you and Daisy were there, after the whole night fell apart."

"What happened?" Karman asked.

"I hit him," Chelsea said, shrugging.

Karman's head jerked back. "*She* hit Aiden?"

"He wanted her to," Shannon said, unfazed by the secondary conversation going on between Karman and Chelsea.

"We're friends now," Chelsea added matter-of-factly. "That's all that matters."

"My boyfriend, who has chronic depression, didn't tell me about the anniversary of his parent's death, the reason behind his chronic depression, and you two being friends is all that matters?" Shannon dropped back on all four legs of the chair.

Chelsea's cheeks reddened under the weight of his stare.

Karman cleared her throat again. "He'll be fine, Shannon."

Shannon shook his head. *No, Aiden wouldn't be.*

Aiden didn't hide from things. He didn't dodge a challenge or go around obstacles. The things Aiden feared were the things that wilted him, and they were few and far between.

Shannon was one of them. His parents were another.

"I can talk to him," Chelsea offered.

"No," Karman and Shannon said in unison.

"Well, fine!" Chelsea fumed haughtily, picking at a mushroom.

The detectives ignored her outburst.

"I can, though." Karman sipped at an almost-empty gin martini.

If anyone knew loss, it was Karman.

Shannon finished his beer. "You can, yeah."

ON APRIL FIFTH, AIDEN SENT a text to Shannon. It said: *I love you, don't come looking*

> Shannon responded four times. He called twice.
> Shannon Wurther 4/5 10:04 a.m.
> *i love you too. i get it but im here ok? let me come get you*
> Shannon Wurther 4/5 3:54 p.m.
> *Aiden please*
> Shannon Wurther 4/6 10:07 p.m.
> *Youre not home*
> Shannon Wurther 4/7 12:15 p.m.
> *you don't have to do this alone*

It was April eighth. The world was a spinning top stuck in place, wobbling back and forth but refusing to fall. No, Aiden decided, he *did* have to do this alone. There was no other way to do it. Alone, he thought, was the only thing that paralleled what happened when before was gone and after loomed on the horizon.

There had always been a before and after, but the loneliest part was the during.

In the space between, when Aiden remembered everything that'd gone wrong, he was immersed in the during. A state of unrest and silence, forged of complexities he didn't have the strength to identify. Memories crept by. The sound of Sasha's irritated voice. *Aiden Maar, you better listen. No son of mine acts up like that, you hear?* Followed by Christopher, a man who lived on in Marcus—his stature, his nose, his voice, everything. *Aiden, listen to your mother. We're leaving the cabin now. No, don't argue.*

Drowned voices. Aiden struggled to remember their faces.

He hadn't been there to hear the wreck, but every time he watched a similar collision happen in a movie, or heard someone slam on their breaks when they almost sped through a stop sign, he imagined what it would've been like. How do sound technicians gather the tools to construct such realistic noises? What does metal sound like it when it slams into another, heavier, denser block of metal? Teeth in aluminum, claws raking dusty glass, a symphony of quiet things made loud in one sudden blow? What do people say right before they die?

Did his mother whisper something, did she think of Marcus, did she think of Aiden, did she think of anything?

Did his father try to swerve, did the tires squeal when he hit the brakes, did he think *this is it, this is it, this is it,* did he assume they would live?

Metal against metal, tires seizing against the concrete, someone gasping, and then he imagined it was over. Aiden didn't have the heart to wonder if they'd died on impact, or if it'd taken a few minutes; if his mother had the chance to look at his father, if his father had the chance to look at his mother; if they had the chance to regret leaving the cabin, regret taking the vacation, regret a lot of things. Aiden wondered if his breathlessness was their ghosts, if the weight on his chest was their presence reminding him that he would never know. He would only ever be able to assume.

Aiden remembered the smell of acrylic paint on Sasha's hands and he walked into the ocean.

Slithering out to sea, climbing high, crashing down—the ocean was a constant loop. Waves tossed him around. His arms reached toward the darkness below while sunlight shot through the water above. Fingers stretched, toes curled in, Aiden held his breath until the breathlessness was overcome by the need to inhale. The cold Pacific numbed him to the bone.

Fate, come out. Fate, where are you. Fate, tell me why.

But fate didn't swim from its hiding place far out where Aiden couldn't see. The heart of the world didn't beat. All those mysteries, all those majesties, they cowered in Aiden's shadow, a cluster of worn, rusted, sharp things, under a shark swimming backward, confused by its inability to breathe.

Aiden was a blatant reminder that fate wasn't gentle. No wonder fate refused an audience. No wonder.

He broke the surface and sucked in a breath. His lungs expanded, jarred by the cold, and he kicked his feet, waiting for the next wave to pummel him beneath the water again. It happened. His limbs, jumbled one way and then another, lacked energy; his eyes stung when he opened them. Sunlight, filtered through navy blues and vibrant greens, fell upon his hands. Aiden looked at them, and then at the rolling swell of a wave as it passed overhead, and he asked again, *fate, why, why, why.*

Fate did not take his face in its hands.

Aiden swam to shore.

The sand was hot on his back as he lay down; he stared at the sun until his eyes began to water. Thoughts were not his own; they came and went one right after the other, and Aiden was not in his body. He tried to think of his name, the name Sasha had given him, but all he could hear was her irritated voice. He tried to think of Daisy, but the only thing about her he could see was black and white, the only thing about her he could hear was his name leaving her mouth a whimper, and a gasp, and a shout all at once.

That was his name—a plea.

That was his name—a something and a nothing.

Aiden thought of Shannon and he took another breath.

That was his name—a something, a something, a something.

A shadow crept across his face and blocked the sun. Aiden opened his eyes, and a man built of ages of wandering looked down at him.

"Where's your cat, wild boy?" Empty Man said.

Aiden turned to look at the cliffs, natural castles above the beach. Empty Man plopped down beside him, as invasive as ever.

"You're gettin' sand all over yourself. Where's your towel?"

"At home, same place my cat is," Aiden said. He didn't know he'd spoken aloud until Empty Man nodded.

"You ever let what goes, go?"

Aiden shook his head. "I'm working on it."

"Doesn't look like it to me, kid. Looks like you're waging war on all the wrong things."

"What do you know about my war?"

Empty Man laughed until he choked, and coughed until he was laughing again. "Still as wild as ever, I see. What were you lookin' for out there anyway? Nothing in that ocean for you except drowning."

"Maybe that's what I was looking for."

"You're too young to drown, too much of a lot of things to drown."

Aiden sat up. He wished there was a pack of cigarettes in his jacket, but there wasn't. His black jeans grew colder, sopping wet and clinging to his legs. It was the only thing he felt besides the breathlessness, a chill that crept through his veins, frostbite beneath his skin.

"If I want to drown, I'll drown," Aiden growled. He picked up a handful of sand and sifted it through his fingers.

"Yeah, sure. But here you are, on the beach, not drowning. C'mon, now. Don't act like you're ready to die when all you're asking for is a way to live."

"Not a way, just a reason."

Empty Man followed Aiden's nervous sifting and tossed a handful of sand on Aiden's lap. "You've got a reason; that's why you came to shore."

"All I've got is myself," Aiden snapped. He swept the sand off his lap and glared at Empty Man. He wore the same torn beanie, had the same weathered face, and his fingernails were still long and chipped. A brown coat, patched and sewn with different colors of thread, covered his shoulders. His shoes, still carrying all the places he'd been, had holes and rips and frays.

Empty Man stared at Aiden, and this time Aiden was sure Empty Man had seen a thing like him before. He looked at Aiden as though he was looking into a mirror.

Aiden wanted to run.

"You don't need any other reason to live than that," Empty Man said.

Aiden grabbed his jacket and stood up. "What do you know about living?"

"I know you've got enough to live for. Go on, eat the heart of the world, swallow it whole, be as wild as you keep tellin' yourself you're not. I see you, wild boy. I see you."

Aiden ran. He zipped his jacket as his feet hit the sand, one right after the other. In the distance waves crashed, and Empty Man laughed, and seagulls screeched, but the only thing he focused on was his breathing. *Inhale, exhale, hold.*

The ocean was a soundtrack.

Aiden's lungs burnt. He ran faster. He ran harder. The sun was high in the sky. It was too early in the day to feel what he felt. That, the spike of heat, the thaw, the surge of spring, of life, of *it's over*, that came when he tried to sleep and couldn't. It was too soon. He wasn't ready to be anything except ashes.

He wasn't ready to be on fire again.

Aiden ran, and ran, and ran.

SHANNON WURTHER 4/8 9:05 P.M.
Is he okay?
Karman de la Cruz 4/8 9:10 p.m.
Sort of
Shannon Wurther 4/8 9:11p.m.
Sort of? What does that mean
Karman de la Cruz 9:15 p.m.
It's up to him at this point

Shannon opened the front door at midnight. It wasn't raining, but the air outside was wet with the promise of it, and Aiden's leather jacket was damp from the fog. He slipped past Shannon's arm and into the loft without a word, with his face turned toward the floor and one hand shoved deep in his pocket, the other holding his helmet.

None of the lights were on, and Shannon kept it that way. He shut the door, twisted the lock, and hesitated before turning around. Aiden leaned against the wall. His helmet—dangling from two fingers—smacked the floor.

"Can you not ask me if I'm okay, please," Aiden whispered.

"Have you slept?" It wasn't *are you okay*, but it pointed in the general direction of the same question. Shannon didn't have to ask, he knew how not-okay Aiden was.

"I don't know."

"I called—"

"Yeah, I know. Can you not…" Aiden tried to take a breath, but it trembled. His chest caved, and he braced his hands on the top of his thighs. "Can you not be the good guy, just this fucking once?"

"What do you want me to do?" Shannon dropped his hands to his sides, looking for signs of life in the darkness. There was a perfect silhouette of Aiden against the wall, helmet rocking by his feet, shoulders rising and falling, but somehow it didn't seem alive at all. Somehow there was emptiness where Aiden should've been. He took a step, and Aiden didn't move. He took another, closer, and reached out. Fingertips brushed the top of chilled hands, then wrists, until Shannon unzipped Aiden's jacket. "Tell me and I'll do it."

Aiden's gaze lifted from the floor; his eyes were ringed red and swollen. Where candlelight used to be—was ashes. He battled with himself, and his lips quivered around unspoken words.

Shannon pushed the jacket off his shoulders, and, before it hit the floor, Aiden's hands gripped his face. Their mouths collided, rough and painful, sending Shannon's complicated reservations falling. He shoved Aiden backward, knocking the air from him. Teeth dug into lips, fingers wound in Shannon's hair, nails scraped beneath Aiden's shirt.

Every ounce of worry that'd been boiling in Shannon's veins burst from him. The sedentary panic and ruthless unease melted into Aiden's mouth. He snatched Aiden's bottom lip and bit, gripped his ribs, dug his thumbs into his hips harder than he should have. Aiden's cold hands tangled in Shannon's hair, holding him in place, keeping him present in Aiden's pain.

That's what this was about, Shannon knew. It was about pain. It was about feeling.

Aiden removed his hands once to strip his shirt off, twice to push Shannon toward the middle of the room, a third time to pull Shannon back against him. Aiden kissed as if he was dying, and it was a frightening, jarring thing.

It scared Shannon, more than when he'd shown up bleeding and laughing with a half-inch gash in his stomach, or when he'd stared back at him from the other side of thick glass. It scared him more than the night Shannon almost used his gun, when Aiden's knuckles had been torn open and raw. This—not Aiden burning away, but already burnt out—was brutally reminiscent of those instances, and so far beyond them.

A phoenix—flames and talons, cinders and soot—refused to rise.

Shannon leaned forward as they stumbled into the side of the couch, trying to catch his breath between Aiden's lips. Aiden surged forward, hips rolling into his waist. Fingernails raked down Shannon's spine, and he winced, rumbling into Aiden's open mouth, nipping his top lip, his chin, until Shannon dragged his lips across Aiden's jaw and tasted salt.

Everything stopped. He set his hands on Aiden's face, and felt warm, wet tears on his cheeks. One complicated emotion by one, Shannon clicked them into place. He pulled back, just enough to see Aiden's eyes squeezed shut and his bottom lip white under the weight of his teeth.

"No," Aiden snapped. "Don't you dare; don't do this right now."

"Aiden, this isn't..."

"Don't." He gasped, eyes flashing wide in the darkness. It was a sad noise. The heaving, shaking, distressed sound of someone who refused to feel what couldn't help but be felt. "I need this. I need you, okay? Don't fucking stop."

Aiden's words left his mouth in too much of a hurry to mean anything. He didn't retreat from Shannon's gaze, and he didn't swat Shannon's hands away, or make vicious, empty threats.

Shannon said, "Not like this."

Aiden fought the crumbling until his knees started to shake, and when his shoulders slumped, head heavy in Shannon's hands, he surrendered.

"C'mon," Shannon whispered. Aiden hid his face in Shannon's neck. "Boots," he added, giving Aiden something to hold on to while he kicked his shoes off. "Pants." Shannon unbuttoned them and Aiden stepped away. His feet dragged against the rug as they made their way to the bed.

The crying came from his chest in hiccuping breaths. His gaze was far off, unfocused. He swiped tears off his cheeks, pulled his knees to his chest, and tucked his hands against his sternum.

"You weren't supposed to see me like this," Aiden said softly. "I shouldn't have listened to Karman. I should've stayed home."

Shannon trailed his fingertips across Aiden's side, his shoulder, the bit of his jaw that wasn't hidden. "If anyone is supposed to see you like this, it's me."

Aiden's breath caught. He rubbed his palms over his eyes, to the top of his head, and pulled himself into a ball. Shannon touched his thumb, his wrist, eased his fingers off his scalp. It took patience to coax him to uncurl, one delicate touch at a time, first his arms, then his shoulders, relaxing a little more on every breath. Shannon ran his fingertips over Aiden's warm skin in gentle reassurances that he wasn't alone.

"Close your eyes."

"I can't," Aiden snapped. Tension gathered between his brows.

"Come here," Shannon mumbled. He tugged on Aiden's arm, but he wouldn't budge. "Aiden, come here."

Aiden glared at him; glassy eyes narrowed dangerously and lips pressed tight together. His top lip twitched, and his nostrils flared: razor-edged villain, displaying a heated warning.

"That," he circled his finger around Aiden's face, "doesn't work on me anymore," Shannon said through a sigh.

"Fuck you."

The side of Shannon's mouth lifted. Aiden didn't appreciate the smile. He snorted and rolled away. Shannon slid closer. "Stop." He eased one arm over Aiden's torso. "Just stop, all right?"

After Aiden's breathing evened and the trembling stopped, he let Shannon wrap around him. Aiden hid beneath Shannon's chin, nose pressed between his collarbones. His arm clutched at Shannon's waist.

Shannon stroked the back of his head and wrote phrases with his fingertips on his nape.

"I wish I would've had you then," Aiden whispered, voice muffled against Shannon's chest.

"I wasn't the same me seven years ago."

"You were enough of you," Aiden said.

He fell asleep, and Shannon listened to him breathe.

00:00

AIDEN WATCHED SHANNON SLEEP FOR close to an hour in the morning.

He didn't move: not to pee, or check his phone, or start the coffee pot. He stayed next to Shannon, who was sprawled out as usual with his arms thrown across his face. Aiden watched Shannon's chest rise and fall, enjoying his own ability to breathe after days of being breathless. He didn't believe in miracles; after being versed in tragedies for so long, miracles seemed mythical. But Shannon was a fucking miracle, if Aiden had ever seen one.

Three-second breaths turned into two-second breaths, and one long inhale followed by a yawn alerted Aiden to Shannon's waking. Shannon's lashes, dark against his cheekbones, lifted and fluttered. He licked his lips, blinked, glanced to the side, startled, and then relaxed as soon as he realized Aiden hadn't left.

"I'm sorry," Aiden said immediately, before he changed his mind, "for being a train wreck. It happens every year."

Shannon flung his arm lazily across Aiden's stomach. "Don't be sorry, darlin'."

"Darlin'?" Aiden barked, face heating. Shannon's accent wasn't always sexy, but sometimes it was, and pet names weren't always Aiden's thing, but sometimes they were. "Well, I am. I'm sorry for being a mess."

The tip of Shannon's finger traced his hipbone. "That was yesterday."

"Yeah, but I was a mess all the yesterdays before yesterday, too."

"Today's today."

"And if I'm a mess tomorrow, what then?"

"Then it's a good thing I like messes," Shannon sighed. He laid his head on Aiden's shoulder.

"I don't think you can clean this one up, Detective," Aiden whispered.

"Don't need to." Shannon pressed his mouth against Aiden's collarbone, his sternum, the edge of his jaw. "I happen to like my mess the way it is."

"Your mess?"

"Your mess is mine; my mess is yours." Shannon slid his hand up Aiden's side, thumb climbing over each rib.

"You aren't a mess, Shannon. But I am, and my mess doesn't have to be yours. You don't have to keep dealing with it because the Clock says so."

"I'm not perfect. I've got messes, different than yours, but messes." He tugged, urging Aiden to lie on his side and face him. Shannon's accent was always thick in the morning. Their noses bumped. "The Clock doesn't make the choice, Aiden. It just makes the match. I choose you, all your messes, too. I choose you when you're pissed and when you're reckless and when you're hurt," he said.

Aiden kissed him, but Shannon kept talking between the parting of their lips.

"When you're distant and when you're right here." Shannon pulled him closer beneath the sheets. "When you're happy..." He paused, allowing Aiden to roll him over on his back. "When you're wild." He took Aiden's face in his hands. "I choose you, all of you."

Aiden touched Shannon's Cupid's bow. "What's your favorite part?"

Shannon bit at his fingers, but Aiden jerked them away. "Wild," he said, "my favorite part of you is wild."

Danger, danger, another wild one born to eat the heart of the world.

Maybe the heart of the world wasn't in the sea after all.

"I love you, Shannon Wurther."

"And I love you, Aiden Maar."

Some advice for you, wild boy, let what comes, come, and let what goes, go, you understand?

Aiden understood. Finally, he understood, and he was never letting go.

DAISY BALANCED ON ONE FOOT, shifted, and balanced on the other.

Aiden wanted to say something to make what he'd done seem better than it was. He'd never been able to, though. This year didn't change that. Even now, even in the after, he couldn't find a way to express what went on, not the breathlessness, not the loss of identity, not the emptiness—nothing. Once it was over, it was over. Once it was gone, it was gone.

"I'm sorry," Aiden said. It was the best he could do, despite having more to say. If he could've strung together the proper terminology, he would've; if he could've formed what he wanted to say in a way that made any sense, he would've. Shannon had been easy. He'd accepted Aiden's mess as his own and moved on, unaware that messes got messier before they got better.

Shannon wasn't Daisy, though, and Shannon hadn't been around to read the book of Aiden Maar's disasters chapter by chapter the way Daisy had.

An apology was all he had to give, and the silent promise to fight harder.

Daisy narrowed her eyes and glared, anger stitched finely across her brow. "Sorry?"

Aiden nodded. "Yeah, for... You know, for freaking out. I shouldn't have."

"You're apologizing for having a panic attack and disassociating?"

"I guess," Aiden stammered. "Yeah, what else am I supposed to say? I shouldn't have put you through that. I should've kept it together. I'm sorry you came back and I'm still like this."

Daisy tilted her head. Her dainty feet dragged against the carpet. Mercy meowed and rubbed against her ankles. The world turned. The world still turned.

"Don't ever apologize to me for that."

Aiden blinked and nodded.

"Take it back," Daisy snapped, suddenly furious. "Take your apology back."

"I take it back," Aiden said, halfway between a whimper and a growl. Confusion settled between his temples, and he thought it might give him a headache. *Apologizing was the right thing to do, wasn't it?* Aiden had been alone long enough to assume the people who quenched his loneliness deserved an apology.

"You're not a burden to me, Aiden," Daisy whispered. "We just have to find a way to fight back, that's all. Don't apologize for not knowing how yet. We'll figure it out together."

"What if there isn't a way to fight?"

"There's always a way," Daisy said.

It was quiet as the world turned. Aiden tried to smile at her; she tried to smile back.

"Your birthday's coming up."

Aiden nodded. "I know." He gathered Mercy into his arms, holding her snug against his chest. "Your timer goes off soon."

Daisy nodded. "I know."

The world turned, and Aiden could breathe, and spring was in full bloom, and for the first time in seven years, Aiden wasn't waiting for fate.

Fate sent Shannon, and fate sent Daisy, and fate sent him a war Aiden wasn't sure he could win. But if living was a battle, Aiden was ready to fight.

SPRING WAS LAUGHTER. ONCE THE beach stopped shivering from autumn's chill and the quiet of winter started to lift, Laguna Beach began to unwind. Soft purrs, windy giggles, sing-song notes, and buzzing bees carried melodies through rustling palm trees and patches of opaque tulips. It was new, and it was bright, and it was great, and Shannon didn't know what came next.

Whatever it was, he would be ready for it.

"He came over?" Karman lifted her martini glass to her lips.

Shannon nodded. "Yeah, he did. He was… he wasn't all right, but once I got him to sleep, it was better. He woke up. We talked. It was fine."

"You should be careful with him, Wurther. People with conditions like that are unpredictable. I saw him that night. He was in a bad way."

"Everyone deals with things differently. It isn't his fault, Karman. Having depression isn't a choice."

Karman pursed her lips. "Everyone makes a choice to be a certain way," she said, condescending her way under Shannon's skin.

"Oh, and how's that going for you?" Shannon gestured loosely at her right hand. "Not everyone can shut it off like you do. Aiden lost both his parents and he blames himself. It isn't his fault he goes through what he goes through. He isn't unpredictable, he's sick."

"He's messed up," Karman said plainly. She lifted her hand and waved it, dismissing whatever Shannon had to say before he said it.

Karman was rarely wrong, but when she was, it was a deep cavern of wrong that she could not crawl out of—such wrongness that it was a sore thing, the kind of wrong that made him ashamed of her.

"He's…" Shannon huffed and rolled his eyes. "He's fine. He's got some shit to deal with; we all do. Why do you feel the need to come down on him so hard? What did he say to make you react like this?"

"Nothing. I tried to get him to come out of his funk, that's all. He spits venom like a cobra, I'll tell you that much." Karman paused, sipped her drink, and added very quietly, "I didn't know you told him about Jay."

"He's my Rose Road, Karman. Of course I told him. He's not a cobra. He's a person who has an anxiety disorder, which comes from his chronic depression, if I haven't mentioned that already." Shannon didn't mean to be sarcastic, but it was that or anger, and he didn't have the patience to be angry with her.

"Well, anyway, be careful. I wouldn't want you to be disappointed if something happened."

"Anyway." Shannon nodded as a dry smile spread across his lips. "That's what it always is, isn't it? *Anyway*, let's change the subject. *Anyway*, Karman has no issues. *Anyway*, let's pick everyone else apart. *Anyway*, Karman gets to pass judgment whenever she pleases, because she got hurt once, too."

Karman straightened in her seat. She flipped a clump of curls over her shoulder and snorted with her brows arched high on her forehead. Shannon had struck a nerve; he saw it spark within her and he caught her snuffing it out.

He waited for her to lash out and scold him, but instead she nodded and ordered another martini.

"People like him are volatile," Karman said. That was her way of being petty, Shannon knew. Dismiss the obvious, circle back to any problem that wasn't hers, and chew on it.

"You're a bitch," Shannon snapped.

"I know that."

"Jay is gone, and it's not your fault."

"I know that, too."

"I'm not going to love him any less because he's got baggage."

"Good for you." Karman shut down. Her voice was low; her gaze was lifeless and long-gone.

"You know..." Shannon paused to laugh, short and sarcastic. He had sharp teeth, too, and sometimes she needed reminding. "I hope Marcus doesn't give up on you as easily as you give up on everyone else. God forbid he sees through that mask you wear and figures out that you're just as broken as his brother."

Karman's face hardened. Shannon watched her jaw flex, hollowing the space beneath her bronzed cheekbones.

"See you at work." Shannon grabbed his messenger bag, slid on his sunglasses, and walked out of the Whitehouse.

00:00

SHANNON THOUGHT ABOUT AIDEN'S BIRTHDAY, and he thought about the Mortez case, and he thought about his bitter conversation with Karman last week. He sat cross-legged on his bed with a science fiction book, reading lines and rereading them, trying to absorb the content and failing miserably.

Shannon thought most about what Karman had said. *People like him are volatile.*

Aiden shuffled around the loft, searching for an old band T-shirt he'd left months ago.

"Babe, what even *is* this?" Aiden held up the remnants of a sock, torn at the toe and with a hole in the heel. His face scrunched and his septum piercing caught the afternoon light. "I'm throwing it out."

Shannon ignored the book and tilted his head to take in the Aiden Maar that was no longer predatory thief, but domesticated bartending photographer: bare feet on the wood floor, jeans unbuttoned, looking as out of place as the bed or the television or the microwave or Shannon.

"Do you think you're volatile?" Shannon waited for a laugh or a snide snarl.

Aiden shrugged and dropped the sad excuse for a sock in the trash can. "I guess, yeah. I don't know. Do you think I'm volatile?"

"No, I don't." Shannon arched a brow. "You responded well to that. I thought you'd be offended."

"We've already talked about me being a disaster, Shannon. Volatile is just a fancy added description." Aiden dug through one of Shannon's dresser drawers until he found the shirt he'd lost. He exclaimed how pleased he was in a flutter of foul language. "Why'd you ask?"

"Just curious. Describe yourself in three words."

"Catastrophe. Tall. Hungry."

Shannon laughed. Aiden did, too.

"Your turn, describe yourself," Aiden said. He tossed his tank top on the floor and tugged his newly found T-shirt over his head.

"Over-analytical. Sophomoric. Also, tall."

Shannon dog-eared the page he hadn't finished reading and set the book on the nightstand. The blood rushed back into his legs as he unfolded them and rose to his knees. He stretched, listening to cracks and pops from his back.

Aiden sauntered closer. Cloud-filtered light beamed in through the poorly dusted windows. It crawled over his shoulders, skipped across his arms, and painted him a curious, breathtaking thing. Seven months had passed, and Shannon still marveled at him, at all that he was and would be.

Shannon smirked when Aiden gripped his face and tapped long fingers against his temples, and fell when Aiden tossed him down against the comforter.

Everyone makes a choice to be a certain way.

"What's wrong?" Aiden said gently. He propped himself on his elbow and touched Shannon's cheek. "What aren't you saying?"

"You're okay, right?" Shannon swallowed, unsure if he should continue. "You won't... You're not still..."

"Shannon, I'm fine," Aiden said.

"Do you still feel like dying?"

That, Shannon knew, was the question he'd wanted to ask for months.

Aiden's playfulness dimmed. He exhaled and tried to smile. Shannon heard him hold his breath. Silence wasn't always a weapon; sometimes silence was a secret. Secrets, to Aiden, were hoarded masterfully, locked away, and distributed at opportune moments or not at all. When something was his and only his, he kept it.

That, Shannon knew, was what Karman feared in Aiden. His dance with death, his obscure relationship with the concept of living, his inability to smother his emotions beneath heaping piles of lackluster responsibility—all of Aiden, all of his war, Karman saw in herself.

But Shannon didn't fear it anymore. He only feared the chance that Aiden might not live, that *they* might not live, a *together*, a *home*, a *something*. Shannon was terrified of losing a *future*.

Shannon was terrified of losing Aiden.

Aiden didn't answer. He bracketed his legs around Shannon's waist. They kissed like the first time, questioning and then colliding. Aiden's lips brushed Shannon's mouth, gasoline, and Shannon craned his neck to catch them, a match striking. Aiden made a wounded sound. His hands glided over Shannon's cheeks, his temples. Shannon cradled the back of Aiden's neck with his palm.

His hair was longer, Shannon noticed. He twirled it between his fingers, strands of gold and dirty snow. His other hand swept across the tattoo beneath Aiden's shirt. Black-feathered phoenix, burning and alive.

Aiden said Shannon's name on a tentative breath. It wasn't an answer, but Shannon let it go. He latched his arms around Aiden's waist and pulled. The force caused their teeth to knock, but neither of them bothered arranging themselves in a way that would prevent it. Closeness was their sanctuary; it always had been.

Shannon remembered the beginning, when Aiden was a ghost manifested out of peculiarity, haunting and dangerous.

You're beautiful. I've never been scared of anything until you. I might love you, someday.

Someday, someday, someday.

"I feel alive," Aiden said suddenly. Shannon's lips were on his throat, and Aiden's hands wound in the sheets. "I feel alive with you."

"You are alive." Shannon's hands smoothed up Aiden's back, pressing on jutting bone, counting piano keys, dragon spines. "You're alive," he said again. "Things like you can't die. The world would die right along with you."

"Someone told me I would eat the heart of the world one day," Aiden said. He leaned back, only enough to rest his forehead against Shannon's. "I've always loved the world, but I never thought I'd find the heart of it, the best of it, the center of it. I did, though. I found it," he added quickly. "Or it found me, I'm not sure which."

"I don't know either, but you've completely consumed it."

Aiden offered a shy smile, one of his gentle rarities, and he kissed Shannon again.

SHANNON LOOKED AT HIS PHONE, debating whether he should answer. Karman's name flashed on his screen with the cartoon image of a video recorder below it. He chewed on his lip, going over every conversation they'd had since their argument at the Whitehouse. Other than work, they hadn't spoken in three weeks.

He slid the tip of his finger across the screen. Karman's face popped up.

"We never FaceTime. What's the occasion?" Shannon asked.

Karman rolled her eyes. "We can't keep ignoring each other, and you don't have anything to be sorry for, which means I'm the one who needs to apologize. So, Shannon, I'm sorry. You're right about everything, you always have been. I don't know how to deal with my shit, which makes it hard for me to accept when other people are having trouble dealing with their shit."

Shannon nodded. "Go on."

"I don't have the excuse Aiden does, not that it's an excuse, but you get what I mean. I have complete control over my situation and I refuse to do anything about it. It bothers me, which makes me angry, and I say things I don't mean. So, there. Yeah, sorry. I'm a bitch."

"You're a *total* fucking bitch," Shannon gritted. "You basically told me to prepare myself for Aiden's suicide, you get that, right?"

"Why do you think I'm apologizing?"

"Well, try again!"

Karman grabbed the phone and held it close to her face. "Shannon Wurther, I am your best friend and I love you and I am sincerely sorry for what I said about Aiden. He didn't deserve that and neither did you. I'll take you guys out sometime this week to make up for it."

"I have to go, all right? I'm meeting him in an hour for his pre-birthday thing."

Karman lifted an eyebrow and tilted the phone awkwardly. "You gonna give him the overpriced flower thing?"

"Yes." Shannon rolled his eyes. "You're coming to dinner tomorrow, right?"

"The Wicked Witch is still invited?"

"Yes, you're still invited."

Karman grinned. "Then yes."

Shannon flashed a grin at his phone before he hit end, stashed it in his pocket, and headed out the door.

SEATED ON THE COUCH WITH Aiden on one side and Mercy on the other, Shannon clicked up the volume on the TV. Boxes of Chinese takeout and beer bottles crowded the coffee table. Aiden gave an impressive impersonation of Jabba the Hutt with his mouth full of chow mien.

"What do you think Carrie thought when she saw the outfit for the first time?"

Shannon shrugged.

"Do you think she thought it was sexy or stupid?"

"I don't know, probably a little bit of both."

Aiden scooped more noodles into his mouth and nodded. "Speaking of first impressions, what'd you make of me, Detective?"

"You aren't an article of clothing," Shannon said matter-of-factly.

Aiden rolled his eyes and waved his hand in a circle. "Yeah, okay, you know what I mean."

"I was trying to arrest you at the time, so."

"You're no fun. Tell me..." Aiden snapped his chopsticks in Shannon's face. "Did you think I was sexy or not?"

"Was I not clear enough with the dozen hickeys? Of course I did, even though you were a criminal at the time."

"It's weird hearing you say it like that." Aiden plucked a piece of shrimp from Shannon's white takeout box. "Using past tense. It's still strange not stealing, you know."

"What made you start? I don't think I've ever asked." Shannon held the box to Aiden as he rummaged through it for another piece of shrimp.

Aiden shrugged. "My mom painted, not professionally or anything, but she was always working on a canvas, sketching, buying supplies, repainting murals on our kitchen wall every summer. When she died, I wanted to keep that part of her, but I couldn't look at any of her work. It... hurt to acknowledge, I guess. So I stole. The first time I took something, it felt dark and powerful, like a secret. I thought it was exchangeable with living—the exhilaration—but I was wrong. It was just adrenaline."

"Do you miss it?"

"Sometimes." Aiden shrugged. He pointed his chopsticks at Shannon and lifted a brow. "I still steal, Detective. Small things, though. Things you'd never notice."

Shannon smirked. "Don't tell me what they are."

"Didn't plan on it."

"Do you want your gift?"

"That depends on what it is."

"You can't eat it, it isn't alive, but I wrapped it."

"Will it break if I shake it?"

"Do not shake it."

Aiden set his box on the table and nodded. "Fine, yes."

"*Don't* shake it," Shannon stressed. He walked to the kitchen counter where the square-shaped gift sat beside his keys and sunglasses. "If you do, it will break, and I will kill you."

Aiden curled and uncurled his outstretched fingers. "Okay, whatever. Give it."

An irritating scratch formed in the back of Shannon's throat. His grip tightened around the corner of the square, wrapped in bright orange paper decorated with cartoon balloons. He'd been waiting a month and a half to give this to Aiden. This, Shannon thought, was something too personal to be simplified as a birthday present. Beyond the wrapping paper was a piece of their past framed and centered, the first of Aiden's many truths—a beginning that started in a state of complicated reverence.

Reminds me of myself.

Shannon handed it to him.

A pleased, raspy hum built in Aiden's mouth; his smile stretched thin. He tore the paper open. Stopped. Looked up. And Shannon froze.

"Shannon, what is this?" Aiden said, quick and clipped.

Aiden's smile ruptured. His bottom lip twitched; the tension between his brows deepened. It wasn't anger, Shannon realized. Aiden was bewildered, and like all things Aiden, his state was interchangeable with many others. Anger took precedence, even if it wasn't the cause.

Shannon chewed on the inside of his cheek. "Open it."

Aiden's movements slowed. He peeled back the paper, carefully breaking the tape on each side, and tossed it on the floor. Long fingertips investigated the glass front of the frame, and he saw the painting within.

"This is a Nichole Scott," Aiden whispered.

"Yeah, it is. *Fortitude Smashed* was sold, but that one was available along with some others. It seemed fitting."

"What's it called?"

"*Catalyst.*"

The Nichole Scott painting wasn't in the nicest frame, but Shannon didn't think Aiden would mind.

The piece, all lavenders and mauves and bursting apple reds, sat in a sea of blue pollen. Tendrils of ivy and dandelion stems coiled into orbs. A merlot calla lily, black at its base and rich purple at its tip, dominated the canvas' middle. The swirl of blossom was separated from the stem, which was an inch lower, and accompanied by tiny spherical vines and bursting tulip buds.

A masterpiece, Shannon thought. The kind people didn't understand, but wanted to.

"Shannon, this had to be like..." Aiden's breath caught. He tapped his fingers on the frame. "Two grand, at least. This—this isn't... I was expecting a new camera strap or something, this is—"

"Say thank you," Shannon interrupted.

"Thank you," Aiden said, and it was grounded and true and wide open. "Why did you do this?"

Shannon shrugged, sat beside him, and glanced at *Catalyst*. Aiden stared at him as vivid curiosity replaced bewilderment masked as anger.

Aiden stole a quick look at the painting before he asked again, "Why...?"

"Reminded me of you," Shannon said. It was easy to say because it was the truth, but if he had to explain it, Shannon feared he might ruin everything.

A sound left Aiden. Shannon had never heard it before—not from him. The winded acceptance of being told an unbelievable something. Aiden would usually scoff, or roll his eyes, or twist his handsome features into ghastly, vicious laughter. But this time, his lips parted and, very quietly, he whispered, "This is artwork," as if to correct Shannon, to say *this is not me, this cannot be me.*

"I'm aware of that."

"And still...?"

"Still," Shannon said. "Happy birthday, Aiden Maar."

Aiden's eyes turned to the frame and candlelight reflected, and Shannon wished he had the courage to take a picture. Aiden, admiring *Catalyst,* a thing so much like him, wearing a whisper of a smile. What a picture it would be.

"Where should I hang it?" Aiden asked.

"Wherever you like."

His thumbs traced the frame, and Aiden set it on his thighs while he whipped his gaze around the living room. "What about there?" He pointed at a space beside a photographic collage on the right side of the entertainment stand. "Above the Vincent Cross sculpture?"

"That's as good a place as any."

Aiden nodded. He swallowed dryly, lips parting and closing.

"I wish I had more to say, but... I don't understand, I'm trying to wrap my head around it and I can't. This isn't just a gift, it's... This is something else. I don't know, I can't figure out how to say what I'm trying to say."

"Don't say anything then."

Aiden picked up *Catalyst* and set it on the entertainment stand, away from the coffee table and Daisy's mess. Quiet knotted between them: Aiden breathing, Shannon holding his breath. Shannon wasn't sure if he should breach the distance, or if Aiden had kept it there for a reason.

"We're still not good at this," Aiden said.

Shannon narrowed his eyes. "Good at what?"

"Talking." Aiden reached across the middle cushion and grabbed Shannon's hand. He stood, hauling Shannon along with him. "We'll get better at it, but for now..." He pushed into Shannon, guiding him clumsily toward the bedroom. "Let's just get on with it."

Briefly Shannon thought, *wait* or *let's talk*, but Aiden's mouth was on his, and Aiden's body was pressed against Shannon's, and it didn't matter. Aiden was all-encompassing. His thumbs stroked Shannon's temples; his fingers dragged through his hair. They fell against the bedroom door, and Shannon hoisted him up.

"I always forget you're cop strong," Aiden mumbled, grinning against Shannon's cheek.

Shannon shoved him against the door, one hand wrapped low on his thigh, the other sliding beneath his T-shirt. "I'm glad you like it," Shannon said.

"The throwing me against things, or the painting?"

"Both." Shannon worked a violet bruise on Aiden's throat. "But I was talking about the painting."

Aiden's thighs tightened around Shannon's waist, one leg slipped to the floor. "No one's ever done anything like that for me. No one's ever listened. I can't believe you remembered. I…" He paused. Shannon bit his jaw, his shoulder. "I didn't think you'd understand what I meant when I told you about *Fortitude*—"

His voice cracked. He clawed at Shannon's shirt and tossed it away. "I never thought you'd see me as anything other than a guy who stole shit. I never thought you'd see me as…"

Shannon would ruin it if he tried to explain. "You're my best kept secret, Aiden. You're the most vibrant thing in the room, artwork unlike any other."

Somehow, in a tangle of arms and legs, they found the bed.

Aiden's fingernails dug into Shannon's shoulders. Shannon hoped they tore him open.

This candlelight, this wolf, this magnificent being—he's everything.

42

SHANNON OPENED HIS EYES. THE ceiling fan spun brisk morning air through Aiden's bedroom. He glanced at the open window, then followed the slanted light to where it cut through the shadows on Aiden's back. He slept on top of the comforter, both arms shoved under the pillow, his nose buried in the mattress. What a view, Shannon thought, and was careful not to wake him while he reached for the camera on the nightstand.

Aiden stirred after Shannon took the first picture and woke as he was taking the second.

"Don't," Aiden hissed, pulling the pillow over his face.

"I have successfully captured your first minute as a twenty-three-year-old; how does it feel?"

"Like that Blink-182 song. Go back to sleep."

"Nope, get up. We have things to do today. Daisy's already in the shower and Chelsea will be here soon." Shannon tried to pry the pillow away, but Aiden gripped it tighter.

"It's my birthday, isn't it? Don't I get to decide when I wake up?"

Shannon rolled over and threw his arm around Aiden's waist. "We're supposed to take the girls to the Hollow, remember? Then sushi for lunch." Aiden made a pleased sound and peeked at Shannon from beneath the pillow. Shannon continued. "You mentioned the Southside cliff, so after we eat, we can go up there. Are we still doing dinner with Marcus?"

"And Karman and Fae, yeah."

"Okay, there you have it, a whole day planned out."

The bedroom door swung open.

"Are you two decent? Not that it matters, lord knows I've seen too much of you both to care." Chelsea grinned, leaning against the inside of the door. A long, white shawl covered a neon pink bikini top, and a pair of frayed jean shorts clung to her hips. "C'mon now, wake up. Aren't you supposed to be takin' us somewhere amazing?"

"How'd you get in my house?" Aiden mumbled, rolling his eyes.

"I let her in!" Daisy bounded past Chelsea, leapt onto the bed and climbed over Aiden's naked back. "It's your birthday! Get up, get up, get up," Daisy chirped, pressing loving kisses against his cheeks and forehead. Bouncing on top of him, she shoved his shoulders. "Happy birthday to you," Daisy sang. Her mouth hovered inches from Aiden's ear. "Happy birthday to you, happy birthday, dear asshole, happy birthday to you!"

"Get off me," Aiden groaned, his gaze fixed on Shannon and a smile lingering on his face despite the wake-up call.

AFTER A TRIP TO THE Hollow and lunch at Aiden's favorite sushi restaurant, they found a spot on the beach and lounged about. An hour passed, two maybe, but it wasn't long before Aiden's restlessness brought them to the top of the tallest cliff in Laguna.

Waves crashed beneath, licking the sides of maroon boulders and jet black rocks. Kelp clung to the jagged edges at the bottom and painted the surface dark green. Far off in the distance, a buoy bobbed against rolling swells. To the right, Main Beach extended down the boardwalk. Tops of umbrella's and folding chairs lined the beach, and the remote sound of chatter filled the air. Sunscreen, aloe, and salt scents wafted around them, mingling with sweet wildflowers and dirt kicked up from their shoes. The sun was bright, dead center in a cloudless sky, overpowering the cool breeze that riled the palm trees.

"I haven't been up here in years," Shannon said.

Aiden tilted his head to welcome the sun on his face. "I come up here a lot."

Daisy balanced on the very edge. Her dress billowed, and the wind tousled her hair: locks of white overlapping black. She swayed forward, arms outstretched for the world to see.

Chelsea stayed put behind Shannon, her hands laced firmly in front of her. "Daisy," she called nervously. "Can you not do that?"

Daisy ignored her. She reached toward the sky with her fingers spread.

"We should jump," Daisy said, her voice carried by the wind.

"No," Chelsea sang. "We definitely shouldn't do that."

Aiden stood beside her, looking over the water. Shannon traced the outline of his tattoo, vivid and raging in the mid-day light. The wings of Aiden's shoulder blades tensed. Shannon never had been good at stringing together proper descriptions. He found that what he thought and what he said sometimes became jumbled, no matter how many times he went over it in his head. This moment, like many moments, was one Shannon would never be able to properly explain. He thought it might have been poetry—the art of it sewn together in a single, easy scene. Aiden standing on the edge of a cliff, beaches stretched on either side of him, and Shannon wondering what he ever thought was beautiful before this—before Aiden Maar and Laguna Beach.

Daisy's chin lifted. She gazed at Aiden, feral and certain and alive, taking the form of one of her fantastic sketchbook creations. What she was constructed of beneath her skin besides bones and muscle and blood? Was there magic inside her, too? Surely there was; people like her, who ran with people like Aiden, had to be some sort of magical.

"We should jump," Daisy repeated, stern this time, ready.

Aiden smiled and said, "Is this how we fight back?"

"This is exactly how we fight back." Daisy slid out of her dress and adjusted the straps on her sleek one-piece bathing suit.

"There are other ways to fight." Aiden leaned over the edge. He kicked off his shoes and stuffed his socks inside them.

"Aiden, don't..." Shannon tried to find something else to say, but there was nothing. All he could muster was a gentle plea, and a useless one. If Aiden decided to jump, Shannon knew nothing could stop him.

"I'm sick of being scared," Daisy said, barely audible over the sound of Shannon's racing heart. "I'm ready to let it go. I found a way for us to fight, and it's this. This choice is our weapon."

Aiden looked at the waves crashing below, and Shannon looked at Aiden.

Instead of trying to plead with him, Shannon simply said his name. "Aiden..."

Aiden glanced over his shoulder. Sunlight played on the slope of his nose; fair lashes fanned over his cheeks. Blue sky against pale skin and pale skin against blue sky accentuated Aiden's strength, cast shadows along the nooks and curves that pulled his body tight, and reminded Shannon that Aiden was a cluster of knives, a shark's mouth.

Aiden's lips parted in a sly smile. "Jump with me."

Shannon swallowed dryly, saliva thick and sticky in his throat. "That's a far fall."

"It always has been." Aiden tilted his head. The sun reflected in his eyes, a little bit like stars, a little bit like candlelight. "I'm not dying," he added, holding out his arms. "This is me deciding to live."

"You *will* die if you jump off that damn cliff!" Chelsea squawked.

Aiden stepped into Shannon's space. Warm hands, fairy tale hands, gripped Shannon's face. Lips, chapped from the wind, pressed against his. Aiden's breath trembled on Shannon's jaw; his bottom lip dragged across Shannon's cheek. His breath didn't taste like soot and smoke, but Shannon remembered when it had. Now it tasted like honeysuckles and green tea. Aiden stepped back, inching toward the edge.

"Jump with me," Aiden whispered. "Live a little."

The world turned slowly, slowly, second by second. Yet Shannon didn't have enough time to form a coherent thought, processing one moment after the next: Aiden's lips, gentle and familiar; his voice; the sound of bare feet against dirt; and Chelsea's strangled gasp.

Daisy and Aiden disappeared over the edge.

Daisy's joyful scream on the way down anchored Shannon to the present, to the sound of one splash and then another, to his name being shouted from the bottom of the cliff. The world jolted into its usual pace.

"Those two are insane!" Chelsea's whole body shook, and her foot tapped against the ground. One trembling hand covered her mouth; the other perched on her hip. She watched him, wide-eyed, before she stumbled over an explosion of words. "Shannon Wurther! No, don't you—don't you even think about it. I am not, I will not! Don't you dare, for one second think that I'm..."

"C'mon, Chels. Let's do it; let's jump."

"Now *you're* crazy! First Aiden, then Daisy, and now you're losin' your mind, too? I can handle you and your boyfriend being idiots, but you are not draggin' me into this!"

"Either we keep being afraid, or we jump in after them. I don't know about you, but I'm done being scared. I'm ready to fight, too."

"Shannon, we can't follow them into every stupid situation they get themselves into."

Shannon pointed over the edge of the cliff, where Daisy and Aiden's laughter rang like faraway bells. "Yeah, we can. We just have to stop being scared to jump."

Chelsea's expression dropped. Her wide cerulean eyes darted around Shannon's face, then flicked from him to the pile of clothes on the cliffside and back to the expanse of ocean in front of them.

"Are you coming?" Shannon held out his hand.

Chelsea stepped out of her shorts, folded them, and set them on top of Daisy's dress. She tightened her bikini, top strings, then bottom.

A deep, unsettled sigh was Chelsea's answer, before she snatched his hand and they ran into the sun.

43

Laguna Beach was a canvas.

The sky twisted colors into shapes, manifested sound into sculptures. Daydreams came to life on the horizon, bursting from the sun as it melted into the ocean. Reflected off the top of the water, segments of the coming night shone and glittered. High above the leftover sunset, stars blinked awake beside a waning moon. Aiden had seen sunsets before; he'd seen them from Top of the World and from the Hollow and from his apartment, but he'd never seen one quite like this.

Perched on the cliff they'd jumped from, Aiden sat with Shannon, Chelsea, and Daisy. Shannon's feet dangled off the edge; god-awful sunglasses settled on the tip of his nose. Chelsea and Daisy shared a towel beside him: Daisy with her chin on top of her knees, and Chelsea cross-legged with her head tipped back as she gazed at the waking stars.

Aiden didn't know what to look at. He was torn between watching the ocean swallow the sun in a pageant of rose-stained clouds, Creamsicle kissing purple above rolling waves, and navy clashing against sleepy gold and Shannon Wurther—witness to it all.

Colors manifested across Shannon's cheeks; orange streaked his bottom lip, pink caressed his brow. He leaned back on his palms, and blue tinted his throat.

"Are you ready for twenty-three?" Shannon asked. His head lolled and he gazed at Aiden over the top of his sunglasses.

"I think so. I think it'll be a good one this time."

"We'll make it a good one."

The sun was a blood-red dome sinking and sinking. Light from it danced on Shannon's face; it cast elongated shadows along the bridge of his nose and deepened the line of his jaw.

Aiden grinned and asked, "What do you think summer will be like?"

Shannon shrugged. "Warm," he whispered, "new, bright...I think it'll be great."

Summer—warm, new, bright—would be a summer unlike any other.

This spring Aiden would remember as the spring he decided to live, the spring of cheap drinks beneath a blanket of stars and the taste of honey between shared breaths, of a day spent trying to drown and a night spent learning to breathe, of "I love you's" against bloody knuckles and artwork meant for his hands. Spring was Daisy singing in the shower and Shannon asking *how was work*. It was Chelsea Cavanaugh, tropical storm of woman, beautiful and captivating. Spring was the world turning radically, wonderfully, unceremoniously, out of a winter of firsts and afters.

A winter of champagne-stained laughter against Shannon's smile and photographs that told the beginning of a beautiful story, of feelings manifesting from a void of uncertainty and a Christmas tree Mercy decided was hers. Winter was *yes*, and *this is it*, and asking fireflies for forgiveness. It was naked trees, and hot coffee, and Shannon's lips on the back of his neck *god, you're beautiful*. Winter was the heart of the world beating louder, and it had come from a fall that shivered.

Fall—constructed of impossibilities—was the tumbling of leaves across his boots and a pair of eyes that reminded him of rain. It was daydreaming about what if's that came true and *you're here* that became *you're home*, a fall of skeletons and cigarettes, lips against lips, and hands against hands, of Shannon's smile memorized, phoenix feathers ruffled,

Clock's that were wrong first and right second. Fall was hunting for *Fortitude Smashed* and finding fate instead.

Summer was on the horizon, leaving behind a spring when he decided to live, a winter of firsts and afters, and a fall that started with Shannon.

The fall that turned him wild.

"What do *you* think summer will be like?" Shannon touched Aiden's hand.

Aiden glanced at the dwindling light leaking from the place where sky met ocean and ocean met sky.

A smile and the brush of fingertips across his shoulders, an almost kiss and *how was work.*

"As long as you're there, it'll be something," Aiden whispered.

One side of Shannon's mouth lifted. He tugged Aiden's wrist to his lips and kissed his knuckles. "Something," he repeated.

The sun was gone, but it was still warm.

Aiden was alive, and Shannon was his.

The world turned. Aiden felt it.

Shannon's arm curled around his back. Their feet knocked together over the edge of the cliff, and Aiden leaned against Shannon's chest. The impossibility of the two of them, an intricate something, was a wild, wonderful, magical thing.

Aiden's lips hovered over Shannon's mouth, which was curled in a patient smile. They kissed, deep and slow and knowing, the kind of kiss that told a story.

Impossibility tasted like Shannon Wurther, and Aiden would never get enough of it.

ACKNOWLEDGMENTS

FORTITUDE SMASHED TOOK A LOT of unpacking. I had a team behind me the entire time, sorting through the mess that gathered as I threw this and that over my shoulder. First was Matt, my reputable rescuer, who knows my befores and afters better than anyone. He has climbed to the top of many, many cliffs with me. He's jumped off some, too. We'll be jumping off more, I'm sure. The team at Interlude Press—Annie, Choi, Candy, Nicki, Linda—you brought this story to life, and I can never thank you enough for that. Mom and Dad, my unshakable support system: Your unyielding love for one another reminds me to believe in fate, even on days when I question it.

ABOUT THE AUTHOR

AFTER FLESHING OUT A MULTITUDE of fantastical creatures as a special effects makeup professional, Taylor turned her imagination back to her true love—books. When she's not nestled in a blanket typing away on her laptop, she can be found haunting the local bookstore with a cup of tea, planning her next adventure, and fawning over baby animals.

For a reader's guide to **Fortitude Smashed** and book club prompts, please visit interludepress.com.

interlude**press**™

🌐 interludepress.com
🐦 @InterludePress
f interludepress
🛒 store.interludepress.com

interlude press
you may also like...

Into the Blue by Pene Henson

Tai Talagi and Ollie Birkstrom have been inseparable since they met as kids surfing the North Shore. Tai's spent years setting aside his feelings for Ollie, but when Ollie's pro surfing dreams come to life, their steady world shifts. Is the relationship worth risking everything for a chance at something terrifying and beautiful and altogether new?

ISBN (print) 978-1-941530-84-9 | (eBook) 978-1-941530-85-6

Luchador by Erin Finnegan

A young exótico wrestler in Mexico City's professional lucha libra circuit charts a course to balance ambition, sexuality, and loyalty to find the future that may have be destined for him since childhood—a story about finding yourself from behind a mask.

ISBN (print) 978-1-941530-97-9 | (eBook) 978-1-941530-98-6

The Star Host by F.T. Lukens

Published by Duet, the YA imprint of Interlude Press

Ren grew up listening to his mother tell stories about the Star Hosts—mythical people possessed by the power of the stars. Captured by a nefarious Baron, Ren discovers he may be something out of his mother's stories. He befriends Asher, a member of the Phoenix Corps. Together, they must master Ren's growing power and try to save their friends while navigating the growing attraction between them.

ISBN (print) 978-1-941530-72-6 | (eBook) 978-1-941530-73-3

CPSIA information can be obtained
at www.ICGtesting.com
Printed in the USA
FFOW03n0713221017
41336FF

9 781945 053368